The Adventures of Pirates

Tall Tales and Other Short Stories

Edited By Evelyn M. Zimmer

The Adventures of Pirates

Tall Tales and Other Short Stories

Edited by
Evelyn M. Zimmer

Zimbell House
Publishing, LLC

This book is a work of fiction. Any references to historical events, real people, or real locales are used fictitiously. All characters appearing in this work are the product of the individual author's imagination, and any resemblance to actual persons, living or dead is entirely coincidental.

All rights reserved, including the right of reproduction in whole or in part in any form. No part of this publication may be reproduced, distributed, or transmitted in any form or by any means, including photocopying, recording, or other electronic or mechanical methods, without the written permission of the publisher.

For permission requests, write to the publisher at the address below:
Attention: Permissions Coordinator
Zimbell House Publishing, LLC
PO Box 1172
Union Lake, Michigan 48387
mailto: info@zimbellhousepublishing.com

© 2015 Zimbell House Publishing, LLC

Published in the United States by Zimbell House Publishing, LLC
http://www.ZimbellHousePublishing.com
All Rights Reserved

Print ISBN: 9781942818434
Kindle Electronic ISBN: 9781942818441
Library of Congress Control Number: 2015916384

Acknowledgements

Zimbell House Publishing would like to thank all those that submitted to our anthology. We chose nine yarn spinners from the United Kingdom, Italy, and the United States to delight you with their unique take of tales on the high seas, including the novella by E.W. Farnsworth, *Pirate Tales*.

We would also like to thank all of those on our Zimbell House team that worked so diligently to bring this collection to press.

Table of Contents

Dead-Man's Chest   9
DJ Tyrer

Don Miguel, The Inquisition, And The Mad Pirate's Crusade   17
Benjamin Fine

Montego Bay   93
Lucy Ann Fiorini

Pleasure for An Hour, A Bottle of Good Wine…   101
Sergio 'ente per ente' Palumbo
Edited and Translated by Michele Dutcher

Pirate Tales ⚓ A Novella   125
E.W. Farnsworth

Sacking Fort Holland   273
DJ Tyrer

Sea Of Blood   285
Matthew Wilson

Seventy-Seven Pounds   299
Eugene L. Morgulis

The Davidof Dilemma   319
Thomas Sheehan

Wake of the Monster	329
Cynthia Morrison	
Contributing Yarn Spinners	349
Additional Anthologies from Zimbell House Publishing	369
New Releases Coming Soon from Zimbell House Publishing	369

Dead-Man's Chest

DJ Tyrer

White surf exploded against black sand and rocks as the longboat fought the surging waves to beach itself upon the desolate and storm-lashed shore. Overhead, the sky was black with clouds that, legend claimed, never parted.

A tall, dark man with weather-beaten skin and muscles like cables leapt from the boat, a rope in his hands, and began to tug it up the beach. Two more men, each marked with scars, joined him and, a moment later, they had it sufficiently far up the beach to avoid the grasping waves. Four more men jumped out onto the black sands, one of who, a tall, thin man in a frock coat and knee-breeches of red with a golden trim, and wearing a long-feathered hat, was their Captain, Henry Rice.

"Lucifer's Revenge cannot last long out there in the storm," said Bosun James, the tall, dark man who had led the way onto the island. Responsible for the men and sails of their vessel, it was his job to know the limitations of both and the ship as a whole. While the sails were furled and the majority of the crew safely below decks, it was only a matter of time before it was denuded of masts and driven onto the rocks.

"Then, we must move swiftly," said the Captain. "We came for the treasure and I won't leave without it."

Treasure, the island, considered by most to be little more than legend, was where the long-dead Captain Harris, known to the ages as Pegleg, had concealed his hoard. Doom had overtaken him and his crew soon after, so that none of them could return to claim it, but Rice's First Mate, known as Thistlebeard, for his particularly-coarse facial hair, had come into possession of a map showing both the location of the island and the treasure hidden upon it. Having braved the everlasting storm to find it, they were determined to leave with it.

Captain Rice had brought his six most trusted men with him and, now, he pointed at the mountain at the island's heart and said, "The treasure is there, in a cave."

Although it was midday, the thick clouds meant it was almost as dark as night and each man carried a bull's-eye lantern to light their way.

The island wasn't large, but it was rocky and difficult to cross. Despite the pouring rain that soaked their clothes and chilled them in the whipping wind, there was no plant life to be seen, no soil, nor any sign of birds or beasts. Everywhere was black rock, much of it glasslike and slippery to walk on and sharp to brush against.

"Careful," muttered Black Jack Jones, nursing a gash on his arm. "These rocks are like knives."

A short distance on, hulking Little William halted as he saw the ravine that gaped ahead of them. A narrow ledge ran along its side, which was slick with rain.

"We should go back."

Captain Rice shook his head. "We go on."

Slowly, with difficulty, feet slipping with every step, they began to edge their way along it. It was worse than clambering about the ship in a storm.

There was a sudden scream and Cannon Joe plunged down into the ravine to land, broken and bloody, upon the razor-sharp rocks that jaggedly filled the bottom of the ravine.

"We're all going to die," muttered the man known, after his tattoos, as Cockles. "If we make it across, we'll never make it back."

Captain Rice snorted. "Old Pegleg made it, and, if he could do it, so can we."

Having made it to the far end of the ravine, they found themselves climbing the mountainside, which was every bit as bad, perhaps worse, being lashed by the storm winds.

"Devil take you," snarled Black Jack, looking at the Captain's back as they struggled to climb the slope.

"I think I can see the cave," said Little William, pointing.

The Captain laughed. "See, not far. We will not be beaten. Move yourselves, men."

They entered the cave, which was like a shaft perfectly bored into the mountainside. The black walls accentuated the darkness, so that they might have been walking along with their eyes closed, save that where the beams of their lanterns struck the glass-like rock or when lightning flashed outside, there was a shining, almost sparkling effect that was quite strange and disorientating.

Cockles crossed himself. "This is the very mouth of Hell."

"Then, you should feel at home," Black Jack sneered, "for is that not where we all are destined to reside?"

"There is something wrong about this place," Little William said. "I'm scared."

"Cease your cowardly prattling," ordered Captain Rice. "Pegleg came here and left alive."

"Alive, yes," said the Bosun, slowly, "but what befell him after he left? We all know the stories. He didn't live long, did he?"

Thistlebeard snorted, "I'm with the Captain. I don't believe in Fate or curses, only cold hard steel, my own skill and the life I carve out for myself. We came here for the treasure, so let's take it."

"Besides," said Black Jack with a chuckle, "if entering this place will bring a curse down upon us, it is too late, for we have already entered this nightmare."

Bosun James sighed. "He's right, of course. We might as well go on along the road to our damnation and see what comforts it might bring us along the way. Perhaps treasure will ease our suffering on the way to Hell."

The tube-like cave descended at a slight angle for some distance into the mountain before opening out into a large chamber. There was a wide pool filling half the cavern, the waters of which seemed as black as tar. On a rise to the left of the chamber was a single large, ironbound chest. On the slopes of the mound, there were skeletons, the bones alarmingly white against the black of the rock.

"Fourteen," counted Thistlebeard. "He left fourteen men to guard his treasure."

"Well," said Captain Rice, "they are in no state to stop us. William, James, fetch it down."

The two big men began to climb the mound, gingerly stepping over the scattered bones that decorated it.

While they climbed, Cockles shone his lantern beam about the cave and settled upon the pool. There was something wrong about it that he couldn't quite discern.

Bosun James and Little William had reached the top of the mound. The chest didn't appear to be locked. James reached out to open it.

Cockles let out an inarticulate cry of terror.

James threw the lid open to reveal not only a pile of coins and jewels but, atop them, the disarticulated bones of a fifteenth skeleton.

The black waters had surged out of the pool. For a moment, it seemed something was rising from the pool, then Cockles realized it was the water itself that had risen. Not that it was water. It moved viscously, but with greater solidity than water, a demonic substance. It flowed up the mound.

James looked down in surprise and swore when he saw it.

"What is it?" William cried.

"The Devil's blood!" shrieked Black Jack, all bravado gone.

Suddenly, as the black liquid reached them and flowed about them, painting them black with congealed darkness, the bones sprang to a ghastly parody of life, and the one in the chest leaping up last of all. Each one held a cutlass in one bony hand.

Surrounded, Bosun James and Little William had no chance. The dead seemed immune to mortal weapons, but the pirates were not and they were cut down in moments.

Then, the skeletons turned to pursue the others, followed by the black tide.

Terrified, Cockles didn't even try to turn to run; the strange liquid flowed up his legs, up his body, and up into his scream-stretched mouth, silencing his cry of terror with an obscene gurgle. Then he turned, cutlass in hand, to join the marching dead in their pursuit of his former comrades.

Black Jack had been the first to flee. Whatever he might joke, he had no will to face such devilish things.

Captain Rice was close behind him, cursing because he had had to abandon the treasure. Thistlebeard was just behind the Captain.

With a scream, Black Jack lost his footing on the slick rock at the entrance to the cave and went flying into space, plunging down the hillside, snapping his neck and shredding his flesh on the rocks.

"Careful," the Captain said as he and Thistlebeard reached the entrance.

The First Mate swore. "We're dead if we run and dead if we tarry."

Captain Rice looked back, wide-eyed with fear. The black-smeared skeletons were barely a few feet behind them. With a roar, he charged at them. With a swipe of his cutlass, he took the skull off one, but that seemed not to affect it a jot. They began to strike at him and though he tried to fend off the blows, he fell to his knees, then collapsed under the relentless assault.

Thistlebeard slid and skidded down the slope, desperately praying he might reached the longboat before the dead caught up with him. He didn't know exactly what had happened, but he was certain it was demonic in nature. They were being punished for their many sins. Had old Pegleg set a trap for sinners such as they? Or, was the darkness in the cave the concealed evil of the man and his crew? Or, was it something older that the pirates had disturbed?

He remembered a verse the priest had recited to him in his youth after he was caught stealing a ha'penny, 'The love of money was the root of all evil.' Perhaps it was. It certainly seemed as if their lust for wealth had brought them to their doom.

He started to sob. Even if he got away, would he remain caught in the vile web of this diabolic fluid?

Thistlebeard looked up to the stormy sky and called out to God for mercy, but nothing changed; the storm continued to whirl about him and the darkness continued to flow down the slope towards him. It seemed as if there was no hope in the world left to him.

But, he continued to run.

DJ Tyrer

Don Miguel, The Inquisition, And The Mad Pirate's Crusade

Benjamin Fine

I

The magnificent Alhambra, the pearl set in emeralds, with its soft red brick walls and adjacent gardens, towered over the city. The hot August sun and the wide, cloudless sky made the stucco homes, sitting on the hills of the upper town, gleam bright white as the sunshine bounced off their walls. The orange tiled roofs of the buildings were burnished a golden hue that framed the whole city against the green of the mountains beyond.

Below the hills of the upper town the four rivers; the Beiro, the Darro, the Gentil, and the Monachil, that came together at the foothills of the Sierra Nevadas to locate the city, were calm and idle on the windless summer day. The heat, oppressive even in the morning, made the sometimes bustling city, have a slow, sleepy feel.

It had been sixty years since the Spanish conquered, or reconquered depending on one's point of view, Granada.

In 1492, the Reconquista was completed, the Granada War was over, and Granada and all of Al-Andalus became part of the great new Spanish kingdom. The mosques and synagogues were now churches, the grand mosque that had been the heart of the city at the main square or Zocalo was now the main cathedral, and the Alhambra was the office of both the Spanish Governor and the city Alcalde, and not the palace of the Almohad king. However, the look of the city had not changed; it remained the same as the Moorish city, constructed by the Muslim rulers for beauty, that it had been for centuries; the capital of the last Moorish Tarifa or kingdom in Iberia and the home of the last Emir. The conquering Spanish were awed by the magnificence of Granada and physically left the town much as it was.

Even the spirit of Granada as a Moorish town partly remained. For two hundred years the Muslim rulers practiced a type of tolerance, called convivencia or 'live and let live', that allowed Muslims, Catholics and Jews to live together in relative harmony. The Jews of Granada especially flourished, and were among the leaders of the Moorish city, both politically and in business. The Jewish quarter was set above the Zocalo, on what was called the Hill Judaica, and abutted the Albaicin, the district where the wealthier Moors lived. The last Emir had made a deal with the conquering Castilians, as part of his surrender, to preserve the convivencia. Within ten years the Spanish, goaded by the strength of the Inquisition, turned their back on their agreement. The Jews and Moors were either killed, expelled or forced to convert. Catholics poured into Granada from the rest of Spain, and rioters partially destroyed the Jewish quarter and took over the Albaicin, forcing the Moriscos or converted Muslims to the lower town. Many Jews did remain though, and formed the conversos, or converted ones, who reclaimed the Hill Judaica. Six decades after the onset of the Inquisition the conversos and the Moriscos still played an important role in Granada, despite the push of the Grand Inquisitor in Madrid.

☠☠☠☠

Mical Joshua bin Mordecai Benzion, known to all as Don Miguel, walked slowly from his home in the converso district on the old Judaic Hill and down the narrow streets towards the Zocalo. It was already past ten in the morning and although his father Don Mordecai, and his older brother Abram, had been in their business office for at least two hours, Don Miguel walked leisurely. The heat had made the day slow and languid and he felt no need to rush.

Tall, strong and handsome with broad shoulders, dark skin and a hawk nose, Don Miguel was an imposing figure. He was dressed in finery and a floppy hat that only the wealthy and powerful could afford. The people he passed along the way nodded in deference. Miguel was a man of wealth and privilege, a man of respect; un hombre de respeto.

Don Miguel lived a life of luxury. His father was Mordecai bin Moshe Benzion, the banker to the Spanish Governor and to the Alcalde. Don Mordecai was the leader of the converso community in Granada and was also a trader, importing and exporting fruits and wines from throughout Spain and silks and fine cloth from Italy and Morocco.

The Benzion family, Don Mordecai his brothers and cousins, had vast holdings throughout the Sephardic world. Mordecai's branch of the family had been in Granada for two hundred years, and now lived in a large stucco home in the Distrito Judaica on the old Hill Judaica where the conversos have been forced to reside. Don Miguel, as the son of this important clan, lived and ate well. He also felt that he had the pick of the finest women in Granada; Spanish, Morisco, and Converso.

Many of the conversos tread lightly when they walked, knowing that their lives and livelihoods hung by a thread on the whim of the Spanish and the Inquisition. Although Granada, six decades after the end of the Reconquista, had settled into an uneasy version of convivencia where Catholic, Morisco and Converso lived in an uneasy but cordial peace, it could change at the drop of a pin. Throughout most of the rest of the new Spanish kingdom, the conversos, those Jews who stayed and converted, were reviled and called Marranos, which signified filth or swine. In Granada, however, some of the spirit of the tolerant Moorish past remained, and the word Marrano was rarely heard. Still, many conversos were timid in walking and talking lest they incur the wrath of the Inquisition. Not so Don Miguel. He walked always with a swagger, as if to tell the world how important he was and how he feared nothing. He was a man of the world, having studied at the University of Padua in Italy, and then spending three years as a commander in the army of the Prince of Sienna. His exploits in the wars between Italian city-states had become legendary among the people in Granada. He was renowned as one of the finest swordsman in Granada and when he returned from Italy and his skill and ferocity as a soldier and swordsman became known, the Spanish governor offered him the command of the Spanish garrison. His appointment was only stopped by the Bishop Llorda, perhaps pushed by the local inquisitor.

"It is not right to have a converso commander. We cannot have it, they cannot be trusted," the Bishop told the Governor. "They are still Jews at heart and remember how the Jews opened the City of Toledo and let the infidels conquer our land," repeating a myth that was accepted as truth throughout Catholic Spain.

Don Miguel, though not the garrison commander, and a converso, was still respected by all. Despite his reputation as a fierce military Captain, the people of Granada knew him as a man of even temperament, who treated everyone with dignity, and was quick to laugh and to joke. He spoke Spanish, Arabic, Ladino, Italian and the Sicilian dialect of Palermo, where a branch of the Benzions were bankers, and while he walked to the Zocalo, he greeted many along the way.

"Good morning Señora Dominguez, try to stay cool today," he said to a woman hanging clothing from her building on the Calle Collina.

"Hola Vincente. It is too hot to work," he joked with the cobbler whose shop was right before the entrance to the Zocalo.

Each person smiled back at Don Miguel and answered politely as if he were their friend.

He entered the Zocalo at the end of the Calle Collina and surveyed the large square. The stalls of the market had already been set up and Don Miguel walked directly to a stall packed with oranges. This was his daily ritual.

"Are these fresh Señora?" he asked, as he did each morning on his walk from the converso district to the Benzion business office.

"Right off the trees from the countryside" she answered. She then handed him several large oranges which he put in a small satchel and he gave her several coins. He then returned to gaze at the square. Don Miguel's greatest pleasure was women, and he admired them all; the converso women with their dark skin, curly hair and sharp wits, the Morisco women with the faces demurely covered and the Spanish women with their straight black hair and fiery eyes. To Miguel's delight, the fashions in Granada showed off the lovely bodies of those he admired.

It was expected by Don Mordecai that he marry a converso woman of high standing like his brother Don Abram had done. Abram had married Rebekka Bat Yehuda the daughter of another converso trader, had two children, and worked as his father's chief assistant. Despite his father's expectations, Don Miguel remained as free as a flying eagle and tried to flirt with almost any beautiful woman he saw. With the women from good families, whatever their religious background, it was difficult, since each was accompanied by a dueña; yet he still tried.

In Italy, he learned the pleasures of lusty Italian women and as a soldier he learned that even married women were not immune to the charms of a handsome swordsman. In Granada, he often went to the taverns and gypsy camps beside the rivers in the lower town, where he enjoyed the company of dark, beautiful women from Romany; gypsy women or gitanas. Often the taverns by the rivers and the gypsy camps were dangerous.

Bandits and thieves preyed on the other customers, many from the upper city. Don Miguel though had no fear. Once, set upon by two would-be thieves he dispatched and killed one of them easily with his sword and chased the other off. His reputation as a swordsman then spread quickly among the people of the lower city and Don Miguel was free to enjoy the entertainment of the river.

As Don Miguel surveyed the Zocalo, he spied Señorita Imelda Navarado y Ortega accompanied by her dueña. Dona Rosa. Imelda was the daughter of Don Luis Navarado, a powerful merchant who had moved to Granada from Navarre. Don Luis was a business rival of his father, but Don Luis and Don Mordecai, while not friends, it was outside of the norm for a friendship between a converso and a Catholic, were cordial to each other. The families often attended the important fiestas and galas thrown by the Governor, and Don Miguel had often tried, sometimes successfully, to flirt with the lovely Imelda, who had coal black hair and fair skin. She was in a dark blue dress of the finest style with a wide skirt and a top that showed off her beautiful young body. There was a black comb holding up the front of her shiny hair. Miguel had often felt that she was the most beautiful of all the eligible women of Granada and he would court her if it were only possible.

Don Miguel walked over to Imelda and doffed his fancy hat at her. "A beautiful day to see a beautiful lady walking across the Zocalo," he said to her and smiled.

Her dueña, Dona Rosa, dressed in black, older and fat with a double chin, tried to step between them, but Imelda ignored her and smiled back at Don Miguel.

"A wonderful day to be complimented by a handsome gentleman," she answered and also smiled.

Dona Rosa spit on the ground. "Don't speak to him. He's a converso," she told the señorita, but again Imelda ignored her.

The young señorita often thought about the handsome Don Miguel, but his being a converso never entered her mind. "Will you be at the Governor's fiesta this evening?" she asked.

"I will," Don Miguel answered. "Perhaps we can share a dance."

"Don't answer señorita," ordered Dona Rosa and tried to push Imelda along.

The young woman stood her ground and again answered with a coy smile. "Perhaps."

Don Miguel began to say more but stopped when he saw his Uncle Arnoldo hurrying towards him. Arnoldo seemed upset and was perspiring heavily in the hot air.

Arnoldo ignored Imelda and her dueña and spoke rapidly to Miguel, catching his breath as he spoke. "You have to come quickly. Your father needs us. Don Mordecai sent a messenger to my apartment and we must hurry."

Despite the agitated state of his uncle, Don Miguel remained calm. "We will get there in due time my uncle," he said and then turned back to Imelda, who Dona Rosa was trying to push along and away from Don Miguel. "Until later My Lady," Miguel said to her. Imelda smiled and then without any prodding from Dona Rosa, walked on.

"Quick let's hurry," his uncle pleaded, but Miguel headed for a small wine stand at the far end of the Zocalo. "A glass of wine Uncle to make the day and the meeting with my father tolerable," he said to Arnoldo.

Arnoldo was only fifteen years older than his nephew, Miguel. In his youth, Arnoldo lived the same life that Miguel lived now; food, women and drink. As Arnoldo aged, he became fat and anxious. He traveled for the Benzion businesses throughout Spain and he had become a constant worrier. He watched the Inquisition grow stronger and more vicious with each passing year and he feared for the safety of both himself and the other conversos. "We only survive by the grace of heaven. At any moment, the Inquisition can turn on us," he often stated.

He suffered from gout and sometimes was in severe pain. He fretted constantly about his health in general. Miguel always pooh-poohed his worries but that day his uncle was even more nervous than usual.

"Your father wants to see us quickly. What does he want? It can't be good that he sent a courier to me." The heavy perspiration had stained his uncle's clothes, but Miguel still wouldn't rush. At the small wine stand, Miguel ordered two glasses of a red vintage from Al-Andalus.

II

Miguel stood at the small wine booth at the far end of the Zocalo and sipped his wine. Arnoldo, now almost in a state of panic, quickly downed his small glass and moaned, "Please hurry Miguel, this is important. My brother will be angry." The combination of anxiety and the extreme heat made the heavy Arnoldo's perspiration even worse. His clothes were totally covered in sweat and as Miguel calmly drank, Arnoldo kept shaking his head.

"Calm down Uncle. We'll get there soon enough" Miguel answered and continued drinking.

When Miguel finally finished, he and Arnold trudged to Don Mordecai's office, which was just a short walk off of the Zocalo. The office was in a large stone building on the Camino Real, the main street leading from the Cathedral, up the hill, to the Alhambra. The front office was an open hall, much like the dining hall in a palace and looked opulent. It had a large desk, visible as soon as one entered the building, and the walls were hung with fine tapestries. This room was used for Don Mordecai's banking interests and he met here often with both the provincial Governor and the city Alcalde. A smaller business office, used as the center of the import-export business was behind the front hall. This room was more functional and contained the records of the Benzion holdings. The back of the building contained the warehouse, holding their inventory of wine, cloth, silk, and porcelain.

Don Mordecai stood with his older son Abram, and Mordecai's other brother Asher, in the center of the entry hall. He glared at Don Miguel and Arnoldo as they entered. Don Mordecai was angry, while Abram and Asher were clearly upset.

"You only work half a day if it's warm?" Don Mordecai snarled at Miguel and pointedly, completely ignored his youngest brother Arnoldo.

Miguel started to say something in explanation, but Don Mordecai shook his head and put his hand up indicating to Miguel that he should say nothing. Mordecai, without speaking, motioned both Miguel and Arnoldo into the smaller office and Abram and Asher followed silently. Mordecai then walked into a meeting room off of the back office. He motioned them all to sit down at a large table that sat in the center of the room. Don Mordecai stood at the head of the table while the others sat. Abram and Asher looked solemn while Miguel and Arnoldo, knowing nothing, waited for whatever was to come.

Don Mordecai was a stern man and as impressive in his way as his younger son Miguel. Sixty-three years old, he had been the leader of the converso community in Granada for thirty years, following in the footsteps of his father, Moises Benzion. Moises had been the secular leader of the Jews of the Moorish kingdom and the banker to the last Moorish Emir, Boabdil. Boabdil had ousted his brother as Emir and then in an attempt to save his kingdom converted to Christianity. He knew the war was lost and made a pact with the conquering Castilians.

As part of his surrender, the Moors, and Jews, would be allowed to remain in Granada if they converted. Many Jews fled, clinging tenaciously to their religion, some to Morocco, some to Turkey and some to Egypt where they were still welcomed in the Muslim realms. Moises though found a rabbi who told him that it was better to convert than flee and that God would forgive him. Whether the rabbi told him this, or whether the powerful Moises ordered the rabbi to tell him this, was never clear, but the Benzions remained in Granada as the leaders of the new converso community.

Don Mordecai even in old age was tall and powerfully built, his hair thick and black. He had a full beard that framed his dark piercing eyes. In the thirty years since Moises' death, he had expanded both the wealth and importance of the Benzions in Granada. As he stood, he looked around the table. His older son Abram sat to the front. Abram was dark like Miguel but slender and balding and he held his head in his hands. Mordecai's younger brother Asher, bearded and dark but not as large as Mordecai, just sat solemnly.

Miguel also looked around the table and thought that his older brother might burst into tears at any second. Arnoldo, still perspiring, sat to the rear. The anxiety of not knowing what was happening made his gout flare up and his face exhibited the pain that he was in. Don Miguel, Mordecai's younger son, sat calmly.

"It isn't good," Don Mordecai began. "I have known about this for about two months, but I thought we had more time. I believed we had until the Day of the Dead in

October, but now we must act immediately." Miguel and Arnoldo had no idea what he was talking about and hung on his words. Abram and Asher nodded their heads solemnly.

"We have to leave Granada," Mordecai told them without much emotion. "There is no saving us now. This must be done." As he spoke, Abram began to weep very quietly. Arnoldo was speechless and he appeared like he was hit by a boulder in his ample belly.

Miguel was astounded. "Leave?" he asked. "Why?"

Mordecai raised his hands up again to silence everyone and continued. "The Governor has told me that the Grand Inquisitor from Madrid comes next week. He brings a Spanish troop with him and he plans to remove us and the remaining Moriscos. The order from Madrid is that the conversos are dangerous to the kingdom. They claim that we are corrupting los Catolicos—the Catholics—and have never really given up our Jewish ways."

"Why run?" Miguel asked. His voice was defiant. "We can fight the Inquisition. We have always survived and flourished. Besides, my Father, you own both the Governor and the city Alcalde."

"You are brave my son, but you are foolish," Mordecai answered. His voice was solemn but direct and unwavering. "It is too late to fight. My information is directly from the Governor. He cannot protect me. He is being removed by the King under the advice of the Inquisitor. He knows all this, but he stays anyway. The Grand Inquisitor told the King that the Governor is too friendly with the conversos, meaning, of course, myself." Don Mordecai was now shaking is head, "Do you understand now Miguel? The Governor expected the Grand Inquisitor from Madrid to come next month and then all chaos would occur. Yesterday he called me to the Alhambra to tell me that the Inquisitor's troop is only several days from here and we have to move rapidly."

Mordecai looked at his son to make certain that he now understood. Miguel nodded and then looked back to his uncle. Arnoldo winced in pain from his gout but nodded also. Don Mordecai then continued.

"I have kept all this information to myself as best I could. No-one must know until we are away. Miguel, you and Arnoldo will stay behind for several days to close our affairs and then follow us. You, as a soldier, are better equipped to deal with the Inquisitor's men than Abram or Asher."

Miguel took in all that his father presented. It was overwhelming, and he was startled and surprised, but from his time on the battlefield he knew how to react quickly. In his mind he had already formulated plans. "When do you leave?" he asked his father.

Before Mordecai could answer, Arnoldo, who looked as if he will keel over, meekly asked his brother, "Why must we," pointing at Miguel, " wait behind?"

Mordecai ignored his younger brother and answered Miguel. "Abram, Asher, their families and I leave tonight during the Governor's fiesta. We hope that we can get away without much fanfare. We are taking fifteen servants with us and the Governor has given me a small contingent of soldiers for protection. We go to the port of Malaga. There is a ship there to take us to Palermo. I have changed, whatever I could, to wealth we can carry."

Miguel, spoke again, thinking now as a soldier and a warrior, "Why run? We have survived before. We can fight the Inquisitor in whatever way we can." As Miguel spoke, Abram wept more, and Arnoldo seemed as if he was about to die.

Don Mordecai shook his head. "Son, again, you are brave but foolish. Listen to me," he stressed. "Even a good soldier knows when he must run. We survived the massacres sixty years ago, but it looks like our luck, our suerte, our fortuna, has changed."

Abram was sobbing and Asher solemnly nodded his head. Arnoldo was moaning loudly from a combination of nerves and gout.

"We have to leave," Mordecai repeated. "There is no other way. The best we can do is take with us as much as possible."

"Father," Miguel asked him, "Why use the soldiers from the Governor? I am the best to protect us."

Mordecai played to his son's pride. "You are my son. I know that, but I need you and Arnoldo to close up here. You are the ones who can best deal with everyone. You have four days and then you also go to Malaga for a ship to Palermo. You and Arnoldo are both younger and better able to take care of yourselves. We will rebuild our family in Italy. I am sorry it has come to this."

Don Mordecai had finished but then Miguel realized that in Palermo the Spanish were still in control and there was still the Inquisition. As conversos, they would have to continue to live submissively. Miguel became angry. "Why go to Italy? Let's leave the Catholic lands. We are not believers. Why not go to Africa or Turkey and live again as Jews?"

Don Mordecai shook his head and spoke as if he regretted something long past. "Miguel your grandfather, my father Moises, made that decision for us sixty years ago. To the Muslims, we are Catolicos and hated and to the Jews we are conversos and hated. Our fate is in Christian lands, unfortunately. My father gave us sixty years of peace, but now we pay the price. There is nothing more to do but flee. Go back to the house Miguel and prepare, you also Arnoldo. Go to the fiesta tonight and tell no one. When the community realizes that I am gone there will be a panic, I am certain. Do what you can for the community but our family must come first. The next time we see each other is in Palermo."

Don Mordecai signaled for Abram and Asher to follow him and they started to walk out into the main office.

Miguel is discouraged that his father is abandoning the other conversos. He called to his father, "Father we must help the others, they depend on us."

Mordecai turned back to his son. "The family must come first. That is what must be done."

Miguel and his uncle sat for a while in silence at the large table. Arnoldo was in pain but said nothing. Finally, Don Miguel stood up and motioned for his uncle to follow. "Come Uncle, there is much we have to do."

The two walked back to the Zocalo and then across to the streets leading up towards the Judaic Hill. Arnoldo was beside himself. "Miguelito my nephew, everything is lost. Our lives are over." He struggled, against the pain of his gout, and the heat of the midday, to keep up with his nephew. "What if we can't get out before the Inquisitor arrives?"

Don Miguel, who has never known fear, assumed that all will work out. Although the pleasures and the good life in Granada have been his existence, he had the mindset of one who adjusts and adapts, a true grandson of Moises and a true son of Mordecai. He tried to reassure the worried Arnoldo. "You'll see Uncle, we'll pick up the pieces in Sicily and it will be as before."

III

In 1492, the Castilian army captured Granada and the last Moorish kingdom fell. It was the end of the Reconquista and Spain was now Catholic. Castile and Aragon united to form the new kingdom of Spain under "los Reyes Catolicos"—the Catholic rulers—Isabella and Ferdinand. Ferdinand and Isabella then united most of the remaining Iberia, including what had been the Moorish lands of Al-Andalus. They also brought the Inquisition and it began a period of terror for the Jews and Moors of Spain. The Jews and their Moorish overlords had lived peacefully for hundreds of years and it was the golden age of the Diaspora for the Spanish Jews, the Sephardim. In Spain it was the age of convivencia, let and let live, and it benefitted Moors, Christians and Jews alike. Even many of the Christians in Iberia fought the Inquisition. In Navarre, after they became part of the Spanish kingdom, the Christians refused to allow the Inquisition to destroy the Jewish community. However, by 1500, the Inquisition, under the terrible Grand Inquisitor Torquemada, who had the confidence of the very religious Queen Isabella, had taken control. The Jews, many wealthy, fled Spain for the other Muslim lands, Morocco, Egypt, Syria, and Turkey as well as for friendlier Christian principalities in Italy. Those who fought to stay were killed or forced to convert. Those who converted continued to live in Spain and were called conversos or Nuevos Christianos but more derisively Marranos, a word that was synonymous with rats and filth. Secretly many conversos called themselves Anusim, which in Hebrew, means forced; many could be identified by the Hebrew names. The Moors were killed by the thousands, yet some managed to convert and became the Moriscos.

Moshe ben Levi Benzion, known by his Spanish name Don Moises, was the banker to the Muslim Emirs of Granada. Moises and his family held great power in Granada and lived in a large white home in the Barrio Judaica on the Judaic Hill above the Zocalo. The Benzions had lived in Spain for over five hundred years and had relatives throughout Al-Andalus. Moises's branch had been in Granada for two hundred years. Other parts of the family were scattered throughout the Sephardic world, and there were many relatives both in Christian lands in Sicily and the Italian peninsula and throughout the grand Muslim Caliphate. Moises had owned a huge estate north of Granada that had been plundered by the conquering Castilian army.

As the Catholic Spaniards approached Granada, a large portion of the Jews fled. Moises had seen the writing on the wall and allied himself with the new Emir, Boabdil, who betrayed his uncle, the previous Emir, and made a deal with the approaching Castilians. Boabdil converted to Catholicism, and his agreement with the victorious Spanish gave both the Jews and Moors of the city of Granada a special dispensation and allowed them to remain. Within ten years, though, the Spanish turned on this agreement and allowed Catholic mobs to plunder the Jewish homes. In the violence that followed, it seemed that the remaining Jews would also flee, but the new Spanish Governor sought out Benzion. The Governor and the city Alcalde needed the Jews money, and he told Moises that if the Benzions converted and convinced the remaining Jews to also convert they could stay in Granada in peace. Moises found a Rabbi who told the community that it was better to convert than flee. Moises converted and became the Governor's banker. The Benzions became the leaders of the converso community in Granada and lived much as they had under the Moors. They were forced to sit in a separate section of the Cathedral and were always suspect by the Inquisition, yet three successive Governors and three successive city Alcalde's protected them. They survived for the next sixty years. Moises, and then his son Mordecai, had the ear and trust of the Governor and maintained an opulent banking office in a building near the Zocalo and near the Cathedral. The conversos rebuilt their plundered homes on the old Judaic Hill.

Boabdil the last Moorish Emir, with whom Moises had allied himself, found that his conversion meant nothing to the Spaniards. They removed him as Granada's ruler and banished him to the Muslim lands. He went to live, disgraced, in the Almohad kingdom in Morocco. As Boabdil left, it is said that he looked back at his beautiful city, the garden of the west, and wept. His mother rebuked him, "Don't cry like a woman over something you could not keep as a man."

☠☠☠☠

Don Miguel and Arnoldo packed what they could of their clothing into small trunks and then he and Arnoldo dined together in Miguel's apartment in a small part of the Benzion compound. They were somber, and whenever Arnoldo, still nervous and fretting, tried to speak, Miguel would silence him.

Later that evening, the two went to the Alhambra to attend the fiesta thrown by the Governor. Normally, Don

Miguel enjoyed these parties, because he was able to flirt with the beautiful women of the city. That night he was too preoccupied to flirt, and for much of the evening he stood to the side by the wine bar, watched the dancing, and sipped his wine. Señorita Imelda, with her ever vigilant dueña, Rosa, by her side, caught his eye and smiled. Miguel smiled back at her, but he was no mood to dance. When he did not come over, Imelda seemed to become angry and turned to talk to another young gentleman. Early during the fiesta, Arnoldo told Miguel that his gout had him in pain and Arnoldo left.

Don Luis Navarado, Imelda's father, walked over to Don Miguel. "Can I buy you a wine, Don Luis?" Miguel asked the older man.

"No Don Miguel, let us walk. We have some business to discuss. Come." Don Luis pointed to an outer patio and Don Miguel left his wine on the bar and followed him.

Don Luis surveyed the patio to make certain that they were alone and then spoke quietly to Miguel. "I know everything. Don Mordecai spoke to me this afternoon. Can I speak freely to you?"

Don Miguel nodded his head and Don Luis continued. "Tomorrow we have to meet about the inventory. I will give you a good price. Is ten in the morning at your offices all right?"

Miguel was wary of saying too much, although he had no doubt that his father had entrusted the information to Don Luis. "Ten tomorrow is fine."

Don Luis then leaned into Miguel and spoke even lower. "Your father and I were rivals in business, but we always respected each other. I've also admired your reputation as a soldier. It is too bad that the times did not allow us to be friends." Don Luis then held his hand out, a gesture that surprised Miguel.

Miguel shook Don Luis's hand and Don Luis said "Until tomorrow then," and walked back into the dance.

Don Miguel stayed late at the fiesta to make certain that his father and brother had time to leave. Most of the wealthier people of Granada were at the gala, and with their absence the departure of the Benzion group would not be as noticeable.

In the early morning, Don Miguel went to his father's part of the compound and found that everyone was gone. Much had been left behind and Miguel, though never religious, thought of the Bible story, that he had read in Arabic, of the hasty departure of the Hebrew slaves from Egypt. Maimonides, the great Sephardic sage, had written that Jews must think of the departure from Egypt as if they had lived it personally. Don Miguel could only smile while he thought of the ancient Exodus, although being a converso had never been that important to him. Now, he hoped that his father and brother would make it to Malaga, and then to Palermo. Palermo, although controlled by the Spanish king, still lived under the convivencia, and Asher's two sons were bankers there. If Don Mordecai and his party made it to Sicily, the Benzions of Granada would survive for some more years.

Miguel and Arnoldo had only four days before they followed the others and made their own way to Sicily. They were left with the unenviable task of closing the office and selling most of what was left. Each day, messengers arranged by Don Mordecai, came to tell them how close the approaching Inquisitor was. The Inquisitor had with him a regiment of Castilian soldiers whose task was to remove the Governor, who was not trusted because of his close ties to the conversos, and then to force both the conversos and the Moriscos to leave Granada. Arnoldo and Don Miguel realized that this meant that Spanish mobs would be urged to storm the Barrio of the conversos and burn the homes, as they had done sixty years earlier. As they prepared, Arnoldo constantly bemoaned their fate, while Miguel prepared as if for battle.

As had been arranged, Miguel and Arnoldo went at ten the next morning to meet with Don Luis and to sell their warehouse material. When they arrived at the office, besides Don Luis, there was a collection of other Christian merchants who had heard that Don Mordecai had fled and that his inventory must be sold. Miguel unlocked the door to the Benzion office and motioned for them all to enter. As the group gathered in the large front banking hall, Miguel pulled Don Luis to the side and said, "You have first priority. My father trusted you and I am a man of honor. First let me deal with these others."

Don Diego Guzman, the leader of the delegation of Christian merchants, and an enemy of the conversos spoke first to Miguel. He made a very low, almost insulting, offer, from his whole group and for the entire warehouse. Miguel dismissed the offer quickly. Don Diego then spoke derisively, "Why should we buy it from you when we can get it from the Inquisition after you flee. Accept our offer or get nothing."

Don Miguel stepped forward and stood right before Don Diego. Miguel drew his sword and Don Diego stepped backward in fear. "My father was a businessman, but I am a soldier. If you repeat that offer you will die right here in this office," Miguel threatened.

Don Diego and the others stepped further backward and now Don Miguel ordered them out of the building.

"Go and come back when you have fair offers. I will not be cheated."

The delegation led by Don Diego left the office and only Don Luis remained. Don Luis told him, "Miguel your father and I agreed that five-thousand golden doubloons would be fair for the building, the wine, the cloth and the porcelain." A servant of Don Luis opened a chest containing the gold and showed it to Miguel and Arnoldo.

"That is more than fair Don Luis. Everything is now yours," Miguel told him. "Uncle Arnoldo, go with this servant to bring the chest to our home."

After Arnoldo had left, Miguel stood together in the office with Don Luis. The older man, bearded and gray then said to him. "Don Miguel, as I told you at the fiesta, I have always admired you and your family. Don Mordecai was a good man, a tough businessman, but I respected him and I admired you. It is bad that the situation does not permit our families to be friends. I never hated Jews or conversos. I wish you luck."

As he had at the fiesta, Don Luis held out his hand to Don Miguel and said, "For better times then–they will come." Don Miguel smiled at him not knowing the secret that Don Luis held.

Miguel then sold the Benzion compound on the Judaic Hill to a wealthy Spanish merchant who had moved from Aragon to Granada. Miguel and Arnoldo had to empty their papers from the office and then had to follow the path of Don Mordecai to the waiting ship in Malaga.

The remaining converso population of the city was thrown into a panic when they learned that Mordecai Benzion has fled and Don Miguel will follow. They now knew that the Inquisition, despite the reluctance of the Governor and local Alcalde, would crack down on the conversos and the Moriscos. As they learned, the Inquisition now considered them a great danger to the good Catholic population of the Spanish kingdom. They were to be killed or exiled as their non-converted brethren had been six decades earlier.

Many of the Moriscos, who lived in the lower city along the rivers, began to flee southward. The Moriscos hoped that they could get to the Muslim lands in Morocco and North Africa, but for them there was the danger that when, and if, they get to Africa, they will be killed by the Almohads for converting.

During their preparations for leaving, Miguel, both in his house and at the office, was approached by frightened conversos who begged him, "Please get us out. Your family has always led us." Miguel was moved by their plight and was ashamed that his father had just deserted them. Despite what his father ordered him not to do, he told them that he will do what he can.

IV

On the fourth day after Don Mordecai's departure, Arnoldo and Miguel fled Granada also. They rode on horses and took three servants with them. One of the servants, the trusted Benito, whose family has served the Benzions for over a century, handled the wagon which contained the chest of gold doubloons, the payment from Don Luis for their inventory. They also had two trunks for their clothing which was extensive for both men. They left much behind.

Don Miguel, over the strenuous objections of his uncle, permitted a group of eight converso families, forty people in all, to travel with them to Malaga. He promised them his protection on the journey and in the early morning of the departure day the caravan gathered outside of his home on the Judaic Hill. Most of the converso group were families of merchants who had their own wealth. Don Miguel did not promise them a ship to leave Spain but did assure them that he will personally guard the group until they reached Malaga. At Malaga, they were to be on their own. Miguel's heart was with these refugees and he did all this despite the commands of his father.

Arnoldo was frightened. "Miguelito," he pleaded, "we cannot protect them. It will slow us down. You know what Don Mordecai commanded."

Miguel shook his head in disagreement. "Arnoldo I cannot desert these people. They are our brethren. My father was their leader here and I am ashamed that he has left them to the vagaries of the Inquisition." Despite his love of pleasure, his temper, and his ferocity, Don Miguel considered himself above all a man of honor.

There were two roads from Granada to the port at Malaga. The mountain road was shorter but closer to the approaching Inquisition forces, so Miguel decided to take the somewhat longer main highway that went from Granada directly to the coast and connected with the shoreline road. Malaga was less than ninety miles away and in former times it was an easy four-day journey. However the well-constructed Roman road, paved with sturdy cobblestones, was in disrepair. The Visigoths, the Moorish emirs and then the Almohad kings, all maintained the road, but the War of the Reconquista, followed by sixty years of neglect by the new Spanish rulers, made the road a stony, rutted, dusty mess. It was nearly impossible for the caravan to travel more than fifteen miles a day as the horses and the wagons struggled. There was constant fear that the caravan would either be captured by the Inquisition troops or set upon by gangs of mountain bandits. It was only the presence of Don Miguel and his servants that gave the travelers some peace.

They traveled on the difficult road, down the mountains to the coast, the whole first day. Evening fell, but Miguel pushed the caravan forward. They had to reach Malaga as quickly as possible. The travelers became hungry and tired and the horses were exhausted. Many of the wagons had been damaged and some were left behind in the haste to get to Malaga. Finally, late that first evening a delegation from the travelers begged Miguel. "Can we rest and eat Don Miguel? We can't go any further?"

Arnoldo, constantly worrying, told him, "We can't stop, we will miss the ship."

Don Miguel understood both sides, but he realized that he had to allow the party to rest. They camped in a clearing by the side of the road. While they ate, Arnoldo told Miguel that he is frightened by any delay.

"Miguelito, I fear that when we get to Malaga, the ship Captain will have betrayed us and left. He already has payment from Don Mordecai but what forces him to honor that?"

"Uncle," Don Miguel nodded, partly in agreement with him, "You ride ahead and go as quickly as you can to Malaga; make certain that the Captain honors his agreement. I will hurry these people as rapidly as possible."

Arnoldo took one of their servants and hurried ahead of the group to get to Malaga. They had only five days before the arranged ship, whose Captain had often dealt with Don Mordecai for importing, and had been paid well, was scheduled to leave. However, in the confusion that was caused by the crackdown of the Inquisition, and which was now known throughout Spain, as refugees fled south, the loyalty of this Captain, was less than certain. The others in Don Miguel's caravan were worried when they saw that Arnoldo had left. Most were wealthy carrying jewels and gold to barter and each hoped to also get on a ship in Malaga and away from Spain.

The party was not harassed by bandits in the mountains and when they reached the coastline the road improved. On the fourth day of travel, Miguel's group arrived in Malaga and headed directly to the waterfront. The harbor area was crowded with refugees from all over Al-Andalus, both Jews, and Moriscos. Arnoldo waited at the port and when he spotted Miguel, he rushed to him. He was clearly agitated, but he proved that he too could handle a crisis.

"Miguelito," he told him breathing heavily, "as I feared, the ship to Palermo left. He was a privateer afraid of the Inquisition. I told him he had to honor his agreement with Don Mordecai, but he ran. I have arranged for another ship to leave, but it goes through Gibraltar to Cuba."

"Cuba? We can't go to Cuba," Don Miguel answered. "We must get to Palermo."

"We have no choice," Arnoldo said, holding his hands up as if in surrender. "My contact here has learned by pigeon that the Inquisitor knows of this party and, as we speak, leads soldiers to Malaga. We cannot remain here. The ship to Cuba is to leave tomorrow morning and we must be on it."

Miguel explained the situation to the other converso families. They begged again for his help. Miguel shook his head. "I protected you until here, but now there is little that I can do."

Don Yussef, another prominent converso merchant, said to him, "Don Miguel, we have money also. Talk to the Captain of your ship and let us pay him also. Cuba is better than dying here in Malaga."

Don Miguel, a bit reluctantly agreed to talk to the Captain. "Arnoldo," he told his uncle," show me to the Captain."

"Miguelito, please," Arnoldo answered. "It was expensive and the others will tie us down. We travel as Spaniards, even in Cuba it is dangerous for conversos. We are Vargas now."

"Stop your moaning Uncle and take me to the Captain. You did well to find this ship, but I have to protect these people."

Despite his fears, Arnoldo brought Miguel to Captain Cozzano, a stocky Italian from Genoa with a thick brown beard. Miguel spoke to him directly.

"Captain Cozzano, I have also brought eight families that must board the ship. They can pay well."

"Are they conversos also?" the Captain asked.

"I am Spanish," Miguel said. "Why do you ask about conversos?"

"I know who you are Don Miguel. You don't recognize me, but you sailed with me three years ago from Palermo. On the ship, you were well-known as a famous commander from Sienna. I was the ship's mate so I know you are converso and why you are fleeing. Your uncle has paid well so your secret is safe and you are Señor Vargas for this trip. As for the families, it will not be cheap and it will be crowded. I already have twenty-six passengers to Cuba, but I will try to squeeze them onboard if they can pay."

"I will tell them," Don Miguel told Cozzano. "Those that can pay will. Those that can't will have to take their chance here in Malaga."

The eight converso families paid the Captain's exorbitant price in gold and they boarded the ship. Cozzano did not say that they were conversos, but it became well-known to the crew members and to the other passengers that they were. It created friction, since now the vessel, although a legal privateer, would be in danger from official Spanish galleons. The Captain put the ship to sea the next morning and from the decks the crew and passengers could see columns of soldiers on the coastline highway accompanying the Inquisitor towards Malaga.

V

As the Spanish Empire grew and the Spanish plundered the wealth of the conquered lands in the Americas, each year, twice a year, two fleets left Spain loaded with European goods in demand in the Spanish-American colonies. The two fleets sailed together down the coast of Africa, and stopped at the Canary Islands for provisions, before the six to eight-week voyage across the Atlantic. When the two fleets reached the Caribbean, they separated. The New Spain fleet sailed to Vera Cruz in Mexico to load silver from Mexico and porcelain shipped from China and then brought overland across Mexico from the Pacific. The second fleet, the Tierra Firme fleet sailed to either Cartagena, Columbia or to Panama, to load more silver and gold from the captured Inca Empire. A few ships went to the Caribbean island of Margarita to collect pearls, that had been harvested from offshore oyster beds. When the loading was complete, both fleets sailed for Havana in Cuba, to rendezvous for the journey back to Spain.

Along with these official, governmentally sponsored trips, privateers and private merchants, such as Captain Cozzano, also made the difficult voyages, bringing materials and passengers to the new world. For the passengers and crew, these were arduous journeys. With the best of conditions, the trip to Cuba took six weeks, usually eight weeks or longer. The passengers, who paid a royal sum for the trip, stayed in the best cabins the privateer's ships offered, but these were still crowded and uncomfortable. Most of the passengers were wealthy and accustomed to living in privilege and luxury, but the conditions below deck, even in the better sections, could best be described as awful. Many animals, sheep, goats, chickens and cows were taken on board to provide fresh meat, eggs, and milk. Many crew members and passengers had dogs and cats. The smells below deck were horrendous and made worse by the primitive sanitation facilities. For the paying passengers, there were cut out seats on the outer deck towards the front (the head) of the ship where waste was emptied directly into the sea. The constant up and down, left and right, and listing of the ships, made many, not used to the sea, horribly sick. Quite a large portion of the passengers were sick for the entire voyage.

The privateers, like the official fleets, liked to travel in convoys for safety. The rough waters of the Atlantic often damaged the traveling vessels, so for security, even the private merchants traveled in flotillas, though not as large as the Spanish fleets. Captain Cozzano had only three ships in his flotilla, the large main galleon, called the Bella Sonrisa, which housed the passengers, including Don Miguel and the families he managed to get aboard, and two smaller sloops that were ocean worthy. The main galleon had six mounted guns on each side, as well as two swivel cannons, in case of encounters with pirates.

As Cozzano's flotilla sailed through the Straits of Gibraltar, and into the open Atlantic, the weather was warm and sunny, and the open sea in August seemed as calm as a lake. It boded well for a safe passage. When the conversos saw, from the deck of the Bella Sonrisa, the Inquisitors's army approaching Malaga on the shoreline road, there was the fear that official Spanish ships would chase them. At Gibraltar, there seemed to be no ships following them, and this calmed the refugees. The conversos happily assumed that the Inquisitor was pleased that they left, wherever their destination.

Each of the passengers, who were well enough and not stricken with seasickness, was allowed to walk and congregate on the upper deck of the rear portion of the ship. The crew worked below them. For the crew, on a merchant vessel such Cozzano's galleon, it was also a difficult journey. The living conditions for the workers were even more crowded and unclean than those of the passengers. The passengers paid for better food, but the crew subsisted on dried meat, hard bread, and oranges. There was also the constant work of pulling on ropes and adjusting the masts coupled with the dangers of climbing the masts to work on the sails high above the ship's decks. The crew, though, were mostly hardened seamen who knew no other lifestyle. There were ample spirits to drink and many worked in a semi-constant state of drunkenness. There was a freedom on the seas that they would not have enjoyed back in their seaside villages. The merchant Captains, like Cozzano, had to be careful in the way they treated their crews. For the merchant seamen, there was always the temptation to join the many pirate vessels that plied the waters of the Caribbean and where there was the possibility of earning great wealth.

Don Miguel took advantage of the good weather in the Atlantic and each day walked in the sunny and warm sea air on the deck. Uncle Arnoldo, troubled by seasickness and gout, stayed mostly below. On the third day past Gibraltar, Miguel was shocked to see Señorita Imelda, together with her dueña and two servants, walking on the deck. She was well-dressed and seemed relaxed as if she were walking in the Zocalo in Granada. Miguel quickly tried to avoid her, but she spotted him and walked over to say hello.

She was surprised to see him also. "Don Miguel, you sail to Cuba also? I was told that the Benzion family went to Palermo."

Miguel nodded and answered, "Señorita Imelda our ship to Palermo left without us and we had to leave Iberia. We had no choice. Cuba was better than battling the Inquisitor in Malaga." He then asked her. "Why are you sailing? Why did you leave Granada?"

Imelda lowered her head and answered in a soft voice, "My father thought it would be wise with all the turmoil for me to leave Spain. My father fears for the chaos that comes now with the Inquisition. I go to live with my uncle in New Spain in Mexico." She suddenly began to cry. "It was so fast to leave home. I don't want to go."

Dona Rosa hearing the weeping stepped close to her and said, "Come, My Lady, this is foolish to cry. Come with me." Imelda though stood still and looked at Don Miguel. He didn't know why, but the tears in her dark eyes made her look even more beautiful to him.

Trying to calm her, Miguel touched her shoulders. "Don't cry Imelda," Miguel told her, "I always believe that things will work out."

Her dueña looked on in disapproval and again attempted to lead her away from Miguel and his touch, but Imelda, holding back her tears, stayed.

"You know that I sold much of my family's holdings to your father," Miguel told her.

"I know" Imelda answered. "My father spoke highly of Don Mordecai and was sorry that things have come to this."

Miguel was silent and thought for a moment. Then, although the sour dueña could hear, Miguel asked Imelda, "Señorita, please do not say on this ship that you knew me. It is dangerous for conversos. My uncle and I are called Vargas now and we travel as Spaniards. Please do not say anything."

Imelda stopped crying and nodded. "Of course Don Miguel, I understand. I will say nothing."

Dona Rosa though, spat on the deck and ignoring Miguel, told Imelda derisively, "Let the Inquisition have him. He's a Marrano."

Imelda became angry. She had never spoken harshly to her dueña or spoken back to her with force. Dona Rosa had been with her since she was a young girl. She knew her dueña better than she knew her mother or older sisters.

"Rosa you must swear not to say anything," Imelda ordered the old woman. Her forceful tone startled Dona Rosa, who had not seen this side of her señorita. "Swear to it now," Imelda demanded.

The old woman shook her head and then lowered it. She reluctantly agreed. "I swear not to reveal anything," Rosa said in almost a whisper.

Many things could go wrong on the passage to New Spain; storms, sickness and even the crew turning on the passengers. When the flotilla finally reached the warmer waters of the Caribbean and the Islands of the Bahamas they might be set upon by pirates. Yet, as the first two weeks passed, the voyage on the ocean was uneventful, the weather behaving nicely for the fleeing hidden conversos. The mighty Atlantic, which killed many seafarers stayed placid as if it were their friend or a quiet country lake.

        Each evening, and into the darkness of the night, Miguel would walk the deck and stare at the moon and stars and then think of his home in Granada. It pierced at his spirit, knowing that he would never be there again. Even during the battles he fought in Italy, he knew that if he survived the fighting, he would return to his father's home in Al-Andalus. Now, perhaps he would never see his father and brother again. The gaiety of his life in Granada and in Padua became just a whispering memory, rapidly fading beneath the truth of the voyage.

        During the daylight, Miguel would also stand on the upper deck and stare at the vastness of the ocean. He was untouched by seasickness and the sea air invigorated him. If it was sunny, he often saw Señorita Imelda strolling on the deck of Cozzano's ship. The young Señorita, like Miguel, was unaffected by the motion of the sea.

        Dona Rosa was affected by sea sickness and her face, sour looking in the best of times, showed the anguish she was in. Yet, even with sickness, she faithfully stayed by Imelda's side. Several times, Don Miguel saw Dona Rosa lean over the side of the deck and vomit. Imelda would rush to comfort the old woman. Rosa, uncomfortable, sick, and out of her element still honored Imelda's order and said nothing of Miguel, Arnoldo or the other conversos.

Uncle Arnoldo was troubled by both seasickness and his gout. He spent much of his time below deck. Confined to his cabin he planned carefully what they would do in Cuba. "Miguel," he told his nephew, "Don Yussef knows a man in Havana who is the secret leader of the conversos there. Many of our people fled there years ago. We will meet with him and then try to get a ship back to Spain. If we can get to Cadiz or back to Malaga, we can eventually move on to Palermo."

"Well thought out Uncle," Miguel told him. "That's what you and I will do, but I hope Don Yussef and the others survive. They have no place to return to. Their lives and fates lie in Cuba and New Spain."

On the deck, Miguel and Imelda often smiled at each other. Miguel began to love her beautiful smile and the intense look in her eyes. However, Miguel, fearing for both their security, thought it best not to be seen together and avoided speaking to her.

One late evening in their third week at sea, Don Miguel stood on the upper deck, as was his custom. They were in the Atlantic, well beyond the African coast, and the ocean could often be rough. However, the ocean and the heavens were still kind to the refugees, and the sea, instead of choppy and cold, appeared like a pond in the mountains. The sky was filled with a multitude of bright burning stars and the full moon hung over the ship, so large that it looked like it could be touched. Don Miguel was deep in thought and as usual pictured the life he had left behind. Trained as a soldier, he took all things as they came, but still the realization that his Granada existence was in the past and never returning, hurt him deeply. His future had been always planned for him; whatever Don Mordecai expected. Now his future was controlled by fate. As he stared at the sky, lost in his thoughts, he was suddenly startled by a touch on his shoulder. He jumped a bit, and by force of habit, drew his sword. A soft voice stopped him.

"Don Miguel it is I." It was Señorita Imelda. "Dona Rosa snores like a sick bear and I could not sleep."

Don Miguel returned his sword to the scabbard on his side and looked at the Señorita, whose eyes shone in the moonlight. "It's not safe for you on deck. On the sea, many believe that it is bad luck for a woman to be on a ship. Some in the crew may take it out on you," Miguel told her.

Imelda shook her head and smiled, "I have three older brothers, I can fight." With this she laughed and then suddenly touched Miguel's cheek. "Besides, why should I worry? I have the great Don Miguel with his sword to protect me."

Her soft touched startled Miguel, and even with all the women he had known, he suddenly seemed shy with nothing to say; no joke, no flirtation.

Imelda then became solemn and serious. "There is something I need to tell you. I swore to be silent for you, so you must swear to be silent for me. Even Dona Rosa doesn't know. If she did, she would leave even as she is so devoted to me."

"What is it?" Miguel asked, "Anything you tell me remains only with me."

Imelda paused, as if she could not get the words out, but then spoke clearly. "My family are conversos also. We have hidden this for all the years we have been in Granada." She was silent as an astonished Miguel took in this information.

Miguel seemed bewildered. "But you are Spanish, Navarado y Alvarez. You always went to the cathedral. Your father was important in the church."

"That is all true." Imelda answered but then continued. "In Navarre we were BenTariq, a Jewish family that went back centuries there. We converted at the time of the union with Castile but were protected by the King of Navarre. My grandfather fled south anyway. When we came to Granada, the Emir treated us as Catholics."

"Have you known this your whole life?" Miguel asked.

"My father has known it his whole life. He told it to me and my brothers when I turned fifteen. It pained him to not be able to tell Don Mordecai, but like your father he protected his family. Now I go to New Spain to an uncle who is the leader in a secret converso community there. It is in the far north of New Spain, beyond even the Aztec empire, called New Mexico."

Miguel was silent for several moments. He thought of Don Luis and his father and he thought of the lovely señorita standing by his side. "I will keep your secret," Miguel assured her and then he laughed. "Maybe I will have to come with you to this place. Who knows what happens in Cuba."

They looked at each other for a few moments, again in silence. Each had always wanted the other, but each was forbidden to act by their positions. Miguel leaned closer and could feel the heat on Imelda's face. He touched her cheeks and they were on fire. He pulled her gently to him and their lips met, first briefly and then in a full kiss under the starlight. Miguel then guided her willing body to him. They were now bound to each other by the secrets they shared and the secret love they could one day openly show.

For the next three weeks each night that it was dry, they met under the stars to hold each other. Their love grew stronger. For Miguel, women were always playthings, but now his heart was completely captured. At first Miguel thought that he would go with the señorita to this strange New Mexico. "My life lies with her," he told himself. Then he thought of his family in Palermo and instead made a vow to himself that he will find a way back to Europe so that he and Imelda could live together once again in the luxury they knew.

VI

After six weeks, Captain Cozzano's small fleet had successfully crossed the open ocean and entered the warmer waters around the islands of the Bahamas. All three ships were in a good condition, something that the Captain told Miguel was rare.

"Señor Vargas," Cozzano said, maintaining the identity that Don Miguel and Arnoldo had assumed, "this has been a wonderful voyage. I cannot remember one that has gone better. My ships are in good shape and my crew is pleased. You and your fellow travelers have tremendous suerte—luck. It is as if you were watched by heaven."

Miguel noticed though that as they sailed by the many small islands that made up the Bahamas the Captain began to constantly have crew members man the twelve cannon that lined the sides of the main galleon. Cozzano said nothing to either Miguel or the other passengers, but Arnoldo spoke to his nephew of pirates.

"Miguel, I have been speaking to Captain Cozzano and now we must be careful of pirates. Twenty years ago a French pirate sacked Havana and piracy is the city's greatest fear. Havana's harbors are well-armed now and safe from marauders, but the waters are dangerous. There are many buccaneers; French, English, and even Spanish turncoats. Cozzano spoke of a madman pirate who has been a scourge for shipping in the Caribbean for months. He calls himself Jerusalem after the holy city and is a religious fanatic. Cozzano told me that he is a giant and he kills the people he captures if they do not join him. The Viceroy in Havana has tried constantly to catch him, but he has twice defeated Cuban squadrons."

"I think he tries to scare you, Uncle," Miguel said smiling, "show you that he's earned the heavy gold we've paid him."

Miguel still noted that as the flotilla passed the many small islands with hidden coves and harbors making up the Bahama chain, and then turned south to Havana, Captain Cozzano maintained a strong vigilance and kept his crew members armed and manning the mounted guns. The two sloops went forward in order to intercept any pirates first if they should encounter them, and allow the bigger ship time to prepare for a battle.

Don Miguel approached Cozzano as he stood in the wheelhouse. "Captain, you know that I am a soldier. I will happily fight alongside your men if there is trouble."

"Thank you Don Miguel" Cozzano answered him, "but I doubt that there will be trouble between here and Cuba. The Viceroy has well protected the sailing routes to Havana. On the voyage from Havana to Mexico, that is where I might need your help."

"You know that my uncle and I plan to stay here in Havana until you return from Vera Cruz. Then, hopefully, we will return to Spain with you."

The Captain nodded but then added, "I could really use you Don Miguel on the sail to Vera Cruz. The pirates now are quite brazen. You could sail with me as a soldier and then return to Spain."

"I will speak to my uncle and think on it," Don Miguel answered.

The flotilla turned west and off their starboard bow they saw the green of Cuba. Soon, in the distance they could see the city of Havana, the jewel of the Caribbean. Havana, sitting on the northern coast of the Cuban island, with its three fine harbors and strong overlooking fortifications, was a bustling community, made rich by the transports from the mainland. The Spanish galleons carried provisions and supplies to Cuba and to New Spain and then loaded them with silver and gold from Mexico. They stopped again in Havana on their return voyage to Spain.

The colonists built Havana as a Spanish city. The white buildings and red-tiled roofs reminded Miguel of Granada. As the Bella Sonrisa entered the harbor and Miguel saw the city before him, a sudden burst of sadness overtook him. Over the seven week journey, despite beginning his love for Imelda, his sadness grew from the realization that he will never return to his home in Iberia.

As the passengers disembarked, they were met by a delegation from the Cuban Viceroy. Accompanied by a small contingent of soldiers the leader of the delegation ordered them into the customs house where the Viceroy, Don Jose Armandez, waits for them. He is finely dressed and looked the group over. He then addressed them.

"I am Jose Armandez y Vega and I am the Governor. I like to welcome all new visitors and colonists to my city. I hope that you have sustenance because I will not allow someone without support or without work to stay in Cuba."

He then eyed the whole group suspiciously and continued. "I hope that none of you are accursed Jews or Marranos hiding out. Here on my island Cristos es Fuerte—Christ is strong. Marrano swine will not be allowed to return to their pagan ways just because they are far from the main Inquisition. This is Don Nardo," a tall priest stepped forward and bowed slightly to the group, "the chief inquisitor here in Havana. He has my total support." The Viceroy then looked directly at Don Miguel. "You Señor with the sword, who are you?"

"Don Miguel Vargas, I am here with my uncle. I was a soldier in Italy."

"A soldier, perhaps I could use you here. Come see me after you settle in."

With that, the Viceroy said no more and left the passenger group alone. Those that had people to stay with moved on, while the others went to find lodging in the Inns and taverns near the waterfront. Imelda and Rosa and her party went to stay with friends that her father had contacted. Don Yussef and his family went to stay with Don Leon Raymondo, the secret leader of the hidden conversos in Havana. Miguel and Arnoldo found rooms for themselves and their servants near the harbor. Miguel sent a message to Dona Imelda; "The loss of my life in Granada is compensated by my love for you. Let us meet and talk."

The next evening, still with no plan as to what they will do in Cuba, Miguel and Arnoldo dined at a restaurant near their rooms. A messenger from Don Yussef found them. The messenger was rushing excitedly and told them, "Don Miguel you must come to meet Don Leon. It is crucial. You must come right away."

Miguel and Arnoldo followed the messenger to the home of Don Leon in the center of Havana. It is a large home, well guarded by a wall, and two guards stopped them before they entered the house. Inside they found Don Leon, an older man, bearded and gray, sitting with Don Yussef and two other conversos who had made the journey with them from Malaga. After introductions, Don Leon had Miguel and Arnoldo sat and then spoke to them and the whole group

"It is dangerous for you here in Havana. The Inquisition is strong and the Governor hates Jews. You must leave; he is suspicious of the new arrivals. Get to Vera Cruz, we have some people there." Don Leon gave them the name of the converso leader in Vera Cruz.

"There is no boat leaving right now," Don Leon said. "The ship you arrived on is supposed to stay for several weeks for cleaning and repair but perhaps Don Miguel, you can convince the Italian Captain to leave earlier. Don Yussef tells me that he has become your friend. Your group must leave and Don Yussef and the others are willing to pay." So almost as quickly as they had arrived in Havana they had to prepare to leave.

Miguel went to the Bella Sonrisa and found only the first mate and a few crew members onboard. The mate told him that Cozzano was in a nearby tavern. Miguel found him sitting with a woman by his side. Some of the crew were also there, sitting at nearby tables, some with local women and most were drunk. "Captain Cozzano," Miguel said, "My party needs to leave with you, but we have to leave immediately."

Cozzano shook his head. "Vargas, that is impossible. My sloops need work as well as my galleon. It will be several weeks before we can put out to sea."

"We have to leave immediately, there is no choice. The group is willing to pay well and they will meet your price. You will become a rich man quickly."

Cozzano mulled over the offer. He knew the group was wealthy and the large payments were enticing. "Señor Vargas, it will cost them to get to Vera Cruz, but I told you I could also use your sword. In Havana, all I have heard is tales of this mad pirate Jerusalem. If you work with the soldiers I hired, then I can delay my repairs until I return here. I let my men have some fun," he pointed around the room. "As you see, most are quite drunk and enjoy these women. When they sober up and we clean the ship, we will leave. The sloops are not sailable. I can only take the galleon and that is risky. In these waters, with the threat of pirates, having only one ship is foolish."

"It may be foolish, but it is a risk that my group must take. We are willing to pay for this risk."

Cozzano set a price and finally agreed to leave with only his galleon. Miguel left to tell the others. He gathered the refugee leaders together and told them the gold they had to pay Cozzano. Most thought it was robbery, but Cozzano was their only chance of escape so they reluctantly agreed to pay it.

Miguel quickly sent a note to Imelda and met her outside of the home in which she was staying. He told her what they now knew and that his group must leave. "Stay hidden my señorita and we'll meet again in Mexico."

"No, I will go with you," Imelda told him, her dark eyes fixed on his. She gently stroked his cheek. "I will be at the ship by the time that we leave."

Despite the objections of Dona Rosa, and those of her father's friend, Imelda, Rosa and their servants join the new refugees with Miguel and Arnoldo.

Two evenings later the refugees of Cozzano's boarded the ship and they cast off at first light. The Cuban authorities had been alerted and raided their rooms almost at the moment that they set out. Cozzano's galleon cleared the harbor and behind they saw a small ship, sent by the Viceroy, beginning to chase them. Cozzano managed to steer the Bella Sonrisa into the open waters of the Gulf of Mexico ahead of the pursuing vessel. The Governor's ship turned around and returned to the harbor in Havana.

VII

The air was warm in the Gulf of Mexico, and the water was calm, yet Captain Cozzano was anxious and maintained a strong watch. He had a crew of twenty and in Malaga he had hired fifteen mercenaries who both worked with the crew and who will man the guns and fight if they were to be attacked by pirates. The commander of the mercenaries was Antonio Ceruzza, another Italian, and an experienced soldier. When the Cuban Viceroy's ship stopped its pursuit and the Bella Sonrisa was able to set a course for Vera Cruz, Cozzano called a meeting with Ceruzza, and Don Miguel.

"Antonio," Cozzano began as they sat a table near the Captain's cabin, you know Señor Vargas, right?"

Antonio nodded, and Cozzano continued.

"He is really Don Miguel Benzion. He was a famous commander for the Prince of Sienna and he is a well-known swordsman. He will fight with us if we are attacked."

Ceruzza looked skeptically at Don Miguel and asked, "Why do you call yourself Vargas? You have called yourself that since Malaga."

Miguel felt that deception was no longer necessary with the Italian and told him directly. "My group and I have fled the Inquisition in Spain. Most of us including myself are conversos. It was safer to be Vargas."

Ceruzza nodded at both Cozzano and at Don Miguel, to indicate that he understood. Cozzano then continued further. "Here is the problem. I was told in

Cuba that this pirate Jerusalem is a madman. The Cubans said that he has over two hundred men. If he catches us in the Gulf, we have to fight. We will have no other option even though we are outgunned and outmanned. This pirate leader is crazy and he is not out only for plunder. I was told that if we are captured he will kill us all. Our hope is to make Vera Cruz without encountering him."

On the third day of sailing towards Vera Cruz, the luck that had followed the refugees all the way from Malaga finally failed them. They were set upon by a lone pirate ship. The pirate vessel was a sloop, smaller than Cozzano's galleon, but as a sloop it was much faster and more maneuverable than Cozzano's heavier ship. Viewing the sloop from a distance Cozzano and Ceruzza were able to count only six cannons but even from the distance they saw the sides of the pirate vessel filled with pirates.

The pirates maneuvered their sloop until it was close to striking distance, but still out of range of the Bella Sonrisa's cannons. A rowed tender with a messenger on board started towards the Bella Sonrisa. The small ferry flew a white flag and pulled alongside Cozzano's ship.

The messenger called up to Cozzano, "Captain, I bring a message from my leader, Jerusalem. Let me board and I will tell you his terms."

Cozzano signaled for his men to throw over a ladder and allowed the messenger to board. Cozzano kept the well-armed troop of mercenaries visible behind him, hoping that the pirate envoy will believe it is a larger force.

The envoy was a thin Spaniard, his skin burnt dark brown by the Caribbean sun. He was dressed as a pirate with a bandana around his head and wearing an open shirt. The envoy was unarmed and ordered his oarsmen to remain in their small ferry.

Cozzano received the man on the deck. Ceruzza and Don Miguel stood behind Cozzano. Very calmly the pirate told them, "I bring greetings from my Captain Jerusalem. You must surrender your ship or you will all die."

"And if we surrender," Cozzano asked, "what then?"

"My Captain will then decide, but you have no other choice."

Cozzano turned back to Ceruzza and Miguel and spoke quietly so that the thin Spaniard couldn't hear. "We die either way. I say we fight." The others nodded in agreement. They each knew that they were trapped and surrendering was not an option. Cozzano turned back to the Spaniard. "Tell your Captain that we choose not to surrender."

The Spaniard looked surprised and snarled, "That is a very bad decision. You are making a mistake." He stalked back to the ladder leading to his ferry and climbed down to the waiting launch.

Miguel and Ceruzza prepared their men for an attack. The passengers were all sent below deck where they hid in fear. The Pirate sloop approached the Bella Sonrisa but stayed out of range of the cannon. Cozzano saw only one pirate ship but even at a great distance he could see the deck swarming with a large army of pirates.

The pirate ship flew a strange flag, black emblazoned with a white cross and inside of the cross a black Star of David. Miguel was startled by the sight of the Star of David. Perhaps, he thought, this madman pirate is a Jew and I can deal with him as a brother. The other passengers were terrified.

"It is the pirate king Jerusalem. He is a madman and will kill us all."

Many began to repeat what they had heard of him; "Larger than life; stronger than two men; with long golden hair and with a wife, a dark islander, a native witch."

The faster pirate sloop deftly outmaneuvered Cozzano's heavier galleon. The pirate ship closed in and pulled alongside the Bella Sonrisa before Ceruzza could fire a broadside. From the pirate vessel, battle hooks were immediately thrown pulling the ships together. The pirates, each heavily armed with sabers and pistols, stormed the deck. The mercenaries fought valiantly and killed many of the pirates, but the crew was no match for the marauders and most were slaughtered. A pirate charged at Don Miguel who easily killed him with a sword thrust. Another came at him and swung his sabre wildly, but Miguel managed to pierce his arm and disable him. The pirates snarled and screamed and were more like animals than men. Cozzano, Ceruzza, Miguel and the remaining mercenaries fell back to the upper deck and the wheelhouse. They formed a battle line and waited for the pirates on the deck below to charge them. The pirates had them surrounded but stopped as the original messenger, the thin Spaniard, stepped forward. "Bring up whatever passengers you have," he ordered. Cozzano ordered his first mate to follow the pirate's instructions. The passengers; the converso families, Arnoldo, the servants, Imelda and Dona Rosa, were brought onto the lower deck and then paraded in front of the pirates before being brought to the upper deck with the surrounded crew.

A pirate, filthy and bearded, took a liking to Imelda. "I want this one," he snarled and stepped toward her.

Miguel, sword in hand, stepped between. "Step back she is to be my wife," The pirate lunged forward with his saber and Miguel quickly cut him down. The other pirates started to rush forward while the remaining mercenaries and Ceruzza stood their ground.

Suddenly, a strange booming voice stopped the pirate charge. It was the pirate leader. "Back away and let me through," he demanded. He was no taller than Miguel, but he had the body of a giant ogre. He had long, white-blond hair to his shoulders and wore no shirt. His chest was immense and muscled like a wrestler and he had huge arms like a blacksmith. A large saber hung from his pants and he wore the sandals of a native islander. There was a fire in his eyes like a lunatic. By his side was a woman, voluptuous and dark, with her shirt pulled up and tied under her ample breasts, wearing a tiny pair of pants. She had long thick black hair and strong legs with skin the color of chestnuts.

"You are a brave fool, Spaniard," the pirate leader said to Don Miguel looking down at the dead pirate at Miguel's feet. "Why should I spare you and not let my men have your woman?"

Imelda huddled close to Dona Rosa, who was crying. Arnoldo said quietly to Miguel, "Let me speak for us. You are too angry." Miguel ignored him and with his sword still in his hand stepped forward to face the giant pirate.

"Are you the Jerusalem I have heard of?" Miguel said to him, not flinching or backing away. "I am told that you are a man of God. I see the Star of David in your flag and I say, Shalom."

Jerusalem eyed him up and down. "A Jew or a Marrano dog?" he asked.

Miguel remained defiant, "I am a converso, a hanesim, forced to convert. To my family, God would understand that we had to live. We were good people."

The pirate was momentarily speechless but then asked, "And the others, Marranos also?"

Miguel answered. "Yes, they are conversos," stressing the word and indicating by his tone, his displeasure at the word Marrano. "We go to a settlement in New Mexico in the north; away from the Inquisition."

Jerusalem looked at the others and then spoke quietly to his woman standing next to him. He then spoke to Miguel, "For now brave fool I spare you all. I take all of you with me. Put down you swords and when we land tomorrow we feast together and we talk." Jerusalem turned to the group of pirates and ordered. "These people are now my guests. They are not to be harmed."

Ceruzza and his men reluctantly put down their weapons and all of the captives were then led below deck. While they stood there, the passengers fearing the worst, the pirates were unloosed to loot the Bella Sonrisa. The refugees who had managed to bring whatever belongings they could, and whatever gold they had, all the way from Granada, watched as the wild band of pirates plundered all of their possessions.

VIII

Below deck, the pirates separated the passengers from Cozzano, Ceruzza, and the crew members that were still alive. Miguel assumed the leadership role among the passengers. "I will negotiate with this pirate," he told the others, "and see if he can be persuaded to take us to the Mexican coast. I know that many of you, besides my group from Malaga, are secret conversos and trying to get to a safe haven from the Inquisition. The pirate leader seems to hate the Spanish and he already has our treasures." Miguel told the group to stay calm and to avoid if possible any contact with the pirates.

Dona Rosa stood by Imelda and listened to Don Miguel. She spat on the ground, as she had done in the past when he said the word conversos. As they fled Cuba, Imelda had told her the truth; the Navarado family were conversos. Despite Rosa's hatred of Marranos her loyalty to Imelda was as strong as any steel chain and she stayed with her young señorita.

For two days after the capture, they sailed to the southeast. Miguel and Captain Cozzano were allowed, alone among the captives, to walk freely about the upper deck. They watched as their captured galleon, now with the thin Spaniard, whose name was Enrique, acting as the new pilot, followed the pirate sloop. Miguel saw the hugely muscled Jerusalem standing with his woman, whose name Miguel had learned was Bargara, and staring at the sea.

They approached a small island and Cozzano's galleon followed the pirate sloop into a hidden cove. From the sea, the opening was barely visible, but once inside, the cove was surprisingly large and formed an excellent harbor. Off to their left, in a large cleared area along the beach, was a makeshift shipyard. There were three other galleons being careened and repaired by a large force of laborers. Next to these galleons, were two other faster pirate sloops, also being careened. Most of the workers were bronze and Miguel assumed that they were the natives of these islands. He had learned that these Indios of the Caribbean, who were called the Caribes and the Boricuas, were different than the fiercer Aztecs in Mexico.

To the right of this shipyard the pirates had built a mooring area, and behind this, they had constructed a small village with several brightly painted wooden buildings;

prominent in the center of which was a tavern. Behind this harbor-side village was a collection of thatch-roofed wooden houses and in the distance the island was a jungle. Between the pirate town and the jungle was a native village with a large array of thatched huts.

The pirates docked the Bella Sonrisa and their own sloop at a strong pier and then forced the prisoners ashore. The group was led into the town and then to the wooden buildings behind. The pirates placed the men in one thatched house with several guards while the women were placed in a separate house adjacent to it. Miguel warned the chief guard, a Spaniard with a scar deep across his cheek, "Remember these women are under the protection of your leader." The guard grudgingly assented.

That evening Jerusalem summoned all his captives to a dinner. It was held in an open area on the beach by the shipyard. The pirates had built a huge bonfire and placed tables around it. There were other tables with bread and meat and of course rum. Miguel sat at a large central dais with the pirate leader while Imelda sat by his side. Cozzano was also invited to sit with Jerusalem. The pirate leader sat with the beautiful woman from the deck. "This is Bargara," he told Miguel. "She is a queen among the Boricuas and is as fierce a fighter as any of my men. The Spanish pigs abused her when they took her island and she hates them as a dog hates a flea. I have you here sitting with me, foolish Spaniard, because you were impressive fighting against my men."

"I was a soldier in Italy, a commander in Sienna. I was only protecting my comrades," Miguel answered. He turned towards Imelda. "This is Imelda Navarado y Ortega. She will be my wife."

"If I let you live," Jerusalem said with no hint of humor.

Jerusalem drank tankard after tankard of rum and constantly spoke and rambled. Most of his comments were wild and could not be understood. Miguel thought that he must be mad.

"My goal," the pirate told them, "is to capture enough galleons to build a strong fleet. Then I will sail to Gibraltar and then on to the holy land and take it back from the Muslims for true Jewish-Christians who love the Lord and don't abuse him by following the corrupt church. The Inquisition is the devil and the foolish Spanish people don't realize this."

"Join me," the pirate, in one of his rambling discourses, asked Miguel.

"I want to go to New Mexico," Miguel answered shaking his head. "I'm tired of fighting the Inquisition. I want to marry and settle down."

"No, join me on my quest," Jerusalem repeated, now appearing to be completely sober and serious. "It will be worth your while. If the holy land means nothing to you, then you will still become fabulously wealthy, and I will leave you somewhere in the Mediterranean with your wealth."

Miguel said nothing but silently pondered the possibility of rejoining his father and other family in Palermo.

"I will think about it," he told Jerusalem. Suddenly the pirate leader turned away and yelled at his men. "It is time for music."

A group of pirate musicians with drums and lyres begin to play a wild dance. The pirates, together with their women, began to move in a frenzy around the large bonfire in the center of the shipyard. Many of the dancers stripped off their clothes to be completely naked and began to make love around the large fire, and within sight of the main table. Don Miguel looked on with rapt curiosity. This was more than he ever witnessed in the camps of the gitanas. Dona Imelda though, turned away and hid her eyes. Her background did not permit her to watch this strange sight.

Bargara then began to perform a sensuous dance in front of Jerusalem; moving her large hips to the pounding of the drums. She unwrapped her blouse and let her ample breasts fly free. She slipped off her tiny pants and danced naked in front of the pirate leader. She then pressed her breasts against Jerusalem's body and continued her movement. Throughout the camp, there was a frenzied orgy of drunken pirates, naked women, pounding drums and lyre music.

Uncle Arnoldo, quite drunk on rum, forgot his gout and his anxiety, and found a young naked islander girl. He danced with her while Cozzano and the other conversos just looked on.

The wild fiesta lasted throughout the night, and by morning most of the pirates lay drunk and passed out. Jerusalem though, despite all the rum he consumed, and Enrique, the thin Spaniard, remained sober. Miguel and the prisoners, many of whom had fallen asleep during the long evening, were led back to the houses. Jerusalem yelled to Miguel as Miguel was led away. "Think of my offer Don Miguel. It is to your benefit and to mine."

VIIII

Back in the captive house with the other prisoners, Miguel weighed and considered Jerusalem's offer. He finally decided that his and Imelda's best chance to get to Palermo and his family was to join the pirates. In the late afternoon, he went to see Jerusalem and found the pirate leader sitting in the shipyard watching his men work on the various ships. The ever present Bargara was by his side. On one of the sloops, Miguel saw that Alphonso, Cozzano's chief carpenter worked alongside the pirates.

"Captain," Miguel said to Jerusalem, "I have decided to join you."

The pirate leader nodded his head and looked straight into Miguel's eyes. "I expected you to decide that way, but I am still happy," Jerusalem told him. "You will be a great asset against my enemies the Spanish."

Miguel then tried to save the others and asked, "For my allegiance to you Captain, I ask that you let my fellow comrades go free and take them to Mexico. They are not fighters. You have their wealth and all they owned; they cannot help you and they cannot hurt you. If you are a man of God, as you say, be merciful to them and I will fight hard for you."

Jerusalem was silent, looked back at Bargara, and then answered. "You are a brave, strong man Don Miguel, and you hate the Spaniards. I can use you. But you ask a lot of me to take these people to Mexico. I will look weak in front of my men." He was silent again for a while and Bargara whispered something to him. He then said, "If you swear allegiance to me, Don Miguel, I will do as you ask, but I need the Italian Captain Cozzano and that other soldier Ceruzza and the ship's carpenter and doctor. The others I will take to Mexico."

After making his pact with Jerusalem, Miguel left the pirate leader and spoke first to his uncle. "I have made a deal with this Pirate king," he told Arnoldo. "I will fight with him in return for letting the others go to Mexico. He plans to sail to Europe and I will go with him."

Arnoldo, enjoying his time in the pirate camp with the young Boricua girl he has met, huffed and answered. "Miguelito, you have to realize that he is loco. It is only death with him, either fighting or capture by the Spanish."

"Perhaps," said Miguel, "but by joining him it is the only possibility to get to Palermo and reunite with my father. If I don't do this, this crazy pirate will kill us all. "

Arnoldo thought a bit and then his answer startled his nephew. "Then I will join him also and go with you. I have no desire to die here or in Mexico. What of your Señorita Imelda?"

Pain showed on Miguel's face as he answered. "It hurts me to let her go, but for her safety I send her with the others to Mexico. If somehow we get to Italy, I will come back for her."

Miguel then spoke to Captain Cozzano and the soldier Ceruzza. Cozzano dismissed the idea and Ceruzza nodded in agreement, "We are not pirates," Cozzano angrily declared.

Miguel reminded them that this was their only way out alive. "If you don't do this, then everyone from the Bella Sonrisa will be killed. It is our only hope. Cozzano, you will still command your ship, but with the thin Spaniard by your side." After much back and forth, Cozzano and Ceruzza reluctantly agreed.

Finally, Miguel told Imelda. He held her in his arms and told her, "You go on to New Mexico and I will come for you."

Imelda stood back, looked him squarely in the eyes, pulled herself to her full height and said firmly, "Miguel, in you I have found the man I love, the man for my life, and I will be with you. I am going with you. There is no other way for me." She was adamant and her mind was set. Nothing Miguel said could dissuade her. She told him firmly, "I will stand by you Miguel, much as this Bargara stands by the pirate king."

Although Jerusalem was a religious fanatic, his men were not. They were a strange mix of Spanish and Islanders. Miguel and Arnoldo, speaking among themselves, said that most of the pirates were more like animals than men. They had wealth and gold from all their plunder, but what good did it do them. The Spanish pirates could not return to any city and the islanders could not return to their tribes. Thus, they reveled in pleasure on their island.

One of the Spanish pirates told Miguel that Bargara had been a shaman or witch among the Boricuas and when Jerusalem had landed here she convinced the islanders that the blonde giant held powerful magic. The islander pirates then obeyed Jerusalem as if he were a god. The Spanish pirates feared and worshiped him also. The same pirate told Miguel that Jerusalem was protected by God and that he had seen him kill three men in battle with just his hands.

Jerusalem preached to his pirate army that they were going on a quest to conquer the holy land. Most had no idea of what he meant, but they followed him as if to some strange dream.

They remained on the pirate island for another three weeks while the ships were careened and prepared. There were feasts and orgies almost every evening and the refugees, although still horrified, came to ignore the excesses of the pirates. Because Miguel, Cozzano, and Ceruzza were now part of their company, the pirates avoided the other refugees.

On the fourth week after the capture, they embarked from the pirate island. It was late autumn with winter approaching, but the Caribbean was still very warm. Jerusalem's fleet had three captured galleons including the Bella Sonrisa, now manned by his pirates, and two smaller sloops. Miguel estimated that there were over two hundred pirates under Jerusalem's command. Jerusalem adopted the Bella Sonrisa as his flagship and he, Bargara, and the thin Spaniard Enrique traveled on it. It was Captained by Cozzano, with Enrique, Jerusalem's chief lieutenant almost always by his side watching him. The refugee group along with Miguel, Arnoldo, Ceruzza, Imelda and Rosa traveled on the flagship. The six of Ceruzza's mercenaries, who survived the battle, had been mixed in with the other pirates.

Honoring his agreement with Don Miguel, and surprising his pirates, Jerusalem had his navigators embark first for Mexico. He told Miguel that his plan was to drop the passengers on the Mexican coast north of Vera Cruz and they would have to make their own way to the city and the protection of the Spanish. After dropping the refugees in Mexico, his fleet would turn for the Atlantic and then on to the Mediterranean.

The third day at sea, they came upon a merchant galleon, who realized they were pirates but had no time to flee. The two forward pirate sloops easily captured it. Jerusalem, with Miguel and Enrique, ferried to the captured merchant vessel. The merchant crew, unarmed and surrounded by fifty pirates, stood on the deck. The frightened merchant Captain, an older Dutchman, was dragged before Jerusalem who forced him to his knees. Jerusalem held a saber over his neck and demanded, "What do you carry?"

"Just porcelain and fruits," the frightened man told him. Jerusalem hit the kneeling man with the hilt of his saber and the merchant fell to the deck. Blood poured from his head. Jerusalem then kicked him in the ribs. Miguel stepped forward to stop the beating but then thinking better of it, held back. "If I find more than porcelain and fruits," Jerusalem snarled, "I will slice you like a roast, piece by piece. Now tell me, only porcelain and fruit?" The old merchant hesitated and Jerusalem hit him again with the hilt of the saber and then slashed into his arm. The terrified merchant started to weep and confessed. "There is silver also. It is all below."

Jerusalem then had his pirates loot the ship. They found eight chests of silver coins as well as a shipment of porcelain. The pirates transferred the plunder to the remainder of the fleet.

The captured ship was smaller than Jerusalem's other galleons with only two small swivel cannons. However, the pirates were prepared to kill the crew and take this new galleon, until Miguel spoke to Jerusalem, "My Captain," he said. "It is better to spare this crew and put my fleeing group on this ship. Have this Captain take them to Vera Cruz. We can then turn right now to the ocean. It is safer for us to do that than to go on to Mexico."

Jerusalem, as by his custom, was first silent in thought and then said, "That is a wise move, Don Miguel. You think like a good soldier and I like that. You are a good aide. We do what you say and leave this old dog to bring your people to Mexico."

The converso group was then transferred from the Bella Sonrisa to the merchant ship. Jerusalem ordered the merchant Captain to transport them to Vera Cruz. Now only Miguel, Arnoldo, Imelda, Rosa and their servants remained from Granada.

The Dutch Captain was brought before Jerusalem, who threatened him and said, "Take these people to Vera Cruz. If you betray them, I will find you and kill you."

The merchant Captain, bruised and wounded but happy to be spared, told the pirate leader that he would do as he was ordered.

As Miguel prepared to leave the conversos on the merchant ship, Don Yussef approached him. "Don Miguel, we have now lost everything but our lives; but for our lives I thank you. Go with God and good luck. You did as you promised and honored your family."

X

The pirate fleet turned eastward towards the Atlantic and back to Europe. It quickly became clear to Miguel and to Cozzano that the pirate leader Jerusalem had no real plan. Each evening he drank rum heavily and ranted of the holy land. It was evident that he knew nothing of either the Mediterranean or how to navigate to Palestine. Miguel never learned anything about his background except that he hated the Spanish. His native language appeared to be Castilian so they assumed he was from Iberia.

Jerusalem's madness grew on the voyage. As the weeks passed, he and Bargara wandered the deck of the Bella Sonrisa. He screamed at either his pirates or to the open ocean, "I will land in Italy and kill the pope before I retake the holy land." Then he boasted, "I am blessed by God himself."

Miguel and Imelda often dined with Jerusalem, Bargara and Enrique in the Captain's private dining room.

Imelda sat at Don Miguel's side and as the trip progressed, she gained strength as a woman. She was no longer the protected maiden from Granada, but a strong young woman, and a fitting partner for Miguel. Dona Rosa still stayed by her side, but on her own accord, had receded into the background, as if Imelda and Miguel were married.

Seeing the pirate leader's growing madness, Arnoldo's anxiety grew. He repeatedly said to Miguel, "He is a madman, this is a death voyage. What can we do?"

"We have no choice Uncle," Miguel answered. "I was not going to spend the rest of my days in some backward village in New Mexico. If he makes it through the straits and into the Mediterranean, perhaps we can get to Palermo. Uncle, the woman I love is with me. I want to survive."

The fleets between Spain and the Americas usually stopped for rest and provisions in the Canary Islands. Even though the Canaries were close to the Muslim kingdom in Morocco, these islands had been controlled by the Castilians since the mid-1400's. They provided an ideal stopping point for the transatlantic voyages because of the prevailing northeast winds and for their excellent bays and harbors. The harbor at Las Palmas, the capital, and main city, was perfect for making repairs before returning to Iberia.

Jerusalem's navigators plotted a course towards the Canaries but Ceruzza the mercenary advised against stopping there. Both Ceruzza and Cozzano realized that only by going with the pirates could they get to Italy and save their lives. If they were captured by the Spanish they would be hung as pirates. It would be difficult to prove that they were coerced into joining. Nearing the Canaries, Jerusalem held a meeting of the pirate Captains on board his flagship, the Bella Sonrisa. Ceruzza addressed the group. His advice was to turn south to Africa. He told them, "I have been to Las Palmas and it is well-defended. The Castillo de la Luz protects the harbor and they have been able to turn back many Muslim attacks. If we enter the harbor and they realize we are pirates, all is lost. I suggest we turn south to the African coast until spring time."

Jerusalem, in his madness, was deaf to Ceruzza's logic. He waved his arms to say no and then ranted, "We go to Las Palmas and take by force what we need. There is no stopping now." He turned to Ceruzza and asked, "Is there a place to land north of the city?"

Ceruzza, realizing that there was no reasoning with the pirate leader, answered that there was another small inlet north of the city that could be used for a beach landing from anchored ships. Jerusalem, on getting this news from Ceruzza, told the group that they will moor there, north of the city and then ferry the pirates ashore. From there they will plunder what they need. Near the islands, the weather turned against them.

At first, the voyage for Miguel back across the Atlantic was as calm as the first voyage to Cuba. Now as autumn turned to winter, the air was cold and damp and cut through his body as he stood on deck. Still, no Atlantic storms that could be fierce, have hit the fleet. "You are a lucky sailor Miguel," Captain Cozzano laughingly told him. "I have never been on two calmer voyages." When Jerusalem and Enrique were not close by, he added, "Perhaps this mad man is in touch with God."

Their luck changed several days from the Canaries. The skies at midday grew as black as night, the winds howled and a huge Atlantic storm struck the flotilla. Driving cold rains hit the decks and the crew had to lash themselves to the deck with rope to keep them on board as huge waves crashed over the sides. The rains poured down so heavily that one could not see their own hands. Imelda, Rosa, and Arnoldo huddled below deck in fear while Miguel tied himself to the wheelhouse as Cozzano tried to keep the ship afloat. Miguel had never seen torrential rains such as these, nor a storm like this, and wondered how they could possibly survive. The ships in the pirate fleet were separated and could not see each other. Each was on its own. The vessels were tossed about like toys in the ocean. On the deck of the Bella Sonrisa, Miguel saw the huge body of Jerusalem, with Bargara by his side, just standing freely in the storm, not tied down, being pelted by the rain and watching the sky.

The rain and winds lasted for hours and it wasn't until dawn and the morning light that the sun broke through and the seas calmed. The Bella Sonrisa had taken extensive damage. There were cracks in the wooden sides and one mast had broken. The fleet regathered and the pirate Captains again met with Jerusalem on the Bella Sonrisa. One sloop was missing and the other Captains assumed that it had been sunk and its crew lost. The second sloop was badly damaged and barely seaworthy. The other two galleons luckily sustained only minor damage.

Ceruzza again suggested wintering in Africa. "We are damaged and we need careening," he told the others. "There are many small coves and inlets along the African coast that we can use for this. We must go there, do the repairs and wait for spring."

Cozzano nodded in agreement, but Jerusalem, completely out of his mind, refused. He was beyond reasoning and had a wild animal look in his eyes.

"No, no, no," he ranted. "We go to Las Palmas to get what we need and then on to Gibraltar."

Arnoldo told Miguel quietly, "This is madness."

Miguel only shrugged. There was nothing that he nor anyone else could do as long as Jerusalem maintained power among the pirates.

The damaged fleet anchored near a shoreline clearing, north of Las Palmas. Jerusalem ferried ashore with his leaders and set up a base camp. A raiding party of thirty well-armed pirates, led by his chief lieutenant Enrique, was assembled. The plan was for the pirate raiders to march to Las Palmas and attack the city's harbor by land. Then they would take food, drink, ammunition and whatever else they can gather from the storehouses by the waterfront, and leave as quickly as possible. Despite warnings by Cozzano and other seamen among the pirates, they would forego any but the most basic repairs.

The town was only four miles from their base camp but ten hours passed and the pirate plunderers did not return. Suddenly, an exhausted pirate stumbled into their campground on the shore and fell at Jerusalem's feet. "My Captain," he blurted out, "we are trapped by Spanish soldiers in a warehouse. They have muskets and have killed several of our party."

Jerusalem quickly chose another group of thirty pirates and ordered Miguel to lead them to rescue the first party. "You are a soldier Don Miguel. Let us see what you can do," the pirate leader told him.

Miguel led the group the four miles into the city. He stood on a hill above the town and looked down at the waterfront. A contingent of Spanish soldiers, with muskets, pikes and swords had trapped the first pirate group inside of a storehouse. Miguel counted fifty-four soldiers and assessing the situation decided that he would charge the Spanish troops from behind. He hoped that when the trapped pirates saw the attack, they would charge from out of the storehouse.

He moved his troop, as silently as he could, to the waterfront and placed his pirates hidden behind buildings. Attention was on the standoff at the harbor so his movements went unnoticed. On his order, the pirates let out a blood-curdling yell and charged the Spanish soldiers. The Spaniards, hearing the yell, had enough time, to turn and have the musketeers fire off a volley that dropped several of the attacking pirates. The remainder of the pirates set upon the soldiers with their sabers.

The pirates trapped in the storehouse now ran out and attacked from that direction. The Castilian troops were engaged on both sides. Their skilled pikemen and swordsmen killed many of the pirates before regrouping and retreating. Miguel gathered all of the pirates together. Enrique was badly wounded and half of the total group was dead. Miguel ordered them back to the pirate camp, although they had taken no plunder. Behind them, at the waterfront in Las Palmas, the Spanish soldiers were reinforced and prepared to pursue.

At the pirate camp, the pirates ferried quickly back to the ships. Many were bleeding and wounded. The Spanish general at Las Palmas had alerted the rest of the islands. The pirates realized that the Spanish now knew they were outlaws. If they headed to the Straits, they would most certainly be attacked by Spanish ships.

However, it was now too late to turn south to Africa. Although his fleet was damaged and there were many wounded, Jerusalem ordered the flotilla to sail to Gibraltar and perhaps certain death. Cozzano told Miguel, "If we make it into the Mediterranean, I will try to avoid battle and head for Sicily. If by some chance we make it there, we will flee this pirate. If we are captured, it is death from the Spanish."

Miguel understood.

XI

The damaged pirate fleet limped northward to Spain aware that they were now identified as pirates. However, no Spanish ships confronted them between the Canaries and Gibraltar.

Jerusalem acted like a complete madman. He stalked about the main deck, oblivious to anyone around him and yelled at the ocean, "God has frightened the Spanish pigs. We will soon kill the pope."

Miguel, and the others of his party, knew that they were headed into a death trap, but Miguel told Imelda not to worry. "We have made it this far my love. We can't give up hope now."

Imelda, now showing a strength and confidence that no one in Granada would have recognized, held Miguel. "We are together Miguel and that is what is important."

The flotilla sailed past Tangiers and then turned east and entered the Straits. Still unimpeded and unchallenged they proceeded into the Mediterranean. Cozzano, the only Captain among the pirate ships familiar with the European sea, set a course for southern Sicily. Cozzano was in complete control of the Bella Sonrisa; Enrique, mortally wounded in the battle at Las Palmas, lay dying in the sick bay. Miguel and the others waited for a Spanish attack, but Jerusalem was oblivious. He was convinced that God had protected him from his enemies and he would soon be able to capture the Pope.

As they approached the waters near Malaga, they were confronted by a squadron of Spanish galleons. The Spanish ships, bigger, heavier and better armed, did not try to contact the pirate vessels but immediately attacked the two forward remaining galleons and the forward sloop. A large Spanish galleon pulled close to one of the pirate galleons and fired a forty gun, broadside. Another Spanish galleon went after the damaged sloop. Cozzano, coming from behind in the damaged Bella Sonrisa, went south and slipped by as the battle began. He then turned his ship and followed the navigated course to Sicily.

On seeing his flagship avoiding the battle, Jerusalem stormed into the pilot house. He stood in front of Cozzano, who held onto the wheel. "Stand and fight these pigs," he ordered.

The shrewd Italian kept his course and told the crazed leader, "We go on Jerusalem to the holy land. Our quest is not here. We only stop in Italy to kill the pope. If we fight here, our quest is over."

The crazed Jerusalem stared at the Captain with the same strange wild look in his eyes, said nothing, and turned and walked back on deck.

In the distance, Miguel saw the sloop sinking and the two pirate galleons being boarded by Spanish soldiers. He saw the pirates fighting the Spanish troops like trapped animals, but he knew they were lost. The Bella Sonrisa, even with its main sail down, sped on and at first no Spanish ship gave chase.

The pirates fought hard and there were many casualties among the Spanish soldiers. The battle was won, but the Spanish fleet delayed while they rounded up the pirates they captured and tended to their wounded. Their delay permitted almost a full day head start for the final pirate ship. A smaller squadron then began to chase Jerusalem's flagship.

The damaged Bella Sonrisa, even with only two main sails, managed to stay several hours ahead of the pursuing squadron. Near Sicily though, the ship began to break apart and the crews could see the cracks in the deck and the side walls separating further. Water began seeping through the openings below deck and filling the holds. Cozzano took the only action he could and steered the sinking vessel into the Sicilian coast. He grounded the large ship on a sandbar near a beach area on the southern shore.

The pirates abandoned the vessel and flocked onto the beach while the ship, filling with water, turned over on its side. Beyond the beach, there was a wooded area and beyond that a mountain range. Rocky trails led in several different directions through the woods and up into the mountains. The pirates stood on the beach and waited for instructions from Jerusalem, while Arnoldo, Imelda, Cozzano, Ceruzza, Rosa and their remaining servants congregated off to the side.

Ceruzza knew the Sicilian coast and quickly said to Miguel, "These paths lead north into the mountains. They are difficult to walk, but this is the time to leave this mad man."

Miguel nodded in agreement but said, "Wait for the right moment. If he sees us fleeing, he will kill us all."

Far offshore they could see the Spanish ships, which have spotted the grounded and sinking Bella Sonrisa and the crowd of pirates congregated on the beach. Jerusalem was silent and stared out at the Spanish galleons. Miguel approached him and said, "It is only death to wait for the soldiers. We must flee into the mountains and regroup there. Ceruzza has been here. These mountain trails are steep and dangerous and it will be difficult for them to chase us."

Ceruzza had picked one path to flee and Miguel directed Jerusalem towards another path leading in a different direction.

Jerusalem turned to Miguel, his face flushed and his eyes burning with fire. "We will fight them here. God is with us. We are still alive and we will defeat them." He turned to his pirates and yelled, "Prepare for battle here. Dig in and we kill these dogs." The pirates found a sand dune towards the back of the western side of the beach and constructed makeshift fortifications. They had no cannon and few muskets, but they sat with their sabers and waited. Miguel quietly moved his people away from the fortifications and towards the eastern side of the sand and close to the wooded area.

In the late afternoon sun, they could see the Spanish, ferrying soldiers to the coast west of them. Miguel understood that the ground troops would then come from that direction. He assumed that the Spanish galleons would sail as close to the shore as possible to rain cannon fire on the pirate beachhead. Each galleon held at least fifty soldiers. This time, they were outmanned and outgunned and it was only a matter of time before the mad pirate's quest would be ended. "Point your men to the west," he told Jerusalem, "that is where they will come from."

The Spanish Army took its time and it became evening. In the darkness, Miguel gathered together Imelda, Arnoldo, and the rest of their small party including Cozzano and Ceruzza. In the confusion, as the pirates waited for battle, he was able to bring his group to the woods at the rear of the beach and away from the pirate fortifications.

"Ceruzza," Miguel started, "take this group and go quickly into the mountains. Go north to Palermo and safety. Imelda, you will find my family. Leave now. When you get to Palermo, tell them you were merchants captured by pirates." He turned to Arnoldo, "Get to Don Mordecai and safety. Uncle, I leave the life and safety of my love, and wife to be, in your hands."

"Don't you come also?" Arnoldo asked.

"I stay and fight," Miguel answered. "I made a vow to this man. Madman or not, I will honor it. God willing I will survive and also reach Palermo. Now go."

Imelda, up to this point as strong as a warrior, suddenly started to weep. "Please come with us now, my love," she begged.

Miguel held her in his arms. "Go, and I will meet you in Palermo, it is my promise."

Rosa, old, bedraggled and exhausted, also started to weep. "Don Miguel, I will not survive the mountains. I can take no more. I am prepared to die here." She sat down on a rock. Imelda weeping, grabbed her and said, "Please Dona Rosa come."

Miguel pulled Rosa to her feet, "No Rosa, you mean so much to Imelda. You must survive." He then called over Benito, his last remaining servant. "Benito it is your task to protect this woman. See that she lives." Imelda hugged Rosa.

In the darkness, Ceruzza led the group away from the pirates and northward into the mountains. Miguel walked back to the pirate encampment. The pirates, concentrating on the attack from the west, had not noticed the group that had fled.

XII

The pirates dug in at their fortifications on the sand dune. They waited and watched as the Spanish troops, several squadrons of musketeers, pikemen and swordsmen, marched towards them on the seacoast. The soldiers were in armored breastplates and metal helmets. Some of the pirates fled into the mountains leaving Jerusalem with only twenty-eight men.

The leader stood with Bargara in front of the sand dune and screamed at his remaining followers, "We stand and fight. It is for God and for justice. We will not lose." He held his saber in his hands while he looked to the heavens. He had totally lost his mind. Jerusalem then raised his saber high above his head and yelled a blood-curdling war cry, as if he were a wounded lion fighting off ravaging jackals. His loyal pirates did the same and the approaching Spanish soldiers could hear the yells and screams as they moved forward onto the sand dune. Jerusalem then stepped behind the sand dune and stood with his pirate army while his woman Bargara, a saber in her hand, stood, as always, by his side.

Miguel knew that it will be a losing battle. It would have been easy for him to step into the woods and flee with the others, but he stayed with the pirate force. He wanted to delay the Spanish troops long enough so that Arnoldo, Imelda, and their group could get to safety.

The Spanish squadrons, at least one hundred men in armor and helmets, armed with muskets, sword, and pikes, marched in formation through the beach and then up onto the sand dune. The pirates, with the little ammunition they had left, fired a musket volley point blank into the approaching soldiers. A few of the soldiers fell dead and the Spanish retreated out of musket range. They quickly regrouped and began again to march to the sand dune.

With no ammunition left, Jerusalem ordered his men to charge the Spanish troops. The pirates drew their sabers, ran down the sand dune screaming and savagely attacked the squadron. Miguel stood to the rear and at first watched what was developing in front of him. Suddenly, he was attacked by an armored Spanish swordsman. The soldier lumbered forward and swung a heavy broad sword that Miguel easily deflected. Miguel then pierced the attacker's arm in a spot unprotected by his armored plates. Miguel fell back further to the rear of the beach and the swordsman, his arm bleeding profusely chased him. Miguel stopped and the Spaniard, hot and exhausted, gathered his breath and raised the big broad sword. He squinted for a mere moment in the bright sun and Miguel was able to drive his sword into the soldier's neck. The Spaniard, blood pouring from his mouth, still came forward and took another swipe at Miguel with his sword, and then collapsed. Miguel then stabbed the man again in the throat. Miguel looked around. They had run quite far from the center of the struggle and Miguel found himself alone in a section of the battlefield.

There was confusion and yelling all along the beach. The pirates, fighting like the trapped beasts they were, killed many of the troops and temporarily forced the Spanish army backward. Miguel thought of his father's words, "Even a soldier knows when he must flee." He slipped into a grove of trees behind the beach and hid. Below him the Spanish pikemen counterattacked and the exhausted pirates fell backward and were being killed. From his hiding spot, Miguel saw Jerusalem, on the front of the beach, the sweat on his huge body gleaming in the sunlight, fighting three Spaniards, his saber thrashing like a blur. Bargara, her wild hair waving like a lion's mane, fought another with her saber beside Jerusalem. Eventually Jerusalem and Bargara both fell, and the mad pirate's crusade ended, not in the holy land, but with Spanish pike thrusts on the southern coast of Sicily.

Miguel waited a bit in his hiding place, and seeing no soldiers pursuing into his back wooded area, slipped onto the trail leading out of the woods and up the rocky hill. From high on the hill, he looked back and saw the Spanish troops force the remaining pirates into a circle. As he watched, the musketeers shot them on the beach. The pikemen moved in and killed any that had survived the muskets. He shook his head in horror; who was crueler, Jerusalem's pirates, the Inquisition or just the army? Even as a soldier it all made no sense to him. There was little time for such thought, and he quickly continued on the steep path.

Slowly, he alternated between hiding and going forward, until he was certain there were no soldiers pursuing him. The Spanish were chasing some fleeing pirates up the different path that Miguel had shown to Jerusalem. A bit more confident that he was not being followed, he began to move quickly north, to try to find Palermo.

XIII

Miguel knew that Palermo was on the northern coast, so navigating by the movement of the sun he traveled northward as best he could. It was a tough climb on the rocky steep path and the mountain footing was treacherous. Still he moved rapidly for a day and a half. On the top of a hill, he stumbled into a small mountain village and found a farmer working in an olive grove. Miguel spoke the Sicilian dialect of Palermo but still didn't understand the speech of the farmer in this remote village. Although he had difficulty communicating with the farmer, he eventually managed to get the man to understand that he fled from the Spanish. The farmer, as most Sicilian peasants, hated the Spanish conquerors and took him into the village and to a small tavern.

A heavy set man, bald with a bushy mustache, sat at a table drinking wine. Two other men with swords sat with him while two others, also armed, stood guard. The farmer kissed the heavy man's hand and said something to him, looking back at Miguel. Miguel's clothes were torn and blood stained from the battle and the long climb. The heavy man signaled for Miguel to come over and motioned for him to sit. One of the guards tried to take Miguel's sword, but Miguel wouldn't give it up. The seated man indicated that he could keep his sword. He then called over the inn keeper and spoke to him.

"Are you Spanish?" the innkeeper asked Miguel in Spanish. Miguel realized that the innkeeper would serve as a translator.

"I hate the Spanish," Miguel answered in the Sicilian of Palermo, "but I am from Granada." Having heard that the Sicilians still had convivencia and hated the Inquisition, he told the translator, "I am a converso and I fled the Inquisition."

The translator related this to the seated man who said something back in the local dialect. The innkeeper then told Miguel, "This is Don Vincenzo. He is the Mafia chieftain in this region and he rules the village and protects us from the Spanish, although they do not often come this high into the mountains."

Don Miguel then spoke directly to Don Vincenzo. He spoke in Italian, but the innkeeper still translated his words into the local dialect. "I fled the Spanish from the coast south of here. I have climbed for two days. I have family in Palermo and I must get there. I know it is north, but I don't know how to travel. Can you guide me?"

The Mafia chieftain listened and pondered and then spoke to the translator in Sicilian. The translator then called over one of the guards who carried a musket and told Miguel, "Don Vincenzo gives you Tonio," pointing at the man with the musket, "as a guide. He will take you to just outside of Palermo. Tonio will not enter the city, it is dangerous for him."

Tonio nodded at Miguel and the translator continued, "Don Vincenzo asks that you sit and eat with him. You'll stay in the village tonight and leave with Tonio in the morning. You are safe here from the Spanish."

The inn keeper's wife, a heavy woman with dark hair, clad in a reddish dress, brought roasted duck, bread, and wine to the table. Miguel and Don Vincenzo ate and drank. During the meal, a group of villagers came to the chieftain. Each paid respect to Don Vincenzo by kneeling and then kissing a jeweled ring on his right hand. Each then asked, in their dialect, for some favor. The chieftain seemed to grant them their wishes.

When this business with the villagers concluded, Miguel related to Don Vincenzo and his henchmen, who stood around them, through the translator, the story of his flight from Granada to Cuba. He told them of escaping the Inquisition, the capture by pirates, the madness of Jerusalem and the battle on the beach.

Don Vincenzo and his men were entranced by the epic, hissed when the Spanish or the Inquisition was mentioned and cheered when Miguel killed the Spanish soldier. Miguel cautiously omitted the wealth of his family and described himself as a soldier from Sienna and his father as a wine merchant.

Late in the evening Don Vincenzo told Miguel, "Sleep here at the tavern. In the morning, Tonio will guide you to Palermo. As an enemy of the Spanish you are my brother."

Miguel, finally feeling safe, slept soundly. In the late morning, the innkeeper woke Miguel.

Tonio waited there with a satchel of food and wine for the journey and he handed Miguel a clean shirt. "You cannot enter Palermo in a blood splattered cloak," he told Miguel and laughed.

For three days, Tonio guided Miguel through the mountains. When the terrain became less steep, they found a wider road which they followed. Finally, they stood on a hill overlooking a city. In the distance, they could see the sea.

"That is Palermo," Tonio told him and then indicated that he can go no further. The guide then left him there and headed back on the road.

Miguel, tired but excited, staggered into the city. Following his instincts, he managed to find the main square or Zocalo. He stopped several people and asked in Italian for the location of the Benzion banking office. Most avoided the shabby looking stranger or said they didn't know. Finally, one person knew the bank and directed him to it. It was near the Zocalo as Miguel had remembered.

The building had no markings and there was a huge wooden door with a large brass knocker at the entryway.

Miguel knocked on the door to the bank and a servant opened it. Before the servant could say anything, Don Miguel stated, "I am Miguel Benzion, son of Don Mordecai."

The servant was shocked, and without saying anything, ran to a back room, leaving Miguel standing there. When the servant returned, he came with Mordecai, Asher, Abram, and Arnoldo. Momentarily, they were stunned, and then the usually unemotional Mordecai rushed to his son and embraced him. Tears streamed down the old man's cheeks and the others also wept with joy.

Miguel simply said, "I survived and I am home."

Arnoldo pushed to the front and hugged his nephew. "What of Jerusalem?" He then asked, "How did you get away?"

"They are all dead," Miguel answered.

Before he said more, Mordecai interrupted, "Tell us all later. Come to the house, there is someone you must see."

The group led him to the Benzion home, as opulent as their compound in Granada. "Wait here my son," Mordecai told him, as Miguel stood in the entry hall. Within moments, Imelda walked in. Again finely dressed, she seemed like the maiden of Granada, not the captive of a pirate. Miguel felt that she was even more beautiful than before.

Imelda and Miguel stood silent for a few seconds staring in amazement at each other. Then they ran together and embraced. They held onto each other as if they would never let go. Their past was over, the future was unknown, but they were together.

Montego Bay

Lucy Ann Fiorini

We pulled into our fore-and-aft rig, the schooner Clara Belle, into Montego Bay just before dusk. Our last haul had been dropped on the mainland and we were running fast with a mostly empty cargo hold, cleaned up and prepped for picking up a load of Jamaican sugar.

I gave the order for the mainsail to be lowered as we settled into port. As we disembarked, the harbormaster approached and met us before we had two feet on land.

"Are you the Captain of this floating mess?" the white-haired codger asked, a ledger book in his grasp and a greedy glint in his eyes.

"Aye," I said, I knew he was looking for either a bribe or a fight and while I was never one to back down from a good brawling, my men had been through hell in the last fortnight and they didn't need me drumming up more for them.

"Name?"

"Captain William Wisdom."

"Crew?"

"Ten souls strong."

The harbormaster's eyes darted up from his ledger book. "Shouldn't this have a crew of twelve?"

I cast a glance back at my men as I answered, "Rough seas. We've lost a few along the way."

The harbormaster was appeased and moved on in his questioning, "License to…"

Before the harbormaster could finish his sentence, I produced a small, worn coin purse from my pocket and extended my arm in his direction. "I have this for a license."

With a nod, he took the bribe and, passing me, headed for the next ship in sight, calling out to them, "Are you the Captain of this floating mess?"

I waved to my men and they followed me into the cobblestone streets of Montego Bay. We sought the rowdiest pub we could find and found ourselves space inside and kept the women coming by and the rum flowing at our table.

After a few hours of this debauchery, I held up my hand. "Steady lads, it's time to wind down. We have a shipment to pick up in the morning and a wide-open sea waiting for us." The men stammered and groaned and complained it was all happening too soon.

"We are two hands down," I reminded them, "so there's more work with fewer of us."

"Then pull in some more men," Roscoe, my first mate bellowed from his seat, wench on his lap and pint in his hand.

"I would if I could," I hollered back, but I didn't think it would be easy to find more souls as strong as ours here in Montego Bay.

As if reading my mind, a strong young man approached our table. "I hear you're looking for some more crew members," he said.

I laughed, "Do you, now? And who are you?"

"Someone who knows his way around a ship," the young man countered. He kept his eyes trained on me, steely gazed and stubborn. I could tell he didn't back down easily.

I put down my drink and looked him up and down, "What my crew needs isn't a man who knows his way around a ship, as much as a man who knows his way around the sea."

The young man looked puzzled, "Are you getting at something, Captain?"

"Aye, I am. Have you ever sailed the breakers way between Jamaica and the Colonies?"

"I can't say that I have," he answered.

"I didn't think so."

"Possibly because that's an idiot's way to sail."

My men, drunk as they were, pricked up their ears at this insult thrown in my direction. "What did you say?" one of them called over, standing up so abruptly that the girl in his lap fell straight to the floor.

I held up my hand. "It's all right. Our fine, young candidate here doesn't know these waters any more than he knows the world ten feet from his mother's side."

The men laughed and started to settle back down.

The young man was undeterred in sparring with me. He was either desperate for the job or desperate for a beating. I decided to let him continue.

"I think you're asking me a trick question."

"Do you, now?"

"The breakers way is full of rocks and dangerous waters…"

"Rocks aren't the half of it!" One of my inebriated crew called out and the other laughed.

The young man continued, "So most ships that go through that pass never come out. There are shorter paths through calmer waters."

"And there are enemies who steal and Navy ships who seize our goods or tax our cargo and many other things afloat in the calmer waters, and those calmer waters are the longer way around. I get my cargo to the Colonies faster and make more money in the process going through the breakers. It ain't for the faint of heart. If you want to sail with my crew, you have to have the stomach for the breakers and you have to obey me at all costs."

"I can do it," the young man insisted.

"We'll see," I said. "Meet me at the port at dawn. You'll help us load the cargo before you help us sail."

"I understand," the young man nodded.

"You won't understand anything until you get to the breakers and you will understand even less when you pass through it."

Roscoe and the rest of the crew held up their pints and laughed at that thought.

"What's your name?" I asked.

"Everett," the young man replied.

I nodded and took a drink. "Everett. Good to know. I'll need it for your headstone."

"We'll see about that," Everett countered as he walked away.

"Yes, we will," I said, in response to his departing form.

Half a day later, our cargo was loaded up and the hold was filled. We were ready to go. Young Everett had proven to be to a big help to us in the loading of the sugar and the rum. We had clear skies and flat seas for the first half of the run to the Colonies until we reached the breakers.

The water got choppier as we approached closer to the rocks. The sky darkened a bit as if foretelling the darkness that was to come.

I gave the order, "It's time." My men knew their positions and hastened to them. They stood where they could handle the sails without looking over the sides of the ship.

"You," I yelled to Everett, "get below deck!"

"Why?" he asked, challenging me.

"The Captain said to get below deck!" Roscoe bellowed back.

"But why?" Everett asked, manning his part of the sail.

"We are almost in earshot," one of the other men called out.

"Earshot of what?"

Before anyone could reply, the sound of singing started.

"Turn away, boys," I ordered, and they did, all except for Everett. He turned to the railing and looked over the edge.

"There are women in the water!" he yelled, but my men knew better than to look. They stayed resilient and kept their backs to the waves.

"Look away!" Roscoe ordered.

"We need to save those women. They're drowning."

I kept my hands tight on the wheel and stared straight ahead. "They aren't drowning. They're Sirens. They're calling us in."

"What's a Siren? Is it a mermaid? They are so beautiful."

"They ain't beautiful," one of my men yelled out. "They are only women from the waist up. They have the bodies of a snake underneath."

"Don't listen to them!" another of the men yelled out. "They need you to come to them."

"Their song is so beautiful, Captain," Everett said.

I kept my hands firmly on the wheel. "Look away and be strong, stay away from the edge. We're almost in the clear. A few more minutes that's all."

But Everett wasn't hearing a word I said. He had listened too closely to the Siren's song and was running full speed towards them, diving over the railing and into the sea.

I watched his body drop head first into the frothy waves. One of the Sirens slid from her rock and into the water, as well. She swam effortlessly to the spot where he had gone under and she too dipped below the surface and came back up a moment later with Everett in her arms. Her claws had pierced his side as she had latched onto him to pull him back onto the rocks. Her once beautiful mouth opened and exposed rows of razor-sharp teeth.

"Just look at that," Roscoe exclaimed, but I didn't look back. I kept the bowsprit pointed straight ahead. We would clear the breakers in a few more minutes and, God-willing, reach the Colonies intact and ahead of schedule.

The sky lightened and everything looked better once the shore was in sight. "We made it through again, lads," I called out and my men cheered in response.

"Once we reach the Colonies, we will take a break and find some men who know how to obey their Captain before we head back to Montego Bay," I informed Roscoe as he met me on the bridge.

"That sounds good," he said. Then, after a pause, he added, "It's too bad about young Everett."

I nodded in agreement, "Well, he was a good man while he lasted."

Lucy Ann Fiorini

Pleasure for an Hour, A Bottle of Good Wine...

Sergio 'ente per ente' Palumbo

Edited and Translated by

Michele DUTCHER

"Caution with others is a must have..."
Old Chinese proverb

    The taverns on Hirado Island were common venues where pirates, assassins, outlaws and individuals of ill repute preferred to stay for most of the day and also into the night. At that time the most famous houses were 'The Long Evening', 'The Captain's Rest', 'A Sea Devil', 'The Sunken Junk', 'The Flowers of Everlasting Summer', 'The Old Tavern of the Lost Days' and a few others, situated on the south side of the forested coastline.
    Although such places were open to all comers, it was easy for small companies of men, banded together by common interests and devoted to similar aims - be they crimes or plans for the next illegal venture ahead - to keep

aloof from casual patrons. These rogues were middle-aged sailors; hot-headed mercenaries; experienced seamen; the terrible waegu - which literally translated to 'Japanese pirates' or 'dwarf pirates' - who raided the coastlines of China and Korea; and the likes who claimed respect both outside the tavern and inside. The landlords granted them whatever privileges the house afforded, knowing full-well that knives could be easily drawn, blood might spurt and a few body parts could be severed, if proper attention was not paid and offense was taken.

Actually, Xiaohui was not exactly a regular customer of such taverns, but it also wasn't rare to catch a glimpse of her in there. This was because inside of those venues is where the kind of men she liked most commonly spent the night while drinking heavily, eating spicy meals, expressing themselves too freely, boasting too much and drinking a lot, again. Alongside their legitimate fishing and salt-making activities, those consummate seamen also excelled at piracy and became very powerful due to their control of important sea routes. Some of their recorded activities included escorting vessels to ensure —at a price— their safe passage; operating toll barriers; and fighting naval battles with cruel adversaries, which occupied most of their time, as a matter of fact.

Xiaohui's usual lovers changed frequently, but that was exactly the way she liked it. She appreciated the Captains most of all, and she also loved their beautiful, huge ships full of capable pirates ready to serve at the command of their bloody masters and, of course, also at her orders - through those men who led their crews. As a matter of fact, the young woman found that all of them were handsome, even though they didn't look alike in any way. The question was, why did they find her so attractive in return? Well, the answer was very simple, Xiaohui was young, being only twenty-years-old; she had long dark, fine hair; her pale face displayed her delicate features; and she had a beautiful, slender body endowed with two perfectly sculpted legs. On top of this, she had a considerable stature, certainly taller than the ordinary woman living in those surroundings – and that truly made the difference.

You could also ask how she dared to love four dangerous pirates at the same time, as was currently the case. How was it possible for her to go from one man to another over the course of months, before coming back to the first one, then on to the second and so forth? Specifically, how could she do this in a world where sexual infidelity was a reason for many a girl's ghastly death who only cast eyes at men other than their husbands or their appointed boyfriends? But here was the explanation; she was different from all the other female partners who dated these outlaws and raiders that sailed the most ill-reputed sea routes among the islands, surely, because of her capabilities and her knowledge of useful herbs.

And why four men, instead of only one? Actually, what fun would there have been in only being with one lover for the rest of her life? Of course, there was always something new on the way, as all those strong and warlike men possessed their endearing qualities and great riches. But the four pirates she stayed with from time to time had one thing in common; all of them loved to drink continuously, so she was always called for in the end. That is, she and her wondrous bottle were called for, actually...

Her name meant 'little wisdom', but she knew she was much more capable and astute than most of the people around her, for sure. That was the reason she had been able to live safe and sound, at least so far, taking advantage of the many opportunities she found along the way in order to improve her condition. And her experience with ancient herbal magic went the extra mile.

As Xiaohui was walking along a dusty street in town, surrounded by the humid climate of the hot summer on the island, she looked on her right and on her left at the flashy though worn-out signs outside of the taverns. She was trying to find the one where her man of that night would likely be drinking at the moment. She had already tried two well-known places before, but with no luck. The woman was sure that now things were going to change. After a while, Xiaohui slowed her pace and thought that she had finally figured out where the man she was looking for probably was. Of course, he didn't know yet that he was going to bed her in a matter of a few moments.

The huge sign outside, on a long wooden plank, said: 'The Flowers of Everlasting Summer'. So, that was the venue she had to go in. As the young woman put her foot inside, a smoky haze assailed her senses, there were many customers who were drinking presently. She reasoned that it was very common at that time, before a battle or a raiding assault, for a wise and very experienced Captain to feast with his crewmen on alcohol and meat. If they won the battle or the attack was good, they would be rewarded with good wine. On the other hand, if a warrior or a seaman on the same ship fell in battle, his fellow crewmen would scatter wine on the ground as part of a memorial ceremony, certainly. Beyond this, it was always possible that men in the common houses were just drinking themselves into a stupor, as that was a common behavior for the men in Hirado, and it was especially true among those pirates.

There were many smells coming from the several tables, the origins of which were mostly imported sweet 'pijiu' and a local spicy drink called 'jiu'. Cheap 'huangjiu', literally 'yellow wine' or 'yellow alcohol', was also a type of common Chinese liquor brewed directly from grains such as rice or millet that usually varied in color from clear to yellowish-brown, or reddish-brown. For this liquor, huangjiu, the grains were polished, then soaked and acidified in order to either create a bitter taste in it or to render it poisonous. That process produced a taste and mouth-feel distinct from other forms of rice wine, beyond this process the water it was mixed with and its mineral content also contributed to the flavor and quality of the drink.

As her eyes kept looking around in search of her target of the night, Xiaohui noticed many details of the tavern she was in now: there were about twenty small tables and some wooden framework. Also, several paintings and carvings had been added to the walls to make them look more beautiful and attractive, or at least this was probably the plan at the beginning, when the owner had ordered them years ago - but now they appeared old and in a very bad shape, as was the overall structure, undoubtedly. Even the posts, lintels and joists seemed to be worn-out today, although some of the windows still displayed exquisite colored appliqué design. There were also a few beautiful starry patterns still visible on wooden pillars inside.

Then the details of a figure caught her attention. It had a short dark beard; two wide shoulders under a gray, polished upper outer garment with a longer lower garment and a jacket that shortened the length of the exposed skirt; and a main circular collar with a sunbathed face on top of it endowed with strong, very recognizable features that made him look handsome and very interesting. Here he was! Xiaohui smiled, satisfied. That was really him, no mistake.

Wang Zhi, also known as Gohô or Ôchoku in Japanese, was a young Chinese pirate - formerly a trader - who already had several followers under his command today. At the time when she first met him, he wasn't a famous waegu yet. Those days he had only one vessel at his disposal, a kobaya, which was a small, open roof ship manned by twenty oarsmen. But over the matter of a few months things had changed greatly, as had his watercraft. It was now a longer and faster seki-bune medium-sized vessel - and his renown had grown as well. Having his hometown as Huangshan City, according to what people believed, he was said to have been aboard the Portuguese ship when it landed on Tanegashima, off the coast of Japan in 1543. This meeting marked the first contact between Europe and Japan, and many supposed he played a part when the Portuguese arrived at Hirado Island seven years later - as that port of call became the first town in Japan opened to British trade.

Now, in 1551 he had already made some dangerous enemies, but his crewmen increased as the overall number of his ships did. It was strange to think that one of his adversaries was the famous and older pirate Xu Hai, who had also been a lover of Xiaohui's, some time ago. The woman hadn't chosen Xu Hai for her purposes today, however, as he wasn't in Hirado this month, unfortunately. Circumstances made unexpected bedfellows, certainly, as Xu Hai was much more powerful than Wang Zhi was now, but she was in a hurry and didn't want to wait any longer. Patience had never been one of her best qualities, the woman was well aware of it.

Now that she had found the man, she knew what to do, of course. So the young woman simply moved forward with decisiveness and reached the table where the drowsy pirate Captain sat. Both of his boots were on the dirty surface of the wooden table, along with showy unpleasant flecks of beer and wine that seemed to be an inextricable part of it so far. She noisily put in the middle of that table a small hand-painted porcelain bottle, similar to the sort of traditional Chinese pottery which was shaped like a nude lady, strange to say. The mixture of minerals that composed such bottles had remained the same since the ancient times and was usually baked in a kiln at very high temperatures. The resulting product was white and hard. However, light could pass through it, so that despite its sturdiness it looked quite delicate and beautiful.

As the bottle touched the top of the table, the pirate awoke and opened one dark eye towards the direction the noise came from, then he raised his head and looked straight at the young woman, so he saw the pottery. Other than the unusual shape, the bottle's exterior had erotic drawings of nude couples that conveyed its meaning to other customers sitting at other tables. She seemed to know very well that men commonly had a quick glimpse at those lascivious depictions and easily understood what delights the night had in store for them.

"I know you!" the Captain exclaimed in a coarse voice that emerged from his beard the same way a vaporous blow came out of a gurgling pot dangling over the fireplace, actually. "Don't I maybe...?"

"Yes, sure thing, Captain...we have already been friends before - well, something more than close friends - if you take my meaning."

The other made a face, as if he was trying to bring to mind some lost memories, then he was going to speak again when the woman anticipated him. "The sands of Rishiri Island in late spring, some weeks ago, and that wonderful night we spent at the lonely tavern. I think that any of your crewmen - if some of them still survive - would easily recognize me today."

"Yeah, yeah..." the eyes of the man seemed to be turning into two brilliant stones now as he looked the attractive newcomer over, head to toe, Xiaohui wore her elaborate, glistening black hair wondrously tied up in a bun; the color perfectly accented her green/blue loose-fitting clothes with long large sleeves; the entire ensemble was made up of a blouse and a wrap-around skirt dotted with drawings of many flowers; and all of that enveloped her lithe though tall young body. "How could I ever forget the great time we had? Xiaohui is your beautiful name, isn't it? And I remember also your beautiful body, of course, all of it..."

"That's the sign of a good memory, my dear," the woman snickered.

"What brings you here, my darling? Is there anything I could do for you? Just ask me..."

"Actually, there is, but we'd better have a drink first. May I sit?"

"Of course! On my lap..." he invited her with a wide gesture.

"Maybe later," she politely refused. "First of all, let's have some drinks..."

"Of course, as you wish!" and with that being said, the man called out and someone nearby quickly responded.

The waiter - or was he the owner of the venue? - came and stood on the right side, next to the table. He wore a chestnut narrow-cuffed tunic tied with a sash similar to a sort of hanfu dress and he was silent, displaying two black, tiny eyes which seemed to be switched off on purpose, at least apparently. He had an unusually wide dark beard with some white streaks that looked like a waterfall flowing down from an outcrop - which was his old, weary face. His nose resembled a curved, pale tree heading down for the far end of a precipice in the distance.

"May I bring you some pijiu?" the man asked the pirate Captain, without even noticing the presence of the young woman at his side.

"No beer tonight, man!" the other exclaimed. "I need some more liquor, so bring us some shaojiu, and let it be one of your best bottles."

As the old person bowed respectfully, Xiaohui openly sneered and turned to her partner with a satisfied expression on her delicate, beautiful features. The woman liked that particular flavored 'hot liquor', also called 'burned liquor' - either because of the person's mouth being 'set on fire', given the fact that such a beverage was warmed for a long time before being consumed, or because of the heating required during distillation. So it was a good thing that the Captains Xiaohui chose as her prey from time to time, still maintained part of their true preferences even when their will was under the spell of her powerful, magical potions. That thought allowed her to argue that they weren't really just slaves who were unable to have their own opinions or to express their true wishes - or at least this was the way she liked to think about all of it.

"Please, have a drink..." she invited the Captain, pouring some tempting liquid from her bottle into a mug on the table.

"I hope you're not trying to poison my stomach. My crew would soon avenge me."

"You're very suspicious," the woman pointed out with a wide smile.

"I have many enemies…"

"Well then, allow me…" she replied, while taking the first drink by grabbing the pirate's mug itself, and immediately sipped the alcohol. "So, surely you don't think I'm trying to poison myself too." Xiaohui knew perfectly well that the magical ingredients she had previously mixed with the liquid in the bottle had no effect on her - given the fact she had already ingested the only antidote known in the world against that preparation - but only on the target of the potion.

Wang Zhi looked at her with both dark eyes, considering her gesture. "I suppose not…"

"Now, if I may, I need to discuss something with you…" she said.

"That being?" the Captain seemed less interested as he heard that statement. By the way he stared at the beautiful female body he had before his eyes, it was obvious he was thinking of something else anyway.

The woman appeared to be wary now, and she approached the pirate as if she didn't want other customers sitting nearby overhearing their conversation. "I know how to get to an unknown, ancient treasure, hidden by priests - as I have been told how to reach it. The only person still alive who knew about it, and passed such news to me, recently died, by chance…"

"What a good chance…" the pirate sneered. "And do you have a map?"

"No, but I've got some useful clues."

"And you need a ship and a crew, certainly…so it's why you are searching for someone like me."

"Well, not only your ship, Wang Zhi, as I have something else on my mind…" and saying that she looked at the man with her lust-filled eyes for a moment.

"Uhm, that does sound interesting. Let's go upstairs and discuss the matter further. What's the destination and how far is it from Hirado island?"

"Too many details for now, maybe later," she objected. "Always pleasure first, then duty…It's my rule."

"Isn't it usually the other way around?" the pirate said in return.

"Not for me, dear Captain. And now, please have a drink…"

"Why not?" and he sipped the liquor in his mug. The effects of the magical liquid soon started to wrap around his mind. He immediately displayed a more pleasing expression, along with a more compliant behavior, and the man's manners improved as well. A sudden feeling of love for the woman was suddenly flowing through his body and it forced him to be seriously attracted by his young female guest. Much to the satisfaction of Xiaohui herself, of course.

In her heart, undoubtedly, the woman was glad that the men she was attracted to appreciated the quality beverages she offered them, and she paid a lot of attention to that part of her plan every single time. However, she was also aware that it wasn't just the superior alcohol that pleased them or let her have a powerful hold on them in the end, but it happened only thanks to an enchanted substance she had previously put in the bottle and added to the drink in secrecy. That was the liquor's real job, of course, with a result that no wine or liquor alone could ever get, certainly, no matter how extraordinary or expensive any famous beverage could be.

☠☠☠☠

While the two were still in the bedroom on the upper floor of the tavern, Xiaohui turned to the handsome pirate at her side and let her small hands feel the skin of the back of the strong man, then smiled, as the whole moment clearly seemed to please her.

As soon as they had entered the room, she had approached him from the back, removing his robe before undoing the buttons concealed inside his garment, touching his chest slowly, very slowly. The woman had moved her hands across his body and did her best to stimulate his senses. The pirate had immediately reacted and turned to her, kissing her arms and her legs which were still wrapped in the remains of the loose cloth. They had made love passionately, and Wang Zhi had proved to be completely bound to her commands, as he had done everything according to her wishes. And it couldn't be otherwise, Xiaohui thought, given the powerful magical potion he had ingested before, even though the enchantment had been unbeknownst to him.

When it was all over, the couple remained on the bed for some time, looking at each other. Actually, the man's eyes appeared to be far more lost and enraptured than hers, given his condition, but that was all part of her game. The young woman told herself that she would enjoy playing with him, just for a while, because she enjoyed having so much fun. "So, tomorrow we'll get aboard your vessel and begin sailing to our destination and the riches that we'll find for us…" Xiaohui softly whispered to the Captain.

"Why do you want for us to leave on this voyage with only my seki-bune and its forty-man crew? I have many larger ships and crews under my command."

"That is a matter to be kept between me and you - and your most faithful crewmembers. No reason to let too many men in on our plans – and no reason to share the gold we'll find with others either. It's also better to not attract too much unwanted attention, don't you agree?"

"You're right. I knew right away that you were an intelligent partner, certainly."

In the dead of the night, as the man was still lying on the bed, the woman stood up and went to the small table where her wondrous bottle was. It had been a very pleasant night, she told herself, still thinking about the love that her partner had given before, so she knew what she had to do. Reaching into a pocket in her robe that was laid over a wooden chair nearby, Xiaohui took out another potion of dusty ingredients that she had in a small purse and added it to the contents of the tiny hand-painted piece of pottery. That would be enough to make certain the pirate Captain was at her feet for another half-day, which was exactly the wish that had crossed her mind as soon as she woke up. It was going to be another session of love and passion, exactly what she presently needed. The treasure and the start of their voyage could wait for a few more hours.

All thanks to a wonderful, magical potion that had been a secret in her family for a very long time!

☠☠☠☠

Their journey across that stretch of the stormy South China Sea had been long and filled with many difficulties, but they had finally arrived at the destination where the woman was sure she would find the final clues that would lead her to the treasure.

Despite all the high waves that their somewhat box-shaped ship had gone through, the terrible weather that had accompanied their voyage for so long, and some bloody curses by the crewmen because of all the problems they had been forced to face, finally they had made it. Xiaohui had never doubted their success in her heart, not even for a moment. After all, weren't the Chinese the people who had improved travel on rivers, lakes, and canals? Weren't they also the ones who invented the first instruments ever to navigate across the Pacific Ocean by positioning a magnetic mineral on wood and floating it in a bowl of water so that it could easily turn until it pointed in a north-south direction, as early as the 6th century B.C.E.?

Such discoveries had made long sea voyages possible because sailors were finally able to figure out where they were heading even without a landmark or a star in the sky to steer by. The Chinese had also made ocean travel safer by improving boat construction and dividing the ships into sections, sealing each section with a peculiar substance that kept out water. So, it was no surprise when they arrived at their destination though it had seemed far away when they first started following that voyage.

The nearest landmass now was Luzon Island in the Philippines. From the wide deck of the seki-bune's prow, they could see the elongated isle in the Zhongsha Islands, next to the Macclesfield Bank. The island stood in the distance and seemed to be a luxuriant place, full of tall trees and white sandy beaches, shores where only a few men had put their feet before. But appearances could be deceiving and she knew that a warlike tribe of primitive humans lived among those thick branches and the short barren hills that dotted its surface. At least that was what she had been told by the person who had revealed that location to her, just before dying.

On this island, inside a small temple, they would find the final clues leading to another mountainous isle that was in the same area, where the treasure had been hidden long ago inside an ancient, bigger ruined temple by some priests who were escaping prosecution by the Chinese Imperial Court. This was all according to the information Xiaohui had been told, which had originally forced her to put her plan into motion.

Wang Zhi's crew was made up of forty clever seamen. All of them varied in height and weight, of course, the same as their weird and skimpy attire, but everyone had one thing in common, they all looked like a bad lot. They were sturdy, snarly and disreputable individuals who were completely at home with the vessel's running rigging comprising the halyards, the downhauls and all the moveable ropes that controlled sails or other equipment aboard. Each one of them had their ears pierced, as was the common practice among pirates, because the value of the earring was meant to pay for their burial if they were lost at sea and their body washed up on shore. No one among the sailors ever questioned the existing relationship between Wang Zhi and Xiaohui, which was easy to understand, as no one wanted to unleash the Captain's anger and to end up being instantly killed. This was good for her, as Xiaohui only needed to have a hold on the man in charge, letting the others simply follow his direct orders, which were her orders, in reality.

Unfortunately, they still had the most difficult part of their expedition ahead of them, the armed crew had to reach the shore, disembark and cautiously enter the jungle, no matter how insidious it might be. But they had to do their best to stay away from and stay out of sight from the wild indigenous warriors living in those jungles. This wouldn't be an easy task. The orders when they set foot ashore were clear; no noises, no laughs or yells, simply proceed in line along the path and be watchful, and make sure that everything was completed very quickly.

But plans often go astray.

It happened when one of the youngest and most inexperienced crewmen fell into a trap the locals had made for hunting wild beasts. It was then that many worries started filling Xiaohui's mind. Such distressing feelings were also filling the Captain's head, but as he was a slave to her potion it was easy to make him eradicate those troubles from his thoughts at once. If only she could eliminate her worries as easily, the woman thought to herself. But unfortunately, there was no sorcery strong enough to do that, as far as she knew, or at least nothing she had at her disposal right now.

Xiaohui knew that they had to leave that unfortunate fellow in the trap without trying to save him and wasting useful time, as every single minute mattered in those thick jungles. So she told the Captain to order the man to be left behind, and Wang Zhi acted accordingly, thanks to the magical power she had over him. But that decision, though necessary from her point of view, caused resentment among the other sailors. Xiaohui thought that such a thing couldn't be helped, as she clearly couldn't use her limited valuable ingredients on all the seamen aboard the seki-bune of Wang Zhi, so to have all of them under her undisputed command. That was why she had chosen to lead the crew, though in secret, through their pirate Captain's mouth after all.

Their first attempt at finding clues proved to be of no use whatsoever, as the primitive locals finally noticed them, and a fierce battle soon followed. The Captain's first mate, a bulky short guy of about forty with almost no hair and a wide nose, was killed just after midday during their wanderings, when two arrows pierced his sunburned head, coming from a position somewhere in the trees.

Hard as it was to have a glimpse of those fierce warriors, or a clear view of their movements, as they knew how to move in the middle of those jungles, and also were very capable of perfectly hiding or walking in silence among the many plants around. In the ensuing two battles the pirates, at least, noticed that the almost nude indigenous assailants had a sort of weaponry which consisted of knives and some strange flatbows. These had non-recurved, relatively wide limbs that were rectangular in cross-section, with a high accuracy against human-sized targets up to nearly thirty-five feet. At least three varieties of arrows, apparently for fishing and hunting, along with untipped ones for shooting warning shots, had been seen so far, but all of them had proven deadly as their fellow sailors kept dropping and their numbers kept decreasing, while their breathless race through the thick shrubs continued.

The remaining twenty-two pirates and the woman wandered through the tall trees like a headless snake, coming and going, guided only by the sun overhead. Over time they stopped doing two things that proved too difficult in their desperate escape; figuring out exactly where they were, which seemed to be the most impossible task of all, and worrying about the newly dead who had passed away because of the deadly arrows fired against them.

Even though Xiaohui told the men that they had to stay together at all times, by means of the Captain's speech and using some decisive words like, "Follow my orders or you'll die" or "If you are alone, you're dead!", some of the crew tried to flee as soon as they all stopped just outside a clearing. This was because they were thinking they could easily take advantage of the oncoming darkness and the predictable difficulties the pursuers would have trying to follow their tracks in the dark. The rest of the group soon lost contact with the ones who wandered off alone, and those men were never seen again, nor did they ever reach the seki-bune. But the remaining eighteen were able to finally get back to the shore where their vessel was anchored.

They finally shoved off and hoisted the sails, placing their ship at a safe distance from the luxuriant and bloody island, even though they knew that it was just a short-term diversion. Obviously, their crew would need to go back to that coast, sooner or later, if they wanted to find the final clues that their Captain's partner still needed in order to reach their desired end.

And she knew very well that there was simply no other way.

☠☠☠☠

A week had already gone by, but Xiaohui hadn't dared to go back to the island. In a way, she was taking a break to rethink her next move and having sex with the Captain daily just to kill time. At least she couldn't say that the voyage hadn't been interesting so far.

In his lodgings, on top of a wardrobe, Wang Zhi had a strange device, a decorated and very valuable mechanical clock that worked by means of a wheel, the size of a wide hand that made one complete turn every twenty-four hours. Dripping water made the mechanism turn; every fifteen minutes, drums would beat; and every hour, a bell would chime. The sounds let people know what time it was. The device was, probably, the result of some plundering that had occurred before, and it looked very complex and accurate. As the woman knew that the Chinese had developed the first mechanical clocks, it was likely that the mechanism had come from some trade vessel the pirate ship had assaulted in the past.

As the resentment among the other crewmen was still visible almost everywhere on the main deck, the woman knew that she had to keep a strong grip on the pirate Captain if she wanted to have everything under control. At times Xiaohui even thought she was becoming too anxious.

So she kept adding more dusty ingredients to the liquid in the bottle that she handed to Wang Zhi every day. Better to be sure that the pirate's will would remain enslaved to the woman's at present, given the losses they had suffered during their previous attempt on the island and the hatred which was spreading among the crewmen. So this was no time to spare her magical potion at present. She needed to be sure that the Captain would execute her orders and act in accordance with her wishes!

Xiaohui turned to her lover who appeared to still be asleep on the bed, just to be certain she wouldn't be discovered. She completed what she was doing in secret, before going back to the man and lying next to him again for a while longer. Then the soft waves resounded on the outside of the ship, along with the yells and the orders of the crewmembers who were at work on deck, as the seki-bune proceeded along its route late in the evening.

☠☠☠☠

It was exactly two weeks later when they attempted to go ashore again, as time was going by quickly and the woman didn't want to waste any more time. She found that she was beginning to feel bored with Wang Zhi's lovemaking.

As they proceeded through the jungles, well-armed and very wary, trying to reach the place where Xiaohui knew the old temple with the carvings stood, their march appeared to be peaceful, without any hindrance, which was good, even though a bit strange. Things changed however as the group got to a clearing where the pirate Captain ordered the others to stop. His action immediately caught the woman unawares, as she hadn't allowed such a stop or ordered her enslaved lover to do any such thing. As Xiaohui was trying to figure out what was going on, the voice of Wang Zhi resounded in a decisive tone. "Now we can go back to our seki-bune, men!"

"What?" the woman exclaimed, "Why are you saying this? I don't agree, we must go on if we want to find the clues that will lead us to the treasure being in the next temple we are seeking!"

"This expedition has already proven to be too bloody, my darling…" the pirate abruptly stated.

As Xiaohui was still considering the entire situation, her hands inadvertently reached into the pockets of the short chestnut robe she wore, and she didn't find what she had been expecting.

"Are you looking for these ingredients?" the man asked Xiaohui with a sneer on his face as he lifted to the sky a small purse filled with something.

A look of awe appeared on the woman's face at once, but she forced herself to behave as if it was nothing. "Do you like to play with the purses of young ladies now? What's the point of that?"

"I saw you taking some strange ingredients out of it and putting them into your hand painted bottle. At first I thought you were going to make me into a drug addict. But then I stole a portion of it, while you were asleep the following night, and served it along with some wine to a seaman in my crew. I was very curious to see what its effects would be. The drug's consequences quickly became obvious as the one who had drunk the liquor started to be attracted to me, much to my surprise. So I figured out that was a sort of potion! And you had been giving it to me for who knows how long...I had some fun while watching the weird behavior of that sailor, but at the same time I considered the whole situation and I began being upset, really upset, at you!"

"Wait, Wang Zhi," Xiaohui said in a soothing tone. "It's not what it looks like!"

But the Captainr didn't let her speak and continued, "And, by seeing the results of your actions, along with all the men in my crew I lost over the course of our voyage, I see that you simply turned me into an enslaved lover for a while. I don't even know for how long! And that makes me even angrier!"

"Please, Wang, listen to me..." a very worried Xiaohui said, in an imploring, low tone.

"Empty her pockets!" the Captain ordered to his men. "Check to be sure that she has no more herbs, tricks or other hellish things with her."

"Listen to me, Captain…you still need me to find the treasure. And you also need me if you want to get out of these jungles without being killed by the warriors living on this island."

"Well, about your treasure, actually I don't believe it's true…and about our life, you must know that it's perfectly safe for now," Wang retorted.

"Why are you so sure? We are very far from the shore, and anything could still happen to us," the woman said in return.

"We made a deal with the people of this island last night, unbeknownst to you, while you were asleep in my bed, in order to save our lives. You know, it's only been two days since I stopped drinking your potion and I've already started feeling much better, and thinking much more freely, as well!" a smiling Wang Zhi revealed. "And I gave a little of your potion's ingredients, taken from this very purse, to every man in that tribe, to be shared. Actually, there are more than sixty men overall, so they each possess some of the power and they have also been told how to put their potion to good use. So, just imagine what will happen when they use such herbs on you, my darling."

Xiaohui remained in silence, seemingly lost and without any defense. The man turned his attention back to the seashore where his beloved seki-bune was anchored, and started walking away with his crewmen. "Now we're going to leave you alone on this wild island, but I don't think you'll remain alone for long."

"Please, Wang Zhi, don't leave me here!" the woman exclaimed.

Without showing any compassion, the pirate continued, a smart sneer appearing on his bearded face, before leaving the place. "I hope you have a pleasant day, lovely Xiaohui, although I think the pleasure will mostly be all theirs…"

Sergio Palumbo

Pirate Tales

☠

A Novella

E.W. Farnsworth

Pirates of Madagascar

    We had been taking ships and plenty of pelf off the Canaries until Captain Morgan decided we might be getting too much of a good thing. One bright morning, the Captain ordered the Sweet Cutlass to sail southeast for the Ear of Africa and then to take the slow route south along the west coast of Africa to the Cape of Good Hope, then after passing through the cold winds and mean rip tides of the crossover at the tip of the cape, to sail up the east coast to Madagascar.

    Not all the crew was happy with this plan, and the Third Mate and two others asked to be put ashore with their share of our current booty. The Captain, always the perfect democrat, called all crew topside to adjudicate the matter. So there the ship lay with its sails furled against a gentle breeze with the Captain and me up by the wheel and the crew gathered down around the mast.

    The Captain calmly asked the Third Mate to tell the crew what he and his two companions wished to do and why. The Third Mate was unruffled, and he said he reckoned that the Sweet Cutlass had gathered as much treasure as was possible during the last four months around the Canaries. He said the month-long voyage around the cape would not be commensurately profitable, so he and his hearties figured they would take their share of what had been gathered now and jump ship. He explained that they would ship aboard some other vessel and continue to work here near the Canaries. Maybe, he said, they would ship back aboard the Sweet Cutlass when it returned from Madagascar—if that ever happened.

The Captain seemed to take seriously what his Third Mate said and nodded his head throughout the man's case as if he were impressed with the plan. When the Third Mate had finished and swelled up with pride for having done well articulating his plan, the Captain asked the crew whether any other of them wanted to join the Third Mate and his two hearties. The crew was silent and suspicious because they knew their Captain's calculating moods. The Captain said he reckoned from their silence that the Third Mate and his two hearties were the only pirates on the ship who were in the deal. His voice boomed out that this was the last call to join the Third Mate or to remain with the Sweet Cutlass on its new voyage to Madagascar. No one answered the Captain's call to join the Third Mate. In fact, the crew shuffled back a few steps to distance themselves from the Third Mate and his two confederates so that those three men stood alone before the mast.

Then the Captain asked me, as First Mate, what the death of a crew member meant with regard to each man's share. I answered that the dead man's share belonged in equal part to the remaining crew. The Captain nodded and asked what each living man should deduce from that fundamental maxim of pirates everywhere.

I said, "More for the rest of us."

Then the Captain rose to his full height and ordered the Second Mate to shove out the plank on the lee side of the vessel because three men had opted to leave the ship and he intended to give them a good send off.

A commotion stirred among the crew while the plank was shoved out over the side. The crew knew the meaning of that plank, for many of their victims had walked off it at sword point into the sea.

The Third Mate had now turned pale, and his two hearties seemed to be having second thoughts about their rash decision to join the man in his undertaking. The Captain cheerily asked the three mutineers who would like to mount the plank first.

While they were deliberating among each other, he ordered the Second Mate to chum the waters on the side of the vessel where the plank extended. He ordered me to draw and cock my pistol and to maintain order during the proceedings because he was going to withdraw to his quarters for a moment to relieve himself.

The Captain went back towards his cabin while I assumed the Conn and kept watch over the crew. Meanwhile, the first fins cut through the clear, calm water where the chum had fallen. Soon the water would be a chaos of sharks seeking blood with their wide mouths open, and the crew became fascinated with the thought of the feast we would soon provide for them.

The Third Mate called me by my name and asked me to intervene. He all but begged for mercy as our victims invariably had done before they had walked the plank. He said he deserved his share and his hearties also deserved theirs.

As if he had heard this plea, the Captain emerged from his cabin with three sacks, which he held up so that all the crew could see. In the sacks, the Captain said, were the shares of loot that the departing men had earned. He turned to the crew and said each sack contained gold and silver coins. He opened one sack and grabbed a fistful of coins and flung it to the deck below so the crew could see the truth of what he said for themselves. No one touched the coins though there was no mistaking the glittering coins for anything but gold and silver. The Captain said that the crew should decide what would happen to the bags of pelf as man by man the Third Mate and his hearties left the ship.

The first man to the plank was the Third Mate himself. The Second Mate bound the condemned man's hands and escorted him to the end of the plank where he looked down into the gently undulating ocean water boiling with hungry sharks. When the man was in position, the Captain raised a sack and asked the crew whether it was fair to give the Third Mate his share knowing his fate. When none of the crew answered, the Captain asked me what I thought.

I said that Davy Jones had plenty of treasure but always liked additional company. "Where the Third Mate is going," I said, "he'll have more treasure than the Sweet Cutlass had ever conceived of," I continued, "in that case, the rule should prevail, 'The more for the rest of us!'"

The crew murmured their agreement with what I said. The Captain nodded, and he said that each man should make the determination for himself. He flung all the coins from one bag down on the deck and said that each crew member could either keep whatever he picked up or fling it overboard to the Third Mate as he saw fit. Then he motioned for the Second Mate to edge the Third Mate off the plank.

So at the same time the Third Mate hit the ocean water with its forest of shark fins, the crew hit the ship's decks picking up coins—all but the two hearties of the

Third Mate, who stood trembling as the Second Mate approached to bind them for their last walk on earth. Down in the water the Third Mate's body was being torn apart by two gigantic sharks when a third even larger shark swam between them and took off the man's abdomen with a single bite. The blood and gore in the blue water drove the feeding fish into a feasting frenzy while the Second Mate readied the next man for the plank.

The Captain looked the bound man in the eye and asked him whether he had trained with the Third Mate so that he could one day become Third Mate himself.

The man answered, "Aye, Captain!"

The Captain raised a second sack and said it was the man's share. He asked whether that was now a fair share given what had just happened. I was about to answer, but the Captain raised his hand to stop me from responding and gestured to the hapless man near the plank to answer his question.

The man looked the Captain steadily in the eye and said, "Captain, with one share re-divided, the amount in the sack, if it be the same as the other that was just distributed, is too small by the amount divided by the number of the crew. So it is not fair."

The Captain looked at the man fiercely and then asked me what I thought of this judgment. Without looking at the Captain, I said that judgment was a rare commodity among seamen and it was worth much more than gold and silver coins. The Captain then asked me what I would do if he was the ship's Captain under the circumstances.

I took a few minutes to consider this, and I answered, "If I were you, Captain, I'd offer the choice of the cat-o-nine-tails or the plank, and if he chose the cat, I'd have a tamed Third Mate. If not, I'd have no Third Mate."

The Captain then asked the man near the plank whether he would choose the cat or the plank, and the man chose the cat-o-nine-tails but with the proviso that his hearty be given the same choice as he.

The Captain looked down at the seething waters off the lee side of the ship and nodded in acquiescence. The third man, grateful for his having been granted the chance at life, chose the cat over the plank, and the Captain ordered the plank withdrawn and stowed. He then ordered the crew to return to their stations on their normal watch routines, all except for the two hearties that were taken by the Second Mate before the mast to sit on the deck and prepare their own cat-o-nine-tails. The Captain returned the two remaining sacks of booty to his cabin while I uncocked my pistol and shoved it into my belt. I stood the watch as we unfurled the sails and sailed southeast with fair winds and following seas on our cruise to Madagascar.

☠☠☠☠

I learned that ocean trade along the West African coast was brisk, and the Sweet Cutlass had its choice of vessels. Most of the trade was conducted in barter but, the trading ships always had some gold and silver aboard. As pirates, we had competition that sometimes wanted to prey upon ourselves. So it was as we entered the Bay of Shrimps under the Ear of Africa, a pirate ship displaying the Jolly Roger came at us from the shore.

Next to the Sweet Cutlass, our competitor seemed a slovenly scow, but its Captain was no fool and called for a gam with Captain Morgan. The Captain agreed and ordered that his whaleboat be launched for the meeting.

No sooner had the two Captains met between our ships than the pirate vessel fired at the Sweet Cutlass. I was ready for such a ploy, and I ordered all our guns to fire at the main brace of the pirate ship while I saw my Captain draw his knife, leap aboard the whaleboat of the other Captain and slay both the man and his coxswain.

Having destroyed the enemy's main brace, the ship could not maneuver, so I took the Sweet Cutlass alongside and ordered the men to board and take no prisoners. It took almost no time for our crew to dispatch the enemy's crew and throw the bodies into the water. Making the Sweet Cutlass fast to the enemy pirate ship, we took our time plundering it of everything of value, especially the guns, powder, cannon balls and scrap shot. Meanwhile, we winched the Captain's whaleboat back aboard with him and the coxswain inside it.

At the Captain's orders, we scuttled the pirate vessel and then maneuvered along the shore until we found the village from which the enemy pirates had come. The Captain anchored out and after dark ordered me to take a prize crew to row the whaleboat ashore to reconnoiter.

I steered by the light of a fire near the shore, and we landed the whaleboat amidst a number of boats along the beach. With our weapons, we advanced on the village where the villagers were assembled around the bonfire that we had steered by. I told my hearties to stand back until I called them. I then proceeded alone to address the villagers, who were startled to see me appear out of nowhere alone with my cocked pistol.

The man in charge of the remnant of the pirate colony laughed at the idea that I would approach him without any apparent reinforcements. When he rose and reached for his own pistol, I shot him through the heart. I called my hearties forward and told the villagers that we had come for treasure and valuables. I said we would do them no harm if they did not resist us, but they decided to take their chances by rushing us with their knives drawn. We slew them all, men and women alike. Then we fashioned torches, lighted them in the bonfire and went from dwelling to dwelling to scout for valuables.

We found the hut that must have belonged to the pirate Captain; because it was full of treasure hidden under some carpets in a chest in a hole that had been dug in the center of the earthen floor. We withdrew with that chest, taking care to set all the huts aflame as we departed. We stove in all the boats that lay on the shore in case some pirates who were absent in the jungle might return to pursue us. Then we rowed with our treasure back out to our anchored Sweet Cutlass.

When I presented the chest of treasure to the Captain in his cabin, he smiled and said he thought other pirates lurked all along the coast. They had done the hard work of harvesting treasure for many years, and the Captain said it would *almost* be sinful not to rob those other pirates of their booty whenever we had the chance to do so. So instead of taking ships that plied the coast with scant treasure individually, we decided to masquerade as a merchant vessel to lure the coastal pirates to attack us. That way we could reverse our roles and do what we had done to the first pirate ship and village.

So our progress south was punctuated by our being raided by pirates whose ships we easily subdued and whose villages we overwhelmed and plundered afterwards. This way we amassed greater wealth by far than we had gathered during our time in the Canaries. In fact, we gathered so much gold and silver, jewels and ores that I wondered aloud whether it would be safe to travel with all that treasure.

The Captain had been thinking along the same lines, so we discussed strategy. We decided that we would have to plant some of our treasure ashore at the earliest opportunity in a place we would surely recognize after many years. We were flying Spanish colors now for disguise and convenience, and we came upon an anchorage crowded with ships with so many small boats rowing back and forth between those ships and the shore that it almost seemed American. We anchored a little further out from the rest, and the Captain sent me ashore to discover the nature of the port.

I was disgusted to find that the rich port serviced the slave trade. Large holding pens held the slaves. The colony, which was designed especially for this kind of human trafficking, was larger than any of the villages we had encountered so far on our African journey. Daily auctions of slaves were held in a public square with posts and chains to hold the slaves while the bidding took place. Slavers brought new slaves from the jungles, received their payments and then retreated to a religious house where they prayed. Security for the slaves was pretty good. Men with pistols, sabers and knives stood guard. Some of those were black. The slaves themselves were fed well and cleaned daily because the better they looked, the higher the prices they could command. The trade was in gold and silver coins and bars, and I was impressed that the storehouse for the gold and silver seemed less well guarded than the slave pens. My mind immediately considered how the storehouse might be relieved of its contents during the night. The biggest constraint, it seemed to me, was the sheer weight of the potential plundering.

Coffee houses and trading posts had sprung up around the square with every conceivable African product from ivory tusks to hides of animals, spices of all kinds, sacks of manioc roots and curious crystals. A fortune teller told prophecies about the right and wrong days for purchases. Liquor, including rum, was available in bottles, casks, and kegs, and a tavern sold African beverages that some said had been made from fermented grains. A row of small cabins was reserved for the sex trade, which was linked to the slave trade because the youngest and most beautiful of the female slaves were used there. Merchants could sample the wares for money before they purchased these slaves. I was surprised to see that the slavers and the slave purchasers all used these slaves. I pretended that I was a potential customer, so I was shown to the amenities. I decided against participating when I saw how young the girl slaves were. When I emerged, I witnessed the public whipping of a very large black slave who had tried to escape. Evidently the stripes made by the whip were considered an adornment by potential buyers who seemed not to regard the pain that was being inflicted on the slave.

I thought about that slave's desire to escape, and a vague plan began to form in my mind. I thought of the slaves as the means to get the gold and silver to the Sweet Cutlass. I thought that the best remuneration for their services would be their freedom. What would have to happen was a very rapid overcoming of all guards at the pens and the storehouse, a quick liberation of as many willing slaves as were necessary to carry the gold and silver to waiting boats that would row out to the Sweet Cutlass. I thought midnight would be the best time for executing this plan. I also thought some form of diversion would be necessary to keep the merchants busy while the treasure was removed. I also considered that the anchored ships were the greatest hazard to the welfare of the Sweet Cutlass unless, of course, some warships arrived unexpectedly.

On a whim, I decided to visit the soothsayer's shop where fortunes were told. I was surprised to find that the soothsayer was a beautiful woman with green eyes and auburn hair. Without a word she took my hand and opened my palm, tracing my lifeline with her fingernail. She tried a half dozen languages until she hit upon English. Quickly with fire in her eyes, she said she had information that I must know and it would cost one piece of gold. I produced the gold coin, and she told me that a French warship would arrive early the next morning to receive the tribute that it collected once a month. She said the vessel stopped at all six slave ports—three to the north, this port, and two more ports to the south, before the great diamond desert, so it would be laden with treasure when it arrived.

The soothsayer said she wanted me to spend the night with her for another gold coin, but I had now to get back to the Captain with the intelligence about the French ship. I gave the woman a second gold coin and told her I would return one day to spend the night with her. Her teeth were white, clean and even when she smiled. She had said before I left her that my lifeline suggested strength and a long life. She said she hoped she would see me again. I told her that she should be careful about the people to whom she sold her information. I told her informants were often killed for information far less important than what she had told me today. She said that from my expression and the lines in my palm she knew I would not kill her, not today anyway. She pushed me towards the door and said I had to run because there was not much time left to do what I had to do.

I returned to the whaleboat and had the coxswain row as fast as possible to the Sweet Cutlass where the Captain awaited my report. I arrived in the late afternoon, and the Captain and I spent a long while discussing what we should do. The Captain was very interested in the imminent arrival of the French warship, but he kept his mind focused on the gold and silver stream. When he had digested all the information I had gleaned, he asked me to bring the Second and Third Mates to his cabin for a conference. There the Captain outlined his plan of action, and it was better than anything I could have devised, though I had my doubts about the details of execution.

According to the Captain's plan, our crew would be divided into four teams, one led by the Captain and the other three led by us mates. We mates would strike that very midnight on the shore and at the anchorage while the Captain with a skeleton crew would sail out to meet the French warship. So in the dark we mates shoved off in the whaleboat with six of the crew. We dropped the Second Mate off at the nearest merchant ship and then continued to shore where I showed the Third Mate where the storehouse was and told him and two men what they were to do as soon as possible after the explosion out on the water. I instructed two hearties to seize and prepare two boats from the many on the beach for immediate departure when treasure arrived. I then took the two remaining pirates with me to slit the throats of the guards and liberate the slaves from the pen.

My hearties and I had eliminated the guards at the pen when the explosion occurred on the merchant ship where the Second Mate had been dropped off. After that the entire shore area came to life in a chaos of shouting and excitement during which I opened the gate of the slave pen and motioned for the strongest male slaves to follow me to the storehouse where the Third Mate and his men had already earned their share by killing the guardians of the gold and silver, and found where the booty was hidden inside the enclosure.

The other slaves from the pen followed me and the slaves I had chosen, and a new idea occurred to me. So in the storehouse, I passed out bags of gold and silver coins and bars of gold and silver to the slaves to carry down to the waterside where they were to put them in the two waiting boats. When all but a couple of bags remained in the storehouse, I threw their contents on the floor and motioned for the slaves to pick up what they could carry and run for the jungle. I then set fire to the storehouse and ran with the others to the whaleboat.

Setting out from the shore in the whaleboat with my men, I saw other men rowing towards the merchant ship that had suffered the explosion. At the same time, my hearties and the freed slaves in the two commandeered boats and me, and the rest of the men in the whaleboat were rowing as fast as possible out to the Sweet Cutlass. From the shore it would appear, I surmised, that the crews of ships that were farthest from shore were prudently returning to preserve their vessels. Looking back at the shore, I saw that by torchlight the denizens were scrambling to discover what had happened at the storehouse and at the pen. Some with torches had spread out looking for escaped slaves in the jungle. No one seemed to be interested in climbing into a boat to follow my crew.

We rowed and rowed, and ahead of the whaleboat appeared the Second Mate swimming in the water and laughing his head off. I swung him aboard just in time before another great explosion rocked the merchant ship that the Second Mate had booby-trapped. The ship was riven by the blast and sank rapidly while the row boats that had tried to help looked on. Our three boats converged where the Sweet Cutlass should have been, but it had weighed anchor and was already proceeding to the north to intercept the French warship.

    I signaled the other boats to pass leaders so that the three boats could proceed as a group in a line to the rear. We then rowed in that line in the wake of the Sweet Cutlass. The wind was not strong, and our ship was undermanned without us. I looked for the Captain's sign at the rear of the ship, and I saw it bobbing up and down in the ship's wake. I ordered the boats to stroke harder, and I fished out the empty keg with the line attached. Hand over hand we pulled at the line while we continued to row towards the ship. I saw that on the starboard and port side's lines were extended, and suddenly the great ship came about in a familiar maneuver. I signaled for the two boats to spread out to the right and left while the Sweet Cutlass continued to come about and then regained its course behind us. As the ship passed, the two boats and the whaleboat caught the lines extended to either side; and the transfer of the treasure and men began in earnest.

    The gold and silver were hoisted aboard the Sweet Cutlass and taken immediately to the Captain's cabin. The slaves were told to lie on the deck by the mast where they were provisioned with rum, apples, and bread. When the two boats we had used for treasure and slaves had been emptied, they were abandoned to the open sea. Meanwhile, we in the whaleboat worked the davits and hauled the boat into place while the ship's watch team unfurled the sails and we all prepared to encounter the French warship.

We sailed the rest of the night hugging the shore as much as possible, but we never found the French warship. Was the soothsayer's intelligence wrong? The Captain laughed at the idea. He said that the French never could be on time for anything, even when gold and silver were at stake.

At dawn, the Captain told the helmsman to reverse course to the south again, and as the sun rose in the east over Africa the Captain went to his cabin to survey the piles of gold and silver bars, the thirty bags of coins and the six bags of uncut diamonds that had been taken in that one night.

The Captain resolved to take the course that the French warship was supposed to have seized and to visit the remaining two slave ports to the south to collect a similar booty. He advised us mates to look lively on watch and to brief the lookouts to be alert to sails on the horizon. We were now, he said, as much a rich prize as any he had ever taken. The Captain also had an idea about the slaves we had taken on board, and he asked me to help him communicate with them.

The slaves were glad to have been freed, but they were apprehensive about their future if they were set back on the shore. The one slave who could understand any language that we pirates knew was the huge black who had been whipped the day before. I explained to him that the Captain would put them all ashore if they liked. If that did not suit them, they had a choice that they must make at once. Either they became members of our crew, or they visited the sharks in the ocean.

The huge black man said a few words in the native Bantu language that all the slaves seemed to understand, and his fellow former slaves murmured among each other.

The huge man smiled and told me they were proud to join the Captain and his crew.

That is how the Sweet Cutlass gained ten of the fiercest fighters I have ever witnessed in a pirate crew. The former slaves adapted well to life at sea. They stood watches immediately under instruction and they learned fast. Our Third Mate became their leader, and I helped whenever special communication was necessary. Problems with morale were handled exclusively by the huge black man, who had a special regard among them. I later learned that he had been a chief among his own people, and it showed in his bearing and attitude.

The two slave ports to the south were much the same as the one we had raided with success. Our credibility among the slave traders was increased because of the presence of apparent slaves on our ship. We did not ask the slaves to go ashore to help us combat the slavers, but they volunteered for the job. They contended that their skills with language were superior to ours for the purpose. So when we struck at midnight on two occasions and opened the pens that held the slaves, our former slaves explained what was happening to the newly freed slaves. They also killed the slavers with such vengeance that I could not withhold them from extending their retribution to the entire slaver community. So we gained much gold and silver on both occasions, and we also gained twenty additional crew members, all former slaves. Because they could be trained by people they saw as their own extended family, the newbies learned quickly. None chose to live with the sharks.

So by the time we reached the Cape of Good Hope, we were a jolly ship, unlike any other pirate vessel the world had known since ancient times. The Captain and crew were extremely happy that they had garnered a fortune from harvesting gold and silver; the former slaves were ecstatic that they had been freed and gone on to free others. The warm sentiments did not help much as we crossed under the Cape of Good Hope and ran through the rip tides and the cold winds that had blown many ships onto the inhospitable shore.

We soon plunged northeast along the east African shore towards Madagascar, and the Captain called for a meeting of us mates and the huge black we called Benjamin, who was chief of the former slaves now.

The Captain said that he had a plan that he hoped would satisfy everyone. He had two problems that needed to be solved, and the only way he knew to solve them both, he said, required the division of his crew into two parts, one part remaining on the Sweet Cutlass and the other part taking control of another ship of the same kind. In effect, he wanted to expand the piratical enterprise by fission and employing two ships working in tandem rather than one ship working alone. The Captain let his words sink in, and then he asked for comments from all of us.

I answered first that the Captain's plan would probably work under certain conditions. First, the Captain would have to find an appropriate Captain for his second ship. Second, the Captain would have to determine how the two ships would operate together and share spoils. Third, the Captain would have to decide how to seize the ship that would be the Sweet Cutlass's companion.

The Second Mate then said that the crew now had natural divisions that were unique. By this, he meant that one portion of the crew understood only a foreign language and only one man could interpret for them. He implied that all the former slaves should be allocated to one ship instead of being distributed among the two vessels.

The Third Mate followed by stating that in any case additional crew members would be necessary to fill out the watch teams on both vessels. The most difficult decision—and it was the Captain's to make—was the fair apportionment of treasure according to pirate tradition since in the past the shares equaled the number of the surviving crew on one vessel. Would shares be according to vessel or according to the combination of vessels? The Third Mate suggested that if they could split into two crews, perhaps in future they could split again, so this fundamental determination had to be made right at the start so that feuding did not break out.

Benjamin, like the Captain, had listened carefully to everything that had been said. He had asked the Captain's permission before he spoke, but when he spoke, he was direct and eloquent. First, he said, the First Mate was every bit ready for command of his own vessel, so the Captain's choice of a Captain for his companionship was already made. Second, he said, the communication problem among former slaves was being solved through work since all of them knew their duties now and fit into the watch teams as they were. He said he could interpret as necessary for both ships. The man known as Reuben, who was Benjamin's second, could serve as his surrogate aboard the second vessel. Third, he said, the problems of recruitment would vanish if the Captain saw a way to increase his crews by freeing slaves just as he had already done. As for splitting treasure, what could be more valuable than freedom? The former slaves had already been given a priceless gift, and they were all very grateful. Benjamin said that the Captain would not only be the leader of his own ship but the commander of both ships together. Shares of all the treasure split across all the pirates would be most fair, but the Captain should have an additional share because of his dual role. Having said these things, Benjamin became quiet.

The Captain was lost in thought for a long while. When he shook his head and became conscious of his fellow pirates again, he said that they should share a few bottles of rum together. He extended that to the entire crew, and the ship was allowed to luff sail and rock in the ocean while everyone had his ration of rum, including the cabin boy and the lookouts that came down from the crow's nest. When the imbibition's had been taken, the Captain called for a meeting of all the crew at which he would make an announcement.

The Captain stood next to the wheel, and I stood by his side when he made his historic, game-changing speech, which was interpreted to the former slaves by Benjamin. First, Captain Morgan thanked the crew for working well together and for earning more treasure in the last three raids than his ship had earned in its entire history. He said that everyone aboard would share in the wealth in the pirates' fashion, with one share for each man regardless of origin, color or time in service. He hesitated for a moment to let that thought sink in. Hearing no objection, he pressed on. The Captain said that he was going to add a ship and split the crew between the two vessels so they could take twice the treasure in raids that could be coordinated.

He announced that his current First Mate would become the Captain of the second ship and that, technically, the second ship, as well as the Sweet Cutlass, would still be under his command though the second ship would have some measure of autonomy. The former slaves, he said, were now full partners in the pirate ventures. They would be split evenly between the two ships, with Benjamin remaining on the Sweet Cutlass. Benjamin would serve as an interpreter for all the former slaves. Shares would be treated on an equal basis across both ships with the entire crew of both ships sharing equally regardless of which ship had the most treasure to its credit. Any augmentations of the crew would be drawn from wherever seemed appropriate at the time, including other newly freed slaves.

The Captain said he could not well predict when all this would happen, but he said it would happen at the earliest opportunity and preferably before the ship ported in at Madagascar. The Captain said that he would have other announcements in the coming weeks about who specifically would be allocated to each of the two ships when the time came. The Captain stopped and looked at his crew taking the time to look each man directly in the eye. Then he ordered everyone to get back to their duty stations with the normal watch rotation.

The stunned crew did as the Captain ordered.

During the ensuing weeks, the crew discussed the Captain's plan quietly among themselves. When the final lists were determined, I and the Third Mate were paired so that when I became Captain, he would become my First Mate. At the transition, the Second Mate would become the Captain's new First Mate. Since the allocations had been determined, all the crew looked forward to our finding the ship that would be the Sweet Cutlass's complement.

We were nearing Madagascar when early one morning we espied what was probably a French-flagged vessel with roughly the same size and rigging as the Sweet Cutlass. The Captain had examined the vessel through his spyglass for fully ten minutes before he passed the glass to me and asked me what I thought of the ship off the starboard quarter.

I liked what I saw and told the Captain it would do as the complement. So the Captain directed a course to intercept, went to full sail and ordered the crew to prepare to board the ship.

It took eight hours to come within striking distance, and our initial volley was the wake-up call for our prey, which raised the Jolly Roger, came about and prepared to ram us. So the falsely flagged vessel was a pirate ship like ours, and now we were in a battle for our lives as well as our ship. The Captain took the Conn and ordered me to direct our fire on the closing vessel's masts. I ordered the batteries to fire at will, so smoke filled the air as the guns went off in a kind of rhythmic rotation.

Simultaneously, the Captain ordered the crew to man the port side and prepared to board with grappling hooks and lines. This confused our prey which failed to understand the Captain's intentions. The pirate ship's Captain fully expected to ram us to starboard and to board on that side, but Captain Morgan was not an easy mark. In the final minutes, he ordered the Sweet Cutlass to come about to port, and the prey found itself unprepared for missing its ram and for a boarding in parallel to its starboard side from our port.

For the Sweet Cutlass, this maneuver was our bread-and-butter signature move and a contributing factor to our success. We added to that surprise, a massed boarding by a predominantly black boarding party holding knives in their mouths and brandishing sabers. I shouted the guns to silence because, in the melee that followed, I did not want friendly fire. The ships became bound by lines with grappling hooks, and now the joined vessels allowed free play of both crews across both decks. The Captain and I were in the thick of the fight, but I knew that the victor would be the crew whose Captain survived. So I ordered Benjamin to guard the Captain with his life, and I spirited myself over the side on a hanging line and raced through the fighting to the helm of our rival.

I did not wait for an invitation but pitched my knife so I held it by the blade and as quickly as I could, I hurled it fifteen feet into the heart of the rival pirate Captain. The man knew he was hit and the game was over, but the fight raged on. I shouted to Captain Morgan that the rival Captain was dead. I noticed that Benjamin was taking down two assailants who had been trying to kill my Captain. Now Benjamin raised both arms and in a terrible, booming voice said something in his native language. The former slaves stood back from their work for a moment to allow their adversaries to hear what Captain Morgan was saying.

The Captain ordered everyone on both ships to lower their weapons because he had an offer for all ears. All pirates from both ships stopped fighting to listen. Captain Morgan announced that his rival had been killed. He gestured towards me, and I pointed to the place where that dead Captain lay.

He then announced that he intended to combine the treasure and the surviving crew members of both ships in a single venture, with no prejudice whatsoever. He said that any pirate who objected to this proposal would be killed immediately and fed to the sharks. All who agreed to join him would be given a place in the new crews befitting his current role. He said he would count to three to hear an objection, and if none were forthcoming, everyone would drop his weapons on the decks and await further instructions.

The Captain did not have to reach the count of three when weapons began to fall on the decks of both ships. Benjamin then ordered the ex-slaves to pick up all weapons and place them before the mast of the Sweet Cutlass. The Captain then ordered the crews of both ships to muster before their respective masts. He ordered those of his own crew who had been designated as members of the complementary ship to gather their belongings and proceed to their new vessel. He told me to take charge of my new command, and I gladly did so.

When I was ready, I asked the three mates of the captured ship to stand forward. The First Mate I offered the position of Second Mate under my command. When he appeared to be reluctant, I drew my pistol and shot him in the head. I then offered the position to the Second Mate, who eagerly agreed to serve. I offered the position of Third Mate to the current Third Mate of the captured vessel, and he also agreed to serve without cavil. I ordered the Second Mate to identify half of the captured crew to ship aboard the Sweet Cutlass within the next ten minutes. I told my First Mate to see that the division was carried out and the identified men left the ship with their belongings and joined the crew of the Sweet Cutlass.

Within ten minutes, the transfer had been completed. I ordered my First Mate to sort out and set the evening watch and to clear the decks of the dead and the wounded. I ordered that anyone wounded too severely to serve, be given the coup de grace and hurled overboard with the other dead. I told my First Mate to repair the damaged rigging and await the order to move ahead based on Captain Morgan's orders. When the First Mate told me he was ready, I then called over to Captain Morgan that I was ready to separate ships and proceed after him.

Captain Morgan asked me what I was going to call my new vessel. I had thought about this for as long as I knew I was going to have my own command. Without hesitation I told him, Night Lightning, at which he laughed deep and long. He then ordered his men to cut all binding ties between the Sweet Cutlass and the Night Lightning, set the evening watch and unfurl all sails.

I did the same, and when the Sweet Cutlass pulled ahead into the night, I saw the light on its fantail and ordered my helmsman to follow it. Satisfied that the Night Lightning was on the right course with the watch set, I proceeded to the dead Captain's cabin and there found silver and gold, charts and maps marked with the location of buried treasure. Hiding in the closet was the former Captain's cabin boy with blue eyes and straw blonde hair. I told the boy he now had a new master, and I ordered him to fetch me a bottle of rum, which he did gladly from a store of bottles and kegs in a special compartment in the Captain's cabin. The boy spoke a little English along with his French, so I thought we would get along just fine. He mentioned that he knew the places where the best ladies lived in Madagascar. He said that they were very good in bed, but they knew everyone and everything that was going on in east Africa.

I then knew I had found a treasure beyond comparison. I told him he was now the Captain's cabin boy for the Night Lightning. He liked the new name for the ship and repeated it to himself so that he would remember it. By the time the First Mate had come to report the ship's status, the boy was asleep in his cot.

The First Mate told me that all was well. He said he would shadow the midwatch, and I told him I would shadow afterward until the morning watch. I showed the First Mate some of the gold and silver pelf that had been hidden in the cabin, but I did not mention the charts and maps I had found with the locations of treasure clearly marked on them. I realized that I was already learning the prerogatives of being a ship's Captain.

The next morning's sunrise was resplendent. A pair of whales swam alongside the ship as if they were traveling in company. The only other ship on the horizon was the Sweet Cutlass dead ahead. The crew mustered after their morning meal, and I said a few words indicating that we should be ready for action at an instant's notice. I ordered a meeting of the mates by the helm to discuss the plan for the day, and they went below on the weather decks to tell the men what I had said in their own ways.

When they had finished and the men were at their assigned duties, the Second Mate and Third Mate came to see me as much to gauge their new Captain as to be sure I knew of their loyalty to me. I told them that I did not care whether they liked me or not. I said I intended to increase the wealth of all the crew through our common labor, but I also demanded of every hearty his total effort to make us a success. Anyone not doing his utmost would be liable to the lash, or worse, instantly, and I said that applied to mates as well as ordinary crew. I instructed the two men to choose others who could succeed them if either of them should die in battle and to give me their prospective replacements' names by the end of the afternoon watch.

I then retreated to the Captain's cabin and reviewed the Captain's log. I drew a line under the last entry that the former Captain made, and I wrote my initial notations in that log. I had just completed my entry when I heard a commotion at my door and the First Mate entered my room to say that the lookout in the crow's nest had sighted a warship on the horizon abaft the port beam with constant bearing, decreasing range. I gave the order for the crew to take their battle stations, and I was very glad we had missed the main brace in our boarding exercise of the previous day.

Both our ships were flying false French colors when the English warship came into close visual range. My men stood by their cannons ready to fire, and the crew lined the port side ready for action as well.

The English ship fell slowly behind the Night Lightning, and I waited for any sign of hostile action from our rear. The wind gave my ship the advantage if the English ship chose to attack, and I wondered why its Captain had so insistently closed as if my ship were his target and then decided to pass astern. I thought it must be clear to the Englishman that we were traveling in company with the ship ahead. By closing on my ship, it had perhaps missed the identity of the Sweet Cutlass entirely.

Perhaps, I reasoned, the English ship was looking for some other vessel sailing these waters. The ship passed astern without any sudden threatening maneuvers, and then it continued on a track orthogonal to ours until it was far too distant for any action against us. I consequently ordered my crew to stand down from their battle stations and to set the normal sailing watch again.

We followed the Sweet Cutlass to a small cove off the west coast of Madagascar and we dropped anchors there. Captain Morgan called for a gam, so we met in between our anchored vessels in our whaleboats where we talked about what to do with our combined treasures. We decided that we would take a portion of our pelf from both ships and bury it at a place in this cove that we could relocate easily. I mentioned to Captain Morgan that just such a place had been indicated on a map among the personal belongings of the departed Captain of my new ship. The Captain affected not to have heard what I told him, and he said we would gather our treasures into two chests and proceed separately in our whaleboats to a point just outside the view of the anchorage and to arrive there at an hour before sundown accompanied by one expendable person and a coxswain each.

    I knew the drill from long experience, and I selected one of the surlier of the captured crew members as my expendable person. He helped me lower my chest of treasure into my whaleboat and rowed around the point of land that put us out of view of the anchored ships.

    Captain Morgan's whaleboat had preceded us, and the Captain and his man were already ashore while his coxswain waited patiently by the whaleboat for their return.

    My own whaleboat made land beside the other, and my man and I carried the chest and a shovel inland after the Captain and his man. We all arrived at a place where an ancient tree hung over an enormous rock. There Captain Morgan placed the heel of his right boot against a slot in the rock and he marched thirty paces directly to the east. There he threw down the shovel he was carrying and told his man to dig.

    I did the same and ordered my man to help dig with the man the Captain brought with him. Captain Morgan then brought out a bottle of rum and invited me to drink with him. We drank together while our men dug, and we had nearly finished the bottle of rum when my man struck something hard and the two men scrambled to unearth what lay below.

My man brought up a skull and what looked like a femur. He showed it to me, and I nodded. Captain Morgan nodded also.

Captain Morgan's man then split the skull of my man with his shovel and pulled his lifeless body next to the hole they had excavated together. He placed the two chests side by side at the bottom of the hole and was about to begin filling the hole with dirt when I cocked my pistol and shot him through the heart.

I then pulled his body into the pit and placed it on one side of the chests. I pulled my own man's body into the pit and placed it on the other side of the chests. I then took a final swig from the bottle of rum and threw the bottle into the pit. With one shovel, I worked to fill the hole, and soon Captain Morgan was helping me fill it with the other shovel. We worked rapidly, and soon we were smoothing the surface to remove any indication that the earth had been disturbed that evening.

When we satisfied ourselves that our work would not be detected, we laid some foliage over the area and retreated to our whaleboats where in semi-darkness our coxswains awaited us. Separately we were rowed back to our ships guided by lights we had ordered to be lit on board at sunset.

Before I retired in my cabin, I consulted the map that showed where treasure was buried to verify that the site where Captain Morgan and I had buried our own treasure had the same location on the map as the mark that had been made on it. I wondered at that coincidence and recalled that Captain Morgan had affected not to hear me when I had mentioned the map earlier that day. Was the map somehow connected to Captain Morgan's prior exploits in this area of the world? Was the location where we buried our treasure the repository of other chests like the ones we buried this afternoon? I made a few notes on the edges of the map and hid it among my belongings in my cabin. I then ordered my cabin boy to bring me another bottle of rum.

He mentioned that some of the gold and silver had disappeared from the cabin and that a small chest was also missing. I told him that I had noticed that also. He rejoined that he had overheard two of the crew talking by the apple barrel. They said that a man had accompanied the Captain ashore in the whaleboat, but the man had not returned. One said that he was glad the man had not come back because he was a very bad man.

I waited for the boy to say more, but the boy had nothing more to say on that account. He asked me whether he could do me another service that night. I told the boy to get some sleep. Tomorrow, I told him, would be a busy day. As the boy settled into his cot for the night, I sipped my rum and brooded over what had happened to bring me to this strange place and to grant my wish of one day becoming the Captain of my own ship.

After midnight, I wandered out of my cabin and walked the deck of my own ship. A late night watch stander bid me adieu. We looked out over the still bay water together at the other ship at anchor there, the Sweet Cutlass, with the orange flame of its stern lamp barely visible. The watch stander smoked a shank of hemp and invited me to look at the stars with him. He said the stars had brought us here. I thought he had a point.

Pirates of Zanzibar

    I anchored the Night Lightning off the main port city of the island of Zanzibar in water so pellucid you could watch fish and crabs active right to the sandy bottom five fathoms below. The Sweet Cutlass was anchored a small distance away. Both ships had spent the last two weeks doing repairs and provisioning after a most profitable sail north from Madagascar. We had raided merchants of all flags along the way north; British, Portuguese, French, and American. As we sailed on the ocean to the east of the island, we increasingly took merchants from Yemen and Oman because the spices and slaves of Zanzibar supplied all the vast desert lands of Arabia. Captain Morgan had rightly figured that our most profitable ventures since we left the Canaries were those tied to the slave trade, so he wanted to see what might be plundered in the waters surrounding Zanzibar, the capital of the slave enterprise in this part of the world.

    Now our ship's holds were filled to the brim with gold, silver, jewels, ivory tusks, animal hides, exotic fabrics and bags of rich spices. Several of the hearties had animal pets like monkeys that ran about the decks and colorful birds that sat on shoulders or flew up to perch in the rigging. Captain Morgan and I had found several small, deserted islands in the channel to the west of the main island where we surreptitiously buried a large part of our gold and silver in the usual way. We still kept aside enough of our hoard to distribute small bags of coins to each of our hearties to spend in the old stone city as they liked.

Before the crew went ashore, we warned them that the Islamic law of the land made our usual carousing, brawling and bullying dangerous to life and limb. While in the stone city we witnessed public beheadings for murderers and chopping off of hands of thieves. We also witnessed more slaves than we ever thought possible in pens and in chains. The slavers were a devilish lot with swords, knives, prods and whips. Though Benjamin was incensed and wanted to free slaves, Captain Morgan managed to restrain him.

The British, he explained patiently, were trying to eradicate the trade throughout the world, but it would be hard going. Zanzibar's entire good fortune depended on the slave trade so it would take at least two centuries, maybe more, to stamp out the trafficking entirely. The massive fort on the island was stocked with troops who had modern weapons. We gauged assault too risky for us, and we resolved to save our piracy for our familiar ocean setting.

Ashore Benjamin and the other former slaves posed as our slaves dressed in fine robes and fancy turbans that we had seized from the merchants we had pirated. I admit that we made a colorful parade when we wandered through the streets and marketplaces. We all wore silk in all colors, exotic feathers, turbans and hides of wild animals. Benjamin's parrot perched on his massive shoulder speaking pirate code to all passersby, "Avast, ye lubbers!" being his favorite cry. Behind Captain Morgan and I, ranged a long line of 'slaves' to bear the provisions that we bought in the markets. When the muezzins climbed into their minarets to call the people to prayer and the religious police roamed the streets looking for slackers, we and our retinue sought refuge in a spacious house that Captain Morgan knew from his former adventures.

The house was near the center of the city. It had high walls like a fortress and no windows. In the center of the walled grounds was a magnificent, square garden with fountains and plants in which colorful songbirds played. Along all sides of this central garden were two score rooms. Beautiful ladies in silk sat outside these rooms and waited for companions to bargain and then go inside the rooms with them. Liquor was available by the bottle or cask. Our crew either went into the rooms with the ladies or sat drinking at tables on chairs under the shade of lemon and orange trees covered with fruits. The whole impression was of an outdoor bacchanal. We Captains sat at a special table on a veranda above one of the rooms where the woman named Alia who presided over the house catered to our every whim because Alia knew that she would be richly rewarded for the information that she imparted.

Alia told us that a great commotion had erupted when two pirate ships began marauding merchant vessels on the rich trade route between Zanzibar and Araby. The Englishmen and Americans had separately met with the Sultan of Zanzibar to offer their warships' services to rid the seas of the pirate menace. Alia said that the sultan was not perturbed. Her spies reported that the sultan had laughed at the foreigners' concern. He then told them that everything was in Allah's capable hands. As far as the sultan was concerned, trade on Zanzibar was his concern.

What happened to the ships that came to, or went from the island was decidedly not his concern. As long as the spices, ivory and slaves kept coming from the mainland of Africa, and as long as they were traded for gold, silver, jewels and silk in his bazaars, he was satisfied.

If Araby wanted to protect their ships, they could do so on their own. The sultan suggested that the best way to deal with pirates was to use other pirates against them. He then regaled his concerned visitors with stories from the fabled *One Thousand and One Nights of Queen Scheherazade* until they tired and went away frustrated.

Captain Morgan and I knew that the English and American warships would try to attack us no matter what the sultan thought. We did not know what to make of the threat from warships of Araby because we knew of no such vessels.

While Captain Morgan went below to have Alia entertain him specially, I drank my rum and observed the crew enjoying themselves as they drank, joked and whored. Soon enough the hearties would be climbing into the rigging of the ships and preparing to board the merchantmen that were our prey at the risk of their lives and limbs. Why should they not enjoy to the limit the life of a pirate ashore when tomorrow they might be visiting Davy Jones' locker in the cerulean sea?

After a long interval, the Captain emerged looking refreshed and robust with Alia smiling and following behind him while adjusting her robe. I rose and whistled loud and long to alert the crew that our business here should be brought to an end. The crew mustered by the exit so that we could count them all, and we processed back into the street outside the house and made our way back to our landing in the port where the whaleboats took the hearties in batches back to the ships.

As was our custom, Captain Morgan was among those who manned the first whaleboat to depart and I was among those who manned the last whaleboat from the shore. That way, one Captain was available on land and the other at sea until all the hearties were safely back on board. I kept the best fighters with me for that final boat because the fewer we were with evening fast approaching, the more vulnerable we became. It was a good thing that I was prudent that day because a rowdy group of sailors returning from the stone city to their own ship decided to pick a fight with us for no better reason than their own hubris.

The fight started with name calling and progressed rapidly to shoving and fisticuffs. Then one of the other ship's crew drew a knife. I could not believe the effrontery of those milquetoasts. Could they not see that my hearties were battle-hardened veterans who loved a fight? My men drew their weapons and flew in a frenzy to kill their enemies. In short order, my men dispatched the other crew to the last man. They were wiping their blades or picking over the corpses when we were espied and the alarm was raised. I did not wait for our own whaleboat to return but ordered my men to seize the whaleboat that the now-deceased crew had intended to use. We pulled away from shore just as the first troops became visible with their torches lit over the hill. My hearties pulled with all their strength.

I lit a torch and held it high to make us a clear target for the pursuing troops. I told my hearties to row for the nearest ship in the anchorage and ignore what was happening on shore. From the shore I guessed it appeared that the whaleboat we had commandeered belonged to the nearest ship out. I could see from the motions and hear from the shouting that the troops, whose numbers were increasing, were preparing to launch boats in pursuit of us, the presumed murderers. I steered the whaleboat to that nearest ship, but when we arrived there, I doused my torch and urged the men to pull around the ship and head in darkness for the Night Lightning as if their lives depended on their efforts.

From their own torches, I observed that the three boats that had pulled out from shore were crammed with troops. The pursuing boats would surely continue on their headings to the ship we had now left behind.

By the time we reached our own rightful ship, we would have to act fast to weight anchor because the troops would know their mistake and might be coming after us next. I saw ahead our own whaleboat from the Night Lightning rowing to shore to pick us up, but I managed to get the attention of the coxswain and had it come alongside.

I transferred half of my hearties to the other whaleboat and ordered them to row fast to the Sweet Cutlass and tell Captain Morgan to weigh anchor and set sail. I said we would rendezvous at dawn, or just after, off the small island just around the tip of Zanzibar.

So now two boatloads of desperate men were making for our two ships. When the boats arrived, the whole crews of each ship were given orders to get underway at once. It was a close thing, but the ships managed to unfurl sail and catch the light breeze in every inch of sail surface before the deceived troops could gain their bearings and follow us.

The next morning at the planned rendezvous, my hearties that had jumped into the Sweet Cutlass's whaleboat were returned to the Night Lightning. Captain Morgan and I had a gam at which I told him my version of what had happened the previous night at the landing. We realized that the chances that warships would be sent out to pursue us were scant. No one who had witnessed the killings aside from our crews remained alive. Who would the authorities blame for the slaughter now that hot pursuit had failed?

Captain Morgan considered this matter as we both had another swallow of rum, and he said that it was high time we got back to our business of piracy. Knowing from Alia how the sultan thought about depredations at sea, we decided that the Night Lightning should proceed up the west coast of the island and take whatever prey it could find there while the Sweet Cutlass proceeded up the east coast of Zanzibar and prey upon the merchant shipping there. I said that the Night Lightning would take what it could in the Zanzibar Channel for the next fortnight and then swing north around the island and meet the Sweet Cutlass one day's sail due east of Zanzibar five days after breaking off from the Channel. We drank to that idea and returned to our separate ships to execute our plan.

The Zanzibar Channel has thick traffic, so we had our choice of target vessels. At first we avoided ships that came from Africa and instead focused on ships that were returning from Zanzibar having traded there. We took a ship each day for fourteen days, careful to kill all aboard and to send the ships we captured with their lifeless crews to Davy Jones. I then decided that I would switch tactics and concentrate on vessels that came from Africa. I did not want to take ships that were transporting slaves, but every ship had some slaves as cargo. In seven days, we harvested ten ships, sparing only the slaves, which we freed and allowed to sleep on our weather decks. I did not know at the time what I was going to do with the newly-freed slaves, but the answer came in a wondrous way.

An English merchant ship closed on the Night Lightning on the last day before we had planned to desist our pirate adventure and turn north. I ordered my hearties to prepare for action, but I saw that the merchant was unarmed with what appeared to be slaves on its weather decks.

Because of the English animadversion to slavery, I was curious why the ship carried so many slaves out in the open. I called for a gam with the Captain of that ship, and we met in our whaleboats between our two vessels. The merchant Captain informed me that his mission was to buy as many slaves as he could find and free them. A wealthy, religious philanthropist had discovered the funds to pay for the men's freedom.

I could not believe my luck—or the luck of my newly freed slaves. I told the Captain that I had sixty slaves on my weather decks that I could immediately transfer to his ship if he would take them aboard. He said he would take all the slaves I could give him, and he remarked that I had what appeared to be slaves working as part of my crew. I told him that I had personally freed and trained those men to be my crew and that they had an equal share in everything my crew did. The Captain, who was a devout man, said, "The Lord's Name be praised!"

So the Captain returned to his ship and fetched bags of gold and silver to pay for the slaves I had already freed. I was astonished at the amount he was willing to pay for those slaves. When I received his payment, I ordered my crew to help ferry the sixty freed slaves in batches. So the sixty freed slaves were transported off our decks working the two ships' whaleboats to take them from the Night Lightning to the English merchant. When the entire transaction had been completed, I realized that trafficking slaves to freedom could be a very profitable business. I was not the only pirate who realized this, as I soon learned.

After the last slave had been transported from my ship, my lookout shouted from the crow's nest that a ship was fast approaching from the south with constant bearing and decreasing range. As a precaution, I ordered my crew to their battle stations. I noticed that the English merchant that had taken aboard our purchased slaves was making rapid preparations to flee to the north. To my surprise, the English merchant seemed to be fleeing the same approaching ship we had sighted. Through my spyglass, I saw the telltale signs that the approaching vessel was a pirate ship flying the Jolly Roger. It was making significant headway and its men were poised to board. I had never seen a ship whose decks were arrayed like this one. I saw chains all over its decks and bales of rope. The ship paid the Night Lightning no heed whatsoever as it passed but kept its sights on the English merchant ship. I surmised the game in an instant: this pirate was preying upon the ship that paid gold at sea to free slaves because it could take both the slaves and the gold and sell the freed slaves to the highest bidder ashore.

I had no stake in the one-sided fight that was going to take place between that lone pirate vessel and the unarmed English merchant with the freed slaves aboard it, but I reasoned that the profitable business of freeing slaves could only continue if it was protected. I further thought that protecting my future investment was good business. In any case, it seemed a good idea at the time for the Night Lightning to blow that pursuing pirate vessel out of the water. I ordered the ship to full sail with a course to intercept the vessel we were now pursuing. I ordered the batteries to prepare to take out the mainmast and main brace with a concentrated volley at my command. I also ordered for the Jolly Roger to be flown. The Night Lightning picked up speed and closed on the pirate ship from its starboard quarter. I ordered my men to prepare to board to port.

At the right time when in the foaming wake of the pirate ship, I ordered the helm to the right and ordered the batteries to fire. In a moment the main rigging of the pirate ship ahead fell in a thousand splinters that flew like spears through the bodies of the pirates on its decks. I ordered the helm to come left and I ordered the crew to prepare to use grappling hooks. As the Night Lightning came alongside the pirate ship, I ordered luff sail and the boarding. So over the side went the grappling hooks and their lines with the hearties binding them fast and rushing across to the enemy's decks slashing and piercing as they raged.

The English merchant continued sailing north while my hearties cut down the pirates to the last man. I ordered my men to search the ship's hold for valuables and hoist them over to the Night Lightning. I left the ship in the care of my First Mate and climbed aboard the prize. I went straight to the pirate Captain's cabin and found enough treasure, papers and logs to fill many sacks, which my hearties conveyed back to my own cabin aboard the Night Lightning.

In the hold of the pirate ship, my men discovered in shackles one hundred twenty malnourished slaves who could barely walk. They also found one hundred elephant tusks, huge stacks of animal hides, spices in great burlap bags, barrels of malmsey and kegs of gunpowder. All these we transferred to the Night Lightning, the slaves unshackled and left to sit and sleep on the weather decks with sufficient food and water for them all. When the entire pirate's pelf had been shifted to my vessel, I ordered that the pirate ship be scuttled and cut free. I then ordered that the Jolly Roger be struck on Night Lightning and the French ensign be flown astern. The Night Lightning then moved ahead to the north at increasing speed while the pirate ship and its dead crew sank behind us slowly beneath the undulating waves. I ordered the helmsman to steer with a constant bearing on the English merchant ship, which had slowed when it realized the pirate vessel was no longer in pursuit.

We overtook the English merchant, and I asked its Captain for another gam. It took the man some time to decide to meet me because he now knew that I captained a pirate vessel, but we did meet in our respective whaleboats. I told him that we had taken on board one hundred twenty emaciated slaves that had been held by the pirate ship. I told him these slaves had been freed by me and now needed immediate attention. I asked whether the English merchant ship could accommodate them all and give them what they needed.

The Captain said he could probably take all of the additional slaves aboard as long as they would stay on the weather decks. He also said he had sufficient food and water for them. He confirmed that he would pay the same amount per man as he had for the former sixty that he had received earlier in the day. I told him we had a deal, and we made the exchange before sundown. On parting, the Captain asked me whether I could work with him to free the slaves at the same rate per slave as we had agreed to. I told him that might be possible, but I had to confer with my partners before I made a firm decision. If I could do business with him, I said, I would be back and find him.

After that the English merchant steered north again and the Night Lightning steered northeast on a course to clear the north of Zanzibar before it turned east south-east so as to meet the Sweet Cutlass at the rendezvous as planned.

That night my First Mate came to my cabin to discuss what we had done during the day. He was frankly amused by the turn of events. We had decided to sell sixty freed slaves to a person who alleged not to be in the slave trade. Then we had captured and scuttled a pirate ship with twice as many slaves in its hold, and we had sold those to the Englishman at the same rate. Finally, he said, we had considered making the liberation of slaves a major business venture in the Zanzibar Channel. He laughed at the idea of pirates becoming altruists.

I admitted that I found the idea ironical, but then I went through the numbers with him. I told him what we had earned in gold and silver coins for selling one hundred eighty men into freedom. In addition to those profits, we seized from the adversary pirate ship spoils that added up to a small fortune that all aboard would share. We had lost no men during the last twenty-one days, which was itself a marvel. We had the option never to return if we found that ordinary piracy was for any mix of reasons a more attractive course to continue. I asked my First Mate what he would have done if he had been in command of the Night Lightning during the last few days.

The First Mate brooded on that question, and then he said that his problem was that he would never have been able to think things through in one-tenth of the time that I had done. He wondered whether he ever could be intelligent enough to be a successful Captain. He was a proud man, so this admission came with some difficulty for him. I told him that I had doubts about becoming Captain of a ship, and that was a good thing for me. I said that Captain Morgan still had more tricks up his sleeve than I knew and that I learned something new from him every time we worked together. I told my First Mate that I hoped he would tell me when he thought he had better ideas than mine. I said that I would listen carefully to his recommendations, but I would make the decisions as long as I was Captain. I would not unilaterally make the decision to continue liberating slaves as a business and that two things bothered me about that.

I was, I said, worried that pirates just like the scum that we had killed this day would be a threat to the liberators as long as slavery was managed on a large scale. I told him I was also worried that men less scrupulous than the good English Captain to whom we had sold slaves today might take his place. That would mean that the slaves we sold might be resold right back into slavery by the people we sold them to. Finally, I said that the more successful the liberators were, the more likely the Sultan of Zanzibar was to reconsider his position about securing the sea lines of control on both sides of the island. After all, he had the English and the Americans lobbying him vehemently to engage pirates with their warships.

The First Mate then told me that he would rather be a pirate than a slave. He said he hated slavery and everyone involved in the trade with every ounce of his being. I uncorked a bottle of rum and passed it to him with a gesture to drink. He did so gratefully and passed the bottle back to me so I could join him. When I had drunk a long swallow, I told him that I shared his hatred of the slave trade and if it were in my power, I would find a way to free all slaves. I said that I had discussed the matter with Captain Morgan, and we agreed that was a bridge too far. Slavery had been around since the beginnings of humankind. I advised him to think instead of what we could do to maximize crew share by whatever we did. If in the process of piracy we could seize coins and liberate slaves, so much the better for us and the slaves. He seemed to be satisfied with that approach.

I asked my First Mate how the former slaves among our crew felt about freeing other slaves.

The First Mate knit his brows and said the former slaves were extremely gratified at what we had done to free the other slaves. They were proud to have had a part in that action. He said that he could not be sure, but he thought they would be proud to die in the process of liberating slaves. He said that one former slave had talked with him about going back to his home village. Slave traders had burned the village to the ground and killed everyone they did not take as a slave. The former slave said that the Night Lightning was now as close to a home that he had, and he was glad to be part of the crew. The man had said that he had no family and no friends except for those he fought with.

I said that the former slave was thinking like most pirates everywhere. On that note, the First Mate went to relieve the watch. I reflected on Captain Morgan's wisdom in sparing this man from being fed to sharks and shook my head. It was certainly true that I learned continually from my mentor, and now I was learning from my protégé also.

As we passed around Zanzibar and intersected the sea lines that extended invisibly in all directions, I kept the crew on their normal watch standing routines and ordered the mates to keep the men active cleaning ship and cutting mare's tails and doing all the tedious daily tasks of sailors everywhere. I had the First Mate organize knot tying exercises and drills. Once I ordered the men to furl the sails and while the ship rose and fell dead in the water, I ordered the First Mate to take the Conn and plunged into the sea. Treading water, I asked everyone else who could swim to follow me. Around half the crew plunged in, and we swam around the ship four times before we climbed up the knotted ropes to the decks again and dried ourselves in the sunshine.

Another time, I organized a contest to see which hearty could climb to the crow's nest fastest. I also encouraged competition in knife throwing and swordsmanship. I had already told each mate to find a man to train as his replacement, and now I rotated those replacements in the watch routine and had the mates perform overwatch to see how they did and what they needed to learn.

We made good time, and one day out from due east of the old stone city of Zanzibar, my lookout sang out, "Sail ahoy!.."

I answered, "Where away?"

And he said, "On the horizon, one point abaft the starboard bow."

There with my spyglass I saw a sail and surmised it must be from the Sweet Cutlass. So I ordered the helmsman to keep a constant bearing on that ship as we closed.

In fact, we did not close because the ship was sailing at full speed to the east. I, therefore, ordered full sail and increased our speed therefore to the maximum. I ordered extra sail too, and we began to close with the target vessel gradually, but it was clear to me that we would not close until well after dark. This was not good because from the south we saw a storm advancing rapidly, and the rains from such storms in these climes came in a deluge in which a ship could become lost. The winds picked up and the storm's effects began to buffet us, so I took up sail and sacrificed speed for stability and safety.

My tactics changed from overtaking the vessel ahead to surviving the onslaught of the storm. That was prudent because the lightning flashed and the thunder roared as if Hades had opened. The sea state rose with cat's paws and then great waves with spindrift. On the southern horizon under the huge black canopy that was rapidly covering the skies danced wispy waterspouts. I could see a wall of rain approaching, but I could do nothing about it except to have my watch standers tie themselves in place with line and keep movements about the decks to a minimum.

When the rain hit us, it came in sheets and then in a continuous torrent. The sea beneath us boiled with waves and winds, and I ordered the helmsman to change the ship's heading directly into the storm so we met each wave head-on rather than side-on. That way we would not capsize, but the sea water swept over the ship from stem to stern and the undulating waves made the oak of the ship groan under stress.

I held myself in place with a rope, and I had tied the helmsman in place with a rope as well. We two looked into the jaws of the storm together, and the helmsman looked up at me as if I, as the Captain, had some power over the elements that would save us all. I had no such power, but I watched carefully as the ship was tossed about for anything that we could do to mitigate the storm's effects. There was precious little we could do. It hardly mattered to my crew that I had seen such storms along the Virginia coast in

America and in the Caribbean. What did they care about other storms when this was the storm that might hurl us down to Davy Jones where we would have all the treasure in the world though we would have no way to spend it? Everyone on board was soaked wet to the bone, and seawater was so thick as we passed through waves that it seemed we would be swallowed up. Everything not tied down washed overboard.

The thunder and lightning kept booming and crackling through the night, and the horrific wind whistled in the rigging like the cry of a Banshee. My helmsman at one point said he saw the Kraken looming up from the waves ahead, but then the apparition was gone. Except when the lightning flashed, we were sailing blind.

The ship was well named this night, I thought since when the lightning flashed, the ship was still there even if it was partially under seawater that fell off both sides of the decks in great streams as the ship was lifted to the top of the next wave and then dropped into the trough again.

I do not know how we managed to survive that ordeal, but sometime after midnight or thereabouts, the rain stopped completely, and the wind subsided along with the thunder and lightning receding behind the ship. The sea still swelled and fell more than normal, but the clouds raced away to the north.

Finally, the ocean lay almost flat and the gibbous moon shone through the breaking clouds. I ordered the helmsman to steer in parallel with the waves now because it was safe to do so. I asked the bo'sun of the watch to tally the watch standers. He did so and reported that all remained on station. No hearty had been lost to the storm. I ordered the watch to be shifted, and the men emerged to take their places and relieve the watch standers who had braved the elements.

By sunrise, when the sea was flat as a board, the clouds were gone and a light zephyr blew from the west, the ship glistened as if it had been cleansed. The crew went about the decks checking for damage and tidying up. One hearty brought me a strange fish that had landed on the deck. I had never seen its like before, but I ordered it scaled, cleaned and chopped into fish stew.

We were not becalmed, and humidity was considerably reduced, so I ordered all hands to be watchful for signs of the Sweet Cutlass. We were now a day late for our rendezvous, and no one could say where we were ourselves located now that the storm had passed. I reasoned that going towards the rising sun was as good a direction as any. So we edged towards the far horizon waiting for a sign.

It was noon around watch change when we had our first indication that our heading was correct. We fished out of the water a piece of wood that I knew well because in it I had once carved the name Sweet Cutlass. It was the stern piece from the whaleboat of my former ship, and it did not bode well for the ship and crew. I ordered an expanding square search around the place where we had found the flotsam.

I dropped an empty keg in the water so we would have a reference, and we kept expanding our search around that keg looking for other remains of the Sweet Cutlass. We also kept our eyes peeled for signs of a sail on the horizon. By nightfall, we had achieved no results, and I began to fear that the worst had befallen the Sweet Cutlass. I considered the irony that a pirate ship that had sailed unvanquished for years finally succumbed to a ferocious storm in the Indian Ocean.

I had visions of Captain Morgan regaling Davy Jones and sharing a bottle of rum with the vast treasure of the deep extending in all directions. The Captain Morgan I imagined had a bloated face, and his hair rose up and down in the depths, but his smile was that knowing, half-malicious smile that meant, "Arrgh!" Since the night was likely to be calm and since we had nowhere to go immediately, I ordered the sails to be luffed and the crew to rest on station when they were below decks or on watch. It was a long night of reflection for every hearty.

The next morning, I mustered the crew before the mast and told them that we did not know for certain that the Sweet Cutlass had gone down in the storm, but we had the evidence of the stern piece of its whaleboat to indicate that it had at least suffered great damage. Because we did not know the ship's fate, we could not mourn its loss but we could not waste more time looking for what might never be found.

I told the crew that we would be returning to the waters near Zanzibar to do what we always had done—piracy. I told them that whatever treasure might have gone down with the Sweet Cutlass was minor when compared with the caches of treasure that ship had sequestered all over the world. All would share in that treasure eventually by the pirate code.

In due course, if the Sweet Cutlass miraculously had survived the storm, doubtless, I said, we would meet her in our adventures because we went after the same prey as she did.

Symbolically, I ordered the stern piece of the Sweet Cutlass' whaleboat to be enshrined in my cabin. That was the sum total of the ceremony that I afforded my former vessel. I then returned to my duty as Captain of the Night Lightning and ordered full sail with a heading due west to Zanzibar.

I headed to the anchorage just offshore from the port of the old stone city. As soon as I could, I had the coxswain take me ashore so that I could visit Alia and discover the news that had occurred in the time since the Night Lightning had left the port hurriedly to prey upon vessels to the west of the island in the Zanzibar Channel.

When I pulled the bell of her house, Alia came to the door herself and recognized me with a smile. She took me in and seated me at the elevated table above her own little room. She brought me a bottle of rum, and I poured her a glass of rum as I had seen Captain Morgan do when we last visited here together. I told Alia that I feared that Captain Morgan had gone down with his ship and crew during the great storm that had passed through ten days ago. She listened to what I had to say with her usual attention, and after a minute's reflection she raised a toast to Davy Jones. Then she informed me of what had transpired since my last visit.

First, she said that coincidentally the same evening we weighed anchor the port was abuzz with rumors about a mysterious set of killings at the landing. The best part of the crew of a merchantman had been ruthlessly slain, and the killers had escaped in a whaleboat belonging to their ship. Troops had been dispatched too late, and they scoured the waters of the anchorage but found no trace of the killers or the whaleboat. At the time they reached the anchorage, it was too dark to see anything, so the leader of the troops decided to return to the landing and commence a thorough search of the port, the landing, and the anchorage the next day at dawn. Alia rolled her eyes as if to suggest that the troops did not have a prayer of finding who did the crimes.

Alia told me that she had been questioned about the killings by a customer from the local garrison. She told him she was nowhere near the landing, so she saw nothing. She said she would report anything that came to her attention or the attention of her women immediately, but nothing had been learned. The Sultan of Zanzibar had been informed of the killings, but his comment was, "The will of Allah be done." After that, the dead men had been buried and the searching by the military was stopped because the troops had other duties and the victims were mere visitors and infidels to boot. The authorities forgot the matter.

The second piece of news had ignited a furious dialog with the foreign powers on the island. Evidently, Alia said, a great many ships that were expected in Africa from the west side of the island did not arrive at their destination. They simply vanished. Certain interests from the African side of the Channel had searched the waters and found no trace of the missing vessels. If only one vessel had disappeared, the Captain and crew of the vessel would have been considered to have turned pirate and stolen the cargo to sell on their own. Under the circumstances of the loss of a dozen vessels, however, some external force was deemed to be operating in the waters, perhaps pirates, but no one could prove this. Alia said that the Sultan of Zanzibar was unimpressed with the rumors that surrounded the disappearance of the ships of his customers. Once business had been conducted, the fate of his customers was in the hands of Allah. The factors on the African side, the great man said, would have to sort out what had happened to their ships because it was none of his affair.

The third piece of news trumped all that Alia said before, and it involved a secret source that the sultan had for slaves. Alia did not know the details, but a particularly strident anti-slavery group was routinely intercepting human traffickers in the Channel and buying the slaves that were destined for Zanzibar. From what Alia gathered, pirates hired by the sultan's operatives had been hired to intercept the English merchant ship that bought the slaves and seize the cargo and slaves to return them to the sultan. When the sultan learned that the pirates had vanished, he became agitated and ordered two of his operatives to be beheaded because he suspected them of paying off the pirates to their own advantage. Since those two operatives were the only persons who knew about the sultan's attempt to seize the slaves from the English, many suspected that they had been killed to cover the sultan's tracks and leave him blameless however things turned out.

Alia had slept with both of the sultan's operatives, and she had learned from them the whole plan, which she thought fantastical at the time. She said she had heard nothing further about the matter although another customer had told her that the English merchant was back doing business buying slaves and that the sultan was scheming how to stop what they were doing. She said that the sultan would be willing to pay a great deal of gold and silver to anyone who would stop the infidel Captain of the English merchantman from doing its dastardly work.

When Alia had let what she had just said sink in and fetched me another bottle of rum, she rubbed her shoeless foot up and down the back of my leg and looked at me in the way women do when they dearly want something from a man. We descended into her little room to sport a while, and when she had done what she wanted to me, I paid her three gold coins, which was what she really wanted, and bid her adieu.

Then I decided to return to my ship to consider the implications of what Alia had told me. I noticed, however, as I left Alia's house that I was being followed to the landing by a shadowy man in a long robe. I pretended to be lost and wandered around the city, but the man kept following me. Finally, I decided to discover what the man wanted, so I ducked into a side street and ran quickly taking three left turns in succession so that I ended up behind the now-confused man with my knife against his back.

The man decided to communicate with me in half a dozen languages until I recognized the English for, "I am the sultan's man. Touch me and die." Since I had already touched him, I figured that I had nothing to lose now but my life. I asked him why he was following me. He said that he wanted to take me to the sultan through a secret passage into the royal house. So forward we marched, looking like old friends. I kept my knifepoint at his back and held his robe so he could not escape me.

The man was as good as his word. He led me down a path into the city sewer system and proceeded to an entry below ground that had a stairway into a small room on street level. There he told another man in fine silk garments that he had brought the man the sultan wanted to see.

I decided to take my chances now and lowered my knife, putting it back in its sheath behind my back. The man in silk was gone for only a few minutes, and when he returned he gestured that I should come with him, but he held back the shadowy man from proceeding further. I was taken down a narrow corridor to a room that must have been one of the sultan's throne rooms. I was asked to remove my shoes. Soft carpets were piled on the floor except for the polished area around a throne-like chair. I was told to kneel and bow because the sultan was coming any minute. I bowed and looked up to see the Sultan of Zanzibar himself with a look of amusement on his face.

The man in silk was the interpreter for the brief interchange I had with the sultan. The sultan repeated verbatim the offer that Alia had reported to me—an offer of great riches to rid the sultan of one meddlesome English Captain who was on an infidel crusade to crush the sultan's slave trade, which extended back centuries and gave wealth to everyone who had been involved in it. The sultan said he thought I might be able to do what he wanted to be done, and he said with amusement that I had a choice. Either I did what he asked and rid him of this infidel and his ship, or I would be taken into the square and beheaded instantly. To make his point, he drew his finger across his neck and smiled knowing he had been witty.

Through his silky interpreter, I told the sultan that I understood him perfectly, and I knew now of the sultan's infinite wisdom because I was exactly the man he needed to do this job. I asked the sultan two questions in the language I knew he understood above all others, "How much are you willing to pay me right now? And how much will you pay me when the job has been completed?"

The sultan clapped his hands twice, and a woman wearing a veil with the most beautiful, oddly familiar black eyes entered with two enormous slaves following. The slaves each carried a chest that, once they were opened, revealed the gold, silver, jewels and pearls that they contained. In one chest was an emerald as big as my fist. In the other chest was a diamond equally large.

The sultan asked me to choose one chest as my retainer, and he said his slave would carry it to my whaleboat for me to take to my ship. He said the other chest would be ready for me to pick up when I brought him proof that I had completed my task. The proof, he said, would be the head of the English Captain of the merchantman that was ruining his slave trade.

I chose the cask with the huge diamond, and the sultan clapped his hands. The slave with the chest with the diamond stood fast while the woman and the other slave with his chest followed the sultan out the door through which they had entered the throne room. Smoothly, the man in silk led me to where my shoes had been deposited and then he led me out a separate door with the sultan's slave following in my wake. We proceeded unmolested to the place at the landing where my coxswain waited by the whaleboat.

The slave set the chest carefully in the whaleboat and then stood back and waited. After I entered the whaleboat and the coxswain shoved off, the man in silk departed in the direction of the palace with the slave following ten paces behind him. I shuddered when I considered that the slave might have been a mechanical apparatus because he exhibited no sense of himself as a person. For that matter, the man in silk was little different from the slave. Only the veiled woman had shown vitality. Of course, she was Alia, and her vitality might have been due to the exercise we had shared in her little room before she had donned her Arab disguise and returned to the palace.

I realized that I had done what was necessary to escape the sultan's palace alive, but I needed to consider carefully my next moves. Back aboard the Night Lightning in my cabin I considered my dilemma. I now had a small fortune in the chest that sat on my desk. To the sultan, such riches were paltry compared to what he had in store elsewhere. If I were to abscond with the sultan's treasure, I would probably never see him again and as long as I stayed out of Zanzibar, I would be safe.

If I were to complete the contract I had formed with the sultan, the English Captain would lose his head and I would lose the chance to earn easy money while freeing slaves, but I had no certainty that delivering the man's head would result in the sultan's delivering the second chest to me. In fact, the more I thought about it, the more I was certain that delivering the infidel's head would seal my fate. I pictured myself being seized by the slave who had carried the chest to my whaleboat and beheaded by the slave's companion because my killing the English Captain was itself a capital offense.

In the end, I could see no advantage to the sultan in letting me live another moment after I delivered the promised head. I had witnessed the sultan's mannerisms in Captain Morgan, and I found it somewhat unsettling that the two men acted alike. After all, they were both absolute rulers of their separate domains. Why should they differ as to motives?

The piece of the puzzle that did not fit was Alia. Surely the sultan knew what Alia did in her house of prostitution, and probably he was her sponsor. She was an intelligence asset of the first rate, and her informants knew the intimate thoughts of their customers. Why did the sultan allow Alia to live? Was it her game to be a second Queen Scheherazade? Did she have to struggle to tell the sultan something that he desperately needed to know each time they met to spare herself from a public beheading?

I thought for a few minutes about the advantages of putting the sultan's head in a sack instead of the English Captain's head, but then I considered the layers of agents and troops that protected the sultan. I stood little chance to survive if I killed the sultan, and what would my killing him gain except freedom from my promise to produce the English Captain's head? The more I thought the matter through, the more flight from Zanzibar seemed the best course of action. In that case, I thought, I should carefully assess what was in the chest to assess what I had gained thus far.

I set the chest on the deck and laid out each item from it on the desk, grouping like with like. My cabin boy watched me with open mouth and bulging eyes as I stacked the gold coins and the silver coins and grouped the diamonds, rubies, sapphires, agates, emeralds, and pearls. There was a large bar of solid gold that I let the boy handle so that he would know pure greed and the root of all evil. At the bottom of the chest was a folded piece of paper that contained a note in a familiar hand.

The note was written by Captain Morgan in his unmistakable hand. It stated that he was a prisoner in the sultan's dungeon and would be executed if I did not bring the head of the English Captain as the sultan directed. The note went on to say that Alia had betrayed him to the sultan and she would betray anyone to save her own life, which was at hazard every moment. Captain Morgan must have smiled when he wrote the final line: "Of course, the sultan will kill us all when you deliver the English Captain's head, so you figure what must be done."

I knew I had very little time to react to what I had just read, and what I did was automatic because I had no time to think things through. I told my cabin boy to put down the gold bar and fetch the First Mate to my quarters with the instruction to bring a large burlap sack with him.

When the First Mate came, I showed him the treasure that the sultan had given me. I told him that I had to accomplish an impossible mission within the next eighteen hours, or everything would be lost. I ordered him to take command of the Night Lightning and sail this very night out of the anchorage to the sea and return to the anchorage and anchor two hours before dawn. Then he was to have the coxswain row him to the landing in the whaleboat. There at the landing, I told him I would meet him. I had him repeat what I had told him twice. I asked if he had any questions, and he did not. I told him that for this service I would give him his choice of any one of the items in the chest. Then I stowed the valuables in the chest and had the First Mate and one of our freed slaves help me take it to the whaleboat where the coxswain rowed me and the freed slave to the landing.

In the evening shadows, I watched from the shore as the whaleboat returned to the Night Lightning. I then watched the ship unfurl her sails and depart the anchorage. I then ordered the freed slave to carry the chest and follow me. We wound our way through the evening streets to Alia's house. There I pulled the bell. When she answered the door, I put my finger to my lips for silence and whispered that she must hide me, my man and the chest immediately in a place where we could talk.

In a special room that was reserved in Alia's house for secret meetings, I showed Alia the note from Captain

Morgan and told her that I wanted to free him as soon as possible.

When she said it was impossible, I opened the chest with the jewels and watched her eyes widen. I said in Zanzibar everything is possible with money, and if she did not help me, I would kill her right now as the sultan would do if she ever crossed him. She shuddered and nodded to say she understood me. I told her the outline of my plan, and she agreed to help. What other viable choice did she have?

Right away she dressed in the veiled robe that she wore in the sultan's palace. She led me and my man with the chest through the streets to the secret entrance through which we reached the palace. She showed me the access way and door to the sultan's chamber and told me that the sultan would be entertaining two of her ladies tonight with no guard on duty because of the impropriety of their activities.

I asked her when the women were scheduled to leave the sultan, and she said they planned to leave at first light as they always did. She said that the man in silk always approached the sultan in this chamber at sunrise to be sure all was well and to brief the sultan on the activities of the day.

When I asked her about the location of Captain Morgan, Alia said the Captain was probably in the underground compartment where special prisoners were kept before they were publicly beheaded. She knew the way there because she had been asked many times to get information from special prisoners before their executions. She said she had not been informed about Captain Morgan's presence in the palace but when she was asked to put his letter into the bottom of the chest by the man in silk, she had read it and discovered the truth. Why the man in silk had included the letter was a mystery to her.

I asked Alia to take my man with the chest to Captain Morgan. She was to pretend the man was her slave, and she was to use whatever she needed from the chest to bribe her way into and out of the prison chamber. I told her to tell the guards that she was on a mission from the sultan himself to question Captain Morgan as she had so many others and that she might need to have her slave bind the man and take him to the sultan if he decided to talk. She liked this plan, and she hurried off with the freed slave while I went directly into the sultan's chamber where he was sporting with the two women in his enormous bed.

I left the three no time to react to my presence. I flew at the sultan and stabbed him in the throat with my drawn knife. I then slashed left and right at the necks of the two women. Blood went everywhere, but I did not care. As the bodies bled out and the people died grasping at their sliced throats, I backed off the bed and arranged the naked corpses so that the sultan's own knife was now in his hand and each of the women held another of his many knives. The bloody scene appeared as if the three had played rough games and suffered a terrible accident together. I washed and dried my hands and my knife in the washroom adjoining the bedroom where the bodies lay. I sheathed my knife in the scabbard behind my back and then sat by the door and waited.

One hour later Alia arrived with Captain Morgan bound and gagged. My freed slave with the chest came behind them. I covered Alia's mouth so that she could not scream when she saw the tableau that lay on the bed. When Alia had recovered from her initial shock, I took my hand off her mouth and unbound Captain Morgan and removed his gag. I then asked the astonished Captain and my man to pull on the two women's veiled robes quickly. The four of us proceeded back the way Alia had led me into the palace. We walked through the dark streets as if I were the master of a house and my three wives followed in my wake at the prescribed distance with the last carrying my chest.

When we arrived at Alia's house, I ordered her to put whatever she wanted to take into a sack and come immediately with us to the landing. There at first light as we had planned, the First Mate stepped ashore from the whaleboat, and we all climbed in to row to the Night Lightning.

We had just climbed aboard the ship when the cannons at the fort fired shots of alarm. The port and landing area soon became a frenzy of activity. Shouting filled the city behind the port. Calmly, I ordered the First Mate to weigh anchor and clear the anchorage as rapidly as possible. Since the sails were still unfurled, the ship was tugging seaward in the morning breeze. When the anchor broke free, the ship rocked forward gaining momentum. I took Captain Morgan and Alia to my cabin with my man following with the chest. There I opened the chest and gave my man his choice of any of the items inside it. He chose the largest of the pearls and put it in a pouch that hung from his side.

I told him to return to his duty station, and he smiled broadly and left. When the First Mate came to report that the ship was underway and out of the anchorage heading for open water, I asked him to select one item from the chest. He chose a large ruby. I then ordered him to return to his duties. My cabin boy watched all this with open mouth. He had never heard of such largesse even in the most outlandish fairy tales.

Now I turned to Alia and Captain Morgan. I shrugged and said we had a lot of catching up to do. I asked whether they were as thirsty as I was, and they were parched. So I told the cabin boy to fetch three bottles of rum and a loaf of bread. The ship was out in the ocean now, so I excused myself to visit the helm and order the mate of the watch to follow the shore to the south to the southernmost point of the island and then turn north and follow along the shore in the Zanzibar Channel. When that was clear, I returned to my cabin to find the Captain and Alia drinking rum and talking about the woman's future.

I wanted to know what had happened to the Sweet Cutlass, but before the Captain told me his tale he wanted to raise a toast to the man in silk. Now there was a man, the Captain said, who knew how to take revenge like a pirate. I suddenly saw the light, and I eagerly drank the man's health. The sun was now rising fully above the horizon and behind us the cannons were booming in frustration because the sultan had been found dead in his bed. We were not frustrated because we had together done the impossible and freed a grateful man and a grateful woman and all it cost was one bar of gold and one fist-sized diamond as bribes from a chest that still brimmed with valuables. It was now time to eat, drink, be merry and tell a few tales.

The cabin boy was chewing on a crust of bread in anxious anticipation of hearing lore. Alia ruffled the boy's hair and smiled. She who had survived by telling tales now was as eager as the boy to hear others tell a few. So now it was Captain Morgan's time to tell tales. So all the way around Zanzibar Island to where the Sweet Cutlass lay at anchor on the west side of the Zanzibar Channel, he regaled us nonstop.

He was still talking when we anchored next to our sister ship and when he descended into the whaleboat with Alia, the chest and the stern piece from his former whaleboat with the name of his ship carved in it. The coxswain rowed him back to his ship while I watched by the helm.

The coxswain told me when he returned to the Night Lightning that Captain Morgan was talking even when he and Alia were hauled onto the deck of the Sweet Cutlass. For all his garrulity, the wily old Captain never fully answered the question I had asked him.

After what I had been through, I decided I did not really care. I knew what I had done, and all I really needed to know was that we were back in the pirate business now. It felt really good to get my sea legs back on the deck of my own ship.

E.W. Farnsworth

☠ ☠ ☠

Pirates of Arabia

I know of no waters like those of the vast Persian Gulf where aquatic life is so abundant from the surface in almost indistinguishable layers right to the depths where fish play among colorful coral formations visible from the surface.

The ships Night Lightning and Sweet Cutlass had taken prizes in those waters and in the Arabian Sea that lay to the south of them for just over one month. We focused first on the outbound traffic from the Sultanate of Oman, but gradually our emphasis shifted to preying upon the much more lucrative trade of the pirates along the southern gulf coast.

Those pirates ran gold from a certain sheikdom to India, which could never seem to get enough of the yellow metal. In this congenial gulf sheikdom, a finite amount of gold and silver bought refuge and, more importantly, loose women and liquor. We pirates could and did for a while gain intelligence and feast upon the international shipping vessels from all over the world. We also had rum and women whenever we liked and a steady stream of actionable intelligence from an unlikely source.

I found living among believers in Islam pleasant only when we had an understanding with the local authorities that allowed us to do whatever we wanted to do.

For sufficient treasure in our sheikdom, we became immune to religious strictures because our sponsors and protectors sheltered us from them. While they beat, maimed or killed their own believers for minor infractions, they left us alone for gold. In the right sheikdom with the right arrangement, we could also repair our ships and get some needed R&R between our marauding efforts in the gulf and the sea that otherwise would have been impossible for pirates without patronage.

When we arrived, we had no contacts that mattered in the Persian Gulf, and we had arrived here by traveling the long way around from Zanzibar Island. We followed the heavily trafficked sea lanes through the Indian Ocean taking our prizes all the way from Zanzibar to Oman. We then checked out that Omani sultanate since it was closely connected with the slave trade of Zanzibar as well as all of Arabia. We saw many wondrous things in our voyage such as sea serpents grey in color as smooth as polished brass and as long as our ship the Night Lightning, the cold fire that lit up all the masts like lightning at night or the phosphor. Of these three phenomena, the phosphor was the most mysterious and fatal to my hearties. Our entire time in the magical realm of Araby was like the night the phosphor came, and I should have taken it as the warning that it was, but I was naïve and blind to the consequences of its secret message.

According to the Night Lightning's log, my ship entered the cloud of phosphorescence around midnight on the 31st of October in the Arabian Sea well south of Oman. The white, fog-like substance permeated the exterior and interior spaces of the Night Lightning, and you could feel a tension all over the ship. No one dared make a sound, and any normal sound was muffled by the surrounding, glowing whiteness.

Captain Morgan had told me over a bottle of rum that he had encountered the phenomenon before in the Persian Gulf and also in the Arabian Sea. That night from my preferred place near the helm, I sent a message around to all my crew that the phosphorescence was normal in these waters and that everything was going to be all right. In retrospect, that was a false message that may have cost my hearties their lives.

When one giant, white tentacle reached out and grasped my port lookout, a few seconds elapsed before I could register what was happening. My starboard lookout was taken next. His scream was quickly muffled as he went below the water's surface. Huge, long tentacles now blindly groped everywhere from focsle to fantail and from the weather decks to the crow's nest. My helmsman was snatched away screaming by one white tentacle. I saw another white tentacle exploring the area around the helm. I dodged the slimy, white, living thing, glad that it had no eyes. It slapped the deck looking for prey. It tried but failed to grasp me at the helm where I stood fast, frozen with fear at its ghostly presence. It was like the hand of a wicked drunken man whose intent was to kill whatever it found. But it passed, and I felt the relief of one who has been reprieved.

Then for a while all was quiet in the cottony cloud. Below on the weather decks I heard the tentacles' characteristic thump-thump-thumping. If the tentacles had reached the below-decks spaces, I thought, it would by now have reached the crew's quarters also. My entire crew might have been taken by a white phosphorescent sea monster. I stood at the helm like a bird fascinated by a viper. I could do nothing to stop what was happening. I could only wait out the night and hope for the best. Meanwhile, the Night Lightning made no headway in the white shroud because there were no winds and no currents. When the sun burned through the white the next morning, my hearties came from below decks and found me all alone above decks at the helm. The phosphor had disappeared taking seven of my hearties with it to see Davy Jones. I ordered the crew to look lively and man their normal watch stations. It had been a very close thing to have survived the night. I did not want to experience the phosphor ever again.

The phosphor was not the only lethal phenomenon we met on this voyage. Within the Persian Gulf another day the tiny, poisonous sea snakes bred. You could see them spread upon the surface and through the upper layer of the hot, salt water like an iridescent, wriggling skein. Local people warned us not to swim when the water snakes hatched because they could bite a bare ear or toe and inject poisonous venom that would kill.

Like everything else in the teeming vat of life that was the Persian Gulf, fish ate those snakes and then were eaten by other, larger fish. More dangerous to my ship though than the poisonous water snakes was the daytime fog that seemed to boil up from the gulf on days so hot I thought the entire waterway would evaporate into salt. Pursuing merchant vessels into that fog was a losing game if the merchant's Captain knew his soundings and sped his ship towards shore.

Yet in just such a fog my socked-in ship happened across a curious dhow manned by local pirates. We took that dhow as our prize and found aboard it below decks gold in every conceivable form—bars, coins, dust, and ore. The dhow's Captain and crew pled that they were under the sheik's protection, but that merely sealed their fate in our minds because we could not become known as pirates who raided the sheik's own ships. After we shipped the dhow's gold aboard the Night Lightning, we forced those pirates to walk the plank and scuttled their craft to eliminate all evidence of our piracy. When the fog broke that evening and the stars appeared in the clear, black Arabian skies, no evidence remained of our piracy, and we believed we had struck a gold seam that demanded our immediate and strict attention.

The sheik that we had bought dearly, harbored a house of pleasure worked by beautiful foreign women who serviced all the sailors who visited the sheikdom. They gave pleasure for gold and silver coins of all nations and precious jewels or pearls as well. All of the women workers were infidels from Europe, Asia, and America. They did not care whether their customers were Muslims, Christians or Jews; they only cared about the color of their customers' money. These women knew many languages and listened closely when their customers spoke. They collected intelligence nightly. Alia understood them because she belonged as one of their sisterhood except that, unlike them, she was born a Muslim.

Since Captain Morgan and I had rescued this Scheherazade from what was essentially slavery to the now-deceased Sultan of Zanzibar, she had lived aboard the Sweet Cutlass in Captain Morgan's cabin and was considered one of our pirate crew with an equal share of the booty that we stole. She earned her share doing what no hearty could have done.

In the gulf when we anchored out, Alia went ashore dressed in her veiled robe. She befriended the women in the house of pleasure sponsored and protected by the sheik to discover valuable intelligence that we pirates could put to good use. When Captain Morgan visited the house, he remained in the great room near the entrance entertaining the guests while his veiled, supposed wife Alia slipped into the back rooms where the women waited and rested between entertaining their customers to garner whatever intelligence would help us in our trade.

In this way, she learned about the dhows from the sheikdom that plied the gold trade into India. She was told the location of the storehouse where the gold was readied for shipment. She learned how the gold was transported to that storehouse in the sheikdom by water and by land. Because one of the women of the house of pleasure was favored by the sheik himself, she had learned first hand how the sheik profited from his smuggling operations. Alia learned from her that the sheik was frenetically concerned that a special shipment of gold had vanished without leaving a trace.

The sheik was a bearded man small in stature but with an enormous capacity for rage. When he learned that his special gold shipment had never reached India, he identified ten men who he thought might have conspired to steal the gold and beheaded them all with his own curved sword.

That was the same special gold shipment that had been seized by my hearties, but we had been very careful to destroy all evidence of our crime. We had also taken pains not to exhibit any of the loot we had plundered from the dhow in the sheikdom or anywhere else in the Persian Gulf region because doing so might have been fatal to our business and our lives.

Yet Alia's new female contacts gave her details about the timing of the sheik's gold shipments that turned out to be accurate, so we made it our business routinely to harvest the sheik's gold. We did not capture every dhow. In fact, we let every other shipment pass through our two-ship moving cordon into India to keep the sheik in business. As long as the sheik continued to send out his dhows, we amassed wealth from our piracy. So we had to keep tabs on the sheik's thoughts and strategies.

On one visit to the house of pleasure, while Captain Morgan drank rum, smoked, told tall tales, and swore in the drawing room to an appreciative audience, Alia was asked by the female consort of the sheik whether she knew of anyone who could provide security for the sheik's gold shipments.

Alia told the woman that she would check around. Perhaps, Alia said enigmatically, something could be done for the right price.

Late that night when Captain Morgan and Alia were rowed out to the Sweet Cutlass in the whaleboat by my coxswain, Alia outlined the plan that the sheik's woman had suggested to her.

In turn, the coxswain told me what he had overheard. In essence, the sheik was so desperate for help that he was willing to give up one-quarter of his gold from his gold trade to protect it. His rationale was that he was already losing half his gold and that he would gain back that half for the contribution of a quarter for guaranteed protection. He figured that would leave him a quarter ahead of the current state of the game.

On their next visit to the house of pleasure, Alia told the consort of the sheik that Captain Morgan would be just the man to provide security for the gold trade. His proposed terms to the sheik were to receive one quarter of each gold shipment in advance as a fee for assuring that it reached India as planned.

The sheik asked to meet Captain Morgan, and they rode camels together deep into the desert to the oasis called Al Ain. The men got to know each other, and the sheik liked the Captain for his candor and confidence. So the two men bargained and struck a deal for protection of the sheik's gold traffic, with one important change from Captain Morgan's original proposal. Instead of receiving the full quarter before a shipment departed, Captain Morgan would receive one-eighth. A second eighth would be due upon delivery of the gold in India. If a shipment for any reason did not arrive, then Captain Morgan would forfeit the eighth he had collected in advance. After the shipment had been delivered, Captain Morgan's interest in the business ended. Once their agreement had been sealed the sheik and the Captain rode out of the desert on their camels, and the Captain returned to his ship to execute on their plan.

For a while, their plan worked perfectly. Captain Morgan collected half his fee, escorted the dhow carrying the gold shipment to India where he collected the rest of his fee. On its return voyage, the Sweet Cutlass would prowl and take prizes of opportunity. Meanwhile, the Night Lightning would shadow the protection operation taking prizes as it could but basically assuring that no other pirates would attack either the Sweet Cutlass or the dhow with its cargo of gold. Not long after we had begun our program, it occurred to me that the most valuable target on our home voyages was the same dhow that took the gold to India because it returned with greater than equal value of the outgoing gold in its hold. So every other trip the Night Lightning would harvest the contents of the returning dhow, kill its crew and scuttle the vessel.

After the third such seizure and destruction effort against returning dhows, Captain Morgan and Alia visited the sheik's house of pleasure where they learned from the sheik's female consort that the sheik was beside himself with rage about the loss of the cargo on his returning dhows. The sheik, she said, was satisfied that he had bought the security of his outgoing dhows, but he now wanted to buy the security of his incoming dhows as well.

Alia told the woman that the sheik could probably negotiate the same deal for the returning dhows as he had for the outgoing dhows with Captain Morgan, so the sheik demanded another meeting with the Captain at the oasis, and there he bargained for the same deal, aware that once he cut this deal he would be no better off than he was when he cut the first deal since he would effectively have paid half of his trade in protection money. Nevertheless, the deal was struck, and the two men returned from the desert satisfied with their bargain.

For four months, the sheik's gold trafficking business went swimmingly. I was mildly annoyed to see that we were taking only half of the treasure that was flowing between the sheik and his Indian factors. I began scheming about how to increase our share without driving the sheik insane because if he reneged on our current deals, we would be a lot worse off than we were before we started the enforcement actions that protected his gold shipments.

So I anchored the Night Lightning off the Indian port where the dhows unloaded their cargoes, and I went ashore alone to investigate what happened to the gold after it had been offloaded from the dhows and delivered to the Indian factors that paid for the cargo. I pretended to be a merchant looking to barter my wares, and I took along samples including gold. Of course, the Indian merchants only wanted to deal with me for the gold because they had other sources for all other commodities I had to offer them. They were eager to drive a bargain, but I held out for a fraction more than I knew the sheik was receiving for his gold. We agreed to terms, so I went back to the Night Lightning and fetched a whaleboat full of gold in all forms. The cargo was handled and guarded by two of my hearties who were among our former slaves.

The transaction went as I had planned, and I sent one of my hearties to witness where the gold had been taken after I had sold it. He returned to report that the gold was escorted to an imposing edifice with gables near the port gateway. I conjectured that a small raiding party might liberate the gold we had just sold and other gold and valuables in the imposing edifice as well, but I prudently wanted to know more about the disposition of the gold before I acted. I therefore went back out to the ship in the whaleboat with the large bags of jewels and pearls that had bought the gold, and at midnight I returned to the port to check out the imposing edifice where my gold had been taken.

I saw that the gold was being transported that very night in a kind of caravan. The heavy metal was loaded onto carts and onto the backs of animals and bearers in heavy sacks and boxes. Armed men guarded the house, the road and the caravan itself. If I had brought my small force, we would not have stood a chance to overcome the security and seize the gold.

Clearly, I thought, the gold was controlled by very powerful people who knew the value of their enterprise and paid well to enforce it. I decided to follow the caravan to see where it was going with the gold. Perhaps, I thought at the time, the gold was heading for a place where other gold had been deposited. Raiding that place might be less risky than raiding the imposing edifice, I thought.

The gold was taken through the night to a huge marketplace where many kinds of goods were set out for sale. I saw that the gold was sold from an enclosure that was very secure and well guarded. During the morning merchants went into the enclosure and came out with small lots of the gold. I deduced that liberating the gold in the enclosure would be too risky for my hearties and that stealing from the many buyers would provide too paltry award for the many efforts it would take. Ships can carry much larger volumes of gold than any other mode of transport, and we pirates know how to capture and pillage a ship.

I had to admit that there was no percentage for my crew working to liberate the gold ashore in India, so I returned to the port and roused my sleeping coxswain to row me back out to my ship. There I brooded all day while I watched other ships arrive and depart.

It was late afternoon when I espied through my spyglass an interesting exchange of very heavy parcels that had been transferred from an anchored ship. Unless the ship was dealing in ingots of lead, I thought, the ship's cargo was surely gold. I surveyed the ship where the cargo originated, and I decided that the Night Lightning would make it a prize to determine its business. The ship flew a Spanish flag, but that did not mean much to me because I routinely used false flags to avoid being remarked as a pirate—until it was time to raise the Jolly Roger in the prospect of a raid.

So when the Spanish-flagged ship I had targeted weighed anchor, I ordered my hearties to heave-ho as well, and we sailed off in pursuit. When we were out of sight of land, I ordered the ship to full sail and to close with the ship as we prepared to board her. I ordered my hearties to their battle stations and raised the Jolly Roger. We overtook the vessel and grappled our way close alongside it, with my hearties swinging aboard with cutlasses and knives drawn. Subduing the Captain and crew was easy, and my hearties knew the drill for dealing with a prize ship. Within an hour the Captain and the crew of the prize had been sent to see Davy Jones, and all treasure and valuables from the prize had been transferred to the Night Lightning.

As a special trophy, the First Mate brought me the Captain's log from the prize ship's Captain's cabin. From the log entries it was clear that the ship had made regular monthly scheduled passages between Oman and India. Specifically, it had carried gold to the east and jewels and pearls to the west. It had also on one prior trip carried a baby elephant from India to Oman.

My crew discovered only token amounts of gold aboard the prize because all its gold had been transferred to factors at the Indian port. I deduced from this that I should plan to raid the replacement for this vessel during the next scheduled passage from Oman, which was scheduled to occur one month hence.

Back in the sheikdom I learned that Captain Morgan was becoming bored with the new routine of protecting the sheik's gold traffic. At the house of pleasure after having consumed two bottles of rum, the Captain began railing about the pedestrian nature of a life without danger and daring. He decided it was time to fire his pistol in the house and stand on a table brandishing his cutlass and singing boisterous, lewd pirate songs. With his parrot perched on his shoulder, Benjamin laughed and pointed at his Captain on the table, egging him on.

Things might have gotten out of hand, but I calmed down both the Captain and his man, and I whispered to Captain Morgan that I had another game than security in mind that might please him well enough. I then told him about the Spanish-flagged vessel I had captured and sunk and about the log entries indicating the monthly passage of gold passing from Oman to India. The Captain scowled and ran his hand over his beard.

When the light of realization came into his eyes, he ordered two more bottles of rum, one for me and one for himself. We drank the rum and plotted head to head until it was time for us to leave the house and return to our ships.

Alia had also learned a few things that would come in handy, so all-in-all it was a good night's work though Captain Morgan with his antics had risked the ruin of our whole livelihood with a few choice words in the wrong public environment. I feared that the sheik's female consort, who had overheard the Captain's remarks about piracy, might be smart enough to understand our subterfuge and greedy enough to inform the sheik about our piratical escapades.

We planned carefully for our raid on the next scheduled Omani gold run. The complication was that the sheik's dhow was going to be in transit during the same interval as the gold shipment from Oman. That meant that we had to navigate so as to protect the sheik's dhow while capturing our prize.

As often happens when the perfect plan hits the reality of operations, we met with surprises and had to improvise. Specifically, another pirate decided it was time to move against our sheik's dhow, and the Omani ship was found sailing in tandem with a ship from Muscat. My lookout spied the three ships coming from different directions across our track. The Night Lightning would ordinarily have intercepted the pirate ship, but I figured that the Sweet Cutlass would be able to handle our security job. I therefore hoisted the Jolly Roger and steered to intercept the ships from Oman and Muscat, both of which were armed with cannon.

The winds were in my favor and with full sail the Night Lightning cut right across the bow of the ship from Muscat, firing a salvo that took out the main brace and caused significant crew loss at the same time.

With that ship unable to maneuver, the Night Lightning continued at speed to ram and board the ship from Oman, which chose to fire cannonballs rather than scrap metal, nails and chains as we did. The result was futile whistling as the cannon balls passed over our lower decks without causing damage.

My hearties used grappling hooks and lines to swing from ship to ship, and the boarding party led by the First Mate began to savage the crew with their cutlasses and knives. I had the remainder of my hearties cut free from the Omani ship, and I tacked to intercept and board the ship from Muscat.

My Second Mate led the second boarding party, and they arrived on board their prize with such ferocity that the remaining crew threw down their weapons and begged for mercy. Mercifully, then, my hearties cut them down to the last man and threw their bodies overboard. Then they raced to search the ship for gold and other valuables.

In the distance I heard a cannon's report and saw my First Mate signal. I thought that the First Mate was ready to transfer the Omani ship's cargo when I was ready to receive it. His small prize crew had clearly managed to take control of the ship's navigation and cannon but the ship was now sailing in a direction away from our position rather than towards it.

I urged the Second Mate to hurry what he and his hearties were doing while I swept the horizon with my spyglass. From the crow's nest I heard, "Ship ahoy two points off the starboard bow!"

I swung my spyglass to see that a warship was approaching the Omani vessel with full sail. I called to my Second Mate that I would be back. I then ordered my remaining hearties to cut free from the ship from Muscat, and we proceeded with full sail to intercept the warship before it caught up with the Omani ship. I ordered my gunners to fire one free shot to get the warship's attention. I hoped to divert that ship from pursuing the Omani ship and make it turn and fight us at a disadvantage because of the wind. My ploy worked, and I saw the warship come about. It fired broadside as its guns to port became unmasked, but its sails slacked for lack of wind and as its gunners reloaded, we gained enough advantage to get a shot off from our port cannon as I came right. The shot hit home on the vessel's main brace and brought the warship dead in the water, and that was my intent. As I passed astern of the crippled vessel, I tacked to bring my stern around to face her. Then I ordered sails rigged to proceed as best as possible keeping our stern pointed at the warship's stern. Through my spyglass I saw the warship's crew trying vainly to splice the main brace, and I knew that once out of the range of the warship's cannons, I could proceed as I wished.

I ordered the helm to steer for the Omani ship and to keep a constant bearing while we plied full sail to meet her. Seeing the Night Lightning approach, my First Mate brought the Omani ship around so he and the prize crew could do their transfer and board us. For a moment I did not see the prize crew on the weather decks, and I surmised that they were below decks scuttling the Omani vessel. When they appeared again, the First Mate and his prize crew made great haste to do the transfer of the gold and scamper back aboard.

After we cut away from her, the Omani ship began to list as it took on water, and soon it lay for a time at an acute angle as it sank beneath the waves to descend slowly to meet Davy Jones. By then I had turned the Night Lightning to give a wide berth to the crippled warship. When I had passed the closest point of approach to the warship, I turned the ship and began maneuvering her to the area where I had left the ship from Muscat in the capable hands of my Second Mate and his prize crew.

That ship was not visible on the horizon, so I called to the lookout in the crow's nest to keep his eyes peeled to all points off the bow as we pressed forward, tacking back and forth against the prevailing contrary wind.

Finally, the lookout called out, "Boat ahoy off the bow!"

I could not make out a contact through my spyglass, so I called for the lookout to point at the boat and keep pointing while I tacked to close the distance. Tacking frequently was rough going, but finally I made out a whaleboat coming towards us with a man waving in it. The

The Adventures of Pirates

man was my Second Mate. His prize crew and cargo were weighing the boat perilously deep in the water. When it was clear that the ship was going to close successfully with the boat, the Second Mate and his hearties jumped out of the whaleboat and held onto its sides to give her more freeboard and keep her from being overwhelmed and sunk by the wave action of the ocean.

In these shark-infested waters, dangling like bait from the side of a boat was a courageous maneuver to save a large cargo of gold from going to the bottom. I urged the men to work fast hauling both the hearties and the gold aboard. I then ordered that a line be paid out to tow the whaleboat behind the Night Lightning, which was quickly gaining speed to intercept the Sweet Cutlass somewhere over the eastern horizon between here and the port of India.

The first indication that we were on the right track was the flotsam from the pirate ship that had tried to intercept the sheik's dhow. Captain Morgan had clearly made quick work of that ship of fools and sent them to Davy Jones. The question was, were the Sweet Cutlass and the dhow safe? It was late afternoon as I approached the anchorage outside the Indian port that I got the answer to my question. There where it had last set its anchor, lay the Sweet Cutlass with her Captain and crew, arrayed on deck, eating and drinking as if they were on a pleasure cruise. After I set anchor not far from my sister ship, secured the sailing watch and set the anchor watch, Captain Morgan set out in his whaleboat to see what plunder I had taken. Alia in her veiled robe and Benjamin with his parrot came along for the ride.

As evening came, we all sat in my cabin with my cabin boy. My First Mate came to the cabin to present the best of his pelf first—eight large sacks of gold coins and three of gold dust from the hold of the Omani ship. He described many other valuables he had taken, and to prove the worth of his discoveries, he showed an enormous ruby, which he placed on my chart table next to my log. I rewarded him with permission to broach a cask of rum with his prize crew for their efforts, and he went off quickly to begin the celebration.

Then my Second Mate came to the cabin to present the best of his pelf—a dozen strongboxes containing golden bars and a sack full of almost perfect pearls, one of which was as large as a cherry. Captain Morgan looked on with approval at the pelf, but he asked with an accusatory look what had happened to the ship from Muscat. The Second Mate said that when his prize crew went below to scuttle the ship, they found that the Muscat crew had already done that work and the ship was sinking fast. He said it was all he and his hearties could do to transfer the cargo to the whaleboat and escape the sinking vessel before it disappeared beneath the waves.

I told Captain Morgan about the man's having jumped into the water with his hearties to keep enough freeboard so that the whaleboat did not sink. At this Captain Morgan frowned and said they were lucky not to have been devoured by sharks. The Second Mate smiled and said they were luckier still to have been found by his Captain. They had run out of rum by the time he found them. At this hint, I rewarded the Second Mate and his prize crew with permission to broach a cask of rum. That pleased the man greatly, and he hastened to begin the night's drinking with his hearties.

The Third Mate came next to describe what we had all done aboard the Night Lightning while the First Mate and Second Mate and their prize crews were busy killing men and taking plunder. Captain Morgan was very impressed to discover my tactics when the warship appeared. He said a few words about it being a pity to leave the ship above the waves when it deserved richly to go beneath them.

I laughed and told the Captain that it was better to have treasure than revenge. He retorted that it was best to have both treasure and revenge.

Then Benjamin's parrot said distinctly, "Bottle of rum!" We all drank to that, and I sent my cabin boy below to fetch a feast, which we shared while we listened to Captain Morgan's tale of boarding the pirate vessel, killing her Captain and all of her crew and taking aboard her treasure hoard. To give panache and point to his story, he asked Alia to show everyone what was in the leather pouch she carried around her neck. She opened her pouch with great drama, pulled it open and shook out five enormous diamonds and a great emerald into her hand. The Captain then asked Benjamin to tell everyone what else that ship contained.

Benjamin rose to the occasion with his bird on his shoulder and smiled. He said the enemy pirate ship had contained many barrels, kegs and bottles of rum, five tuns full of malmsey, dried and salted fish, dates and apricots, bags of sundry grains and an armory of guns, powder, swords and very sharp knives. Benjamin smiled when he described the rich garments, animal hides and materials, colorful African bird feathers, six caged lovebirds, three pet green monkeys, four chimpanzees and a pair of gorillas. His face clouded over when he said that they had also found deep in the hold six slaves, four males and two females. They were bound together in tight-fitting chains.

Seeing that Benjamin was now feeling profound emotions, Captain Morgan said that these men and women were now free of their chains and resting on the weather decks of the Sweet Cutlass. They had been given food and water and rum. He said that Alia had provided the women with robes, and the crew had donated their clothes for the men to wear. Without looking at Benjamin, the Captain said with a fierce look that brooked no opposition, "Those fine men and women will never be slaves again." The Captain went on to say that he had received their recompense for safe delivery of the dhow's gold to the Indian factors and for escorting the dhow on its return voyage. Since the dhow was not scheduled to return to the sheikdom until three days hence, Captain Morgan said he wanted me to show him the local sights with particular attention to the port's gold repository--that imposing edifice I had described to him.

So early the next morning Captain Morgan and I went ashore to survey the imposing edifice. We walked all around the edifice discussing the merits of piracy over robbery, but I saw a familiar glitter in the Captain's eyes when I told him how much gold I had seen taken from this edifice and conveyed by that caravan to the great open air market that lay a night's march away. I reviewed the security features of the edifice and the procedures that accompanied the transfer of the gold from port to edifice and from edifice to caravan and from caravan to the market compound.

The Captain said that among the clothing that they had seized from the pirate ship were garments worn by Islamic merchants. Then he asked me where we might find two dromedary camels, and I knew what he was thinking. Once the Captain made up his mind, there was no changing it, but I reflected what the short remainder of our lives would be like in a filthy Indian jail while we awaited execution for murder and theft.

Since our First Mates had been left in charge of our ships, we had no compunction about staying ashore overnight. Just as before I watched the nighttime transfer of the gold from the edifice to the caravan, only this time Captain Morgan's eyes watched the process with mine. He pointed out where the vulnerabilities in the process lay. Then we shadowed the slow procession of the caravan to the marketplace, and Captain Morgan again remarked on the vulnerabilities in the bends of the path and the darkness between the torches that the security guards carried. Around one o'clock in the morning a group of a dozen brigands attacked the caravan, and they were easily killed or repulsed by the guards. The Captain shook his head at the clumsiness of the brigands' approach. He said they were not professionals but a ragtag group probably trying robbery for the first and last time. He said we should break off from following the caravan and instead follow the two brigands who had escaped being killed.

One of the surviving brigands had been wounded. He was bleeding badly and growing weaker with every step. His companion saw that the man would die, so he drew his knife and slit the man's throat. He left the man's body in the vegetation by the side of the trail and went forward with us following him right to his hideout in the forest. He was met there by three men and two women with torches. They seemed to berate him for having been unsuccessful in his venture. All went into a makeshift building where they evidently lived and stored their ill-gotten wealth.

Captain Morgan drew his knife and went for a visit. I followed him through the door with my own knife drawn. Inside the building, we surprised the six people and had no trouble killing them all because they did not know how to fight at close quarters. We quickly surveyed the stores their group had amassed, and we were pleasantly surprised to find among them gold and silver that they had presumably stolen from other caravans. The brigands were surely not amateurs as we had thought.

In fact, there were so many sacks of riches there that we could not carry away more than a fraction at a time. So we found a place under the roots of a huge tree where we could hide what we had found, and we made two score trips from the building to the tree carrying heavy sacks and parcels. Finally, we selected four huge bags of gold coins to take with us on our return to the port. By morning, we reached our whaleboat where we roused our coxswain to row us to our ships with the gold.

We did not wait on our ships but brought a prize crew of twelve in two whaleboats, one of which was from the ship Muscat. We went back to the brigand's hideout where we discovered that other brigands had come looking for their brethren. We were glad that we had found a hiding place for the gold that was not visible from the main building from which we had taken the gold. So stealthily we went to our hoard under the tree roots and, each man taking two huge bags of gold, we retraced our steps and returned to our whaleboats. By the time we reached our ships, it was evening, but a pirate's work is never done.

So once again Captain Morgan and I returned to the shore and went back into the forest to the brigands' building. The brigands were absent when we arrived at their hideout, so we waited outside and watched for their return. In the very early morning, a dozen of the brigands did return carrying heavy bags and two badly wounded men. While the men carried their bags into the building, the man we thought was their leader dispatched the two wounded men by slitting their throats. He ordered the others to bury the two bodies in the forest and then he went into the building.

I told the Captain that I thought that eight men were occupied burying the bodies and four men including the leader were now inside the building with the treasure. I could not make out the Captain's face in the darkness, but I heard his familiar, "Yaar!" I felt him move forward and I knew his knife was drawn, but I managed to pull him down just as another group of brigands came out of the forest from behind the building with more treasure.

I could not believe our good luck. We had narrowly missed being detected, and the treasure we had come for was increasing by the hour. We lay flat watching as the leader of the second group of brigands and the leader of the first group emerged from the building to talk strategy in a language neither of us understood. The upshot of their discussions was evidently that they would take their groups back immediately to make another raid on the caravan before first light. I thought that was a very bad plan from a pirate's point of view because of the visibility that daybreak gave to the defenders.

We, on the other hand, were fortunate because the brigands were going to leave their store unguarded and we had the rest of the night to remove the treasure from the house to our secret hiding place under the roots of the giant tree.

When the men who had been sent to bury their dead comrades returned, they joined the brigands who were waiting to get back to raiding. The two groups departed as a single force in the direction of the main path through the forest.

We waited to be sure none would circle back to their building, but none did return. We then went up to the door of the building, but Captain Morgan cautioned me about barging right in. Instead, he looked for another entrance. There was a high window with a sill.

The Captain forced the wooden covering over the window and together we entered through the orifice that was revealed behind it. The Captain struck flint on steel and started a flame with which he lit a candle that he had brought for the purpose. He showed me with his light how the brigands had rigged a devilish booby trap inside the front entrance that would impale anyone who opened the door. He disarmed the device temporarily so that we could use the door to remove the gold and then he produced a large, red candle by which we would be working to remove the gold.

We hurried to carry the heavy bags of treasure through the door to hide them in the place beneath the tree roots. We worked hard for over two hours to clear all the treasure out of the building. Aside from the pelf we stored under the tree roots, we left four sacks of gold bars on the ground in front of the building. Satisfied that we had not missed anything, the Captain carefully closed the front door and rearmed the devilish booby trap in such a way that anyone trying to disarm it from the outside would trigger the device.

Leaving our large, red candle burning on the floor as a kind of token, we climbed out of the building through the window that had let us inside, and the Captain and I restored the wood covering over the orifice. We then took the four huge sacks of gold bars that we had laid aside with us as we departed the area.

We saw no sign of the brigands as we returned all the way back to the landing where our coxswain was waiting for us. He rowed us to the Sweet Cutlass where we decided that we would return that very night with enough hearties to carry all the gold we had hidden back to the whaleboats, of which we would need three this time instead of two.

I was once again glad that I had towed the whaleboat from the Muscat to the anchorage behind the Night Lightning. The Captain summoned Benjamin to muster a party of twenty strong men to do the heavy lifting and asked me to return to my ship and bring ten men in my own whaleboat for the venture. With ten men in each of three whaleboats, we shoved off an hour before nightfall and landed on the shore where we set out in three parties so as not to arouse suspicions about our intentions. We formed a single group on the main path around an hour's walk from the port, and the Captain led us to the area where the brigands' building lay.

While the hearties hid and waited, the Captain and I went forward to get a view of the building. There, as we saw from hiding, the two groups of brigands, approximately forty of them, sat in circular rows around a large bonfire they had built in the clearing in front of the building. We could make out two men sitting on the ground outside the circular groups that surrounded the fire.

I recognized the bound men as the leaders of the two groups. The brigands had evidently decided that their leaders had betrayed them by spiriting away their gold.

While we watched, four brigands lifted each man and threw him into the bonfire alive to roast there. The familiar stench of roasting human flesh filled the area, and the vain screams of the leaders as they roasted were to me most eloquent expressions of the rage and pain they must have felt.

The brigands laughed and pointed at their roasting leaders, and they pitched more wood on the bonfire to be sure the leaders would be entirely consumed by the flames. One brigand then went to the bonfire and raised a firebrand from the fire. He yelled a few words in a strange language and then hurled the flaming torch into the wooden building. The building smoked a while and then burst into flames. While the brigands continued to have their fun, we slipped back into the forest to get our hearties to work retrieving what had been the brigands' treasure.

In groups of ten, our men picked up the loot from under the tree roots. The Captain and I also hoisted two sacks each, and we all made our way back to the main trail out of the forest. We hastened along the dark path as best we could so that we could return to the landing of the port before first light. We stowed the treasure in the waiting whaleboats and rowed the boats and men back to our ships where hearties hauled the bags on board in nets let over the side and took them to the Captains' cabins. By sunrise our work was completed. We rewarded everyone who had participated in transporting the treasure with rum and rest for the rest of the day and the night as well because the next morning we weighed our anchors and accompanied the dhow back to the sheikdom as we had contracted to do.

When we arrived safely at our usual anchorage off the sheikdom, Captain Morgan and Alia went immediately ashore and visited the house of pleasure. There they were informed by the female consort of the sheik that the sheik had had conniptions about the high price he was paying for protection. The potentate wanted to terminate the whole deal and take his chances on the shipments. He also planned to banish the Sweet Cutlass and the Night Lightning from his sheikdom because he felt he had been snookered and betrayed.

Captain Morgan, having anticipated the mercurial temperament of the sheik, asked the female consort whether she could arrange for him to present the sheik with gifts that he had brought back from his last venture. To grease the way forward, Alia handed the greedy woman a bag full of gold coins as a personal gift to use as she liked. The woman said she would see what she could do at once. In the meantime, she invited Captain Morgan and Alia to enjoy the pleasures of her house.

When the woman returned, she said that the sheik would entertain Captain Morgan the next day at noon in the space before his palace. There all his people would be assembled for the meeting. Captain Morgan thanked the woman for arranging things, and he rushed Alia down to the whaleboat to return to his ship to prepare. He had the coxswain swing by my ship and asked me to join him in his cabin on the Sweet Cutlass for an urgent meeting. I was perplexed by this hasty meeting, but I went as the Captain requested. He had already broken out a bottle of rum before I arrived, and he handed me one of the same. He was not in a good mood, but as we spoke his mood changed and before the end of the meeting he was ebullient because we had evolved a plan.

At the outset of our meeting Captain Morgan put our situation succinctly. He said that the sheik was planning to receive the gifts he had brought and immediately to have him executed in public to demonstrate his power to his people and to regain face with his female consort, who had called him a fool for making a bad bargain with foreign pirates. He said our time doing security for this sheik had come to an end, and he asked how we might arrange a swift and honorable departure without losing our heads in the process. I thought over the case as the Captain put it, and I had a few ideas for his consideration.

First, I said, the sheik had a lot of gold in his storehouse that needed liberation. This perked Captain Morgan up considerably. Second, I said, while the sheik had no further need of our services, we certainly had no further need to be his servants. We had found another source of revenue that was less boring and more lucrative because we did not need to share it with a little potentate. The Captain brightened and took a swig of rum. Third, I said, we had enough time to arrange for the appropriate gift for the sheik to receive before his assembled people. We only needed to borrow the sheik's own personal slave to help us convey the gift to his Highness's presence.

At this, the Captain slapped the table and was about to rise to do a dance when I rapidly conjured a plan and asked him to tell me what flaws he could determine in it. The Captain liked everything he heard, and he agreed to proceed ashore immediately with Alia to do what I asked.

That afternoon the female consort returned from the sheik's palace with the sheik's enormous personal slave, a man well over two meters tall with musculature like a man in the circus. We saw the slave to a private room in the house of pleasure and gave him rum that we commanded him to drink while he waited for our return.

That evening my hearties were busy all over the sheikdom. In the house of pleasure they beheaded, gutted and trussed the female consort of the sheik and placed the woman's head in a sack and her body in an empty tun, which they filled with rum and sealed with wax. The tun was attached to a cart that was drawn by one of the sheik's racing dromedaries outside the house of pleasure.

Along the shore, my hearties stove in the bottoms of all the sheik's dhows so that they could never be sailed again or easily repaired. At the storehouse, they overcame and killed all the sheik's armed guards, beheaded them and impaled their dead bodies on long spears fashioned in the manner of Tamerlane so that they stood on tiptoe with their heads lying beneath them all around the now-empty storehouse. The storehouse was empty because the huge hoard of gold that had formerly been inside it had been extracted and was now being stowed on board our two pirate vessels in the anchorage.

Finally at dawn just before we left the sheikdom in our whaleboats never to return, Captain Morgan summoned the slave from the room in the house of pleasure where he had been drinking. He commanded the slave to carry a large, heavy sack in one hand and to lead the dromedary camel by a tether in his other hand to the open area in front of the sheik's palace. When he arrived there, the slave was to call forth his master in the loudest possible voice and to continue to call him forth until he came. Then the slave was to present the sack and the tether to his master and to say, "Compliments of Captain Morgan!" I rehearsed the slave so that he had the words down pat before he strode confidently forward to do as he had been ordered to do.

Captain Morgan and I then scoured the house of pleasure for all the rum that we could find and took them with us in our separate whaleboats to our ships. We laughed all the way out to the anchorage, and I thought I heard Captain Morgan's voice singing pirate songs while his hearties heaved ho and hauled up his anchor.

We had a good morning breeze to take us where we intended to go without much tacking. Soon we were sailing like innocent twin ships on a merchant adventure to the north in the Persian Gulf. Looking landwards with my spyglass I saw the tall slave with the camel and sack standing in the square in front of the sheik's palace. I plainly heard the slave's voice mimicking the words I had taught him. He bellowed again and again, "Compliments of Captain Morgan!" I then turned my spyglass to the Sweet Cutlass where Benjamin was looking through Captain Morgan's spyglass at the figure of the slave in front of his master's palace. He lowered the glass and began to laugh. The parrot on his shoulder spread its wings and ruffled its feathers. It seemed to be laughing with him.

It was time to set the underway watch, so I called the order to the First Mate who relayed the order to the crew. The watch rotation went like clockwork, and soon we were sailing through the greenish, clear water as the sun rose higher in the eastern sky. Fishing boats maneuvered to avoid the Night Lightning and the Sweet Cutlass as we unfurled our sails and increased speed. I took station behind the Sweet Cutlass and ordered the helm to keep the ship in a line with the ship ahead. Then I relinquished the watch to the First Mate and went to my cabin.

My log entry for this last day in the sheikdom had promise to be a masterpiece of colorful prose, but all I wrote was, "Weighed anchor at dawn and sailed north in the Persian Gulf following the course of the Sweet Cutlass." When I had completed my log entry and read it over, I wondered about how little a Captain's log told about a pirate's true adventures.

A poetic pirate like Captain Morgan, who loved verses and songs, might have given his log entry a certain flourish. The next time we enjoyed rum together I decided to ask him what he wrote in his log this day so that I could compare that with my own record. For now I just looked forward to getting back to our marauding in these target-rich waters where dreams of Araby met the harsh realities of life in Muslim-dominated waters.

E.W. Farnsworth

☠☠☠☠

Pirates of the Andaman's

On both of our pirate ships the hearties sprawled on the weather decks in almost no clothing, sporting their battle scars and basking in the relentless sunshine while we sailed towards the fabled Andaman Islands east of India and north of the Strait of Malacca. The prevailing winds and currents were in our favor, and that meant we were swiftly putting India's Bay of Bengal behind us. After our midnight raid on the gold bazaar high on the West Indian coast inland from the tiny smugglers' port, we thought we would probably not be welcome on those shores again. That was just as well, I thought, because pirates like us belong at sea.

Captain Morgan hatched the plan to steal the Indian gold, and as usual I executed his plan to perfection—with luck and the help of those of our hearties who formerly had been slaves. We had only just finished our circumnavigation just off the Persian Gulf littoral during which circuit we captured, looted and sank three dozen prize vessels. We had then sailed down into the Arabian Sea through the wide bend of the Strait of Hormuz.

We had been careful before we made the strait to steer clear of the sheikdom where we had left the sheik with the comely head and body of his concubine as a grisly farewell present. Once we were well south of that bit of trouble and out of the Gulf, Captain Morgan called for a gam on the becalmed water to discuss how we might steal the mountain of gold that lay near a now-familiar small smugglers' port in India.

We plotted in our tethered whaleboats drinking from bottles of un-watered rum. We were visible to both crews as we sat between Captain Morgan's ship the Sweet Cutlass and my ship, the Night Lightning. As was his habit, the Captain sang the pirates' song, "Fifteen Men on a Dead Man's Chest," and talked about the gold and then sang again about a beautiful woman with a strange disease, "The Lady Should Have Told Me but She's Dead." The more the Captain talked, the better his idea of getting the gold settled in my mind though I did not like making a steady business of doing piracy on land.

In the event, I need not have worried as much as I did about our being attacked by troops during our approach to the bazaar's gold repository or during our taking of the treasure while we were there.

I should, however, have worried about the ever-present brigands who appeared out of the forest on our way back to the port and tried to relieve us of our hard-won treasure of gold. They made a lot of noise, but we discovered that brigands know nothing of fighting with cutlasses and knives as we pirates do. We cut the brigands all to pieces and then debated rifling their new hideout, but we did not know their hideout's precise location in the dense forest and we were already loaded down with gold and running late, so we returned to our waiting whaleboats arriving an hour before dawn and returned with the treasure to our two waiting ships. As for the scope of our pelf, it was beyond our wildest expectations. As our ships sailed south in tandem while hugging the Indian shore, we Captains counted the mounds of yellow coins and bars in our cabins.

Later we found a secret place to bury part of our treasure ashore in the pirate way near the tip of the continent. When our gold, pearls and jewels were securely underground with a fresh female corpse to guard them until we returned to exhume them, we turned our ships to a northerly heading, always remaining in sight of land while looking for prize ships offering booty on the bounding main.

I thought that the Captain would not miss his woman Alia because she had betrayed him with Benjamin. The Captain had cut off her head in a drunken rage when he found the two naked with her moaning in ecstasy under the enormous black man. He did not threaten Benjamin for having had his way with the fickle woman, but he snatched Benjamin's beloved talking parrot from his shoulder, wrung its neck and plucked its colorful feathers.

To show his displeasure, the Captain ordered Benjamin to roast the dressed bird for his supper. The next day when we left the ship to bury our treasure, the Captain ordered Benjamin to carry Alia's head and body inland to be interred with the treasure. In the hole where the treasure lay when Benjamin laid Alia's body atop the chest and put her severed head next to her headless neck, I thought the Captain would kill him on the spot. Instead, the Captain brought out a bag of colorful parrot feathers and scattered the feathers over the woman's cold, naked corpse and head. He laughed, drank rum and sang bawdy sailor songs—"She Surprised the Sailor with Her Charms" and "Bawdy Wench a Long Time Seeking"—while Benjamin filled in the hole and tamped it down. The former slave then carefully smoothed over the surface and covered it with cut foliage so that the place would not be found.

Captain Morgan told me he had sailed in the Andaman's as a young sailor, and I believed him because he had experience of the whole world. He was impressed back then with the simple, happy lives that the Andaman islanders led. He said the young men traditionally set out on the sea to find adventure and possibly wives because there were so few eligible women among them. They were not congenital pirates like the Malays, so they had no earthly ambitions. Captain Morgan called them "the lotus eaters" because they were as innocent as if they had been born in Eden and desired no possessions on account of their nomadic lives on the sea where possessions would be a hindrance to their movements. Those nautical young men and boys, the Captain said, made excellent replacements for pirate hearties that had been lost in battle.

So Captain Morgan planned for us to shanghai a dozen or so strong, young men each to fill out our crews that had been thinned by our constant fighting. He had seen this done to good effect on the ship he had sailed when he was here last. He said that kidnapped Andaman islanders had adapted readily to the seagoing life, and they apparently never regretted sailing far from their home islands. They had no loyalty to any place or person, so they were natural pirates if only they could discover the right leadership.

When we reached the north islands, for a month we sailed around looking for men and boys we could lure onto our ships to augment our crews. For the promise of food or rum, or both, they flocked to ship aboard, and we had the fittest of those to choose from. We each selected twelve young men, and as we continued to scour the islands, we substituted a better new recruit for a worse among the former selectees. This did not faze our kidnapped males because they saw that merit was rewarded on pirate ships and that pirates ate well—far better than those who chose to make their home in the islands. The mates were in charge of the training of these new pirates, and individual hearties were identified as mentors to show the boys the ropes.

Before six weeks were over, our new watch standers were being schooled to watch the horizon for ships, to furl and unfurl sails and to do the thousand odd tasks that a pirate had to perform on the average day or night watch at sea. They each received a knife to use as a weapon, and we taught them to throw the knives and to use them in close combat. They lived with their new weapons and kept the knives razor sharp. A few we taught to use cutlasses and swords also. Before long these men were going to need skills; without skills, the new men as pirates would surely die.

As we moved through the halcyon waters around the Andaman's, we saw divers pulling seafood, sponges and coral from the depths of the sea. They brought these treasures to us as gifts. Some bays were sandy, others were rocky, and some were so crowded with tangled green vegetation there was no way to penetrate to the island's interior without hacking through with our cutlasses all day long. Weather in the islands was mostly sunny, but rains came too in sudden storms that filled our empty water barrels with fresh water.

Our new sailors liked to be out on the weather decks in rain and shine. They were sure-footed as they climbed the ropes and rigging and ran up and down the ladders extending from below decks to the weather decks. They quickly learned to drink rum and sing our pirate songs.

Their needs were few, and they never complained of bad treatment when the hearties lost their tempers. One newbie named Hamad, who was raised as a devout Muslim, seemed to command respect among all his fellows, and he was a quick study. So I ordered my First Mate to groom this lad as the future leader of the islanders for both ships. Hamad was a natural leader and excellent interpreter for his people, and he made friends with Benjamin, who as the natural leader of the former slaves was his counterpart.

No matter what else pirates do in their times between maritime battles, they prepare for what they must do in the dangerous trade of piracy. They practice throwing grapples, swinging through the rigging, sword fighting and knife fighting. These exercises are not games, but by encouraging the hearties to compete, I discovered that they could excel above their expectations.

So I encouraged completion among the Andaman islanders and among the former slaves as I did among the hearties. Once a week for a bottle of rum I would have the crew throw knives and swords at targets, climb the rigging to the crow's nest, run from the weather decks down the hatches to the keel and back again, dive into the sea and swim around the ship three times without being eaten by ever-present sharks. The winner of each event received a long pull at a bottle of rum. The crew would vote the best overall performer, and he would claim a whole bottle of rum as his reward. Captain Morgan did the same among his crew, and once a month we practiced our skills by conducting boarding exercises from one ship to the other. Captain Morgan also liked to swap the crews so that half of his came to my ship for a week while at the same time half of mine went aboard his. We did this to give our hearties a sense of comradeship across both ships.

We used our time in the north Andamans to bring our crews together and to overcome the petty differences that sometimes arose when the pressures of sailing soared while at the same time the experience levels vastly differed among the crew members. The old hands were used to the changes wrought by bringing new crew aboard, but the former slaves were frustrated if the islanders did not respond perfectly the first time when ordered to do a task and every time thereafter.

I kept reminding the mates and the hearties that not long from now we would be up against bloodthirsty opponents like the Malay pirates who knew nothing about mercy. My hounding sounded extreme to the crew until we had our first introduction to the fierce south islanders.

The north islanders knew the south islanders as a different race. Where in the north everything was assumed to be shared by everyone, in the south the islanders fought for what they individually owned and captured whatever they could from others. I frankly liked the fighting spirit of the southerners, and I was bewildered by the insouciance of the northerners about treasure.

When we were anchored off the southern islands, the inhabitants would swim out to our ships and climb aboard any way they could. They would steal things and leap into the sea. So I offered a bounty to my crew for stopping the marauders, dead or alive. Hamad took this to mean that the southerners should be killed rather than captured. So the north islanders of my crew began to repulse the south island boarders, and often when a south islander managed to get aboard and steal something, he met with swift justice in the form of a thrown knife in the back or a throat slit ear to ear.

When Hamad brought me a living south islander who had been trussed, I asked him what he thought should be done with the captive. Hamad did not answer in words but drew his razor-sharp knife and slashed his captive's throat. He then threw the body off the Night Lightning into the water while his fellow north islanders applauded him. From that day I was sure that the new recruits could do what was necessary for successful piracy.

As we sailed from island to island in the south of the Andamans, we became aware of the large number and great variety of creatures that populated the land and waters of the region. We also noticed that in the north islands the people lived a Spartan life with modest dwellings and few possessions. In contrast in the south islands the people lived a sybaritic life with large, permanent dwellings and many possessions. Where in the north a few shells or native fruits were bartered, in the south the natives looked for gold and silver coins in all our exchanges. In the north, we never feared that the islanders were a threat to us, but in the south we saw good reason to be afraid of the denizens' perfidy.

One apparently mild-mannered south islander grabbed one of the north islanders and drew his knife blade over the man's neck. He had seemed to be friendly right up until he committed his hostile act. Just after his crime Hamad's knife found the man's back, and the man died in agony, but Hamad was inconsolable about the loss of one of his people. He told me that he would henceforth kill any south islander who came aboard my ship. He said this with such conviction that I knew he had been changed since his departure from his island—for the better from the pirate's point of view.

Our first taste of Malay pirate blood occurred while we were still in the south Andaman's. A pirate ship crowded with Malay pirates aspiring to loot the Night Lightning came head-to-head to ram us and board. As they maneuvered to come alongside, three score grappling hooks came flying through the air, and right afterward the pirates swung like a myriad of monkeys towards our decks. The mates had readied the hearties for just this form of attack, and they moved to the sides with cutlasses and knives slashing every which way.

This show of resolve was new to the Malay pirates, yet they pressed their attack anyway with increasing vigor and savagery. I ordered my boarders to swing onto the Malay ship and fight their way below decks to scuttle the enemy ship. Meanwhile, I ordered my mates to be alert for the Malays to do precisely the same thing when they swung aboard the Night Lightning.

In the melee I saw two of the new sailors and one of the former slaves cut down by the swarms of Malay pirates, and over the din of the shouting and fighting I heard the loud report of a cannon followed by the hollow sound of a tremendous explosion. I guessed correctly that my boarding party had reached the pirate ship's magazine and fired cannon filled with shot directly at the pirate's powder room as they had been instructed and drilled to do. Immediately afterward the Malay pirate ship began to list to starboard from taking on water below decks.

My hearties pressed against the Malays forcing them either to return to their sinking ship at once or to die and be cast off the decks of the Night Lightning. Hamad and the remaining islanders ran amok at the Malays who were still on board our ship. They slashed in frenzy on all sides, and the Malays could not make a stand. To avoid being hacked to bits, the Malay pirates swung back on board their ship and feverishly began to cut all lines that led to our ship.

As a result, the Night Lightning broke free and came about while putting distance between itself and the rival ship. Four of my hearties kept slashing at the pirates on the Malay ship, but they saw the way the battle was going, so they jumped into the shark-filled water and swam as fast as possible towards the Night Lightning where their mates had dropped lines over the sides so the swimmers could be hauled up onto our deck. Only one of the four swimmers was actually taken by a shark, and he died screaming. The other three swimmers made it to the lines and pulled themselves out of the water while my hearties on deck raised the lines to bring their comrades up to the deck's level and safety.

The Malay pirate ship that had attacked us did not sink all at once. It slowly rolled onto its side and continued to take on water yet stayed afloat a while. The remnants of the pirate force aboard her saw the feeding frenzy of the sharks in the water, and they knew that soon they would become the fishes' dinner. Some jumped into the water holding onto planks and other flotsam from their vessel, but their legs and arms were easy targets for the massive sharks that snapped at anything that moved or hung down into the water.

I offered no quarter to that vicious Malay pirate crew. In fact, I mused that if they had remained aboard my ship and we had taken them captive, they would now be walking a plank and falling into the same fish feed that they were soon going to experience. When the Malay pirate ship finally did sink, all the remaining pirates thrashed in the water until one by one they were taken under the surface by hungry predators. Finally the sea was entirely clear of all bodies and body parts. Everything indicating that a raging battle had taken place was reduced to a stream of bubbles that rose to the surface from the submerged and slowly sinking pirate vessel.

I asked the mates to muster the crew before the mast and report. We had lost six men including two islanders, one former slave and the hearty who had been eaten by the shark. Three hearties had also been wounded, one so seriously that I gave him the coup de grace myself and ordered my hearties to add his body to the watery feast with the mantra, "More for the rest of us." I saw that the other two wounded had their flesh wounds bound with cloth tourniquets. I ordered a rum ration for all hands for a job well done. The crew had gained good experience fighting the Malay pirates together, but ours was a costly lesson. I vowed that we would suffer fewer casualties the next time around.

While my ship, the Night Lightning, fought one Malay pirate ship, Captain Morgan's ship, the Sweet Cutlass, fought another just like it. They also slew all the pirates but instead of sinking the vessel, they towed it while the Captain's crew raised the ship's treasure and valuables from its hold. The Sweet Cutlass had lost seven men as the Night Lightning had done, and four of those had been among our former slaves. When we held our gam to assess the damage and decide what to do next, Captain Morgan said that we should ship aboard replacements to bring our crews to complement before we headed south through the Strait of Malacca to confront the rest of the Malay pirates on the sea lane and in their lairs along the Malay coast. Since we had a third ship now, the Captain suggested that we use it as both a training vessel in the short term and a lure in the long term.

So we sailed north and visited the Andaman Islands, to the east instead of the west this time. Hamad was our recruiter because he spoke the islands' citizen's languages and could tell personal tales of his recent acts of bravado and daring while fighting against the ruthless Malay pirates. With his credibility among his people, we had no trouble adding fifty young men to our stable in one week.

Captain Morgan wanted not fifty, but one hundred prime recruits and he wanted to cull out the weak and unfit early. He told me that we should bring aboard at least two hundred men and by testing and training work the number down to one hundred. So we sailed from island to island for three months growing our pool of north islanders as recruits and swapping out the better from the worse. We kept the recruits aboard the Malay pirate ship rather than the Sweet Cutlass and the Night Lightning. Our third mates were put in charge of training, and the two alternated as Captain of the training vessel, which we renamed the Black Lagoon. That gave them experience of command at sea that they could not have obtained in any other way. It also created a third entity in our cabal, but we did not foresee the trouble that portended at the time.

Our three ships made a handsome sight when with full sail they raced and maneuvered around the Andaman Islands. Each day we all practiced closing and boarding, swordsmanship and knife handling, swimming and grappling and seamanship. At one point we had two hundred fifty able bodied recruits, and through attrition they became one hundred twenty-five and then one hundred. Only three men were killed during our training exercises. Carelessness and incompetence were the causes of two deaths, and an argument of one recruit with Hamad caused the other. Hamad made his leadership over his people clear by slitting the throat of the would-be competitor before a direct challenge to his authority could be raised. After that incident no one else ever tried to challenge Hamad's authority.

Captain Morgan placed his own first mate in charge of the Black Lagoon when it was time to move south towards the Strait of Malacca. Fifty of the best, hand-picked recruits were integrated as two equal groups into the crews of the Sweet Cutlass and the Night Lightning. Captain Morgan stationed Benjamin on the Black Lagoon to serve as a kind of second in command and master at arms. As I look back on this choice, I discerned the Captain's malice aforethought. What better way to achieve his revenge on Benjamin for sleeping with Alia than to send him on an impossible mission against bloodthirsty Malay pirates with a green crew?

The mission of the Black Lagoon was to serve as a lure for pirates in the Strait. They were to fly the French flag, unfurl maximum sail and speed well ahead of our other two ships with her crew sunning themselves on the weather decks and appearing to have no real defenses against predators. When the Malay pirates tried to board her, the crew would bring their weapons from hiding and return the favor of the pirates by taking the attacking ship captive. Captain Morgan and I decided we would lend a hand if necessary but otherwise we would let the chips fall where they may.

We thought it was a good plan at the time. What we had envisioned was one attacking pirate ship, but when the Malay pirates attacked with three ships it was clear that all our forces had to mass to repel them. Two of the pirate vessels boarded the Black Lagoon to port and starboard simultaneously while the third rammed her astern and boarded her from there. The four ships were in minutes bound by lines with grappling hooks so that all four decks featured a melee of killing with men swinging from ship to ship.

Captain Morgan and I struck our false French colors and raised the Jolly Roger. We came outboard of the knot of four ships on either side and fired our cannon at close range to disable the mainmasts of all three pirate vessels and do as much damage to the structure of those ships at and below the waterline. We boarded from port and starboard with grappling hooks and lines fusing our ships with the others.

Now the Malay pirates fought us at the center on the Black Lagoon where the casualties were many and across the decks of all the other ships. Since the Malays could not escape, they fought desperately, for they were without hope. We saw the meaning of the word amok for the enemy fought in desperation, wildly and without discrimination.

I sent my second mate with a small party to scuttle the pirate ship next to the Night Lightning and simultaneously sent my third mate with another small party to scuttle the pirate ship that lay astern of the Black Lagoon. Captain Morgan, seeing that the crew of the Black Lagoon was beleaguered and had been decimated by the fighting, sent most of his hearties into the thick of the fight keeping only a few on board to defend the Sweet Cutlass.

I saw an opportunity to join the fray to kill the three pirate Captains and seized it. I brandished my cutlass, grabbed a stray line and swung aboard the adjacent ship in the area of the helm, where I beheaded the Malay Captain. I then hewed left and right through the enemy until I saw a way to jump aboard the stern of the Black Lagoon and then immediately jump to the focsle of the pirate ship at her stern. I had a long way to cut and slash through Malay pirates to reach the helm area, and I picked up a pirate's cutlass with my free hand so I could slash with two weapons at once as I proceeded.

At my side suddenly was Benjamin with two cutlasses in his hands. So like a two-man killing machine we lopped hands and heads all the way to the helm. There I let Benjamin have the honor of beheading the enemy Captain and slaying those who tried to defend him.

Meanwhile, I made my way back to the Black Lagoon and swung over to the pirate ship that lay next to the Sweet Cutlass. Thereby at the helm I saw the Malay Captain shouting orders vainly to his dwindling crew. He did not see me come alongside him until it was much too late for him to react successfully, and as he raised his sword to strike me, I hewed his neck and his legs simultaneously so his head, his torso, and his legs fell separately onto his deck with his useless sword all at the same time.

Now that the Malay pirates were without leadership on any of their ships, it was time for me to fight my way back to the Night Lightning. Two of the pirate ships were listing in the water because my hearties had scuttled them. When I reached my flying bridge, I yelled out for my hearties to cut all lines between the pirate ships and ours. I saw that my hearties had brought treasure out of the holds of the pirate ships they had scuttled. They were transferring the treasure to the Night Lightning before they shipped back aboard themselves. I understood and allowed the transfer but urged haste.

The denouement was balletic, I thought, as my hearties grabbed lines like dancers to swing back aboard and simultaneously cut all ties with the sinking pirate vessels. The remaining pirates had swung back to their sinking ships learning only too late of their mistake. The

Night Lightning drifted out to port from the two sinking pirate ships while the Black Lagoon drifted to starboard. Because of the blood in the water, a great many giant, hungry sharks had begun to gather for a feast, and the still-living Malay pirates learned to their horror that they would soon be food for those sharks.

 I saw that on the other side of the Black Lagoon, the Sweet Cutlass was pulling off to starboard while the pirate ship to its port was listing badly and starting to sink. The hearties of the Black Lagoon were working frantically to cut all lines binding the sinking pirate ship to its starboard. Finally, she broke free from all the pirate ships sinking to her port, starboard, and stern. The hearties aboard all three of our ships then scoured the decks for the bodies and limbs of dead Malay pirates and our own crews. As they cleared the decks and threw the human remains overboard, the fins of feeding sharks swirled in the blue and the water seemed to boil with feeding activity. The pirates on the sinking ships joined the feeding frenzy as food when their ships sank beneath them. Those who attempted in desperation to swim to one of our ships were torn apart by ravenous jaws and dragged down to the depths.

☠☠☠☠

 In a gam in the aftermath of the pirate raid, Captain Morgan and I reviewed the status of our crews. In our whaleboats, we enjoyed some of the liquor that we had seized from the pirates. The Night Lightning had lost five hearties and the Sweet Cutlass had lost four. Of the crew of the Black Lagoon twenty had been lost. All had gone to Davy Jones along with all hundred-odd Malay pirates. Treasure seized from the three pirate vessels included; gold and silver coins and bars, jewels, pearls, rich corals, ivory tusks, spices, bottles of wine, and casks of liquor.

The Captain opined that it had been a good day's work, but with far too many casualties. He said that we should try the same gambit tomorrow and hope that the Malay pirates came in a single ship only.

I told him that Benjamin had done valiant service this day, but the Captain only scowled in response and did not want to hear the details of Benjamin's service. We had lost none of our mates, he said, so we would not have to shift any of the crew. As for losing the north islanders, they were green and the survivors were now battle hardened. The lessons would make the survivors twice the men they were before the fight for their lives.

At first light the next day, the Black Lagoon sailed well in advance of our other two pirate ships, and it sported the French flag as before. A single Malay pirate vessel sped to intercept and board to starboard. The pirates were surprised that the apparently docile French ship turned out to be full of battle hardened pirates who cut down all those who tried to board her. The Black Lagoon quickly reversed roles with the pirate ship, and after killing the enemy pirates took her time to rifle the stores of the pirate ship before scuttling her. After the pirate ship went down to Davy Jones, Captain Morgan and I sailed close enough to ask whether the Black Lagoon needed any assistance. Benjamin waved us off with his broad ivory smile and held aloft by its hair the severed head of the Malay pirate Captain.

The Black Lagoon then proceeded to unfurl its sails while the other two ships luffed sail to lend some distance between the vessels. In the mid-afternoon, a second Malay pirate ship intercepted the Black Lagoon and tried to board her, but it met with the same success as the prior pirate ship.

This time, some of the Malay pirates threw down their weapons and surrendered, but they were not held captive long before one by one they walked the plank into the shark-infested waters. When all her treasure and valuables had been transferred to the Black Lagoon, the pirate ship was scuttled and sank to Davy Jones.

Throughout that day, the Black Lagoon only lost five of her crew, three during the first attack and two during the second. She celebrated her victories late into the night with rum for all hands because tomorrow promised to be a very busy day. The pirate coast was drawing nigh, and Captain Morgan's plan was to hug close to shore so that the Malay pirates would come out of their bays and attack in large numbers. Each ship was to be its own lure, surprise its attackers, seize the pirates' treasure and scuttle their ships.

The ruse worked like a charm. By evening, each ship had attracted three Malay pirate marauders. In the end all the enemy pirates had been killed, their treasure seized and their ships sunk. Two of the crew of the Black Lagoon had perished, but none had died on the Night Lightning or the Sweet Cutlass.

At our evening gam, I joked with Captain Morgan that we were doing the good work that the great powers should have undertaken to rid the sea of Malay pirates. The Captain responded by having a long pull of rum and singing some of his bawdy pirate songs including two of his all-time favorites, "The Wench Wore the Pirate's Pantaloons" and "His Behind Arrears Before the Mast." I could tell the man was bored sick because the action in the Strait of Malacca so far had been unchallenging. He told me that he intended to pull out into the main and go after merchants instead of preying on the Malay pirates any longer. He said he needed for the Night Lightning to provide over watch for him in case a warship tried to interrupt the fun.

I suggested that the Black Lagoon accompany us since it would otherwise be naked to attack by Malay pirates in great numbers.

In retrospect, it was prescient of the Captain to want me to watch his back because he spied three rich Dutch merchants sailing in company and needed all three of our ships to pillage them. So each ship intercepted one of the Dutchmen and their sailing in company did no good for their security because none was a warship. We pirates had easy pickings. Each of our ships drew alongside her target and grappled aboard. All Dutch treasure, valuables, food, liquor and water were transferred to our ships before their ships' Captains were beheaded and their ship's crews were forced to walk the plank. We sank the three vessels rather than leaving them adrift in the Strait; with the three ships safe with Davy Jones, there would be no evidence of our piracy.

As evening fell, my lookout shouted that a warship was on the horizon, so we steered for shore and our fellow pirate ships followed us to an anchorage for the night.

Patrols of warships are mysterious to us pirates. I would prefer not to combat them because of their superior armor and firepower. They have a few things of great value, like small arms, gunpowder, shot, cannon, victuals, potable water and sometimes rum, but the sacrifice of crew for that kind of plunder is often not worth the bother. Running before the wind in flight is preferable to picking a fight with a warship, and only when you absolutely have to fight do you look for the best angle of attack and tactics that will mask your intent.

The next morning we observed that the warship we had remarked the night before was keeping station offshore from the location where we had chosen to anchor for the night. The warship's intention was clearly to board and inspect as many ships as it could while seeking pirates and treasure.

I did not like waiting for warships to come to me, so I set sail early with full sails and the French flag flying. I was trying to make it appear that mine was a pirate vessel trying to escape the one-ship blockade. The warship noted my tactic and set out to intercept. It fired cannon over the bow of the Night Lightning, so I luffed sail and waited for the ship to approach. My crew was all on the weather decks trying to look innocent while concealing their weapons, all except for my gunnery hearties.

As the warship drew alongside and prepared to board, my cannon took out their main brace and the shot leveled the troops on the enemy's decks. Then my hearties uncovered their grapples with lines and hurled them so as to capture the warship. Over side swung my hearties as our cannon balls broke through the warship's hull and found the magazine with a dull explosion. The marines aboard the warship had been surprised by a hardened force like ours, but they were nonetheless formidable enemies because of their courage. Our desperation and innovation won over their heroism and drills.

My hearties slashed and stabbed their way across the warship's decks to her flying bridge where they slew the Captain and bound the helm with line. Then they made their way below decks to haul up plunder while their comrades tidied up by killing all forces from the crow's nest to the keel. My hearties set up a high line for conveying the arms and pelf, and the transfer began in earnest when rum was discovered below.

I went aboard the warship for a time to see what was in the recently deceased Captain's cabin. I returned to the Night Lightning with papers that held much needed intelligence for me and gold that the Captain had hidden in a compartment that I had no trouble finding because I had one just like it in my own cabin. I also shipped aboard my ship the warship's deceased Captain's private collection of fine vintage wines.

When I take a warship, I want no loose ends. I saw the last marines walk the plank and all that was left of the munitions, swords, knives, pistols, powder and shot transferred to my ship. I then had my hearties fire the warship's own cannon so that her bottom would be breached. All my crew returned to my ship before the warship keeled over and sank beneath the waves. I kept as a trophy the brass plate with the name of the warship that I took from the Captain's cabin, but that was the only remnant of that once proud warship after she went with her Captain and crew to see Davy Jones. The papers that I found in the deceased Captain's cabin described a strategy for using many such warships as we had just sunk. They were supposed to be spaced all along the Malay coast to roust out the pirates in an operation that was meant to end the Malay piracies once and for all. This was bad news for pirates of all origins including mine, and I had to get this vital intelligence to Captain Morgan as soon as possible.

When I returned to the anchorage that I had left earlier that day, I discovered only one ship at anchor, the Sweet Cutlass. I anchored nearby and called for a gam immediately. With Captain Morgan, I intended to discuss strategy for dealing with the situation of the warship blockade of the Malay coast.

The Captain told me that when I had set out to draw the warship away, the Black Lagoon had set out in the opposite direction to escape the blockade and go pirating on the main.

I told him that, under the circumstances, the Black Lagoon might now be in grave danger. The Captain seemed to be preoccupied with his rum and his pirate songs, and he looked out on the Strait with a distracted expression as I told him the dimensions of the warship blockade. When I had finished, the Captain said that we were likely to lose one or even two of our ships within the next two to three days. He advised me to drink and eat heartily and to give rum rations to my hearties because tomorrow we might all die.

I told the Captain what else I had found on the warship I had sunk, and he nodded as if he did not think that mattered much in the long view. Then we returned to our respective ships. After brooding in my cabin for a time, I decided that I did not want to chance fate by just waiting for it to knock on my door, so I weighed anchor and sailed out into the Strait to see what had become of the Black Lagoon.

In fact, I discovered that the Black Lagoon had experienced a very good day of piracy and plunder. She had taken a French merchantman and transferred everything of value to its hold before scuttling the vessel and sending it to Davy Jones.

I had a gam with the now-Captain, who was of a mind to go on his own now that he had achieved a number of successes. I told him about the warship blockade, but he scoffed at the idea of that being a hindrance to his good piracy. When I asked him whether Benjamin was of a similar opinion, the man gave me a fierce look but he agreed to let me speak with Benjamin for a few minutes. I therefore ordered my coxswain to steer for the Black Lagoon, and when we came alongside the Black Lagoon, I called Benjamin down into the whaleboat and explained the situation to him.

"Benjamin, warships are covering the entire Malay coast. They mean to root out pirates, and that will include us if we remain in this vicinity. Your Captain wants to break away from Captain Morgan and me and go pirate all on his own. That may or may not be a good idea, but it is certainly a dangerous idea at this time. We might be stronger if we stayed together than if we go alone. I know how you and Captain Morgan feel about each other after Alia's death, but I beseech you to come with me and let the Black Lagoon find its own path."

"Captain Abe, you've always told me the truth, and I appreciate it. Captain Morgan and I will never be friends after what I did with Alia. I won't drive wedges between you and him, and I have allegiance to the Black Lagoon now, so I have to return to my Captain and crew. I'll see you when we meet Davy Jones together."

That was the last I saw of Benjamin, an honorable pirate to the end. After we had conferred, I ordered my coxswain to return our whaleboat to the Night Lightning.

Once on board I immediately set sail for the shoreline where I wanted to talk more strategy with Captain Morgan now that I had learned that the Black Lagoon had decided to strike out on its own. That evening in a gam by torchlight, the Captain raged and fumed, but he knew that nothing could be done now to remedy the situation with the Black Lagoon. In a very black humor, the Captain drank rum and sang dark pirate songs of death, ghosts, loss and loneliness, like "The Pirate's Ghost Danced for Davy Jones."

The Captain told me that in his opinion the only option available to us was immediate clandestine flight to the South China Sea. He said he was setting sail that very night, and he advised that I should follow him. We agreed to use Dutch flags as our cover, and by dawn we were pretending to be two Dutch merchants sailing in company in the middle of the Strait, both heading slowly on the usual commercial passage to the South China Sea.

As it happened our course intersected that of the Black Lagoon, which was being boarded by marines from a warship that had found her suspicious. A second warship stood off covering the first making rescue not only risky but also nearly impossible. We had the option to try to save the Black Lagoon, but we no longer owed the ship anything. We decided though as with a single mind to interpose.

The Sweet Cutlass headed straight to intercept the warship that was conducting overwatch. The Night Lightning headed to intercept the warship that was now boarding the Black Lagoon. We took the warships completely by surprise since they considered no opposition was likely or even possible. As we approached, we hauled down our false colors and raised the Jolly Roger. We saw that our approach heartened our comrades on the Black Lagoon because they began to fight fiercely and loosed their cannon in a series of volleys as the boarders fled from her decks to defend our oncoming vessels.

The Sweet Cutlass rammed the warship that was her target, and she came athwart ship and let forth a volley from her cannon that leveled the troops that stood on her decks and took down her main brace.

The Night Lightning turned hard right and brought all her cannon to bear on the warship that was tightly coupled with the Black Lagoon. Withering volley followed withering volley, and the above-decks personnel fell while the masts split and shattered with splinters flying all over her decks. Another volley of balls aimed at the waterline breached the warship so badly that she began to list in a direction away from the Black Lagoon, whose crew cut all lines for fear of being pulled to the bottom as she sank.

Captain Morgan was not going to let this exercise be profitless, so he closed on his target and boarded her, with grappling hooks and lines flying and his hearties flying even before she made fast to her prey. The slaughter began immediately, and it did not cease until all the marines aboard were dead and sloughed off board to become shark meat. When all men were dead on their prey vessel, the hearties quickly made off with all things of value from the warship's armory to the hold of the Sweet Cutlass. The Captain's first mate went to the cabin of the warship's Captain and came away with the gold the now deceased Captain had sequestered there. All the warship's stores were high lined to the Sweet Cutlass, and when this had been accomplished, Captain Morgan ordered the warship to be scuttled.

Meanwhile on the Night Lightning I saw that the warship had rigged the Black Lagoon to be breached by her own cannon and sunk. There was nothing I could do to prevent the outcome. A tremendous explosion rent the ship in twain, and she sank at once with all hands. This was an affront to us pirates that I could not countenance, so I ordered our cannon to fire unrelenting until no trace of the offending warship remained on the surface.

There was no sense searching for survivors of either vessel because the sharks feasted on all who hit the water from both the warship and the Black Lagoon. Thus I never saw the bodies of the Captain or of Benjamin. Unlike Captain Morgan, I did not have the sweet profit from the venture of destroying the warship that had sunk the Black Lagoon. I had only had the satisfaction of sweet revenge. My hearties told the mates that they were gratified that we had taken our revenge because they had comradeship with the members of the crew of our sister pirate ship.

When it was clear that the encounter with the warships had been resolved in our favor, the Sweet Cutlass and the Night Lightning hauled down the Jolly Rogers and hoisted false Dutch flags again. As if nothing extraordinary had happened beforehand, we then sailed forth into the South China Sea passing vessels sporting many different flags that were coursing both ways in the busy seaway that was the southern entry to and exit from the Strait of Malacca.

After we had sailed through the Strait, I followed Captain Morgan's lead as he steered a course along the eastern rim of land that marked the boundary of the Asian landmass. We began to see in these crowded waters, junks of all sizes that in hundreds pursued fish and small cargo vessels that carried freight from port to port along the coast and then to mysterious China, hermit-like Korea and martial Japan. We knew that the pirates of the Philippines were active farther north, but for now we had no competition in our piratical trade. Therefore we began to pick our targets carefully and continue to do what we had always done.

We found that Dutch merchants and English were the richest to be plundered, but the American ships were good targets also. So we came alongside and boarded almost four dozen vessels in the course of five weeks, and we took on gold and silver, jewels and pearls, silk fabrics and exotic minerals like jade and jadeite.

Until we reached the Philippines we brooked no opposition, and we pleasured ourselves by sending many vessels to see Davy Jones with all their crews. Sometimes we anchored off islands that were nothing more than seamounts, and sometimes we luffed sail to ride out typhoons and monsoon rains in the open sea. Once we saw the clouds turn golden by agency of a fine dust that blew out from China's vastness over the sea. We anchored off lands whose rivers emptied into the South and East China Seas, and there we let the hearties spend some time ashore buying women and trinkets while we took on water and provisions.

We had come a long way from the Persian Gulf, but we were still in sight of Asia. Captain Morgan and I considered what we should do in these waters, and we decided to plunder the ships that were heading to or returning from China, Korea and Japan. Our expectations were fairly certain. We thought that those merchant ships that were inbound would be carrying gold and silver mainly and that those that were outbound would be carrying the goods of East Asia. It turned out that the cargos were mixed.

The best we harvested were warships because they carried gold and rum. There was, of course, a limit to what we could do with warships because nations under threat could band together against a common threat. That is why our time in East Asia was limited. So before five months had passed, at a gam off northern Japan, Captain Morgan and I began to consider what we would do next. He had been in these waters long before, but not much had changed in the interim. He suggested that we should provision ourselves well and then follow the trade routes across the vast Pacific towards the Americas, taking prizes as we went, and then follow the coast to Tierra del Fuego and sail around Cape Horn. That sounded fine to me.

I frankly liked the exotic East, but I knew that the pirate spirit in me would win out against my healthy but unprofitable curiosity. Besides, I had found a beautiful and daring young girl named Xiaohong at a Chinese port we had visited. She had decided to join me in my cabin and explore the world with me. My cabin boy had long since grown into a man who needed to join the hearties to grow in the trade. So he was now on watch in the crow's nest, and gentle Xiaohong was in my bed. Captain Morgan liked her so much he wrote a pirate song about her, "Red Port and Red Lady a Pirate's Love Affair."

That was about the simplest summary of my trip to China, and the woman, the farthest thing from a curse upon my vessel, turned out to be worth her weight in gold.

☠☠☠☠☠

Pirates of Tierra del Fuego

The winds were very cold, and the sea state threatened all but the most stalwart of sailors and, of course, us pirates. Of all the passages in the world, Cape Horn was the most unforgiving, and it is impassable three to four months a year. Two great oceans, the Atlantic and Pacific, come together there like the clapping of giant, watery hands, and large ships have been known to capsize and sink straight to Davy Jones in less than five minutes with all hands lost. Even sailors lucky enough to be left on the gelid water's surface would die of the cold in ten or fifteen minutes, their only consolation being the comatose state they would reach after the first five minutes overboard. The shores of the land called Tierra del Fuego are littered with the flotsam and jetsam of centuries of shipwrecks, and in between raids on the main, I sent my hearties scavenging because you never knew what useful things might be found among the jumbled remains of those hundreds of lost ships.

We had been hunting for merchants in those treacherous waters, sometimes sailing to the Atlantic side to catch a ship as she tried to get her bearings after passing around the Horn, but mostly we worked the west side of the Cape where ships, having passed the most dangerous trials, would drop their guard and become easy pickings. We had sailed northwest out of the East China Sea when the Japanese warships made things difficult for pirates off their island shores. We finessed Korea because little of value went into or out of that hermit kingdom. Captain Morgan's grand plan was for us to sail around the great Pacific Ocean until we reached Cape Horn where we would never lack for prizes if we could stand the elements.

It was a good thing we had the company of my woman Xiaohong, who now shared my bed in the Captain's cabin, because she was the scion of a nautical Chinese merchant family and therefore knew how to dress for sailing in the frigid northernmost and southernmost climes. She warned us to sail first to the northern strait between the two great continents of Asia and America where she advised us to gather the warm skins and garments that we would use whenever we reached Cape Horn.

So we had sailed into the land of ice, sish, slush and snow, and we traded with the Eskimos for huge mounds of their skins and hides. With those raw materials Xiaohong fashioned me, her and each of my hearties on the Night Lightning a warm suit of clothes that made Captain Morgan's crew jealous. Xiaohong then made cold weather garments for the Captain and all the other pirates of the Sweet Cutlass as well.

We wore those garments as long as we sailed in the Arctic waters, and when we boarded merchantmen who dared to sail those waters, we looked like Eskimos with our cutlasses and grappling hooks. Our captives were freezing and their teeth were chattering. Their vessels hung with ice. They put up no resistance, and only when they walked the plank into the green, icy waters did they realize the meaning of surrender.

Our time in the Arctic was excellent training, and we learned how to deal with chilblains and frostbite. Captain Morgan liked to shake out his long icy hair and his icy mustache and beard, and he would laugh for the fun of the experience and drink his rum. He took aboard his ship an Eskimo woman who had lost her husband on a walrus hunt.

Eida was her name, and she knew how to make meals from the fatty creatures of the region. She and Xiaohong became famous friends, and they shared Xiaohong's clothing when we sailed through milder climes as we headed south along the western coast of the Americas. When they worked side by side, I could tell the women apart, but at a distance and wearing the same clothing, they appeared to be identical twins. They both worked constantly to make us Captain's happy, and they were cheerful and sometimes playful with the hearties, who always treated them with respect.

Before we headed south, in addition to fresh water, we took aboard barrels of whale meat, walrus meat and ivory, tuns of rendered whale oil, slabs of dried fish, skins of Arctic foxes and hares, three huge chests of old, blue Russian trading beads and twelve kayaks with oars—six kayaks for each ship. We followed the old Russian trading route along the western shore, and we anchored out off Indian villages to trade, hunt and take on our usual provisions.

Captain Morgan received gifts when he went ashore, including a totem pole that he fastened to the mainmast of the Sweet Cutlass so that its many faces looked him in the eye when he was in the area of the helm.

We did not meet any Russian traders as we passed through those waters, and we were well south of the farthest reach of the Russians when we began to encounter large Spanish merchant vessels, many of which became our prizes.

By then we had shed and stowed our Eskimo clothes and once again paraded around the decks in our pirates' rags. The warm sun felt better and better as we approached the Equator, and the hearties grew brown and orange on the weather decks. Xiaohong and Eida wore fewer and fewer garments also, and they lifted the spirits of the hearties by sunning themselves where everyone could see them.

We knew that we would not see much by way of silver and gold as we transited towards Tierra del Fuego since the days of the Sixteenth-Century Spanish galleons with their loads of fabled yellow and white metal cargo had largely passed. We did not see a Spanish merchant we did not like for piracy regardless of their cargos. We did like the tuns of Spanish wines and liquors that we took from the holds of some of those Spanish merchants. Wherever the Spanish had sailed, they planted trees, shrubs and crops that could be harvested by later Spanish mariners and others also. Where we found them, we harvested those same Spanish-planted fruits and vegetables and included them in our diet.

Captain Morgan liked to squeeze oranges, lemons, limes and grapefruits into his rum and into red Spanish wines. Sometimes he would eat an orange or a lemon whole with peel, seeds, pith and all because he thought oranges and such were healthy. He encouraged his hearties to eat them, and some ate them with rum.

As we passed the Equator and the midday and early afternoon sun pounded the sea like a hammer does on an anvil, Captain Morgan would lounge under a canvas parasol on his flying bridge and sing his pirate songs and toast his hearties. I could hear him from my deck as I watched Xiaohong comb out her beautiful black hair with a cunning comb she had brought with her from China.

She sang her own songs, and sometimes she taught me what they meant. Her family had been pirates, and her songs told of her family's exploits in the East China Sea. One haunting song told of a woman who had drowned at the mouth of a great river called the Yangtze where it met the sea. The drowned woman's ghost haunted the intersection where it waited for the man who had betrayed her and left her a spinster without hope of a child. When Xiaohong sang that song, the salt tears streamed down her face, but she would not tell me why she was crying.

We passed down the coast and heard tales on shore of other voyagers who had come from far to the west in the time of the native peoples' ancestors. Since we were not Spanish, we were a novelty but the people, particularly their priests, were suspicious of us.

One Holy Father asked Captain Morgan in his cups whether he was a pirate. The Captain told him that he was a pirate when the mood struck him to be one, and he asked the Father whether he had any objection to that. The Father unfortunately began to lecture the Captain about changing his ways and renouncing his chosen vocation. Captain Morgan listened intently to the Father, and then he drew out a pouch with a string around it and placed it on the table.

He asked the priest what he would do with twenty gold coins if he had them. The priest answered that he would use the money to build a new chapel to honor the Lord. The Captain then opened his pouch and poured twenty gold coins on the table. He said the priest could take the coins as his offering and build his chapel and give any residuum to the poor.

The priest was now in a quandary because if he took up the gold coins, he was taking stolen money from an acknowledged pirate, but if he did not take up the gold coins, he would not be able to build his chapel or feed the poor. Captain Morgan laughed heartily and began to recite the Nunc Dimmitis. He then recited the Ave Maria and Pater Noster.

I who was there beside him had never heard the Captain utter as much as a word of Latin before. I had never suspected him of knowing anything about the papist religion or any other religion for that matter. When Captain Morgan was done with his recitations, he stood up from the table and departed the establishment leaving the gold coins and his empty pouch lying on the table.

I followed him out the door, and when we had reached the village square, the Captain burst out laughing and slapped me on the back. He drew a bottle of rum from his pocket and offered me a swig. Then he took a long draught, smacked his lips, and told me that he once had studied to be a priest. He laughed again, and he said the trouble was that he liked women more than he liked the men who did not like women. Then he became meditative and we walked back to our whaleboats by the shore in silence.

The Captain had heard of a place where gold ore was mined and the ore was refined and the refined gold was shipped to Spain. Spanish merchant ships came to pick up the gold in bars and returned an equal amount in weight of gold coins. So Captain Morgan wanted to assess whether it was true that the gold in bars was of equivalent weight to the gold in coins. The only way to do that, he said, was to

The Adventures of Pirates

obtain both and do the comparison. So he hatched a plan by which he would stand off the port where the Spanish merchant anchored. While I went ashore with my hearties to liberate the gold coins that had been traded for the gold bars, Captain Morgan would liberate the gold bars from the Spanish merchant ship. He said we would meet off the coast a few miles to do the comparison.

When we reached the small port, we both anchored out and I took my whaleboat to the shore to reconnoiter. I saw a fort on a hillside with soldiers patrolling its ramparts. I saw soldiers guarding a storehouse at the center of the village square. The problem with the Captain's plan was clear to me: it would be impossible to steal the gold coins on shore without undue risk to my hearties. I decided to look into matters further, and I discovered from the village prostitute that I visited that the soldiers had not been paid for many months. They were expecting to be paid their arrears when the merchantman came the next day with the coins that were to be used for payment. The prostitute said that many soldiers owed her in arrears for her services, so I gave her two gold coins and told her that I would give her two more gold coins if she told me when and how the gold bars that would be traded for the coins would arrive.

She laughed heartily and told me that everyone in the village and the fort knew that the gold bars would come by carriage two hours before dawn on the road from the refinery. She said that many soldiers guarded the refinery and the storehouse, but only two guarded the gold bar shipment itself. I gave her the additional two gold coins and departed the village and went back to my ship at anchor. I signaled to the Sweet Cutlass that I wanted a gam with Captain Morgan. At the gam, I explained the situation and outlined a revision to our plan.

That evening I went ashore in my whaleboat with five of my fiercest hearties with spades, and we walked down the road to the refinery. At a likely spot just after a slight bend in the road with foliage that could hide us, we stopped to dig a wide, steep rut in the road and we rolled five large rocks to block the passage beyond that. We lit some hemp and brought out bottles of rum that we had brought to pass the time and waited. At the same time Captain Morgan weighed anchor and sailed out in darkness to greet the Spanish merchantman that was to bring the gold coins to exchange for the gold bars from the refinery.

Three hours before dawn, I heard the report of cannon out over the main, and I suspected that the Spanish merchant had been cheerily greeted by the Sweet Cutlass. When the carriage with the gold bars came an hour later, it fell into the rut the hearties had dug and broke its front wheels while the horses pulling the carriage reared in confusion and my hearties charged the two soldiers that were guarding the treasure. The whole business was done in two minutes. We harvested the gold bars and used the untethered horses to bear them to the landing where we loaded the bars into the whaleboat and departed just before dawn. As we had planned, the Night Lightning had weighed anchor and was waiting for our arrival to depart the anchorage. Dawn came and no ships were visible in the anchorage. Three miles offshore the Night Lightning and the Sweet Cutlass made a rendezvous and a gam.

Captain Morgan was indignant at the gam. After carefully weighing the gold coins and gold bars, we discovered that the gold bars outweighed the gold coins by three to one. The exchange, we thought had been utter piracy. Spain was making two hundred percent on its investment!

Our piracy was at least honest labor that required nothing from anyone except, of course the gold. The Captain and I drank rum while we inveighed against the greed and deceit of the world powers, of which Spain was only one. Then the Captain began singing his pirate songs, and I knew it was time to return to our ships and unfurl our sails.

To be fair, we split the coins and bars down the middle, though I had argued that perhaps I should keep the bars and he the gold. He may have seemed drunk beyond reason, but Captain Morgan spotted the problem with that deal immediately. As he rowed off with his share, the Captain sang a song that ran, "Pirates be good to fellow pirates, else 'Avast!'"

So we sailed south, and the weather became increasingly cold until we sighted a village that may have been the farthest habitation to the south before Tierra del Fuego. By then we were all wearing our Eskimo clothes again, and we were anxious to see how bountiful our new hunting grounds would be. When we had anchored and gone ashore, we found the village was long deserted. We noted that livestock pens were still in good repair and the buildings were in need of only minor alterations to be livable. We decided that the village was as good a habitation for pirates as we could hope for, so we brought the hearties ashore to fix things up. We named our village Hearties Village, and in no time it was shipshape. Naturally, the best two dwellings in the village were reserved for Captain Morgan and me, and our two women were delighted to have arrived at a place on land that they could call their own. Xiaohong and Eida made homes out of their two houses, planting trees, bushes and flowering plants and setting up kitchens.

Dwellings were also identified and set aside for the first, second and third mates from each ship, but those mates and their hearties preferred to remain at sea and live on board their ships rather than become comfortable ashore as landlubbers. Instead of occupying the dwellings, they made one of them into a tavern, and we provisioned it with casks of rum from floor to ceiling along one wall and casks of wine from floor to ceiling along the opposite wall.

Across from the tavern's entryway was a wall that the hearties knocked down to form a large open hearth where a roaring fire raged all night long. Tables and chairs made the place a kind of mead hall for pirates, and we Captains, as well as the crew, drank and held forth there when we were ashore. Since the other dwellings were empty, we prudently made them storehouses for our pelf, and such was our success at piracy that it was not long before those storehouses were full to capacity. We eventually had to build new storehouses to accommodate our growing wealth.

Hearties Village was perfectly situated for piracy because the prevailing winds carried us right down to our prey running in both directions around Tierra del Fuego. After first transiting around Cape Horn, we became accustomed to the rip tides, currents and winds where the oceans collided. We also learned how we had to maneuver to our advantage so that we could plunder the merchants that we wanted and avoid the warships that would certainly come in due course.

I sailed down once to examine the ice continent that lay far to the south of the Cape, but I saw no advantage in spending time there. I did see huge flocks of penguins frolicking and thought they might serve as food if we ever had need of them. I also sailed close to the eastern shore of the extreme south of the Americas for a half day's voyage. I saw no advantage on that eastern side of the continent for a village such as Hearties Village was on the western side. We had done well with our choice of habitation, I thought at the time. If only we had animals to fill our empty pens, we would have lived in Paradise.

We began a routine that worked like a properly wound clock. On average each of our ships seized, plundered and sunk three or four merchants each week. Since we had created additional storehouse space on land, we offloaded our excess valuables and stores at the end of each week, regaled our hearties with rum in our warm tavern and set out again at the beginning of the new week to continue our work off the Cape. We took Spanish, Dutch, German, Italian, Portuguese, French, English and American ships.

I raised flag poles around the village to sport the colors of the nations whose ships we had captured and sunk. It was our game to find a prize with a flag we had not taken, but we soon found that most of our booty came from only a few nations' merchantmen.

The Asian trade and the Spanish colonial trade were the two main commercial enterprises that made the water off Cape Horn an important choke point in world commerce. Nations depended on the trade that crossed the Atlantic and Pacific around Cape Horn.

Therefore, Captain Morgan estimated that it would take six to nine months before the big maritime trading interests would become wise to our piracy. He said that factors would report ships we had sunk as missing, and those who insured the ships' passages would have to pay for their lost cargos. In due course, insurance rates would rise.

Consequently, important moneyed people would start wondering why so many ships rounding Cape Horn were disappearing all of a sudden. Those people would want answers, and they had the power to influence governments. Warships would be sent to assess the threat of piracy.

Then, the Captain said, our game would have to change. I understood what the Captain said, but I could not hold his ideas with the same burning sense of conviction that he did. He told me that it would be unwise to let Xiaohong and Eida know about the transitory nature of our stay in Hearties Village. When retribution came, we would either have to fight and die in defense of what we had built or pack and flee beforehand and never look back.

I have never believed in panic because I have seen what that does to men. It makes them craven cowards and breaks their will to survive. I did see the wisdom in porting some of our pelf from Hearties Village to a new location. So I decided to look again for a storehouse venue on the eastern side of the coast leading to Cape Horn.

I told Captain Morgan I would do a scouting mission for a week while he continued to plunder ships around the Cape. Accordingly the Night Lightning proceeded north and east along the track I had already taken, but this time I was alert to nuances in the landscape that would permit us to hide our treasure and valuables at least temporarily. I sighted a river's mouth emptying into the Atlantic and figured that fresh water could be had there, so I anchored out and went ashore with a few men to scout the areas to the north and south of the river.

I recognized the general lie of the land as perfect for burying pirate treasure. I had an eerie feeling that other pirates had reconnoitered this place before, and someone

The Adventures of Pirates

had perhaps buried treasure here. I looked for likely landmarks and found an ancient tree. With two of my hearties I circled the area around that tree in an expanding spiral looking for loose ground or the slight declivity that might mean a former burial. We found such a place thirty paces to the north of that tree, and I asked the hearties to lend a hand and dig. Six feet below the surface they hit solid wood, and they worked fast to uncover a skelefive over a chest. Unearthed, the chest revealed gold and silver coins, a pirate's hoard for certain. My hearties were glad to carry this unlooked-for treasure to our whaleboat and then to the Night Lightning.

Meanwhile I continued to look for other signs of pirate hoarding, and I found the hearties that had searched to the south of the river. They had found a stone with a crude marker near it in the form of an arrow. So we followed the direction of the marker and found a mild depression, which I ordered the hearties to investigate by digging a hole three feet wide and as deep as they could delve. The hearties quickly dug through scrabble and finally struck a skull with a chest below it. They unearthed the chest and saw the gold and silver treasure that was within it. They took it to the shore and, when the whaleboat returned, the coxswain rowed us all and the found treasure back to the Night Lightning. We had thus in a single landing uncovered two stores of pirate treasure worth a king's ransom.

I had to ask myself how it was that this treasure had become interred in this godforsaken place. I guessed that the treasure must be the result of other continuous pirate ventures in the area surrounding Cape Horn. I began to think why the treasures had come to be buried where they were found, and I had a wild surmise. What if, I thought, pirates had inhabited Hearties Village just as we had, and they had seen the future clearly and decided to hide their treasure on the opposite side of the Cape? They must have done, I thought, exactly what I did. Coming to the river, they hid their treasure to the north and the south in the usual pirates' way. They evidently had never returned to retrieve their wealth. But why? The only answer I could devise was that they were all killed. If they had found a congenial safe harbor in the village that we now called Hearties Village, they had been systematically exterminated or forced to flee without their treasure. It was more likely, I thought, that they had been exterminated. I now feared for Hearties Village, and as I set sail to return there, I began to devise a plan for our next steps because it would have been madness to continue as we had done for the last few months.

While I was finding pirates' hoards, Captain Morgan had experienced the pinnacle of piratical success in his ventures against rich merchants rounding Cape Horn. He had taken five ships in my absence, and he was feeling invincible when we had our gam outside the anchorage for Hearties Village. I told him over a bottle of rum what I had found on shore on the other side of the Cape. I explained what I had reasoned about why the gold and silver had been hidden and why the former villagers had disappeared. At first I did not think the Captain had heard me because he began to sing his usual pirate songs and took long draughts of the bottle of rum. But he had moments of absolute clarity, and his eyes pierced me to the soul when he said that he knew that pirates had preceded us because he knew who they were and why they would never be returning.

Captain Morgan then launched into a horrific story of pirates who became too soft because they had discovered a good thing. They had taken women and done all the things that a landlubber does to guarantee the futurity of his women and children. They had been discovered by troops of one of the nations whose ships they had plundered. The Captain thought in this case it had been the English. They had been wiped out in a concerted attack. All their ships had been sunk, and the English had gone ashore to kill everyone: man, woman and child in their pirate village. Captain Morgan said that if he stretched his brain he could tell me which warship and which Captains had been involved because only a few competent Captains knew how to eradicate entire pirate communities. But he said it did not matter what had been done in the past. For now, he said, the same was about to happen, and we had to make a plan.

I told Captain Morgan that I had formulated a plan while I returned from gathering the treasure on the other side of the Cape. I told him that the treasure I had found dwarfed all that we had amassed in the time since we had arrived in this region. He seemed to like my plan, but he said Xiaohong and Eida would not like it, not one bit. I now took a long draught of the rum and told Captain Morgan that it was only a matter of a little time before we had to execute my plan.

The Captain agreed with me, and he said he had a few modifications to my plan. I listened with increasing interest because he seemed to have thought everything through beforehand. I was convinced when we had finished our gam that we had to act at once. We anchored our ships, and I went directly to Xiaohong and told her the situation. She was not surprised. She told me that her people always had to keep on the move. They never rested because they knew that their pursuers would never relent.

So she said she was ready to leave everything that she had built tomorrow. I knew then that I loved her, and I told her that she should prepare and be ready to leave when the decision was made. In the meantime, she should gather what she treasured to take with her. She answered that what she treasured most was me.

I met Captain Morgan in the tavern, and he told me that Eida had told him much the same thing that Xiaohong had told me. So I suggested that we execute our plan as soon as possible. He was, as always, a step ahead of me. He had already prepared his hearties to transport half the treasure and valuables that we had amassed to the Sweet Cutlass, and he advised me to have my hearties transport the other half of our pelf to the Night Lightning.

He said that we should leave the village exactly as we had first found it, so everything we had done had to be undone. All this took another two weeks of hard labor involving the crews of both our pirate ships. Finally, the village was empty and as void of evidence of recent habitation as when we first came upon it with our women living again aboard the ships and the village looking as deserted as it had been when we had arrived. The one exception was the flags of many nations that hung from poles at the village's center and played in the winds. Liking what we saw, we weighed anchor and made headway as the sun rose that final day off Hearties Village. We were not leaving under the threat of immediate attack; instead we were leaving on our terms with our treasure and all our hearties alive and our women content to make the shift to other quarters.

As we rounded Cape Horn with our false Spanish colors flying, we passed a group of American warships that may have been sent to discover our whereabouts and destroy us, but we would never know the truth of that since we had already vanished from our haunts. I was too wise to think that we had escaped just in the nick of time or any such rot. We had made a business decision that required our relocating. We had not waited to be evicted or to be threatened with extinction. Rather, we had taken what we had earned and departed.

We were not challenged by the American warships because to them we were apparently innocent Spanish vessels involved in an innocent trade. There was no reason for the Americans to detain us because they sought the pirates that would maraud such ships as we appeared to be. We were riding heavy in the water because we had loaded all our treasures, but we were still seaworthy. We continued within visual range of the shore up the Americas, stopping to take on provisions and trade. Because we saw increasing signs of genuine Spanish vessels, we shifted to the false flags of the Netherlands. Neither off Portuguese Brazil, nor off Spanish Argentina, were we challenged as we sped north with full sails.

We reached the Caribbean Sea before we stopped worrying about pursuers because we were now too far away from Tierra del Fuego to be considered credible perpetrators of what had happened there. No one would suspect that the empty village had been used by us pirates. No one would check on the opposite side of the landmass to find the exhumed remains of the burial of treasure that had been removed. Captain Morgan reasoned that Davy Jones himself would have to be subpoenaed to testify against us in a court of law, but he did not care who had sent vessels his way. He reveled in the mayhem on the high seas because everything on the sea finally ended in his domain on the sea bottom below it, and Davy Jones' locker attested to his gains and the mariners' losses.

Captain Morgan did not believe in looking backward. He was now again in prime hunting grounds that he knew—the Caribbean. He had been around the world again searching for better, but he had not found it. I had to agree that we had seen the world together. Partly because of the Captain's former experience, partly because of our combined ingenuity and partly because of luck, we had survived our ordeal and returned to tell our tales.

The Captain's songs reflected what he had seen this time around. He sang of an Eskimo lady whose husband had not returned but she had found a pirate who loved her better than her former mate. He sang of a fool who fell in love with a Chinese woman who knew he was a fool and would betray him. He sang lots of new songs that I'm sure he composed on his own because he was a genius poet, as well as a genius pirate, as well as a drunken rogue.

We buried treasure all around the Caribbean in the pirate way. Eida may have marked one such hoard because she disappeared on the day Captain Morgan set out in his whaleboat to hide a large part of his treasure in Dominica. Xiaohong may have marked another because she disappeared the day I set out to bury a hoard of gold bars and coins in Haiti. That was what the hearties thought, and we did not contradict them.

As I look back over our escapades since we left the Andamans, I saw a broad continuity of our actions. Pirates are romantics, and our treasures are extensions of ourselves. I laugh when I think of leaving all those flags of all those nations at our village near Tierra del Fuego. If the flags survived, they would have tantalized the warriors who pursued us. What would they have learned from those flags? Perhaps they would have learned that pirates have a sense of humor. Perhaps they would have learned that pirates know when to fish and when to cut bait. Most likely though, they would have learned nothing. In their single-minded pursuit of an unknowable enemy, they would have missed the point entirely. They would have arrived where we had enjoyed a few months of perfect piracy only to find that their prey had fled they knew not whither.

At a tavern in San Juan, Captain Morgan and I decided we would go our separate ways. He said he had taught me what I needed to know to survive. He said he had circumnavigated the world with me and that we had nothing to teach each other anymore. We drank rum, and he sang pirate songs. He stood on the table and brandished his sword. He railed at the host and he called for the ladies to parade before him naked. Then he collapsed, and I asked two hearties to help me carry him to his whaleboat where his coxswain was waiting to take him to the Sweet Cutlass.

What happened to Captain Morgan from that time forward, I do not know. I heard rumors of his having had many adventures on the seven seas. I heard that he went to Davy Jones and bested him for all his treasure. I heard that he had retired from the trade and gone to a place he had prepared for himself in Dominica where he now lived with Eida, who was alive and well and entertaining whoever her now-husband wanted to bring home. I thought that was the least likely of the possible outcomes, but it had the ring of truth.

By my lights, at least, it had that tone because my Xiaohong and I live well in Haiti in a spacious house with a view of the harbor. She accommodated quickly and well to the new environment, and she loved the vegetation that luxuriates without her tending or care. She laughed when I told her I was going to give up being a pirate, and when I am sad she goads me by insinuating that I will fly the Jolly Roger again one day. We have five children, who are the light of my life. I know where untold treasures hide around the world, and I could sail tomorrow to dig up whatever my family needs. I have a good life, and the past is forgotten because by now all my hearties have gone to Davy Jones or been hanged by landlubbers who have no earthly idea what piracy really means.

I compiled all of Captain Morgan's songs that I remember, and I want to have them properly published someday. I will not own them because he composed and sung them, but the pirate songs were not as much his property as they were the product of the rum, his fertile brain and the people and situations that they evoked. I thought of Captain Morgan's women, and I wondered that all those various females could live with a pirate with such wildly varying moods. I thought of his numberless women on shore and how they served as his intelligencers and seers. I thought of the man's vision and insight into human beings. He was a leader among outlaws, and his presence evoked allegiance. He won mine, surely. I felt the attraction of his personality, and it changed my life entirely. He was my mentor, my teacher, my brother and my friend. I would miss him if his memory were not always with me somehow. I sometimes fancy he will pop up in a whaleboat singing his songs with a bottle of rum at the ready and invite me down to talk about some new scheme for piracy.

The Sweet Cutlass, I am told, was sunk by a British warship that took out her mainmast and then volleyed a broadside at her waterline before scattering shot across all her decks killing all aboard. Captain Morgan had long departed before that sinking ended a legacy. The Night

Lightning, I am also told, was sunk by an American warship that boarded her, killed all the hearties aboard at the time and stole all her gold before scuttling her.

Both pirate vessels suffered ignobly at the end, but then a ship is only to be known by the spirit of the men who sail her. When Captain Morgan and Captain Abe departed, those ships changed utterly. We changed too. Now I am the entity I hated most when I was a pirate sailing the main; a landlubber. Xiaohong and the children like the change, but I know that if we had to set sail again, my wife would sail with me as she always has done in the past. We would set sail together without looking back and have treasure whenever we want to dig it up again all over the globe.

Sacking Fort Holland

DJ Tyrer

Fort Holland was known by all to be impregnable, yet Josiah Hawkstone, Captain of the Black Swan, was sailing towards the peninsula upon which it stood with the intent of sacking both the fort and the town of Port Orange that it protected. Hawkstone was a man of such violence and cruelty that his rivals, even his very crew, feared him as if he were the very Devil himself. Such was his ferocity that his men might have been cajoled to sail against the fort in an attempt to seize it in a wild frontal assault, but the Captain was in possession of a map that offered the means to succeed where his every predecessor had failed.

Black sails were stretched taut by the wind as they drove the ship forward, its prow, shaped like a black swan, its neck extended towards their destination, pointing the way. On board, the crew sharpened blades and checked their powder, readying themselves for battle.

Old Hanse moved his whetstone back and forth in rhythmic fashion along the blade of his cutlass, honing the blade to razor sharpness. He glanced over at his companion with the hideous features, 'Pigface' Pete, and said, "Map or no map, we're all doomed."

Pigface laughed. "You always were a prophet of doom. Or, is it regard for your fellow Dutchmen?"

Hanse swore. "I have no love for them. They would have hung me had I not managed to find my way to the Captain. But, that doesn't change the truth of the matter; the fort is impregnable."

"Says you."

"Says everyone."

"Well, I've got faith in the Captain..."

Going by what was known of the fort, Hanse was correct. It was impossible to assault it from the landward side as the low-lying ground was mosquito-infested marsh and the hillside leading up to the fort itself was thick with a vicious thorn-forest that would flay flesh from bone with ease. The fort could be approached from the sea, but an attack was impossible due to the shoals and reefs that formed a maze-like network that held would-be attackers at bay while the fort's batteries reduced their ships to splinters. Impossible, that is, unless you were in possession of the map showing the one safe route through the maze.

The Captain stood at the prow, his head craning towards the speck on the clifftop that was their destination in the manner of the figurehead below him. Once, Hawkstone had been a privateer with letters of marquee from his Queen, but he had soured on being an attack dog for a distant monarch, constrained by whims and treaties. Having slipped his leash, he found a life of piracy much more suited to his temperament.

"Long Tom's dead."

The Captain turned his head to see his First Mate, his right-hand man, a Frenchman named Louis Le Boeuf, standing behind him. Le Boeuf was better known to all as 'Hook' after the large butcher's hawk that was currently stained with fresh gore.

"When we are done," said Hawkstone, "I want De Quincy's head. Nobody suborns one of my crew to steal from me. I'll have my revenge."

Long Tom – what was left of Long Tom – had paid a protracted price for his treachery at the hands of the First Mate with his hook and butcher's knife.

"The crew are ready and the Swan is running at full sail," called Christo, the Bosun, in a surprisingly gentle voice. In charge of the men and sails, he was the complete opposite of Hook. As he passed them, crewmen would smile and nod. Where the First Mate implemented orders through terror, and discipline through violence, Christo built a rapport he maintained through good cheer.

The fort on the hillside was slowly growing from a speck to a blob. The Captain took out his spyglass and extended it to its full length. Through it, he could see the fort in more detail. There were the first signs of movement.

"I do believe they've seen us," he said to Hook. He chuckled. "Doubtless they imagine that, if we are fool enough to continue our approach, they will easily smash us apart as we founder on the shoals."

Hook laughed.

They drew nearer.

Then, Hawkstone spotted a tell-tale puff of smoke from the fort.

"Ready, lads," he shouted.

It was only a ranging shot and fell two ship-lengths short. The second fell just behind them.

"Ready!" he shouted again, knowing third was certain to hit them.

It did. A ball of polished stone clipped the rear port side of the ship and cables whipped free where the fastenings were torn away in a shower of splinters.

They were almost at the outer shoal; it was here that ships would blunder into trouble and the fort would unleash all that it had, destroying them.

"We need full sail!" Hook shouted at Christo.

"Aye, aye!" The Bosun quickly gave the orders to ensure that every available square yard of sail was catching the wind. Speed and the deft hand of the Captain's fellow countryman, Isaiah, on the tiller were all that would let them survive.

Although they expected it and were seasoned marauders, when the fort's batteries all opened fire, it was a terrifying experience. Possessed of the firepower of a flotilla of warships, it was a worse bombardment than any of them had experienced. Only the fact that they continued to move rather than running aground saved them from the worst. But, nonetheless, chainshot tore at the rigging, cannonballs shattered decking and shells burst to deadly effect. The noise was horrendous and splintered wood and splashes of blood flew everywhere.

But, then, it ceased. To be exact; the bombardment didn't immediately stop, but, other than some ongoing musket fire, it was no longer hitting the Black Swan and slowly petered out.

Hawkstone laughed and pointed up at the cliff-top fort. "Their guns cannot be inclined downward far enough to hit us, this close to the fort."

The shoals might have been the fort's best defence, but the reliance on them had proven, now, to be its greatest weakness.

"Ready the boats and return fire," ordered the Captain, leaving the prow. He would lead the assault.

While the fort was almost impotent now, they were perfectly placed to bombard it with impunity. The Black

Swan swung about to present its side and opened up with as many cannon, swivel guns and muskets as could be inclined sufficiently upwards. Those cannon that couldn't be, were used to bombard the jetty where supplies were landed, seeing off most of the small party of defenders and preventing more from reinforcing them.

As the bombardment of the fort began, longboats were lowered on the far side of the ship, each full of vicious corsairs.

The waters were still and it took little time to row around the Black Swan and across to the jetty where they leapt ashore.

"Make me proud, you scallywags!" Hawkstone shouted as he ran a hapless defender through with his epée.

The Dutch marines were sturdy fellows, but having already faced cannon fire and being outnumbered, yielded control of the jetty and surrounding area with little fight.

But, while getting ashore had been simple, making it up the steep slope would be nowhere as easy. The marines who had fallen back had taken position behind rocks higher up. From there they could snipe at them, and were supported by their fellows in the fort above. This produced a killing ground of musket fire that turned the pale stone red with blood as their fire claimed several of Hawkstone's men as they attempted the ascent.

"Come on, my boys!" Hawkstone shouted, taking the lead of the charge himself, before it could falter and stall completely. Beside him were Hook and an enormous man with dark, leathery skin, covered with a thick layer of hair, known as the Bear for both his appearance and a bloodthirstiness that even Hook found hard to keep in line. However, that rage was exactly what they need at this moment.

A musket ball struck the bear, but he just kept going, swinging his heavy cutlass with an awful ease, cleaving heads and limbs free of bodies.

Hook spotted a marine desperately reloading his musket behind a rocky outcrop. He fired his pistol and the man dropped his gun in pained surprise. Then, he leapt onto the rock and swung his hook down in a single, smooth motion, impaling it into his neck. Blood spurted and the man shrieked.

Hook didn't pause, but just kept moving, dragging the yowling man along like a hunk of meat as he followed the Captain up the slope. Horrified at the sight of their comrade being so brutalised, the marines lost heart and fell back towards the fort.

Below the fort itself, were gun emplacements, but they faced out to sea. One gun crew had clearly attempted to turn a gun around to defend against the coming assault up the slope to their right, but they had equally clearly abandoned the attempt. It was unclear if they had fled or were among the bodies scattered about as a result of the Black Swan's bombardment which, now the pirates were almost at the fort, were slackening off.

A few of the marines that had made it up the slope alive had elected to make a stand here: the cannon made for effective cover and barricades to defend, but served them little better than the rocks had.

"Kill 'em!" Hook shouted, leading the way, mouth frothing with berserk fury, flicking the corpse free from his hook with casual ease as he ran.

Whether preferring to charge armed men than disobey the First Mate, or understanding that taking the fight to their foes offered not only a chance at victory, but the best odds of survival, the others followed him. The Captain and the Bear, were close behind him.

Hook leapt up onto one of the cannon – such nimbleness was a necessary skill aboard ship – and brought the cruel curve of the metal he held down to impale a man through the shoulder. The marine howled in pain. Hook lifted him off his feet, then swung him so that he went flying, slamming into one of his fellows, bowling him over and leaving them both prey to the pirates following after him.

Those other pirates were upon them, too, now. The Bear might have been less sure-footed than Hook, but he took hold of a cannon, behind which a marine cowered, half lifted it, and swung it so that it slammed into the man, who fell backward. The cannon smashed down onto his legs, shattering them. The Bear stepped around the gun and looked down at the sobbing man. It was the work of a moment to kill him.

Captain Hawkstone was fencing with a rather dashing officer in a fine uniform in what was the closest to being a fair fight amongst the cannon. Back and forth they lunged, parrying and riposting, trading blows, each earning a sense of the other's strengths and weaknesses, while attempting to gain an advantage. Then the officer fell dead, stabbed straight through the heart.

Hook and the Bear continued to batter their way through the remaining defenders, followed by the rest of the crew who were equally agile, if not as brutal.

Within minutes, those marines who had chosen to make a stand outside the fort were dead.

Now, they were at the entrance to the fort.

Fort Holland had been carved, in part, out of the rock of the cliff-top with loopholes for cannon to fire through.

Higher up, huge blocks of stone, quarried from the landward side and during the carving out of its lower parts, rose in sheer walls that, once, would have been an impassable barrier. However, the bombardment the fort had suffered had smashed holes in its walls and blown apart the double set of doors intended to seal it tight. Rather than an impregnable fastness, it was wide open to their attack.

The usual custom at this point would have been to offer the defending garrison quarter if they would yield, but the Captain and his crew were in no mood to do so. Fired with bloodlust, nothing less than the slaughter of all those who stood against them would do.

"Come on, you scallywags and spawn of Satan!" Hawkstone bellowed, charging towards the shattered gates. "Victory awaits us! Slay all who stand in our way!"

The marines garrisoning the fort had done what they could in the short time available to barricade the entrance, but compared to the mighty gates that they replaced, were quite pathetic, a tangled pile of furniture and crates with a few boarding pikes jammed in, point outwards to create a crude, yet bristling barrier.

Behind the barricade were massed a number of the marines, some bloodied by injuries sustained during the cannonade.

The boarding pikes made an agile assault impossible and held them back so that musket and pistol fire could whittle away at them as they ineffectively tried to return fire. But, it was easy enough for the bolder men to snatch the pikes and pull them free, allowing ingress to their fellows, who began to leap onto the more stable parts of the barricade and take the battle to the defenders.

Once again, it was the Captain, Hook and the Bear who led the charge, each fighting as fiercely and effectively as ten men.

The Captain stabbed and parried with his epée, while the Bear swung wildly with his cutlass, cleaving off limbs and heads, and Hook slashed and jabbed with his namesake; some wounds tearing away chunks of flesh and flaps of skin, were intended more to terrorise, sending his victims reeling back in fear and pain, but others were well aimed to rip open arteries and kill, leaving him splattered worse than a slaughter-man.

Again, the fight was a short one, the marines either falling dead or falling back in disarray as their morale collapsed.

With the entrance in their possession, the fall of the fort was merely a matter of time. Too many men had died in the bombardment and in attempting to deny them entry, and too many of the survivors were injured or their spirits broken, to allow any meaningful resistance. Scattered through the fort, marines made their final stands singly or in twos or small groups, but the end was inevitable. Some tried to surrender or fell to their knees to beg for their lives, while some barricaded themselves in rooms or stood firm to sell their lives dearly, but always the result was the same. Not one of the defenders would be allowed to survive – there was no profit in that compared to the fearsome reputation their slaughter would inspire – and soon the fort was richly painted in crimson, while a stink of death hung about it.

"We have the fort," said Pigface. "The servants have been rounded up and locked in one of the dungeons. There are a few defenders left, but Hook says he'll soon have them."

"Good," said the Captain. "Signal Christo and let him know it's safe to sail into Port Orange."

With the fort gone, the port was defenceless. It was a rich prize, with warehouses bulging with goods and ships at anchor they could commandeer to carry their spoils away, and which could be sold for a profit later.

Meanwhile, there was the treasure kept in the fort to search for; the taxes and tribute collected by the governor were stored in a vault here until they could be sent back to the Netherlands. If the intelligence they had was correct, the despatch was due in the near future and the forts coffers should be full. Of course, if it were wrong and they had played their hand too soon...

"I want a prisoner alive," shouted Hawkstone; "I want to know where the vault is."

A few minutes later, Hook brought him one, dragging the man along, his hook impaled through his calf.

Captain Hawkstone stood over the man who was brokenly saying a prayer and said, "Where is the vault? Where is the treasure? Tell me and I promise you that you shall die quickly..."

The man continued to mutter.

"Tell me, or your death shall be slow and agonising."

The man sucked in his tears and began to blather out directions to where it lay in the bowels of the fort.

"Good," said the Captain. Then, he looked at Hook. "Kill him. As slow as you like."

Hook grinned and took out his butcher's knife as the Captain strode away.

The man's screams followed Hawkstone as he headed to the vault.

But, while the Captain might have imagined he could just take the treasure on a whim, it would not prove so easy. The Governor and his remaining men had sealed themselves in the vault and would not yield, no matter the threats Hawkstone uttered.

"Bring black powder," Hawkstone ordered. Several small barrels had been brought over on the longboats for the replenishing of powder horns, but the speed of the assault and the reliance on fighting toe-to-toe had seen them abandoned on the jetty.

It didn't take long for two such barrels to be brought up to the fort. Pigface, who had some skill at such things, carefully placed them against the ironbound door to the vault. He attached a fuse and lit it as they all retreated up the stairs.

The enclosed space added to the force of the explosion, sending smoke and dust up the stairs and the sound of it leaving them all momentarily deafened.

Then, they ran down the steps, along the corridor and through the doorway, now devoid of door, and into the vault. The Governor's richly-detailed uniform was as torn and burnt and grimed as those of the six men with him, one of whom lay dead on the floor, a shard of the shattered door impaled in his chest. All of them were stunned and deafened and they were slow to react as the pirates charged into the room.

The Governor drew his sword, but already Hawkstone had lunged and run him through. Pigface fired his pistol, killing one of the marines and the Bear, unable to swing his cutlass in the confined space, used its hilt to smash the jaw of another. Hook caught a third in the neck, releasing a spray of blood. Others followed them in and killed the other two guards with brutal alacrity.

Although their imagination had tended to envisage the treasure in the form of a pile of coins and jewels sprawling across the floor of the vault, things were actually orderly with them packed away in chests and crates and the softer items, such as feathered cloaks stolen from the natives, neatly bundled up in rolls. Only one chest, damaged by fragments of the door smashing into it, had spilled its contents in the manner they had imagined.

"Gather it all up and take it down to the boats," Hawkstone said, pausing to kneel down and run his hand through the cascade of spilt coins.

They would load up the longboats and, when the Black Swan returned from sacking Port Orange, row out to be taken back onboard.

Pigface hefted a chest in his arms and began to carry it out of the vault. He couldn't wait to see Hanse's expression when he returned from the port and saw all the treasure they had taken.

"A great success," said the Captain as he observed the boats being filled. The Dutch would doubtless desire revenge, but he had little fear of them; they had shown they could best them. "Our reputations are assured."

"I spy the Swan returning," Hook said. He folded his spyglass.

"Good." Hawkstone chuckled. "Once we have disposed of our gains, we hunt down De Quincy. I will have his head."

Hook grinned. Today was only the start.

Sea Of Blood

Matthew Wilson

Gravelines, Calais. 1588.

The battle was over, and though men still died of injury and illness, Marlowe couldn't allow a murderer to wander free on his ship. The sinking sun was hidden behind the smoke of distant burning Spanish ships half submerged, and the cold waters were filled with pockets of men struggling against the weight of their armor, still trying to fire their weapons as they drowned.

Longing, Marlowe stared at the ember burnt skies and covering his mouth with his thick, snuff spread scarf, headed quickly down into the ships hold before his mind could construct a valid reason to go against orders and let his men get killed on their own.

Carnage ruled in the low light as wounded soldiers yelled as they were stepped on, screaming for wine and their mothers. Things had gotten so bad in the last desperate moments of the battle that the cannon men had resorted to firing chains at the enemies. The Armada was broken, but the war was not over while they were still close enough to threaten the English coast.

"Phil!" The main gunner waved a tobacco stained fist through the gunpowder smoke, knocking thick flies from the air. Though he was expected to be something of a role model, he'd let himself get tardy in the barrage of bullets and wagged a torn sleeve like a snakes molted skin. "What brings you down here, old boy?"

Richard Manning's fat sweaty face stretched as he seemed to see some misadventure in Marlowe's eye and winced as if he stood barefoot on thorns. "Has he been killed?"

Marlowe knew immediately he spoke of Drake - the battles golden boy in his bloody Hind. By no means the first man to circle the world, but the only one who came back alive, and filled with Spanish gold no less. "Nay, man. I doubt God himself could take our good luck charm."

Marlowe hit his head on a timber and wished Richard would address him as sir, since Drake had given him command of this ship for plucking those three drowning lads out the sea who'd tried to impress the boss and batter a lost shark to death.

Old habits die hard and since they were beaten in school and then beaten in the navy and royally beaten on distant battlefields, Marlowe and Richard had grown close through their mutual hardship. Every night, they would sneak on deck and play poker over wine. But Richard didn't like to be addressed by his first name in front of the men. He'd been Captain less than twenty-four hours and with his ship badly gutted to the cold Atlantic, he thought it hard enough to get respect.

When victory was assured, he could call him Sandra. Until then, order had to be maintained, and all its evil necessities.

"Then you're here to take one of my boys," Richard moaned. Of course he'd heard the rumors. That cannon twelve's explosion had been no accident. The men had run it so many times, they could clean and fire that beast with their eyes closed. Now in a battle of five-hundred dead, the supposed murder of fifteen souls mattered. Someone spoke of sabotage and though Marlowe had dragged his feet, he couldn't put this off any longer.

"You want to string someone up for an accident," Richard said and Marlowe became aware that even people with one bloodied eye were watching him with disgust.

"We have to be civilized," Marlowe tried to explain. "We can't have law and order with a murderer in our midst. For God's sake, he might even be a Spaniard under cover—"

"Civilized!" Richard's throat cracked at the attempt of a laugh in so bad an atmosphere and lunged at the remnants of flat wine at the bottom of his flask. "We just killed hundreds of men, how can you call this carnage civilized?"

Marlowe had his orders from Drake personally. He had framed the pretty lettered page in his new room of plundered finery. "Are you gonna fix that sleeve, man?"

Manning seemed to notice it for the first time. "Damn, must have caught it on a nail. Don't look at me like that; the rulebook says we have to be spit and polished but we're standing to our ankles in guts and before long I'll have to ask more young men to die protecting that virgin safe in her tower."

Marlowe had told Richard to whisper his displeasure at the crown. Though there were no stakes to impale his head on, if news reached the shore that men were strangely dissatisfied with sailing towards certain death for the glory of the empire, then Elisabeth may be inclined to see how well this sailor swum in an iron coffin. Marlowe had to swerve the topic to safer waters, over which he had control. "Show me how this works."

Richard straightened his spine in a final act of denial, but lack of sleep worked against him. He submitted, seeing only a Captain and no comrade now.

"Jarvis, Banners, Cooper. Cease dying and be of some use to the Captain."

Three men lay breathing heavily in one corner like exhausted poets. One red-haired lad, less than twenty, was lazily hacking the floor with a mop head, hardly cleaning away the blood. They all moaned dramatically as they struggled to their feet.

"How much are we being paid again?"

"Shut up, Jarvis," Richard sighed. It was too hot to argue.

Marlowe saw his suspects and headed over, sidestepping the mole hill splashes of sand to cover the vomit of cowards in the previous hours, "You, lad. Show me how the cannon works."

Marlowe flinched; unaware that Richard had followed him and repeated, "Jarvis, sir."

Marlowe watched the pulsing mess that had once been the young man's right ear; a Spanish sniper must have gotten lucky and blasted it off from across the no-man lands of floating bodies. There was an attempt at a moustache on his top lip; it quivered with the weight of sweat. "It don't work, sir. It exploded three rounds in."

"It's all right, lad. That's why I'm here. Show me on this one," Marlowe said.

Jarvis nodded, kicking weakly at his friend's feet until they were fully beside him. They had just faced hell together; the least he could expect his friends to do was have his back in some damn interrogation. "There's no gunpowder, sir. We sent a lad to get us more...if the

Spanish come back we'll be killed quicker than any court-martial—

"That's enough," Richard cut in. He didn't agree with the witch hunt after these young men had defended their nation against king Phillip's might, but it fed mutiny if the lower ranks questioned the man in charge, however brief his reign may be.

Jarvis gave a practiced salute as a way of apology, "Sir. Come on, lads."

Mumbling, weak with dehydration, they limped toward cannon thirteen, apologizing as they moved the dead bodies out the way and after taking a moment to collect their thoughts, quickly fell into position like a well-practiced dance troupe. Jarvis took an imaginary wad of gunpowder and inserted it into the long cannon tube.

Banners, a dark-skinned man who fought for Drake after being freed by Bahamian pirates sleepily lifted an imaginary lead ball and came forward.

"Nothing theatrical or forced. Just as you would in a combat situation," Marlowe explained.

"Hurry, lads. I want it done in fifteen seconds," Richard had a standard to maintain. He'd promised Marlowe over better times and foreign wines that he would run a good ship and much of the last battles victory was down to the superior volley of fire his men had ejected from the ship.

"Powder," Jarvis said.

"Load," Banner said, stepping back and patted Cooper on the arm who raised an imaginary lit torch and made sizzling noises as he put a spitty finger against the charred wick poking out the cannon tip.

The men waited, expectant as a child awaiting his grade. Had they done good?

"Bang," Richard said helpfully. "Could the men have water now?"

"Again," Marlowe said and the cannon crew looked for some patch of half clean floorboard they could lay down upon and pretend to be dead on.

"It isn't right the men be treated like this, sir," Richard pressed.

"I have every respect for the men, Manning. But my job here is to uproot a murderer."

"If a murder has occurred, sir. The enemy were firing at us at the time."

"Then it will be my honor to inform their families they died in the line of duty. Rather than be killed by a traitor's hand." Marlowe looked at the men looking at him. "I said again."

Like children, asking the nicer parent for additional food, the cannon workers looked at Manning's fat face, pleadingly.

"Sorry, boys. This is the Captain's ship now."

Marlowe was pleased with the support and having been through two military campaigns thought he'd been called every word in the English language until Cooper summoned up his strength and managed to say, "Undead, sir."

Marlowe blinked. "What did you call me?"

"The lad has fever, sir," Jarvis explained. "The explosion of cannon twelve threw him some distance. He hit his head and thought he could see the undead bodies of our friends dancing in the water."

Marlowe looked at Richard. Was anyone on this ship sane? "Did anyone act strange or different to the standard routine seconds or minutes before the explosion?"

Jarvis shook his head. "No, sir. Things were working as usual. Mr. Manning headed over and gave us extra water and then a small sun seemed to explode in our faces—"

Marlowe raised a hand, interrupting the narrative. "Richard approached you?"

"Aye, sir?"

"So I'm a suspect now?" Richard asked in a tight, angry voice.

"Your orders were to remain on deck and ready the men in case the Spanish tried to board us."

Richard shook his toad like cheeks which spread like a hand sized kite in the wind. "Those men were ready for anything in the fresh air. They had space to run around. I was worried about my lads down here in this lunatic asylum. It's tight enough to send the strongest minded fellow mad."

"He was keeping up our morale," Jarvis said and silenced when Marlowe let the light leave his eyes like Drake had taught him in the face of any enemy, "Sorry, sir. Just trying to help," Jarvis mumbled.

Marlowe sighed. These men would be lucky to last the night. "All right, let them have their water."

"May I ask who put this idea in your head of murder?" Richard asked too carefully and Marlowe told him there would be no keel hauling on this ship for any tattle tales.

"But hanging is fine?"

"For the murderer of fifteen men? Yes."

Richard threw up his hands and let his wine flask fall to the floor. It shattered into pieces like an asteroid smashed on a dead moon, glittering pieces remained in the many fires dancing on the fuel filled waters. "Forget the weak stuff, fetch something to make us dream of women."

Richard stopped speaking when the long howl of a horn emanated from the crows-nest. Marlowe's greatest fears were realized. The enemy had licked their wounds and were returning. Guns blazing.

"There may be no more dreams for any of us," Marlowe said, and trusted every man to return to their positions, besides these three who moved onto cannon thirteen. He hoped the unlucky number bought them more glory than last time.

☠☠☠☠

The cannons blew away the dark and Marlowe remained at the wheel with a spyglass at his eye. Drake had trusted him to die at his station and as his queen rallied troops at Tilsbury, Marlowe knew he had to weaken the; enemy as much as possible before they got there. Without God's intervention, there would be no hope for victory. Marlowe knew this when flagships of King Phillip's color came out the gun smoke.

"We'd need a bloody earthquake to break that wall of ships but I lost count at five hundred, sir," Richard called through the cry of seagulls feasting on the eyes of dead men.

"How many do we have still sea-worthy?" Marlowe called back.

Richard fidgeted into his armor. "Not that many, sir." Even from here, Richard could see excited Spanish sailors collect like monkeys in tree branches in their ships rigging, armed with muskets. Perfect sniper positions to find fools with medals glittering in the little light.

"Can I have a number, old friend?"

"I think the lads feel the odds are against them as it is, sir. Thank god they didn't have a good enough education to count." Richard stopped speaking; his lower jaw hit his chest in awe as he saw the red sail of an English ship break formation and charge the Spanish front ranks. It's cannons discarded for added speed.

"Where's he going?" Richard asked, but no one had a tongue to answer.

Marlowe squinted. Only one man was allowed so fine a color as red. "It's Drake," Marlowe's elation was doused at the idea he'd failed Drakes order to find the killer. El Drago would be disappointed. "I guess he can't count either," Marlowe said as Drakes ship faced five hundred alone.

"We got a blind maniac for a hero, boys," Richard cheered, feeling all great men had madness in them. The stars were suddenly blotted out as behind Drakes ships followed eight smaller vessels chained to the Hind. Eight rotten, creaking ships that barely remained afloat and had no valuable use beside junk. But Drake had found a use for them. He had coated them in fuel and set them on fire like a bizarrely decorated over-sized birthday cake. Aided by the wind, he came at the Spanish surrounded by fire like a peacock with eight long strands of an orange tail.

"We got ourselves a battering ram, boys."

"Shut up, Richard," Marlowe watched, willing this insanity to work.

Drake had a good run up and when he reached top speed, severed the chains which held the burning junk ships to his, hoping they had enough momentum to reach the Spanish front lines. Even from here, Marlowe could hear the panicked screams of the enemy. The Spanish had brought all their armored might forward in one large convoy that would crush anything before it like an avalanche. It was impenetrable.

Yet all wood burned and when Drakes plan was discovered, the ropes holding the Spanish ships together in tight, organized formation were ripped out and scattered like hay in the wind. The ships began to separate and Drake raised a green flag beside the red.

The order to attack.

Marlowe lowered his spyglass, "All right, you lovely bastards. These Spanish gentlemen have come a long way to say hello. Let's welcome them warmly now."

For a moment, the Spanish ships were lost in a blanket of bluish-grey smoke and then reappeared as their cannons ceased. It took a second for the sound to catch up and lead ripped through the air. Men screamed in the crow nest as Marlowe's sails ripped and fell like a mutilated wedding dress on the deck.

"Fire back, damn it," Marlowe cried, holding his hand, cut by splinters of wood.

"We gotta get within a hudnred yards, sir," Richard said. "Their armors twice as thick, we gotta get close enough to punch through."

Marlowe watched a second blue-grey cloud cover the turning Spanish ships and a galleon exploded to his left. They must have hit their ammo supply. Another supposed accident? Men covered in fire like a yellow coat leaped into the sea which smothered their screams. Few managed to struggle to the surface, sucked down by the weight of the sinking ship remains.

Marlowe heard his men cheer and looked back at the Spanish who had lost all sense of direction as Drake's fiery ships clattered into their ranks like skittles, rolling over them, infecting them with fire. Explosions lit the air as the fire grew legs and ran along the unprotected innards of the vessels caught on their half-finished turns.

Ships crashed into each other in this unorganized traffic, like snarling wolves biting each other for the sake of their own escape. More stores of gunpowder lit up and Marlowe's men cooed like excited children on bonfire night at the many pretty colored explosions rising up into the sky.

Despite his fascination of Drakes ship and the brightening hope of success, Marlowe continued counting the distance between him and his enemy. "A hundred yards," he said finally, "Time to earn your money, lads. Open up all portholes."

Marlowe held onto the wheel as cannon fire erupted from below, the recoil slid the ship backwards through a crowning wave filled with broken timbers of other doomed ships.

"Forward men, blast 'em back to Spain!" It would take the gunners fifteen seconds to reload and give the buggers another bang. Marlowe tried not to laugh as blood pumped quickly through his head. He was so excited. There was a chance they'd make it out alive. God bless Drake, that beautiful maniac.

"Looks like we'll have time for dreams after all—" Marlowe stopped speaking when he saw the terror on Richard's face, the popping of his plans. "Oh, shit. It was you, wasn't it."

Richard wiped his eyes, angry at himself. "Damn that Drake. We all knew the Spanish were too many and too strong. Of course they were going to wipe us out, but they would have let me live if I did this. Why did he have to save us now?"

Marlowe thought of Richard's torn sleeve, he was supposed to serve the evidence, yet he had blinded himself for the sake of friendship.

"We can fix this, Richard," Marlowe gestured to the dark waters. "There is an easy way out. You can kill yourself and your name will have no black mark. No one will speak ill of your family—"

"There's no way out for all of us, you idiot," Richards voice shook with cold hatred that his efforts had been overlooked. That Marlowe had been given command of this ship when he was the smart one. The one who had been beat so often in school and through military taking the blame for Marlowe's mistakes. The Spanish had promised gold for traitors' aid and if England was doomed to burn, then Richard would take his reward overseas on a ship of his own.

Marlowe's chest tightened like his buttons pin had pricked him. "What have you done?" He was nearly thrown to the floor as cannons erupted below deck, pushing the ship back twenty feet like a hockey puck across black ice.

"What I did last time on a bigger scale. Cannon thirteen has a small enough problem to show the Spanish my loyalty even from here—"

Marlowe lunged for him. "You bloody fool!"

Richard pulled a pistol, shooting the feather from Marlowe's black hat as a gloved hand slammed down on his wrist. Empty, Richard wrestled free and swung the gun like a club. One attack caught Marlowe's ear and ripped out his favorite gold stud.

"This ship should have been mine!" Richard's blind rage gave him power but shrank his focus, his feet caught on something and he screamed briefly as Marlowe shoved him and watched him fall forever over the side.

"Richard?"

There were only a froth of bubbles as a reply and when Marlowe shook the ringing from his ears, remembered cannon twelve. Woozy as if drunk, Marlowe struggled to his feet; his father had suffered sea sickness and swore never to visit his son on the sea again.

"Jarvis. Jarvis, hold your fire!"

As he headed down into the hold, needing his voice, he resisted the need to cover his mouth with his snuff-scented scarf again, and quickly became lost in the organized mess of cannon smoke and shouting men.

Everyone wanted water or more lead shot.

"Jarvis, where are you damn it? You, where's cannon thirteen?"

A blond Cornish lad coughed like a tobacco fan and admitted he couldn't count.

"I'll kill that red-headed—" Marlowe squinted when he saw a flash of crimson as bright as Drakes flag, "Jarvis?"

The cannon runner had a lit torch in one hand.

"Jarvis!" Marlowe screeched womanly and ran at him. He felt his legs ready to give out and jumped the last few feet, landing heavily on him, knocking the torch to the ground before Jarvis could light the wick and set off the chain reaction that Richard had conceived.

"Ow, you broke my bloody arm," Jarvis wailed, trying to sit up, but with two-hundred and fifty pounds of Captain on his back, found this a difficult venture. Breathing hard, holding his stitch, Marlowe apologized as he watched the sinking Spanish ships break apart and set the cold Atlantic water on fire.

"Sorry about that, lad, but the battles ours."

Jarvis let his tiredness overcome him. "Does that mean we can rest, sir?"

Marlowe nodded, handing him one of his medals for the hell of it, "Aye, lad, dreams for everyone."

Seventy-Seven Pounds

Eugene L. Morgulis

In polite company, to that extent any existed among pirates, Captain Isabella Boggs would say she inherited her ship from her father, the well-loved buccaneer Bartleby Boggs. But the truth was more complicated. She had in fact, at the age of twenty-three, fought and defeated three of her father's hands, each of whom had vied for Captaincy of The Breach.

Isabella thought about that day often. She'd expected such treachery from Jonsey and Black Pete, and those two bitter salts had fallen easily beneath her sword. But Arnold Capshaw's challenge was difficult to stomach. Arnold had always been kind to the young Isabella. And though no man under her father's command would have dared touch her, Isabella wouldn't have minded so much if Arnold had tried. She had even got to thinking that, if her father allowed, she and Arnold might have a life together. That all changed when the man tried to stand between her and The Breach—a ship her father bought as a wreck for a mere seventy-seven pounds, and which he spent the rest of his life turning into the swiftest and most feared pirate vessel in the Caribbean.

Isabella was thinking about Arnold's sea-green eyes, and how they clouded over when she ran him through, as she nursed a glass of Mama Comfort's best rum.

Isabella had never been fond of brothels. But she went to sit at the bar anyway, knowing that her crew treated the ladies better when she was around. It was the least she could do for these girls, whose pirate fathers abandoned them without schooling, protection, or a second thought. And anyway, Isabella enjoyed putting her boot to any fool drunk or suicidal enough to proposition her. Which was precisely what she was about to do to the misguided wretch who'd stumbled over. Luckily for him, he caught himself just in time.

"Beggin' ya pardon, Miss Boggs," he said, fumbling to close his trousers.

"Captain."

"Captain. O' course. My apologies. I, er, mighta had me one too many."

"Then I suggest you go home and sleep it off, sailor."

The man gawped at the Captain. "No need to be a spoil-sport, Miss Captain," he said grabbing her shoulder. Before he could continue, Isabella kicked his knee and yanked down on his collar, plunging the man's chin into the bar. Owing to the remarkable effect of alcohol, he bounced back up instantly and stood over the counter in a daze. After several moments of half-lidded stupefaction, he wandered out into the night.

"Maybe next time you be waiting until after he pay," said Mama Comfort, the brothel's proprietor, who was tending bar.

Isabella tucked her dagger back into her belt and motioned for another drink. Mama, despite her bulk and incalculable age, swooped instantly to fill her glass. Isabella drained it in one go, and pounded for another. To her surprise, the old madam laughed.

"Child, you got the same manner, " she said.

"As who?" asked Isabella. "My father?"

"No," said the woman. "Your mother."

Isabella blinked. She'd never known her mother. Nor had she heard anyone, not even her famously gregarious father, speak of Josephina Boggs, except to acknowledge her untimely death. Growing up on a ship full of men, Isabella stopped thinking of mothers as standard issue, just a luxury for the rich and loved.

"You knew her?" asked Isabella, trying to conceal her curiosity.

"Knew her? I employed her!" Mama said with proud yellow smile, which melted into an exaggerated pout when Isabella didn't respond. "Oh, so you don't be approving, huh?" she teased with a swish of her hand.

Isabella slumped over the sticky bar, and rested her chin on her forearm, mulling this flare up of uncharacteristic priggishness. Was that a pang of shame, she'd felt? Or pity?

"It's not that, Mama," she said finally. "I just...no one ever told me."

"You never asked, my Lady Captain. And you know how your papa didn't like to speak of her."

The elder Captain Boggs had always called the memory too painful, but now Isabella wondered whether he'd also been ashamed. She dismissed the thought.

"What was she like?"

Mama leaned back and closed her eyes, clucking to spur her memory. "She was beautiful, you know. Skin a bit darker than yours. Good teeth. And she wore her hair with a yellow ribbon. Oh, and she sang!" Mama flung a hand to her chest and swayed silently for a moment, recalling a melody Isabella would never hear. "She was a nice girl, Captain. A real nice girl."

Isabella felt herself welling up. It was a nice sensation, and in another setting, she may have indulged it.

"Thank you, Mama," she said after clearing her throat. "That's a fine thing to hear. But I believe that's all for tonight." Isabella reached into her waistcoat for a few coins, but Mama Comfort stayed her hand.

"Tonight's on me, honey. For your mama."

Isabella signaled to her crewmen, who had all already finished up and were milling about. As she pushed out of the doors, Isabella thanked Mama Comfort again for the rum.

"Don't you worry about it, child," she called. "Your daddy done overpaid when he bought her anyway."

Isabella almost turned back, but the tide of men had already swept her outside.

"She say something 'bout Old Fuss?" asked Thom Jankey, her quartermaster, using one of Bartleby Boggs' many nicknames.

Isabella ignored the question. "Prepare The Breach," she said. "We sail for Port Collins at first light."

"For business or pleasure, Captain?"

"For answers."

☠☠☠☠

Isabella woke in her cabin before dawn and dressed quickly by lantern light. Out of the corner of her eye, she caught her own reflection in the grimy, mostly uncracked vanity. Normally, she had nothing to do with the silly old thing—it had been her father's, a famous and unrepentant preener. But this morning, looking at her darkened reflection, Isabella tried to picture her mother.

It was difficult. Her father's features showed prominently on her face. So Isabella focused on other things. Her mother's hair would have been longer, she supposed. Shoulders likely narrower. Hips shapelier. As soon as Isabella tried to superimpose a frilly dress over the image, she realized that she wasn't thinking of her mother at all. She was just picturing herself as one of Mama Comfort's girls. It was an unpleasant thought, but not nearly as unpleasant as the thought of her father buying his wife like a hundred and twenty pounds of salt pork.

The sound of boots on the deck snapped Isabella back to herself, and the mirror's reflection showed true once more. Satisfied with what she saw, Isabella donned her hat and clambered out into the rising sun.

They docked in Port Collins in the bright afternoon. Once the Breach was secure, Isabella strode down the gangplank with her quartermaster.

"Provision the Breach, Mr. Jankey. I want her fully stocked by day's end."

"Consider it done, Captain."

"And get our jerky from MaryAnn this time. I think Mr. Paulson's been feeding us cat."

"Aye, Captain. Going ashore?"

"Just visiting an old friend. I don't expect to be gone long."

Isabella strode past the bustle of the docks to the mercantile district beyond. It did not take much asking to find the directions she needed, for her target was that rarest of creatures, a retired pirate.

She found his home on the outskirts of town, far from the businesses and the shanty houses that weaseled up to them, where the island's original forest still grew partly untamed. It was a bright yellow monstrosity, in the French style, with tall, white-trimmed windows and a stucco exterior that reminded Isabella of a wedding cake. The baroque doorbell was still singing when Abraham Jefferson Scripp cracked the door and peered through the gap. His eyes went wide.

"No!" he croaked and tried to slam the door. But Isabella's boot was already wedged inside, and she threw her shoulder into the wood. The door flung open, sending Scripp to the rug with a poof of dust.

"I'm not here to kill you, Mr. Scripp," said Isabella, stepping through the doorway. She walked over and helped the old man to his feet, brushing off his wrinkled purple robe with a few ungentle slaps.

He coughed painfully. "As I recall, last time I treated with the Belle of the Breach, you threatened to nail my nethers to your maidenhead."

"I believe it was to my mast," said Isabella. "But that was a long time ago, and I was upset. May I speak with you a time?"

Scripp grumbled and led her to the patio, where he was preparing to take tea among the encroaching greenery. The old pirate offered Isabella an elaborate wrought-iron chair, which she declined in favor of a footstool to avoid having to remove her sword belt. Thus they sat eye to eye, despite Isabella's having a head on the man.

"How have the years treated you Miss Boggs," asked Scripp as he poured tea from a white and blue porcelain pot.

"Well, Mr. Scripp," said Isabella, choosing not to correct him. "You may have learned for yourself had you stayed on with my crew."

Scripp laughed. "I've done well enough, as you can see. Better than Fuss and I ever dreamed when we started out." He gestured to his surroundings. "And I wasn't about to bow my head to a know-nothing trollop who hijacked my dearest friend's ship. So if you've come to gloat or to—"

Isabella held up a hand. "My apologies Mr. Scripp. I did not come to speak of that. But please know that I do not begrudge you your choices."

Nor did she, any longer. To be sure, eleven years prior, Isabella swore vengeance against all those in her father's employ who abandoned her once she'd taken control of The Breach. For the new Captain, who'd grown up among those sailors, it was like losing half a family. Some, like the invaluable Mr. Jankey, mercifully stayed on, but The Breach struggled for several hard years with a skeleton crew.

"Mr. Scripp, I've come to ask you about my mother."

Scripp, who'd been applying some sort of cream to a redness on his neck, raised a fluffy white eyebrow. Isabella poured him another cup of tea.

"I want to know," she continued, "whether she was my father's wife or his property."

Scripp groaned and sipped his tea slowly, stalling. "You know Old Fuss didn't care to speak of her."

"Old Fuss," shot Isabella, "my father is dead. Been so eleven years, and I know because I threw the body overboard myself."

The old man patted his forehead with a napkin and blew his nose into the same. "You never cared before."

"I care now."

Isabella stared intently at him, until Scripp finally exhaled in frustration and sank like a deflated bladder.

"Your father loved Josephina. You got that?"

Isabella said nothing.

"And men bought her for a night or an hour or whatever their pleasure long before he did. You know how he was—so particular. Didn't like the idea of other men touching what was his."

"So?"

"So yes, he bought her for himself. Considered it a rescue, I suppose."

Isabella snorted. "She was his slave."

"She was his wife!" Scripp pounded his fist on the table, sending a sugar spoon flipping into the forest. The tinkling of the glassware subsided after a moment, leaving only the chirping of birds and the chattering of monkeys. "And she gave your father three good years and a good-for-nothing daughter before she was taken."

Isabella rubbed her eyes. Sitting on the stool was aching her back and she was sick of the old man's condescension and excuses. But something prevented her from rising to leave.

"What do you mean taken?" she said. "I thought my mother died."

"Taken. Dead. What's the difference?"

"Taken by whom?"

"We never learned. It was the boom time. Any man could make a small fortune snatching up a dark girl, forging some papers, and selling her off. Your father was devastated. He bought The Breach to go find her."

"With the seventy-seven pounds he won in a game of Dead Man's Dice—I know the story. But I never knew why."

"Well there you have it. I cannot say for certain that Josephina had passed. But she may as well have. And after years of fruitless searching, your father must have agreed."

"So you believe she was sold?"

"Perhaps, perhaps. Or simply used and murdered. I know not." Scripp spooned a lump of honey directly into his mouth.

Isabella rose uneasily. Her knee creaked and the bitter tea sloshed unpleasantly in her belly.

"I see that look in your eye," said Scripp. "Whatever you're aiming to do, know this; if you dig up what's dead and buried, you'd best be prepared for the smell."

"Thank you for the information, Mr. Scripp. And the tea."

"Not at all, Miss Boggs."

"It's Captain."

☠☠☠☠

Isabella's longboats crept soundlessly through the moonless night toward the eastern shore of Fort Santiago. On the opposite side of the island, the fortress for which it was named loomed like a massive stone drum over neat rows of slaves' barracks. Once in position, five-hundred feet from land, Isabella whispered the hold order. The other boats drifted to a stop behind hers and waited for the signal.

If Josephina Boggs had indeed been sold in the eastern Caribbean, she'd have gone through here. And there would be a record. That was, at least, according to Isabella's boatswain, Benjamin Toppa, a man whose own intimate experience with the slave trade was memorialized in the scars that crisscrossed his body. It was a longshot, to be sure, but Isabella had set her mind to it. As for her crew, Santiago's rumored gold reserves were enticement enough, even in the face of seventy-five Portuguese soldiers and a score of twenty-four and thirty-six pound cannons. Whatever their reasons, there was no turning back now.

Fort Santiago's western wall exploded with such force that Isabella felt the shockwave clear on the other side of the island.

"Too many shots like that, and the damn thing bound to collapse before we get there," whispered Jankey.

"Then let's pray Mr. Lawrence doesn't get carried away with his temporary command of my ship," replied Isabella. "Alright," she said after a few more breaths. "Forward, slowly."

The longboats slipped ashore to the furious clanging of the warning bell. As expected, most of the company was rushing toward the fort to fend off attack from the west, leaving only a few soldiers behind to guard the slaves' barracks on the eastern part of the island.

Isabella kept low and moved quietly through the rows of wooden housing, ducking behind a barrel when she heard the approach of two soldiers speaking anxiously of the unfolding attack. When the men had passed her, she sneaked behind. In three quick strokes, Isabella thrust a dagger into one's kidney, slashed the other one's throat, and finished off the first. She waved her crew forward. The pirates spread out among the buildings, dispatching stray guards in silence.

"That's all of them, Captain."

"Thank you, Mr. Ortega," said Isabella. "They must have sent the rest to the fort."

"More than expected, Captain," said Jankey. "We won't be able to take it with that many men defending."

Isabella stood up straight and spoke in her normal voice. She was done being quiet. "Then let's invite a few of them back. Mr. Toppa, would you kindly bring the packages from the boats."

Toppa tapped two seaman to accompany him and jogged off. As they left, Jankey threw Isabella a worried look. He did not approve, and she knew it. But the Captain had made her decision.

With the butt of her cutlass, Isabella smashed the lock of the nearest barrack. A few of her men ran among the others, smashing and prying open their doors as well. Slowly at first, then seemingly all at once, scores of frightened men and women filed out into the gloomy night. Isabella knew her mother would not be among them, but that didn't stop her from searching each face for a hint of resemblance.

"Listen up!" she called. "There is a small dock to the north, where you may find some boats. It should not be guarded, but take these in case it is."

Toppa and the other men unrolled several large blankets before the crowd. Inside were all the swords and weapons The Breach could spare.

"Seek what haven you can. If you wish to stay and fight, I offer refuge aboard my ship as freemen."

Isabella repeated the speech in French and Spanish. Toppa did the same in several more languages. Eventually, most of the freed women and men collected the arms and hurried north to an uncertain fate.

Jankey watched the group escape. "They'll be slaughtered," he said with a bitter sigh.

"Some will. Some won't," replied Toppa. "Same as before. But those who die, die free."

Jankey shook his head. "They'll die screaming."

"Don't we all?" said Isabella.

The two men looked at her. She was facing the fortress, her pistols unholstered. Her eyes were keen, and a faint smile rested upon her lips.

"Here they come," she said.

Up the way, soldiers were scrambling from the fort in no discernable formation. Someone must have observed the escape and hastily dispatched a contingent to stop it. But the troops were panicked and disorganized. Easy pickings.

Isabella took two men down with her pistols, and ducked behind cover. She'd managed to reload one, when she heard charging footsteps. Isabella and spun out just in time to run her cutlass through a man's belly. A second got a gunshot to the cheek. But the third caught Isabella with her sword stuck and her pistols spent. He thrust with his bayonet. Defenseless, Isabella could do nothing but grit her teeth and prepare for the plunge.

But it never came. The soldier fell dead half a step short of spearing her. Isabella looked up and saw that Franklin Dunn had shot him from his perch atop the nearest barrack. Dunn was a good lad, and apparently, a good marksman. She would remember that.

Just as Isabella nodded her gratitude, Dunn's barrack exploded in a geyser of wood and dirt.

Disoriented and deaf, Isabella was only vaguely aware of a tugging and then a dragging. When she regained her senses, she saw that Jankey had pulled her behind an overturned cart. She was about to speak when she saw another explosion obliterate a barricade of barrels and three of her crew with it.

Jankey turned his face from the rain of debris. "Mother of God! Are you supposing that's—"

"A sixty-eight-pounder. Always wanted to see one," said Isabella, reloading her pistols. "We won't last against it."

"Then we retreat!" said Jankey, grabbing Isabella's sleeve.

"Like hell we do!" she shouted. "If we push closer to the fort, we'll be below its range. Understand? The plan is the same, Mr. Jankey."

Isabella peeked out from the cover. Soldiers trickled from the fort, but they were too scattered to mount a unified defense. The path was as clear as it would get.

"Charge!" she bellowed.

No fewer than thirty soldiers stood between the pirates and Fort Santiago. And no fewer than thirty were sliced, stabbed, bludgeoned, and shot as Isabella and her crew fought their way to it.

The fort's portcullis hung agape, as there was no one left alive to close it.

"Mr. Toppa and Mr. Stanwick, you're with me. Mr. Ortega, you have your squad and the late Mr. Wallace's. Take out as many of those damned cannons as possible. Mr. Jankey—" Isabella saw her quartermaster clutching a bullet wound on his left bicep. "Can you fight?"

Jankey's voice was raspy but buoyant. "Just a bee sting, Captain."

"Fine," said Isabella over the chuckles. "See the rest of the men to the gold room on the lowest level. Transport as much as you can to the longboats. All understood?"

The men shouted "Aye," and set to their missions.

The records room lay on the third floor. Isabella encountered no trouble on her way there, but as soon as she stepped inside, her face was peppered by a burst of stone shards. When the smoke cleared, she saw a bookish celery stalk of a man, feverishly reloading his pistol. He'd missed her by inches.

Before the bookkeeper could set another round, Toppa slapped his gun away and slammed him down on the ink-stained table.

"Mr. Stanwick," called Isabella, "Barricade the door." The big man nodded and set to work.

The space was larger than she'd expected, over two stories tall, and lined with shelves containing thousands of books and ledgers. All of the island's bloody business flowed through this room at the heart of Fort Santiago.

Owing to The Breach's cannonade, the room was missing its outer wall. Through the gap, Isabella could smell the hot, salty air and see her ship floating in the distance. Though she'd been marked and splintered by the fort's cannons, Lawrence had kept her afloat so far. Isabella smiled proudly. It seemed that Santiago's sixty-eight-pound cannon had nothing on Captain Boggs's seventy-seven-pound ship.

She turned to the bookkeeper, who was trapped in the crook of Toppa's arm.

"Thirty-four years ago, a woman called Josephina Boggs was sold here. An account was made. Show it to me!"

The man stared at her, not seeming to register the request. A slap brought him back to his senses.

"Up there, perhaps" he said, pointing to a space near the ceiling. "If you'll allow me, I can fetch the year's records."

Once freed, the man grabbed a ladder and placed it along the shelves. He hurried up the rungs with practiced movements.

"Do you know the date of the sale?" he asked as casually as if he were inquiring after a sack of grain.

Isabella bit her lip. "It would have been no later than autumn," she guessed finally.

The man ran his fingers over the shelves, plucking a ledger every so often. When he could reach no further, he clambered down and handed Isabella a stack of yellow ledgers.

"Those should contain the Js," he said.

First names only, she thought. Of course. Isabella's heart was pounding. The impulse to scream or to laugh or to murder the bookish filth where he stood was overwhelming, but Isabella restrained herself. The time for revenge would come.

She handed a set of ledgers to Toppa, and offered another to Mr. Stanwick, who shook his head.

"'Fraid I'm not much for letters, Cap'n," he said.

Isabella rubbed her eyes and exhaled sharply. "I'll see you remedy that, Mr. Stanwick."

She hesitated for a moment before cursing and handing a stack of ledgers to the bookkeeper. She kept some for herself as well.

"Josephina Boggs," Isabella said sharply. "Find her."

Jack, Jacob, Jacques, Jacqueline, Jadie, Jago, James, Jane, Janelle, Jasmine, Jay, Jean-Baptiste, Jennie, Jess, Joby, Joe, John, Jonah, Jordan, Jordy, Joseph, Joshua, Juliet, and on and on but no Josephina.

"Anything?" asked Isabella.

"No," replied Toppa and the bookkeeper in unison.

"Keep looking."

They did, ignoring the pounding outside the door, which was growing louder and louder.

She nearly missed it. Her eyes skipped over the name "Jo," but managed to catch "Boggs" on the same line. Isabella knew it was her. And yet, something was wrong.

"Captain!" shouted Toppa. "Ships on the horizon!"

Isabella looked up from the ledger and out to the water but struggled to see anything in the distance. Her eyes were not focusing properly.

"What do you see, Mr. Toppa?"

"Two frigates, perhaps larger, coming toward us."

The Breach could outfight or outrun any ship on the sea, or so Isabella liked to think. But even she couldn't stand against a pair of warships and the fort. Isabella quickly tore the page from the ledger and stuffed into a wax pouch.

"Mr Toppa, Mr. Stanwick. It's time we leave."

Isabella ran to the great jagged hole in the wall and leaned out as much as she dared. On the ledge below, a handful of soldiers crouched behind a cannon, firing their muskets to hold off Ortega and his squad, who were advancing toward them. Isabella had a clear shot, but no bullets.

"Mr. Toppa, have you any rounds left?"

"Out, Captain."

"Mr. Stanwick?"

"Same 'ere, Captain."

Isabella spat. "Hell's bells! Does anyone have any goddamned shot?"

"How 'bout 'im?" offered Stanwick, jerking a thumb toward the terrified bookkeeper.

Despite his slight physique, the bookkeeper dropped like a stone, crushing two of the soldiers below. Ortega's group took advantage of the opening and overran the rest. They raised a cheer to their Captain above.

But there was no time to waste. Her sword and pistols would only weigh her down, so Isabella stripped them off. She needed only a breath to calm her nerves before hurtling through the break and diving into the black sea below. Two splashes followed her, Toppa and Stanwick.

It was a long swim to The Breach, and Isabella realized after only several strokes just how exhausted she was. But she pressed on, paying no mind to her burning muscles.

It was Jankey who pulled her out. Isabella looked around and saw that the longboats had rounded the island and caught up to them. Toppa and the other men, including Ortega and his squad, were all climbing into the boats as well, and cheering when they realized they shared passage with chests of gold coins.

☠☠☠☠

In the end, the frigates did not even sail within firing range of the Breach before she caught a good wind and escaped. But not before Isabella reduced Fort Santiago to rubble.

Once safely docked in a friendly port, despite their collective exhaustion, the crew of The Breach celebrated for hours. Only the Captain and dead abstained.

Isabella sat behind the desk in her cabin with a bottle of rum, ignoring the clamor out on the deck. She had not changed clothes since her swim, so her tunic and leggings clung damply to her. An awful stinging lingered around her left eye, where the shards of stone had punctured her, but she paid it as little mind as the uneaten hunk of salt pork on the plate before her.

There was a knock. "Captain?" Jankey ventured cautiously.

Isabella made no response, but Jankey entered anyway, meek as a virgin.

"My apologies for the interruption, Captain. The men are toasting to your bravery, but there's a rumor you were gravely injured. I came to check."

Isabella looked up at her quartermaster and friend. "I'll live," she said. "How is your arm, Mr. Jankey?"

Jankey touched the fresh bandage. "Fine, Captain, fine. Mr. Beauregard says that if it heals right, I might even keep it." Jankey cleared his throat. "Ain't sure if you heard, Captain, but Mr. Stanwick did not make it."

"Oh?"

"Aye. He was shot while swimming to the longboats."

"I see. That is truly a shame." She reflected a moment. "Will there be anything else, Mr. Jankey?"

Jankey breathed in deeply before speaking. "If I may ask, Captain. Did you happen to find what you were looking for?"

Isabella reached down and tossed a crumpled piece of paper carelessly toward Jankey. He was still unfolding it when Isabella spoke.

"'Jo'," she said. "Just 'Jo.' Who knows what happened to 'sephina.' I would have missed it entirely had I not seen 'Boggs.' How odd, I thought, that they would put the slave's last name under the seller's column. I fancied I was confused or not seeing properly. Or perhaps it was an error of transcription." She swallowed hard. "But then I saw the price."

Jankey looked at the paper in awe. "Seventy-seven pounds."

"There was no mistake, Mr. Jankey. He sold her. My father sold his wife to buy a ship."

"Captain, no." Jankey looked closely at the paper, frowning and grimacing as he read the entry over and over again. "Fuss'd never—"

Isabella looked him in the eye, not bothering to hide her tears. Only one other man had seen her cry since she was a child. It was Arnold Capshaw, who found her sobbing the day her father died. He'd held her then, chastely but with an intimacy that left a mark on Isabella's soul. Maybe that's what made Arnold think she was soft, or that she'd stand aside as he claimed her ship. Isabella proved him dead wrong on both accounts. Back then, she'd have done anything to keep The Breach. It was her father's legacy.

☠☠☠☠

The flames rose high that night and colored the sails in the harbor orange like a setting sun. All around the dock, the Breach's former crew watched groggily, clutching their sacks of possessions and plunder. There were a few bitter grumblings among them, but the shares of gold weighing down their bundles prevented any from feeling too sore.

And everyone whooped in amazement when the powder stores blew.

Isabella stood apart from the rest, watching the fire devour the ship that had been her life. She had nothing but the clothes on her back, the coins in her pocket, and the sword on her hip. Suddenly, she felt a hand on her shoulder as well.

"She was a fine ship, Captain." It was Toppa, smiling warmly, with his sack slung over his shoulder.

"No, Benjamin. She wasn't." replied Isabella. "And I am no longer your Captain."

"Then what now, Miss Boggs?"

Isabella pulled her mother's page from her breast pocket and handed it to him.

"Look here."

"Carolina," read Toppa. "In the American colonies?"

"Aye," said Isabella, squinting past the flames. "She would not be so old now."

The Davidof Dilemma

Thomas Sheehan

Yuri Stanilaf Davidof, a personable teacher of the old language, enamored of pirates and the seas they sailed on, as was his father before him, heard the sounds of the sea calling to him on dark nights, alert or in dreams. Passages in his mind knew a sail cutting the wind in half, the creaking of a yardarm, or the metronomic rattling of an anchor chain as the sea lent music to its swing. Those vibrations as well as battles that imaginative pirates waged set loose in his blood a rhythm as serious as a heartbeat.

On slow days in the quiet mountain village of Kmiekev, he counted on that heartbeat. Yet as deep as any desire may go, Davidof knew he was destined to save his own village rather than realize any dream he might have harbored.

The young teacher, whose father had taught the same course for young students headed toward higher learning, leaned against the chalkboard of the small schoolroom. The village looked west where, with the swells and the moon at midnight, a pirate's prize might sway like a silver buoy in the tide change. Pictures rushed through his mind. Sails furled on spars, bones of masts and yardarms shone with mist, and a hull snug with gold and perfumes from the east made for perfect ballast. Salt and pepper and wild spices waiting particular tastes, and honeys rich as the gold itself, carried the air with a separate imagination. Booty would include cured furs waiting shoulders to adorn, leathers waiting unshod feet, and silks set aside for women of his other dreams.

From high in the Ural foothills, his intense gaze nightly directed itself out the single window, and across the distance holding the Ob, Yenisey and Lena rivers, to the sea. There the pirates he dreamed of raided and exploited the Khabaronsky Krai and the Kamchatka Peninsula from their hide-out ports in the Kuril Islands. With strikes as if from nowhere they battled richly-laden ships to a standstill and took their plunder. Ships' Captains, first mates, and penny-ante tycoon passengers were set adrift. Beautiful women, at a whim, were kidnapped and forced into ships' ranks or were used to decorate pirate strongholds. On occasion, flags were transferred to hardier ships. The sea was their oyster, their rich pearl.

The Kuril pirates were rough and ready for all encounters, boasted of tight commands and tended to brag about their deeds in noisy ports of call. On days given to lively entertainment of his dreams, Davidof read to his students, in the old language of course, stories about the pirates that reached him through various sources. Every stranger passing through the village underwent Davidof's subtle search for books and pamphlets about piracy. Students, at length, enjoying the diversion, applauded the break in lessons and told their parents of Davidof's gift of making pirates come alive right in the classroom, as if those riotous souls had passed through the room during the previous night. They swore their senses had been touched by such realities.

The Adventures of Pirates

The truth was that everybody in Kmiekev knew one day they would lose the young teacher. To a person, they knew his imagination and all the dreams it could muster departed him continually in a reach for new adventures.

Personable as he was, with green eyes a cat had let go of, or a mountain creature few hunters had seen as yet, and a stoutly-based youthful black beard, which maidens watched with joy as he twirled its small pastures of delight, Davidof nevertheless managed to portray the character of an older man.

"He has matured markedly," said one old veteran of wars, "as if he has been in significant battles upon which history turns and is measured. He moves like a veteran at civil tasks."

To the entire village, Davidof was the answer to many quandaries, as though he was a creature of split generations, the explosive young and the sedentary old.

"Balance is what he offers," said another old timer, as they discussed the young teacher on another occasion. "We may be locked into one mindset because of what we have experienced in the past, but he melds the old and new like the pinochle dealer shuffling two decks of cards."

The old man, a shopkeeper, had the floor, and had his say. "Davidof has the other attraction drawing on him, those phantom pirates of his. Perhaps they will be an unendurable weight and need resolution. We have to be prepared for the day he might leave. Hunger comes in many forms, as we all know."

Davidof held his ground on dreams lest he be known as a vacillator. In the village given over to a hard life of toil, nature's gifts were few and man had to wage the best battle to gain an edge. They hunted long hours, farmed small garden plots, and dragged trees to ax and fireside with their horses. To be called a vacillator in such an environment would settle its name on a man as if a large black cape had been thrown over his shoulders. The truth of the village structure said the number of men able to do such labor had lessened in a short time; departure, accident, and mortality making hard claims.

Gradually, with the melding of disparate existences, two persons in the one, Davidof taught, dreamed, and aged along with his students.

And one day, spring crawling out of hiding in the mountains after a rugged winter, but the lower meadows beginning to bloom in myriad colors by fantastic leaps to the horizon, a strange group of travelers came into Kmiekev. The dozen of them did not come from the sumptuous valley below, but from higher in the rugged Urals. None of the visitors showed the wear and tear that such a trip might have induced or a winter stay in such a place would have earmarked. They were jovial and outgoing in nature, promised work in trade for food and temporary quarters, and conducted themselves in a gratuitous fashion.

The leader, one Gustav Dmitricof Tarpenko, twice as tall as he was wide, legs that braced his upright frame steadily against the mountain winds, arms long as half his size, wearing a thick animal coat, a fur hat a rabbit could nestle in, greeted Davidof at the edge of the village. The voice he let loose belonged in the mountains, one could tell, as if he called from hilltop to hilltop in his communications, frightened off big black bears.

"Ho, friend, I am Tarpenko pushing this team of friends towards the seas beyond all of this. To the man, we are tired of toil on land that shows little promise. We are bound to sail on broad waters of the seas, to gain an edge in life, and have decided to sail with the pirates we have heard so much about. Have you, sir, heard about the pirates out there laying waste to all they encounter, and getting rich off the riches of those who have too much for so few? Such a song and such a dream haunt us."

Tarpenko, in his fuzzy, tight hat of black fur, had no idea of the response he would get from the young man who had exited from what appeared to be a schoolhouse, though as small as any building in the village.

"Why, sir," Davidof said, "I am privy to many tales from the sea." Oh, he thought, what a chance to do a good deed for the village. He sat comfortably on a village bench. "Let me tell you about my grandfather's participation with those sailors of adventure, with noted Captains of pirates, the one and only Gromikov, The Sea Turtle, and The Black Buggar, curse of all seas. Their slow ships kept many prize ships in their harbors. Though they could not often bring them to quarters of the open sea, they owned them when they went to port, sometimes trailing them for weeks at sea, following their scurvy waste. It was their specialty of holding them under their guns until they surrendered their ship, their prize. Often it was done without firing a shot."

"How did they do that?"

"They trailed some long boats behind them, and they were quite efficient in keeping the crews of such ships from getting to shore, picking up supplies, or fixing other needs, with guns pointed at the prize ship and the port itself. This was especially tactical in those ports that did not have deep water where ships tied up at a pier. Often, others made the secession of rights, like the starosta or viit of besieged ports or the collection of the local communities or villages making up the port."

"Tactics like that worked, from the open sea?" Tarpenko said.

Davidof smiled with his reply, "With cannon pointed down your throats, cannons that are invariably accurate, decisions are often made on the spot."

His sense of timing at storytelling came into play. "That's not the end of my tales. The plank is the best part, or the worst, depending on where you're standing when it is utilized." His eyebrows raised a silent exclamation.

Tarpenko appeared as alert as the others of his crew, so Davidof continued. "They get a questionable character slightly tipsy, blindfold him, and tell him it's a sobriety test. They tell him that he must walk on a plank raised above the level of the deck without falling off. They do not say how high, or where on the ship the plank is placed, but swear it is strong enough to hold the subject. But it is put over the side of the ship, and always in a rolling sea. A small breeze, an unruly wave, a quick roll of the ship, a blindfold, and all, and you're food for sharks and turtles of the deep. Poof! Like that!" He snapped his fingers under the nose of the leader. "The sea has a law all its own. And that's the Captain of the ship. Every Captain. Every ship. Without exception. They own the soul of every sailor aboard the ship, and that's without question."

From the group came a voice, not quite timid, but close. "Tarpenko, have you told this man that none of us are capable of swimming, that we have never learned how to do so?" The speaker was buried in his coat and hat and heavy boots, afraid of the weather that hung over the mountains, looking as if he would be so dressed the whole year long.

"Not one of us can swim," the speaker continued, "though you have suggested it is not needed by sailors who cannot possibly swim the open sea to the nearest shore. It would be useless, you say, a dreamer's plot at stupidity. What would such a state do for us? We who are basically workers of the land, of the earth."

Davidof spoke again. "I have a story to tell you that might change your minds or frighten you out of your boots. It happened off the Kuril Islands when the Czar sent a raiding ship to catch and punish all pirates on that section of the sea."

"Is it a true tale or is it made whole in your mind?" Tarpenko leaned in close to Davidof, trying to settle his curiosity in one vein or another.

"Oh, no fabrication here," Davidof said. "But none of the involved personalities in the escapade are hereabouts anymore because they all went at the end of the tale."

"It seems that another group wanted to be pirates, share in the sudden riches, come back, buy some land, and live like the mini-Czars they wanted to be. They were found out, what they wanted to do, get rich and run, so the Captain, one Bluebeard or such, stabbed a small pig and tossed it over in the midst of a school of sharks. They went wild, tearing the thing apart, the sea red with blood, and then he made the quasi-pirates, at the point of a sword, jump from a plank into the same water. If they made it to shore they would be free. It is said none of them got any further than twenty meters."

"Do you think that's enough to deter anybody who really wants to be a pirate?"

"I do. Don't you in all honesty?"

"Yes. Perhaps we could become hunting guides to rich people."

"That is wisdom in action."

Davidof said, "One other story I heard is this, which seems typical of pirate lore; the despicable pirate Captain, Black Buggar, knew of traitors on board, mutineers plotting to kill him and take control of his ship. In truth he trusted very few of his men, maybe the first mate, at least in a sea fight, and the cook who was an old friend whose family lived on property that his brother owned. That association locked up his loyalty. There was no way he might extend his full trust otherwise.

"From one of the crew he learned of a possible ringleader, Tizur the Red, and Black Buggar plotted to get him in a compromising position, like a spot of his own on the plank. The sharks, if baited properly, if set afire in their hunger, would take care of him in a hurry. Black Buggar held a knife up his sleeve as he walked the deck, accosted a crewman at random near mid-ship and managed to drop the knife in a scuffle the crewman had not expected.

"He tried to stick me with that blade. Foul mutineer is he!" Black Buggar yelled out with great alarm. "Over the side with him. Feed him to the sharks. Now, lads. Now."

And three crewmen threw the frightened sailor over the side. The sharks, following the ship for a few days as Black Buggar had often dropped baited food from the aft end of the ship, made quick work of the poor sacrificial lamb.

Then the plotting Captain said to Tizur the Red, in a huddle on the deck, "The leader of this escapade is that little scurvy pirate who calls himself Sigmund of Salzer. We'll have to get him close to the side to drop him over. Any suggestions?"

"Why, Captain," Tizur the Red said, feeling he had successfully maintained his identity as the real leader of mutineers, "let's rig the plank and make him walk it. The sooner the better." He bristled with impatience to get the deed done.

"Noble idea, my dear man. Noble idea. Set it up." And Black Buggar made a ringing announcement to his crew. "We have found a traitor in our midst, a foul traitor to the cause, a danger to the wealth we have accumulated, to all of us once we hit shore. We must take care of him now and spread his share amongst those loyal to our cause."

He made sure Tizur the Red was close enough to Sigmund of Salzer to grab him, and then said in that fearsome voice of his, "Have at him, Tizur, have at him. Make him walk the plank. Force him out there. We will split his share. Make him walk the plank. Bind his arms and make him walk the plank. Treat well the traitor, the mutineer."

Perhaps the sharks sensed more food coming their way, for the sea became frothy with their intent as Tizur and two other men situated Sigmund up on the plank.

"Here," Black Buggar said, and handed Tizur a long rod with a V formed at one the end. "Force him out along the plank with this. Death to the traitor. Death to the mutineer. Death to the infidel. He no longer flies our flag." He pointed overhead to a Skull and Crossbones flying in the breeze, and yelled out, "ура для нас." A cheer went up from the crew as they heard Black Buggar saying, "Hurrah for us."

Tizur the Red nudged Sigmund along the plank, pushing, urging him outward, getting him nearer to the end and a fall to the frenzied sharks, with the ship all the while rolling in the waves. Tizur, just about to shove the screaming Sigmund off the end of the plank and who was almost out of his mind, felt the pressure of another rod on his back side. Turning he saw Black Buggar holding a second rod squarely on his backside. A shipmate was helping the Captain.

"Foul traitor, Tizur. Foul traitor," Black Buggar yelled out. "You go with your henchman to your death," and shoved him so that he too fell to his immediate death. Some of the crew believed both men were dead before they hit the water, such fear rode about the ship.

And there in the mountains, in the village of Kmiekev nestled in sharp crags and steep walls, was abounding silence when Davidof completed his tale of the pirates. The rugged mountain men, the men who could not swim, who were fearless when facing bear and boar and wolf, were fully engaged in measuring the reality of their dreams upon the seas. Soon realizing the folly of their quest, they decided to stay in Davidof's village to become guides for rich urban people who on a lark would climb here to hunt their prey of the mountains.

Wake of the Monster

Cynthia Morrison

She clenched tightly upon his blue woolen coat tails as they embraced in a farewell. Anne Sedgewick, a self-made pirate Captain, could feel the warmth radiate from her brother's British royal navy uniform.

"Anne, now promise me that you'll send for me if you ever need assistance."

"I will Victor, I promise."

"Should I be engaged in battle I should still send some of my men to attend to your matters."

The petite, feisty and independent maiden of the sea smiled at her handsome brother Victor as he made way upon her Majesty's ship to resume the ranks of Quarter Master. What a contrast that family portrait presents. Mother and Father seated with the likes of their children standing at each side and behind them. The Royal Naval officer next to his sister the Pirate! Since an early age Anne had shared her brother's passion for the sea. However, Admiralty Regulations stated that women were not allowed to be taken to sea and that '... no women be ever permitted to be on board.' A rule that Anne had set her sites to break by attaining her own ship through undermining means. And that she did.

☠☠☠☠

Seasons passed when Anne finally landed on good fortune. She won a bountiful treasure. She was also fully convinced that she had found the devoted first mate she had only wished for when she took on the bonny lass 'Cinders' as part of the crew on the Mourning Star. Although, this wide-eyed adventure seeker found herself at times, biting off more than she could chew during rough circumstance. Cinders had a lot of heart but unfortunately not the stomach for ranks on the dangerous waters. She usually ended with reminding herself that the road to hell is paved with good intentions as well as her guts spilled over the side followed by her hanky wiping the likes of her peaked complexion. Cinders preferred to live in denial of her sea sickness spells to enjoy the benefits of freedom as the rebellious Victorian woman.

Although Anne had taken the trunk of coin and jewels, she reminded herself that everything has its price. This time the price happened to be the lives of the evil corsair Captain Iridius of Muxloe and his mate Emery. She constantly reassured herself that the sword combat incident was in self-defense. For they came to her with threats and she gave fair warning. Did they actually think that this 'petticoat' of slight stature, having acquired her own sailing ship, would be deficient in skill at arms? Ha! Surely such ignorance must summon allowance for the sins of desperation. Words of regret. Words of explanation. Words of her Captain's log. She read aloud as such:

"Pushed his remains overboard to the sharks. Here's a toast to you Captain Iridius, Master of the Seven Seas. You soon forgot Sir, that without the sun upon you, that you're only a man without a shadow. Nothing more. But now, you're not even that. You're simply nothing! A shame really. As beautiful as you were. But so ugly inside.

Dancing Seas the Autumn winds did fold,
Waters rise to meet young sailing Lips
Helmsman amused as she shakes and rolls
The Mourning Star now blamed for bending hips

His handsome presence did find a place
Davey Jones locker that awaiting fate
Seeking fortune of other and that he tried
Behind you Captain! I heard my Friend cry.

The endless Journey has now unfold
Bluest eyes, ever so handsome but cold,
For we are mere women and that of the sea
How dare that Pirate even think it should be he!"

Captain Anne and Cinders made their way to a remote and unfamiliar Island in the Caribbean sea where Anne had plans to hide the bulk of her treasure.

"Alright Cinders, We'll anchor here and I'll take the longboat onto shore. You wait here on ship."

"Aye Captain. Hmm, So you don't trust me enough to go with ye?"

"Someone needs to stay with the ship. If you haven't noticed Mr. Kinney is not with us anymore."

"Captain you don't have to be so harsh. Poor Mr. Kinney. I really liked him you know. A kind man he was."

"Indeed he was. May God Bless his Soul! But now I'm only looking out fer you! If ANYONE has an idea that you know where the treasure lay then they'll be torturing you to gain that information. Remember, Dead Men don't tell tales. Women either."

"Alright. Alright. You made yer point. I'll be right here. Be sure you take yer pistol. If you need assistance, just give a shot in the air."

"That I will."

"...and don't be kill'in anyone..."

"Oh Cinders. Sometimes you send me round the bend with yer ideas. Sheesh who ever heard of a compassionate Pirate!"

"I just like the Sail'in Ma'am. Not the Kill'in."

"Here, help me get the chest in the boat then. Make yourself useful."

The two seafaring women manage to load the chest into the Longboat.

"Remember Captain. One shot and I'll be on me way to ya."

"Right you are. And you do the same if any scurvy swabs happen to appear while I'm out."

"Aye Captain."

Captain Anne approached the shoreline of the Island in her longboat when she noticed groups of large rocks sitting near the shore. She decides it will be easier to drop the booty amongst the rocks then to bury the colossal trunk on the Island and chance someone finding it. She takes a look over her shoulder to see if Cinders is watching. Perfect timing. There's no sign of her at the moment as Cinders made her way below deck for an extra pistol, just in case.

The Captain struggled to flip the heavy trunk overboard. She barely hung on to the longboat as the trunk nearly flipped the boat with it. Anne managed to steady her poor excuse of a vessel. She reassured herself that her choice was the right one.

"There we go lady Captain. Any scurvy scalawags will be giving these rocks a wide birth. A superb hiding place if I do say so me self."

Captain Anne began to row the longboat back toward the Mourning Star. Cinders was making her way back to the deck when suddenly the monstrosity of a scaled serpent arose from the depths of the waters surrounding the rocks.

ARRRRRRRGH! The deafening screams found the hairs of the Captain's arms standing on end.

The fearless lady pirate shouted to her first mate, "Great Scot! A giant sea serpent. The treasure chest hitting the rocks must have awakened the monster."

"Captain what's that?! Heavens be. Shoot it Ma'am. Hurry!"

"No Cinders. Don't shoot it. That's our watchdog that is. Do you have any more smoke bombs?"

"Aye Captain. I'll go get one."

"Fly on girl. Hurry!"

Captain Anne, now overtaken by a steady surge of adrenaline, began rowing double-time and a half. The sea serpent taken by surprise and regaining consciousness from sleep, swam as though it was stricken with confusion. Luckily for the Captain, this gave her space and time to attempt safety of her beloved Mourning Star. Cinders arrived back on deck with the smoke bomb in hand.

"Here's the smoke bomb Ma'am. Now what?"

"Listen to me. With the wind direction as it is, you're in the right spot, so pull the plug and let the gas out of it."

"But Ma'am you will suffer the consequences of it too."

"Just do it Cinders! I will recover. I'm almost there. Right now we need to get him off my back so I can make it to the Mourning Star for Gods sakes. Do it! Now!"

"Aye Ma'am. Here goes."

Cinders pulled the plug off from the smoke ball. The wind currents made passage into the nostrils of the serpent. The burning sensation from the poisoned residue stopped the serpent's weaving through the waters. After the heightened shrill of screams from the monster, it made its way back into the warm Caribbean waters to seek relief.

Cinders attempted to assist her Captain shouting, "The gas is taking effect Captain. The monster is swimming away from it. There he goes back into the rocks. Keep rowing! Hurry, he may come back."

"Ah Crickey, I made it. Take me up Cinders. Get me out of these waters. We got lucky with the wind change. I'm alright."

"That was a close call. I've never seen anything like it before, have you?"

"No. But I've heard tales of them enough."

"Captain, actually I have seen one before."

"What? Are you serious? Where?"

"In a book that the Nuns used to read to us. There were pictures and drawings with this type of creature. They say that there are actual sightings of these sea serpents and they still exist."

"Aye. I've heard the same rumors. No worries. He's close enough to keep an eye on me fortune."

"But Captain, what if you be need'in some of yer coin? Then what?"

"No worries Cinders. I've kept enough out of it for us to be liv'in mighty high for years to come. If I ever be need'in more then I'll just have to get me some more of the lovely, but hideous smoke bombs now won't I?"

"If you say so Ma'am. Uh, if you don't mind Captain. I'm need'in to go to me quarters to change me bloomers after that one."

Captain Anne, being highly amused by Cinder's comment, displayed a hearty laugh then granted Cinders her request. Cinders made her way to the cabin to change her clothes. Captain Anne noticed a sailing ship and began to investigate it closer through her handheld scope. Cinders returned to the deck.

"That fast as promised. I'm back. What you lookin' at Captain?"

"Just as I thought. It's the Scarlet Dagger."

"What? Are you sure?"

"As sure as we be stand'in here. Take a look through the scope."

"Right you are. I wonder who's taken her on?"

"I'll bet you that I know exactly who man's her now. Give me that scope. Yep, there he is. Barbados himself."

"Captain shall I fetch more weapons?"

"No. Barbados knows better than to try a takedown. He wouldn't hit me right now. He must establish himself. And a crew. He's simply out and about showing off his Prize."

"Oh, look. He's waving at us."

"See? I told ya so."

"You're too smart for your own good sometimes Ma'am."

"I'm not sure if I agree with that statement. Although, cleverly spoken."

"Oh no. The sickness. Here it comes again."

Cinders began holding her stomach.

"The sea kicking at you again girl?"

"No Ma'am it was the wake of the wretched Monster."

"I've got an idea. Let's go back to Slappy's and ask Mathalda if she knows of any remedy for your motion illness. If anyone knows a cure it would be her."

"I agree. Mathalda is like our second Mum. Right you are Captain, let's go ask her."

"Only for you Cinders. God love ya."

"Thank Ye Ma'am. I'm sure she can direct us on how to approach my condition. In fact I overheard her telling Rose what to do for all the mosquito bites on her backside."

"On her backside? Go on, you're pulling me wooden leg with that one."

"I'm not Ma'am. She went walking in the jungle one evening with Pistola Pete when he was in port."

Again, Captain Anne was highly amused at Cinders remark and lets out a hearty laugh.

"Oh Cinders you're killing me. Did she really?"

"Aye. I swear it. I heard her asking Mathalda what to use for all the Mozi bites on her bum."

"Pistola Pete. Well, I hope he was worth it. Bzzzzzzz."

"Captain, do you really have a wood leg?"

Captain Anne suddenly stops laughing as she wonders if this is a legitimate question from her first mate.

"Nooo, you silly seafaring Lass. It was just a figure of speech."

"I didn't think you did 'cause you walk too straight."

"I think the sea has unbalanced your thinking as well as your gullet Cinders. Hang on! I'm taking her a hundred and eighty to the north-west. Slappy, here we come!"

Once the Ship was safe and secure at Burladero and next to some friendly seaman, the two ladies made their way to Slappy's public house. There they were met by Mathalda. She and the pub owner, 'Slappy', have had a partnership in business and in life since the day he finally convinced her to leave her undesirable and abusive sailor beau.

"Well, shiver me timbers look who it is. Captain Anne and Cinders. Twice in one week. Alright, what's ailing you?"

"How did you know that Mathalda?"

"When's the last time I seen ya twice in a week?"

"Can't remember"

"Exactly Captain. Come on, cough it up."

"Cinders already has."

"Cinders you sick?"

"Not now. But I get sick a lot from the ship movin' about so much. When it's rough. We was wonderin' if you knew a remedy for it?"

"I have none here. But I can send you to see the Medicine woman. She lives alone. She was the head hunter's wife, but he threw her out because she snored too loud and wouldn't bathe often enough so they say."

"Blimey. He has a low tolerance doesn't he. Can't say that I blame him."

"Captain, you know the fork in the jungle path and how you bear to the right to find the Port?"

"Aye."

"Well, just take the left fork. You'll see a big stone altar. They don't use it anymore. That's the old village. She went back there to live on her own. Her name is Eshe.

Go to her hut and call her name, E–She. When she arrives at her door with a spear just say "Mathalda". Then she will know that you are a friend and that I sent you."

"Oh great. Now let me think. Would I rather continue to spill me guts over the side of the Mourning Star, or be skewered by a headhunter spear? I think I'll just keep feeding the fish."

"Trust me Cinders. You'll be fine. Eshe is not a headhunter. She was simply married to one. She's all about Life. In fact, that's the meaning of her name. Life. That's why she's a medicine woman."

"No wonder they split up. Talk about 'Opposites attract'. I'll go with you Cinders."

"Oh that will be fine. Uh Captain, the man that just walked in. He's staring at ye rather strong."

"Where? Oh yeah, that's Barbados. I told you don't worry 'bout him. He's harmless. I can suss 'em out. He's not a fighter. And I don't think he's staring at me either. I think he's making eyes at you Lass."

"Me? Well, I don't…"

"You see Cinders? Here he comes."

"Captain Anne. Good day to you Ma'am."

"Good Day, Mr. Barbados. I'm still not hiring ya if that's what you're here for."

"Actually I was hoping you'd introduce me to yer fair little swab here."

"She's not a swab. She's a First Mate, and her name is Cinders."

Cinders being flattered by his straightforwardness reached out her hand to greet him.

"Miss Cinders, it's my pleasure."

"Mr. Barbados. We only just passed you in the Scarlet Dagger."

"Aye. I was testing her timbers. I took Captain Anne's advice and claimed her. She's a right nice sailing ship."

"Well done Sir."

"Miss. Cinders. It's too fine a sunset to spend inside a smoky old public house. Would you fancy a walk on the shore?"

"Uh, Captain Anne?"

"Go on. You don't have to ask me. You're a free woman. I'm your Captain, not your Mother. No worries, you know what I said before. Just be back to the ship at a decent time for some rest. We have some walking to do on the morrow. You know. To visit Eshe."

"No worries Captain. I'll have her back."

"I'm not concerned Mr. Barbados. But *you* should be, in case she doesn't make it back."

"You have my word, Ma'am."

"Words are quite inexpensive now aren't they? Be gone with you both. Cheers."

"Are you lettin' her go with that mangy looking corsair?"

"She's her own woman now Mathalda. That's why she left the homeland to sail and be free. Besides, between you and me I don't think she's been on many strolls along the shoreline. Let her be. You know what they say, 'They'll be back when they're hungry.' Think I could get me some grub and a pint? It's been a long day."

Mathalda brought the Captain some fish and potatoes along with a pint of dark ale. They continued to chat about past times back in England. They never missed the cold, wet weather of course, but often reminisced of the quaint little villages where they grew up. A place where folks harvested their own little gardens in order to provide fresh vegetables in hard economic times.

"Well that's me. Got to get back to the Ship. Don't like leave'n her too long. In the morrow Mathalda. Good night to Slappy for me."

"I'll put it on your tab. Good night Captain."

☠☠☠☠

The next morn Captain Anne tilted the brim of her tricorn hat to shade her eyes from the bright sub-tropical rising sun. She often wondered if any man of science, in her lifetime, would ever harness the intensity of the burning sphere. Oh what she could do with all that power. She made her way to Cinders quarters.

"Cinders. Come on shake a leg. Rise and shine and all the rest of it. Time to be makin' our way to the Witch Doctor…Uh I mean the Medicine Woman."

Cinders snarled and faintly acknowledged Anne's attempt.

"Oh Captain, just another hour please? I've only been back a short while."

"I warned you to get back at a decent hour. Not my fault. Come on I'll even splurge and pay for a horse and carriage to take us, so you don't have to walk. How's that then?"

"Alright. Let me get me clothes on."

After a surprisingly pleasant and educational visit at Eshe's hut, Anne and Cinders made their way back to Slappy's Pub.

"Here. Let's sit at a table today and have some nosh shall we. Look, here comes Mathalda."

"Now don't you two look a real sight. Did you make it to Eshe's?"

"We did and Cinders is ever so grateful for your direction. Aren't you Cinders?"

"Aye. She's give' me some Ginger root and tethers to tie round me wrists. They have a stone in the middle that needs to be placed at just the right place under me wrist. She swears by them."

"Good. Now you'll stop feed'in those fish and watch where you're goin'."

"We're ever so hungry Mathalda. What's the dish today?"

"Slappy's Blowfish soup and Crab Pie."

"I'll think I'll blow the soup and go with the Crab Pie."

"Make it two please Mathalda, and a coconut milk."

"No Soup? Don't know what yer missin'. Alrighty, two Pies it is."

Mathalda made her way to the kitchen with the order.

"Last time I had Blowfish soup it made me bloated. So tell me Miss. 'fair little swab', how was your walk on the shore last night, hmm?"

"Aye Captain, I wanted to talk to you about that."

"Now why do I smell trouble from that statement."

"It was ever so exciting. Barbados wants me to sail with him."

"Cinders, are you serious?"

"Now don't get upset Ma'am. I told him I would discuss it with you and that I thought it was too soon to make such a transition. He told me he loved me at first sight and insists that I marry him."

"You don't believe that I hope."

"Well, why shouldn't I? He's not harmed anyone that we know of. You said yourself that he's not a fighter so how bad or deceitful can he be?"

Anne sat her hat on the table and brushed her short auburn hair back into a ponytail.

"You really want to know? 'cause I'm gonna tell you anyway. I had a feeling about this Barbados character right from the start. When I knew that you two were on the beach last night, I went aboard the Scarlet Dagger and I found his Journal."

"Captain, I can't believe you would do that!"

"Ah-Ha! It was with good reason, and my hunch was right. Now be quiet and just listen to this entry made by him in the Journal, and I quote:

'I learned at an early age how to pretend. I created a tent from my Father's old Tartan wooly blanket. It had a moldy stench to it that added to the atmosphere of the fabricated military camping quarters that I was constructing. I then also crafted a Bow and Arrow from the hedges in the front garden. I lay hidden within my tent whilst I hold so tightly to the Bow. Knowing full well that my brother would arrive home soon from his day of lessons. Upon his arrival I planned to bring him into the world I had created and place him as being an invader. The thought of my courageous attempts grew even more as I clenched onto the Bow.

However, my plans did not take the direction of my intent. Brother was delayed in his journey due to his visit to the market to collect the bumper crop apples for Mother.

The Somerset harvest was good that year. We all had the pleasure of tasting the sweet Cider that we refer to as nectar from the Gods. The monotony of the wait whilst staring into the same pattern of squares on the tartan blanket induced an afternoon nap. I ultimately missed my opportunity for sibling rivalry. And most importantly my chance to once again exercise the creative energies involved with the childhood process of learning to pretend."

"Captain what does this have to do with...'

"Wait! There's only a bit more on the page. Let me finish. He continues with this:

'there seems to be a social forgiveness with relation to child's play. However, the same actions by an adult are shunned. Although these entertaining actions of deceit are well rewarded with respect to professional Actors. Who said Life was fair? Pretending has become an important part of our lives. I shall keep it ever so close to me.'

"So what?! He's written about a childhood experience. Does that make him criminal?"

"Alright Cinders, that doesn't make him a criminal. But in my book he's a con-man. I could see right through him when I met him."

"I need more proof than that for you to convince me. Sorry Ma'am."

"Alright. Remember when he said he claimed the Scarlet Dagger? Well, he didn't claim it! I'm the one who unleashed that Ship. But I didn't need it or want it. In my conversation with him on the docks, I handed it over to him for the taking. But now he falsely presents that he 'claimed' it. I'm the one to answer for the lives lost with regard to that vessel. Not him! Can't you see Cinders?

"He is a Pretender. And a con-man. Just think about his name. Barbados. It's not just a place, it's an entire island for God's sakes. Think with your senses girl and not yer sand-flea ridden bloomers. Now listen' Cinders, I can see that yer likin' the man but in any relationship you must allow time to tell the true meanings. I've been around a few more years than you have."

"Forgive me for saying this but anyone can see your bitterness towards the opposite gender. I don't condemn you for it. I only ask that you do not attempt to thwart my relationship."

Anne knew she had to move fast before the sly fox Barbados could have a chance to take one of the best first mates Anne had ever known. Possibly the secret of the treasure's resting place as well.

"Oh Cinders, Cinders. Come. Let's do this. I'll try to be as open-minded as you for once. I at least owe you that. Let's go invite Barbados on an exploration voyage tomorrow. This will also allow him to present his skills as a seaman. Let's see if he's at least worthy of that. Agreed?"

"Alright. Excellent idea. Let's get some fruit, bread and cheese from Mathalda for the journey, shall we."

"Right you are my friend. And don't forget the coconuts. Now get busy on that Pie. It'll be cold soon. "

The Autumn wind next morning allowed the Mourning Star to move under all sail. The emerald waters seemed to welcome the bow of the ship as it peeled away from its timbers.

"That was right kind of ycu Captain Anne to be inviting me out with you today."

"No problem, Mr. Barbados. Sometimes we anticipate needing an extra hand for certain journeys. Which reminds me. Can you take your hands off Cinders waist for a few moments and fetch me that pole. We'll be gett'in close to shore today and I want to be able to push off before we get too set in the sea bottom."

Cinders raising an eyebrow decided to give Captain Anne her opinion of that last statement.

"Must you be so blunt in your descriptions ma'am?"

"It's important for a leader to be clear. We're not out here to play Blind man's bluff."

Barbados handed the pole to Anne.

"Well done matey. I actually need you to go towards the bow of the ship with the pole and soon I will join you as we approach the next tiny Island."

"This place looks familiar. Isn't this the Isle we visited just the other…"

"No Cinders. It only looks similar."

"I know this Island. There is a boiling pool of water. Some say it's a small Volcano just waiting to erupt. That's why no one claims it or lives on it."

"Is that right Barbados? Thanks for the warning. I'd like to get close and have a look with me spyglass from offshore anyway. Slow her down Cinders. You stay at the Helm. Barbados and I will move forward to look for rocks. Take her slow and easy. I want to get as close to shore as possible."

"I'm almost certain that this is the same Isle…"

"Who's the Captain here Cinders?"

"You are ma'am."

"Then please do as I ask. Now let's move forward with that pole. Barbados, I need you on the aft side close to the edge and watching closely for any signs of rocks. Cinders, keep her slow and steady. Keep looking Mr. Barbados."

"We're getting mighty close."

"Alright, Barbados. Just keep looking off the side."

"You're doin' just fine Cinders, but look behind you. Is that ship flying a Jolly Roger?"

Cinders turned herself to find what her Captain was attempting to see. Suddenly there was a splash! Cinders turned back around to find Captain Anne near the place where Barbados stood. She was looking down into the waters where Barbados had joined the creatures of the sea. Anne quickly shouted, "Man overboard! Cinders stay where you are and don't let go of the helm! Stay with her and take her out away from these rocks. I'm looking for the rope to throw to Barbados."

Cinders noticed there weren't any ropes on deck. How could she have overlooked such an integral part of sailing? She suddenly realized her thoughts had been elsewhere on this journey.

"The Ropes! They're always on deck...where are they?!!!"

ARRRRRRGGGH! The familiar shrieking screams filled the atmosphere. Once again the monstrous sea serpent arose from its monolithic refuge to terrorize those who dare invade such territory.

"I knew it, Captain! This is the same Island that we was at two days ago to drop the treasure. It's the Monster. Oh no, he's got Barbados! Captain Anne do something!"

"I just can't believe those ropes aren't on deck. Where could they have gone? Did someone come aboard and steal the blasted twine? Oh Cinders, there's nothing we can do now. The Monster has taken him below."

"Take the helm, Captain, I'll climb the mast to get the hang'in Gaff to throw."

"Stay on that Helm. That's an order Cinders!"

"No one comes aboard a ship to thieve ropes! Something just doesn't fit right here. How did he fall overboard?! I turn my back for ten seconds and now he's gone forever."

"Now listen here, young Lady. I hope you're not accusing me of this accident? He slipped. That's it in a nutshell. I am truly sorry for you. That's a Pirate's life Cinders. A hard lesson learned."

"I absolutely adored him. Oh God, I'm gonna be sick."

Cinders began to vomit and cry.

"Here Cinders, take some Ginger."

"I don't want any Ginger. I want Barbados."

"Here now. There's no more we can do. I feel your hurt, but you must bid him farewell and let's depart from these God forsaken waters. I've had more than enough for one day. Go on down to your Quarters girl and I'll take her back to Port."

"Aye. Oh, I just can't believe this. What have I done to deserve this?"

☠☠☠☠

Later, back at the docks Captain Anne records the horrific circumstance in her log.

"Captain's Log November 4th, 1890. An exploration voyage with ship's guest known as Barbados has ended in tragedy. During his watchful efforts of a threatening shoreline, Mr. Barbados did fall overboard into the sea. He was then taken to the depths below by the unknown Island's resident sea serpent. Due to the dangerous reputation of the Island I sought passage out with the Mourning Star. First mate Cinders is quite disconcerted by the incident. We rest now in the safer haven of Burladero's port."

Only nautical miles away, the soaking wet beach sand offered very little assistance as Barbados crawled onto shore of the Island. After expelling the salt water from his lungs, he managed to verbally proclaim his avenging intentions.

"I always knew I would use that boot knife one day. I don't think I killed the monster, but he'll be learning how to navigate with only one eye, that's for sure. I need a vine to stop me leg bleeding. Wood and sea bean to build a fire for when the next ship passes. Captain Anne will soon be meeting her match once I gain passage back to Burladero 'cause I've got somethin' to stick into that Haybag!"

Contributing Yarn Spinners

Benjamin Fine

Dr. Benjamin Fine is a mathematician and professor at Fairfield University, in Connecticut, in the United States. He is a graduate of the MFA program at Fairfield University, and is the author of ten books (eight in mathematics, one on chess, one a political thriller), over 130 research articles, and outside of mathematics, several short stories.

The included novella represents a lifetime fascination with pirates. His memoir told in interwoven stories is called, *Tales from Brighton Beach: A Boy Grows in Brooklyn*. The stories detail his growing up in Brighton Beach, a seaside neighborhood on the southern tip of Brooklyn, during the 1950's and 1960's.

Cynthia Morrison

Cynthia Morrison is a graduate of Palm Beach State College and the Burt Reynolds Institute. She is a writer, performance artist, stage combat director, and an award-winning playwright. Her works tend to lean towards historic content. Although she also specializes in works that speak against the suppression of women.

Morrison's performance art is featured inside "Ripley's Believe It or Not!" She is co–producer of the *"Wild West Show of South Georgia"* presented at the Andersonville Outdoor Theatre. She is also a member of the Horror Writers Association.

Cynthia's short plays have been featured in Manhattan, New York theaters, *Off Off-Broadway*.
You may follow her work at: www.cynthiamorrison.yolasite.com.

DJ Tyrer

DJ Tyrer is the person behind Atlantean Publishing and has been widely published in anthologies and magazines in the UK, the USA, and elsewhere, including A Grimoire of Eldritch Inquests, Volume I (Emby Press), State of Horror: Illinois (Charon Coin Press), Steampunk Cthulhu (Chaosium), Tales of the Dark Arts (Hazardous Press), Cosmic Horror (Dark Hall Press), and Sorcery & Sanctity: A Homage to Arthur Machen (Hieroglyphics Press), and in addition, has a novella available in paperback and on Kindle, The Yellow House (Dunhams Manor).

DJ Tyrer's website is at http://djtyrer.blogspot.co.uk/

The Atlantean Publishing website is at: http://atlanteanpublishing.blogspot.co.uk/

Eugene L. Morgulis

When not sailing the high seas, Eugene Morgulis lives and works in Boston, where he is a member of the GrubStreet writing community. His other short fiction has been accepted for publication in Fantasy Scroll Magazine.

E.W. Farnsworth

E.W. Farnsworth lives and writes in Arizona. Forty of E.W. Farnsworth's short stories have been published in 2015. His collected western stories, spy stories, and a romance will also appear in 2015. Bitcoin Fandango, his mystery/thriller appeared in March 2015.

He has two novels coming out in December with Zimbell House Publishing, Engaging Rachel, and the John Fulghum Mysteries.

To follow his works: www.ewfarnsworth.com.

Lucy Ann Fiorini

Lucy Ann Fiorini is a writer and poet and moderates a creative writing group in addition to working full-time. She is based near Washington, D.C. when not traveling. Lucy Ann holds a B.A in English, a B.A. in Communication/Journalism, and an M.A. in Humanities/Literature. She is a former college professor of English literature.

Lucy Ann currently writes mysteries, historical fiction, and poetry. Her paranormal western, "January at Fort Wayne" was recently published in the anthology: Stanger Worlds: Luna's Children.

Matthew Wilson

Matthew Wilson has had over 150 appearances in such places as *Horror Zine, Star*Line, Spellbound, Illumen, Apokrupha Press, Hazardous Press, Gaslight Press, Sorcerers Signal* and many anthologies with Zimbell House Publishing. He is currently editing his first novel.

Sergio -ente per ente- Palumbo

Sergio is an Italian public servant who graduated from Law School working in the public real estate branch. He is also a scale modeler who likes mostly Science Fiction and Real Space models, some of his little Dioramas have been shown in some Italian (scale model) magazines like Soldatini, Model Time, TuttoSoldatini and online on the American site StarShipModeler, MechaModelComp, on British SFM: UK site and Italian SMF.

Sergio has published an illustrated Fantasy RolePlaying manual, *WarBlades*, and has been widely published in many sci-fi anthologies.

☠☠☠

Michele Dutcher, aka Bottomdweller, lives in a carriage house in Old Louisville Kentucky with her border collie–Daisy Dukes. She has a BS degree in Elementary

Education from Indiana University with minors in theology & sociology and has been writing Science Fiction stories for about a decade. She edits all the first drafts of Sergio's short stories.

Thomas Sheehan

Tom has 28 Pushcart nominations. His latest books are *Sons of Guns, Inc.* from Nazar Look, Romania; from Pocol Press are *In the Garden of Long Shadows*, and *The Nations*, about Native Americans. Their next publication is *Where Skies Grow Wide*. His print/eBooks are *Epic Cures; Brief Cases, Short Spans; A Collection of Friends; From the Quickening, Korean Echoes*, nominated for Distinguished Military Award, and *The Westering*, nominated for National Book Award. eBooks, from *Danse Macabre*, are *Murder at the Forum, Death of a Lottery Foe, Death by Punishment* and *An Accountable Death*. He has work in *Indiana Voice Journal, The Path, Rosebud, Linnet's Wings, Copperfield Review, Literary Orphans, Frontier Tales, Belle Reve Journal, Provo Canyon Review, Eastlit, Western Online, Wilderness House Literary Review, Serving House Journal, You are Here, Nazar Look, 3 A.M. Magazine*, etc. Sheehan served in the 31st Infantry Regiment, Korea 1951.

Additional Anthologies from Zimbell House Publishing

Reflections: Michigan 2015
Reflections: Seasons 2015
The Fairy Tale Whisperer
Puppy Love: 2015
The Mysteries of Suspense
Garden of the Goddesses
Elemental Foundations
Romantic Morsels
The Steam Chronicles
Pagan
Tales From The Grave

New Releases Coming Soon from Zimbell House Publishing

Curse of the Tomb Seekers
Dark Monsters
Travelers
On a Dark and Snowy Night
Where Cowboys Roam
The Key

☠

Made in the USA
Middletown, DE
08 November 2015